D1288169

A NEW KIND OF WAR

ANTHONY PRICE
A NEW KIND OF WAR

THE MYSTERIOUS PRESS

New York • London • Tokyo

The Mysterious Press, 129 West 56th Street, New York, N.Y. 10019

Printed in the United States of America

First Printing: July 1988

10 9 8 7 6 5 4 3 2 1

Library of Congress Cataloging-in-Publication Data

Price, Anthony.
    A new kind of war.

        1. Greece—History—Civil War, 1944–1949—Fiction.
I. Title.
PR6066.R5N4   1988   823'.914   87–40385
ISBN 0–89296–281–X

For Ceri

A NEW KIND OF WAR

Part One

Eve of Scobiemas

Greece, February 2, 1945

The eagle continued its effortless wheeling and gliding far above them, like a spotter-plane safely out of range, as the last echoes of gunfire finished knocking from peak to peak below it. Obviously, the bloody bird had heard a machine gun before, and possibly from the same godforsaken hillside. In fact, it was probably just biding its time, waiting for its supper.

"Do eagles eat dead bodies?" As Fred watched, another eagle swept into view. So that meant they bloody did, for sure, and years of war had taught them to steer towards the sound of the guns, with the prospect of succulent glazed eyeballs for an hors d'oeuvre.

"Eh?" Kyriakos had been busy studying the tree line on the crest of the ridge above the path. "What was that?"

"I said 'So much for your bloody truce, Captain Michaelides." Fred was conscious of his own as yet unglazed eyeballs as he stared reproachfully at Kyriakos.

"You didn't say that." The Greek transferred his attention to the track below them. "But . . . not my truce, old boy—your bloody truce."

3

The track was empty, and the mountains were as silent as they had been before that sudden burst of machine-gun fire had startled them. And even allowing for acoustic tricks, the sound had come from over the ridge, certainly; and from far away, hopefully; and possibly even accidentally? Some peasant lad shooting his foot off? Or impressing his girlfriend?

"Not my bloody truce." A tiny green shoot of hope poked through the arid crust of Fred's experience: when things were not as bad as they seemed, that was usually because they were preparing to be worse. But this returning silence was encouraging. "I'm just a tourist passing through—remember?"

Kyriakos chuckled, and then coughed his smoker's cough. "A tourist?"

"You were going to show me Delphi, as I recall." As Kyriakos himself began to relax, Fred's miraculous green shoot flowered. Back in Athens they had said that there'd be eagles over Delphi, so maybe it was just a welcoming party up there. "That makes me a tourist."

"If that's what you wish to be . . ." The Greek shrugged. "But I was actually going to introduce you to Mother as one of our liberators. Just like Lord Byron, I would have told her—

Fill high the cup with Samian wine!
Our virgins dance beneath the shade

—although I can't guarantee any virgins locally, after having been away so long. But I do know that Father bricked up some good wine at the far end of the old cellar in the winter of '40. He knew what was coming, by God!"

"I'll settle for the wine." And this blissful silence! "What do you think it was, Kyri? A *feu de joie*?"

"What for?" Ever cautious, Kyriakos was scanning the ridge again.

"Christmas Eve?" To his shame Fred found the prospect of the temple of Apollo at Delphi insignificant compared with that of good wine and a soft bed, with or without an attendant virgin. But then almost anything would be an improvement on his Levádhia billet.

"Christmas Eve? On February the second?" Suddenly there was something not quite right in the Greek's voice. "No—don't look! Keep talking, old man—just keep talking—look at me!"

"Yes?" It hurt his neck not to look up the hillside. "What did you see?"

"Perhaps nothing. I am not sure. But it is better that we do not both stare, I think. So . . . you were saying?"

Fear crawled up Fred's back like a centipede. "There's an outcrop of rock about twenty yards ahead, Kyri. We'd be a lot safer behind it."

"Yes—I know. But we're having a conversation, and we haven't seen anything yet." Kyriakos brushed his mustache with heavily nicotine-stained fingers. Fred remembered that when he'd first seen that mustache in Italy, it had been a well-groomed Ronald Colman growth, along the road beyond Tombe di Pesaro, on the Canadian Corps boundary. But now it had bushed out and run riot, perhaps symbolizing its owner's own reversion to the traditional banditry of his native land.

"It was a Spandau that fired just now." When he didn't speak, Kyriakos occupied his silence. "That's an *Andarte* weapon. And if they've got another one up there trained on us, we wouldn't get ten yards—if they think we've seen them. So . . . talk to me—wag your finger at me—as though you had all the time in the world, okay?"

"Yes." But words failed Fred, even as he raised a ridiculous finger.

Christmas Eve! he thought desperately. *It wasn't Christmas Eve—it was February the second, not December the twenty-fourth. February the second, anno Domini 1945, not December the twenty-fourth, 1944!* "Yes."

"Go on—go on!" Kyriakos waved an equally ridiculous hand at him, as though to disagree with the ridiculous finger. *"Talk to me!"*

"Yes." *But on the other hand, it was Christmas Eve,* thought Fred. *Because General Scobie had abolished Christmas Day, 1944, for the British Army in Athens. It just wouldn't have sounded right for the British Army—the Liberators—to have caroled "Peace on earth, and goodwill to all men" when they'd been busy killing their erstwhile Communist allies, with their twenty-five pounders firing over the Parthenon, and the cruisers and destroyers in the bay stonking targets along the Piraeus road, and the Spitfires wheeling like eagles overhead!* "It's the eve of Scobiemas, I mean, Kyriakos."

"Ah! Of course—I had forgotten! Scobiemas is tomorrow, of course! But we Greeks do not keep Scobiemas. Or Christmas, either—remember?"

Dead right! Fred remembered. *And General Scobie had been dead right too, because the Commies had launched a midnight attack on the Rouf Barracks garrison, Christmas Day–Boxing Day, on the otherwise reasonable assumption that the British would be pissed out of their minds by then; whereas in fact, thanks to General Scobie, they'd been stone-cold sober and ready—and bloody-minded with it . . . also thanks to General Scobie, by God!*

But he had to talk—

"I went to a party on Christmas Day, actually."

"You did?" Kyriakos took a step towards him, turning slightly and draping a friendly arm across his shoulders. "I thought that all the parties were forbidden then." He glanced sidelong, uphill.

"It was for Greeks, too." Fred let the friendly arm propel him forwards along the path. "What do you see?"

"Nothing . . . slowly now . . . for Greeks, you say?"

"Greek children. Some Fourth Div gunners gave it." Fred let himself be pushed towards the rocky outcrop. "I saw one little kid gobble up four days' M and V rations all by himself." It seemed a very long twenty yards to the outcrop, at this friendly snail's pace. "And a couple of platefuls of peaches after that, plus a pile of biscuits."

"Yes. I heard about that." The arm restrained him. "But it wasn't a gunners' party—it was Twenty-eighth Brigade RASC, Fred."

"Well, it was a gunner who took me along." They were getting closer, step by step. "But you're probably right: trust the RASC to have the peaches!" Fred shivered—slightly at the memory of the bitter wind that had chilled him before and after the party, as he'd helped the gunners find a position in suburban Athens free of electricity cables (which they had not been allowed to pull down; and there was the added problem of the Parthenon, high up and dead ahead, which had worried one classically educated subaltern mightily)—but mostly it was the last three agonizing yards, shuffled step by slow step, which frightened him.

"There now!" Kyriakos released him at last, under the safety of the rock. "Home and dry—eh?"

Fred watched, wordless and fascinated, as the Greek slid a stiletto from his jackboot and began to excavate a hole in the detritus beneath the rock.

"There now!" As he repeated the words Kyriakos fumbled inside his battle-dress blouse to produce a succession of documents—paybook, letters, and military identification—which he then buried in the hole, smoothing the surface above them. And then, finally, he fished another collection of even more dog-eared papers from his other boot, which went back into the empty battle-dress pocket.

The power of speech returned to Fred. "What the hell are you doing, Kyri?"

Kyriakos grimaced at him. "Not *Kyri* or *Kyriakos*—'Alexander'—or 'Alex,' for short . . . *shit!*"

"Sh—?" Fred failed to complete the obscenity as Kyriakos reached beneath his leather jerkin, first on one side and then on the other, to unbutton his epaulets so that they each hung down over his arms. Then he flipped the stiletto and offered it to Fred.

"Cut them off!" he commanded.

"What?" Fred had already admired the smart khaki green Canadian battle dress that Kyriakos had acquired during his service with the British Columbia Dragoons in Italy: to rip that uniform, never mind the badges of rank, seemed a blasphemy. "Why?"

"Cut them off—hurry up! Don't argue, there's a good chap."

Fred hacked at the straps left-handed, clumsily at first, and then with greater success as the sharp steel divided the stitching.

"Pull the threads out—go on—make a proper job of it, then." Kyriakos admonished him casually, yet the very gentleness of the admonition somehow urged its importance.

Fred finished the job as best he could and then watched the Greek pick out every last shred of evidence. "You did see something—just now—didn't you!"

"Thank you." Kyriakos took the epaulets and the knife from him, hefting the epaulets for a moment as though weighing their rank. Then he bent down and opened up the hole again with the stiletto, to add his badges of rank to his identity. "Our best intelligence is that this area is clear, all the way to Mesolóngion. And we've got the gulf patrolled now." He started refilling the hole again. "The word was that the Communists were pulling back into the mountains north and south of it—they don't want to be caught with their backs to the sea, come spring. Or whenever." He replanted a straggling little piece of desiccated greenery on top of his handiwork, and then bent down to blow away the telltale regularities left by his fingers. "But . . ."

"But?" The Greek's casual certainty that his civil war would resume its murderous course depressed Fred, for all that it hardly surprised him: the British had imposed the truce by overwhelming force of arms, but there had been too much bloodletting in those first dark December days, with too many scores left unsettled, for any compromise settlement to last—that was what all his better-informed elders said. "But what?"

Kyriakos sprinkled a final handful of dust on the hiding place. Then he looked back at Fred. "But I think I want to be careful, just in case."

"In case of what?" Fred resisted the temptation to answer his own question.

"In case our best intelligence is wrong." Kyriakos showed his teeth below his mustache. "My friend, perhaps I imagined something . . . But if I did not, then *they* will most certainly have observed *us*. And now they will know that we are behind this rock. So—"

The Spandau on the other side of the ridge cut Kyriakos off with its characteristic tearing-knocking racket, only to be suddenly cut off itself by prolonged bursts of fire from first one, and then another, LMG.

"Ah!" Kyriakos breathed out slowly as the *knock-knock-knock* of the answering machine gun died away. "So now we know!"

So now they knew, thought Fred tightly. It was a familiar enough scenario, reenacted endlessly in no different and equally hated Italian mountains these last two years: the rearguard or outpost machine-gunner getting in his first murderous burst, but then, if he was so unwise as to remain in his position, being outflanked or bracketed by the vengeful comrades of the first victims.

"Brens, the second time." Kyriakos unbuttoned his webbing holster and examined his revolver. "So that must be our people, I would think, okay?"

Fred stared at him, conscious equally of the weight of his own side arm and of his left-handed inadequacy. "Not *our* people, Kyri."

"No." Kyriakos replaced the revolver in its holster. "Not *your* people—*our* people. But that at least gives us a chance." He removed his beret, grinning at Fred as he did so. "Lucky I didn't wear my proper hat. So maybe I'm lucky today."

Fred watched the Greek raise his head slowly over the top of the rock, trying to equate luck with headgear. Unlike his fellow officers, who wore bus conductors' SD hats, wired and uncrumpled and quite different from his own, Kyri often wore a black Canadian dragoons' beret, complete with their cap badge. But then Kyri was an eccentric, everyone agreed.

"Nothing." Always the professional, Kyriakos lowered his head as slowly as he had raised it. "I think I am still lucky, perhaps."

"Bugger your luck!" A further burst of firing, punctuated now by the addition of single rifle shots, snapped Fred's nerve. "What about mine. This is supposed to be my Christmas Eve—I'm your bloody *guest*, Kyriakos!"

"Ah . . . but you must understand that *your* odds are a lot better than mine, old boy." Kyriakos grinned at him.

"They are?" Somehow the assurance wasn't reassuring. "Are they?"

"Oh, yes." The grin was fixed unnaturally under the mustache, the eyes were not smiling. "If our side runs away—your pardon! If *my* side withdraws strategically to regroup . . . If that happens, then the *Andartes* will outflank us here"—Kyriakos gestured left and right, dismissively—"or take us from below, without difficulty, I'm afraid."

Fred followed the gestures. There was dead ground not far along the track ahead, and more of it behind them. And they were in full view of the track below.

"I know this country, this place." The Greek nodded at him. "There's a little ruined monastery over the ridge, which the Turks destroyed long ago. I have walked this path before, with my father, in the old days: it is the secret back door to the village, which is below the monastery. So . . . I am very much afraid that our people have made a mistake—the same mistake the Turks once made. They have come up from the sea to attack the monastery . . . if that is where the *Andartes* are . . . when they should have come out of the mountains, over this ridge—up this path, even—to take it in the rear and push them down to the sea. . . . That will be some foolish, stiff-necked Athenian staff officer who thinks he knows everything, as the Athenians always do."

The firing started again, this time punctuated by the distinctive *crump* of mortar shells—a murderous, continuous shower of them.

Kyriakos swore in his native tongue, unintelligibly but eloquently, and Fred frowned at him. "What's the matter?"

"Those are three-inch—they'll be ours. So our people are well-equipped."

That didn't make sense. "So they'll win?"

"Too bloody right!" Kyriakos swore again.

"So what's wrong with that?"

"I told you." Kyriakos was hardly listening to him. He was studying the landscape again. "I know this place."

"Yes." The eagles were still on patrol, wheeling and dipping and soaring over the highest peak, out of which the ridge itself issued in a great jumble of boulders piled beneath its vertical cliff. "So what?"

Kyriakos looked at him at last. "This is the path the villagers took when the Turks came. Over this ridge—this path—is the only line of retreat. If our side is too strong . . . we're rather in the way, old boy."

The Greek shrugged philosophically, but Fred remembered from Tombe di Pesaro days that the worse things were, the more philosophic Captain Michaelides became. "Then hadn't we better find another spot in which to cower, Kyri?" He tried to match the casual tone.

"Yes, I was thinking about that." Kyriakos turned his attention to the hillside below them. But it was unhelpfully open all the way down to the track along which they should have driven an hour earlier, happy and unworried—only an hour, or a lifetime, thought Fred. And that further reminded him of the Michaelides Philosophy: being in the Wrong Place . . . or there at the Wrong Time . . . that was *"No fun at all, old boy!"* And now they appeared to have achieved the unfunny double, by Christ!

But the unfunniness, and the patient eagles, concentrated his mind. "If you did see someone up there, Kyri . . . couldn't he just possibly be one of yours—ours?" He threw in his lot finally with the Royal Hellenic Army and the bloodthirsty National Guard.

"Ye-ess . . ." Kyriakos shifted to another position behind the outcrop. "I was thinking about that, too."

Fred watched him raise himself—*never show yourself in the same place twice,* of course; and the poor bastard had had a lot longer in which to learn that simplest of lessons, ever since the Italians had chanced their luck out of Albania, back in the winter of '40. But then he remembered his own manners.

"My turn, Kyri." He raised himself—*too quickly, too quickly, but too late now!* And he wanted to see the crest of that damned ridge for himself, anyway.

The surface of the rock midway between them burst into fragments in the same instant that the machine gun rattled down at them, with the bullets ricocheting away into infinity behind them.

This time the echoes—their own echoes, much louder that those of the firefight over the ridge—took longer to lose themselves as he breathed out his own mixture of terror and relief.

(*"Missed again!"* That was what Sergeant Procter, ever cheerful, ever efficient, always said, when he himself had been shaking with fear, back in Italy. *"If they can't hit us now, sir, then the buggers don't deserve to win the war—do they!"*)

"That was *deuced* stupid of you, old boy." Somewhere along the line of his long multinational service since Albania in 1940, Kyriakos had picked up *deuced*, probably from some blue-bloodied British unit, which he used like *too bloody right,* a ripe Australianism, in other "no fun" situations.

"I'm sorry." The ridge had been thickly forested on the crest, with encircling horns of trees to the left and right; so the machine gunner's friends would have no problem flanking this outcrop, thought Fred miserably. And Kyriakos had certainly observed all that already. "A moment of weakness, Kyri, I'm sorry."

"But not altogether useless." With typical good manners Kyriakos hastened to take the sting from his criticism. "That was a Browning—a 'B-A-R,' as our American friends would say . . . a nice little weapon."

"Yes?" Fred let himself be soothed, knowing that Kyri was using his hobby to soothe him, deliberately. "I bow to your experience, Captain Michaelides. But what does that mean?"

"Not a lot, to be honest. It goes back a long way, does the BAR. . . . We had some of them in 1940—Belgian FN variants. . . . But, then so did the Poles. And the Germans and the Russians inherited *them*, as well as ours, of course. . . . But so far as I'm aware, *you* never used them, old boy."

Lying back and looking upwards, Fred caught sight of one of the eagles making a wider circuit. Or maybe the bloody bird had pinpointed his dinner now. "So those aren't our friends, up there?"

Kyriakos thought for a moment. "Ah . . . now, I don't think we have any friends at the moment, either way." Another moment's thought. "Because we're not part of the action: we're an inconvenience, you might say."

The firefight continued sporadically over the crest. By now the commanding officers on each side would be estimating casualties and discretion against the remaining hours of daylight and their very different objectives. And sudden and overwhelming bitterness suffused Fred. Because the bloody Germans were one thing, and bad enough. But the bloody Greeks were another—and this really wasn't the war he had volunteered for. Even, until now, it wasn't a war that he had been able to take seriously. It was Kyri's bloody war, not the British Army's bloody war—and especially *not his*!

All of which made him think of the unthinkable, which nestled in his pocket, where he had put it this morning, freshly laundered. "How about surrendering—for the time being?"

"Yes." Kyriakos nodded. "I had been thinking about that, also."

The lightness of the Greek's voice alerted him. "The truck talks . . . we could claim flag of truce—couldn't we?"

"We could." The Greek had his own large white handkerchief. "But . . . if you don't mind . . . we will claim it my way"—he shook the handkerchief out—"okay?"

Suddenly Fred felt the breath of a colder wind within him than that which he had already felt on his cheeks. "Kyri—"

"No! You are quite right, old boy!" Kyriakos shook out his handkerchief. "We wouldn't get ten yards. . . . This way . . . there's a chance, I agree."

"No—"

"Yes!" The Greek nodded. "I am 'Alex'"—he patted his battle-dress pocket—"and you wanted to visit Delphi . . . you can bullshit them about your classical education, and how you are a British socialist—tell them that you don't like Winston Churchill, if you get the chance. . . . But say that Spiros in Levádhia— Spiros the baker—*he* recommended *me*. Okay?"

"Spiros, the baker." Fred echoed the order. "In Levádhia?"

"That's all. Let me do the talking, old boy." Kyriakos drew a breath, and then grinned at him. "If they're in doubt they won't shoot you—they can always trade you; you're worth more alive than dead at the moment—*don't argue*." He raised his hand quickly to preclude the argument. "*I* know what to say, if we can only get them to talk. And since this is their only line of retreat, I think they'll talk—at least, to start with." He qualified the grin with a shrug. "After that, it will be as God always intended."

Fred bridled, already bitterly regretting his suggestion. "I don't know, Kyri." The truth, which he had quite failed to grasp in half-grasping, was that it *was* this man's own bloody war, truce or no truce. And that meant . . . that if it was true that a British officer had some value as a prisoner, it was even more true that a Greek royalist officer was certain to be shot out of hand if caught in the Wrong Place at the Wrong Time. In fact, Kyri himself had said as much, and he had replied with cowardly stupidity, claiming guest rights on Scobiemas Eve—*I'm your bloody guest, Kyri!* "I don't think so."

The Greek frowned. "Don't think what, old boy?"

Fred shivered inwardly, aware that he could never explain his shame—that would make it worse."I don't think I care to take the chance. I think I'd rather shoot it out here." He clawed at his holster with his right hand, only to find that the damn claw was as useless as ever—more useless even, in its very first real emergency. "Damn it!" *Damn it to hell! Now he had to reach across with his fumbling left hand!* "What I mean is . . . we can just slow them up and wait for our chaps to come up behind them, Kyri." *The bloody thing wouldn't come out—it was snagged somehow. Damn it to hell and back!*

"Too late, old boy," the Greek murmured almost conversationally, raising himself, and then raising and waving his arm with the handkerchief on the end of it. "There! Never done that before. But there's always a first time for everything, they say. And I'm told it always worked a treat with the Germans—with their ordinary fellows, anyway . . . eh?"

"Oh . . . *fuck!*" Fred almost wept with frustration as his left hand joined the claw's mutiny. "*Fuck!*"

"Such language!" Kyriakos tut-tutted at him. "We made a pact, remember, old boy?"

That was also true, thought Fred as he gagged on other and

fouler expletives in giving up the struggle. Only hours—or maybe only minutes—before they had discussed the degeneration of their everyday language under the influence and pressure of army life, in the light of their imminent meeting with Madame Michaelides (who countenanced no such words) and Fred's eventual return to the bosom of his family (who would certainly be equally shocked); and while his own persuasion had been that it would be no problem—that some automatic safety valve would activate—Kyri had not been so confident and was unashamedly more frightened at the prospect than he seemed to be now, at another prospect, as he waved his large white handkerchief.

"Don't you forget now, eh?" The Greek also waved his finger, admonishing him for all the world as though they were about to meet his mother, instead of more likely God Almighty, Whose intentions they were now supposed to be anticipating. "I am Alex, the friend of Spiros, okay?"

It was also, and finally, true . . . what Sergeant Procter always said: that you could like a man and hate him at the same time.

Kyriakos smiled again, turning the knife in the wound. "So now we wait?"

"What for?" The mixture of unpleasant noises from the other side of the ridge had become increasingly sporadic while they had been arguing. But now it seemed to have died away altogether, so maybe that was a silly question. "Not for long, though?"

"They'll flank us." Kyri gave the handkerchief a final vigorous wave and then pointed first left, then right. "Where those gulleys from the top peter out—'peter out,' is that right?"

"Yes." Five years of English education, followed by another five of military alliance, had rendered the Greek almost perfectly bilingual. But more than that, Fred at last understood how Kyriakos had seen their positions through an infantryman's eye. While their refuge could easily be flanked from those treacherous gulleys, it also had to be eliminated because they in turn had a clear view of the lower slopes and the track below. "I understand, Kyri."

"Good. Then you watch the left and I will watch the right." He paused. "And understand this also, old boy. The moment you see anything, you put your hands up—and I mean *up*—up *high*, my friend. Because we'll only have that one moment, maybe. Understood?"

"Understood." He didn't want to add to the man's burdens. "And then you're my guide, Alex . . . recommended to me by Spiros the baker." He wondered for a moment about Spiros the baker. Was he one of Captain Michaelides's ELAS suspects? Or one of the captain's double agents? But then, other than sharing the general British Army distaste for the mutual barbarities of the Greeks' December bloodbath, he had never really attempted to understand their politics. The distinction between Captain Kyriakos Michaelides, of the Royal Hellenic Army, and Kyriakos Michaelides, the son of Father's old friend, was not one he had even thought of seriously until now. "But I don't speak halfways decent Greek, remember—okay?"

"Don't worry about that." Kyri threw the words over his shoulder, forcing him to concentrate on his own gulley. "I'll do the talking. Just you be an outraged British ally to start with, old boy—and be angry with me for getting you into trouble. And—" He stopped suddenly.

"And what?" He fought the urge to turn towards the sudden silence. "Have you spotted something."

"And . . . *nod* . . . nod and *smile* when I mention Spiros, okay?" The Greek spoke with unnatural slowness. "Ye-ess . . . I think maybe I have . . . *so get ready!*"

Fred still couldn't see anything. But the muscles all the way down his arms wanted to get his hands up even before his brain transmitted its own instructions. "Nothing this side—"

"YOU THERE! STAND UP!"

The shout came from his side, out of nowhere.

"Get up," Kyriakos snarled at him from behind.

Fred and his arms shot up simultaneously, his boots digging into the scree beneath them so urgently that he almost over-balanced; and it was only when he'd rebalanced himself that the reason for his failure to react instantly came to him.

"DON'T SHOOT!" He hadn't imagined in advance how he was supposed to obey an order given in a foreign language. But there was suddenly no problem about how to reply to an order in the plainest Kyri's English. *"BRITISH!"*

Kyri shouted something, also. But Fred was too busy staring at the figure that had risen out of the dead ground of the gulley no more than thirty yards away from him.

"KEEP 'EM UP! DON'T YOU DARE MOVE A FUCKING INCH!"

Fred was suddenly impaled on the prongs of disbelief and relief, any last doubts about the identity of his captor dissolved by that beloved obscenity, which sounded sweeter in his ear than all the music of heaven, which could never be foul and harsh again, it was so beautiful.

The welcome figure advanced cautiously towards him, cradling a gangster's Thompson machine pistol in its hands, until it had halved the distance between them.

"KEEP 'EM UP!"

Relief had started to lower his arms. But as they instantly went up again, disbelief still clogged his tongue.

"Say something, old boy!" Kyri no longer snarled, but his voice was nonetheless urgent. *"Say something!"*

"Yes." As Fred's tongue unclogged he felt himself leap from cowardly gratitude to outraged dignity with one five-league stride. "What the hell are you up to"—the man was so close now that he could see the chevrons on his arm—"Sergeant?"

"What?" Now it was the sergeant's turn. "What?"

"Why did you fire at us?" The unmoving Thompson kept his arms at full stretch, but his sense of outrage began to stretch beyond them.

The sergeant stared at him for a full second. "Who the fu—" But a sudden caution gagged the word, and he restrained himself. "Who are you?"

Anger took hold of Fred. "I am Captain Fattorini—Brigade RE, Fourth Div, Sergeant. Who are *you?*"

The sergeant assimilated that information slowly. But then, after having turned it over in his mind, he switched momentarily to Kyriakos before coming back to Fred himself.

"Identification." What the sergeant had plainly seen hadn't reassured him, because the muzzle of the Thompson jerked slightly, but didn't leave Fred's stomach area. "Slowly, now— *identification!*"

Fred reached inside his tunic . . . slowly, because the sergeant had the gun. But there were limits. "Sir, you call me, Sergeant."

"What?" The sergeant frowned. *"Sir?"*

He could understand the sergeant's doubt. But with that reliable weapon pointing at his guts he needed to resolve that doubt as soon as possible. "Aren't officers 'sir' in your unit, Sergeant?"

The sergeant stared at him again. But then something seemed to tighten within him. "Put it down on the ground . . . and then take three steps back . . . and keep your hands up—put them on the back of your neck, right?"

Something deep inside Fred tightened also. This wasn't how it ought to be. But then, this wasn't a situation he had ever encountered before. And this, also, was a new variety of sergeant.

"Do what he says, old boy," said Kyriakos from behind him.

He had quite forgotten about Kyri.

"BERT!" The sergeant shouted past him, and past Kyri. *"WATCH THEM!"*

So they were flanked from the other gulley too then, thought Fred. A careful man, this sergeant.

He took his ordered steps back, until he sensed Kyriakos right behind him, and watched the sergeant retrieve his identification.

But enough was enough. "Just what is going on, Sergeant?"

The sergeant took his time with the identification, giving Fred a long moment's scrutiny against his four-year-old photograph held up shoulder high for easier comparison. And even at the end of this examination his suspicions were by no means allayed, judging by the stony expression he maintained as his attention shifted to Kyriakos. "And who might he be . . . sir?" He pronounced the last word grudgingly.

"Can I lower my arms now?" He had been half-expecting the question, but half-expectation hadn't helped him choose the right answer. Because if the sergeant was still suspicious of his identity, how much more so might he not be with an evident Greek if that evident Greek admitted to two identities, one in his pocket and the other artistically concealed a yard away?

"No!" The Thompson, held one-handed, jerked menacingly. "No, *sir*."

"For Christ's sake!" Fred had hoped that Kyri would decide for him, but for once he seemed cowed in silence. "How long do you intend to keep this bloody charade up, Sergeant?"

"Sir?" The sergeant weakened for a fraction of a second under his onslaught, but then his chin lifted. "For as long as I say so . . . sir." The moment of weakness passed. "Who is this *person*, sir?"

"Please, thank you!" Kyri leapt into the breach at last. "*Riris*, sir—*Alexander* Riris—driver and guide. And good friend to British *officers*, sir." He laid heavy emphasis on *officers*. "Speaking English well—and with copious personal documentation, please—thank you!"

"Oh, yes?" The sergeant sounded as though he had heard similar protestations of friendship all the way from the Suez Canal and was long past believing them. "Well, let's have a *look*, then—*STOP!*" The weary disbelief vanished instantly, and Fred's identification fell to the ground as the sergeant caught up the Thompson with both hands. "What's that under your jerkin, Johnnie? Lift it up, *slowly* . . . the jerkin, I mean, you silly bugger! *Watch it!*"

Fred stood like a statue, if there had ever been a statue of surrender, aware that the sergeant had seen the bulge of Kyri's holster.

"He has a side arm, Sergeant." As Fred intervened, the reason for Kyri's earlier emphasis came to him belatedly. "With my permission." The sergeant was scared, perhaps. But he was also a well-trained soldier, almost certainly Field Security, although he

16

wore no badge or flash, only his stripes. "Where's your officer? You get him—I demand to speak to him, Sergeant." Well-trained—and cautious and observant. A good sergeant, for his dirty job, just as Sergeant Procter was a good sergeant for his dangerous and unrewarding one. And . . . somehow that was reassuring. "Then I think we can resolve this situation, right?"

The sergeant didn't relax. Even, Fred's shift from that peremptory demand to a more reasonable statement increased his wariness.

"Jacko!" The shout came from behind, from the other gulley—that must be *Bert*, with the Browning.

Still no relaxation. *"Yes?"*

"Tiny's down below—with Hughie and the lads, Jacko."

Sergeant Jacko gave "down below" one lightning-quick glance. "Well . . . you're in luck, sir." But even now he didn't relax: that was the difference between the men and the boys. All he did was to raise one eyebrow. "You wanted an officer. So here is one . . . sir."

Fred took that as an invitation and looked down into the valley. There were two vehicles on the track, a jeep and a 15-curt, each with twin Vickers-Berthiers mounted on them, which were manned and trained on the ridge, while the other occupants fanned out on each side, sinking behind what little cover there was.

"Give 'em a wave, Bert," ordered Sergeant Jacko.

Three figures rose on Bert's wave and started uphill, the rest remaining under cover. The most diminutive of them, presumably "Tiny," struggled under the weight of a backpacked wireless. As for the other two, one carried a rifle, and the third and largest—Hughie?—appeared to be armed only with a walking stick. So Hughie would be the officer, thought Fred with an inner sigh. But from his Italian experience he disliked officers who carried sticks. Majors or above, they were usually outrageously brave, and often arrogant with it, and given to chivying the poor devils of sappers required to build their bridges and clear their minefields under fire.

"May I lower my arms *now*, Sergeant?" It would probably be a most uncomfortable interview, because the intrepid major wouldn't thank them for disrupting his operations, however accidentally or innocently. And he would probably be rude to Kyri, who was most likely on a short fuse now, after having been shot at and held up by his allies in his own country. But at least they were safe now.

"What?" Sergeant Jacko paused. "No, keep 'em up . . . sir—

17

and you, Johnnie, *up*, that's it. Until I say you can put 'em down, you keep 'em up, *sir*. Right?"

Fred fumed in silence as he watched the figures approach. The large major was well in the lead now, unencumbered either by caution, like his rifleman, or by equipment, like the little wireless-man, who was falling farther and farther behind. Yet, even as he fumed—the sergeant's caution really went beyond the bounds of prejudice—he identified a tingle of excited curiosity. That the Greeks on both sides might be indulging any opportunity to settle up during the truce really came as no surprise. Their private scores dated from long before the war, so it seemed from Kyri's chance remarks, which were all the more bloodcurdling because by Greek standards he was an unusually *un*bloodthirsty and liberal royalist, thirsting for peace and wine and women after five years of war, but apparently resigned to achieving only the last two for the foreseeable future. *But this was quite obviously a British operation, regardless of the truce.*

The intrepid major was a very young major, as well as a very big one, he observed as the major closed the distance with immense upwards strides. And young majors, role-playing in their elders' image, were always the worst ones.

But . . . if it was a *British* operation, what the hell was the British Army doing breaking their own truce so deliberately?

A *very* young major.

"Sergeant Devenish! What the blazes are you up to?" The young major heaved himself over a larger obstacle in the sceen below them.

"Sir!" Sergeant Jacko—Sergeant *Devenish*—kept his eyes on both of them as he started to reply. "We spotted these two coming up behind us, and—"

"Then why the b-blazes didn't you c-c-call in?" The young major stuttered with anger as he cut the sergeant off while slithering and stamping up the scree over the last few yards.

"The set's on the blink, sir. We couldn't raise you." The sergeant sounded not so much overawed by rank as weary of his faultfinding majors.

"W-what d'you mean 'on the blink'?" The young major anchored himself on his stick for a moment, but took a closer look at Fred and Kyri for the first time, scowling horribly as he did so. "You mean, some bloody fool dropped it?" He stopped as he shifted his scowl back to Fred from Kyriakos.

"The set was not dropped, Mr. Audley." Sergeant Devenish answered the young major with quiet authority, still without taking his eyes off them. "It's the one we've had trouble with before. It's a duff set, is what it is."

Mister Audley? The young major's sheepskin jerkin concealed his badges of rank, and Fred couldn't identify the impossible heraldic quadruped on his cap-badge. But at this close range the man's extreme, almost *beardless*, youth was simultaneously as apparent as his considerable ugliness. (And he hadn't been so much scowling as perhaps frowning nervously?) And then the full significance of the sergeant's *Mister* Audley and his slight disdain clinched the matter.

"What the devil d'you mean by shooting at me?" Fred snapped at the youth, even while keeping his hands close to the back of his neck with the sergeant's eye still on him. "And who the devil are you?"

"W-what?" The scowl-frown returned. "Sergeant, who is this?"

"Captain Fat—" The sergeant paused momentarily. "Fat-O'Rhiney, sir."

"O-what?" The youth blinked.

"O'Rhiney—Captain Fat-O'Rhiney, Mr. Audley, sir," repeated the sergeant before Fred could correct him. "Royal Engineers."

The youth raised his eyebrow at Fred. "What jolly bad luck! F-Fat—F-Fatto . . . what?"

Fred clenched his teeth. "Fattorini. Brigade Royal Engineers. Who are you, may I ask?"

The youth frowned again, this time staring at Fred with peculiar concentration. *"Fattorini?"*

Kyriakos cleared his throat, but mercifully didn't spit. "Captain Frederick Armstrong Fattorini, Royal Engineers, GSO Three, Brigade Staff," he said, with deliberate public school King's English clarity.

The youth shifted his frowning stare to Kyriakos. "And may one ask who the hell *you* are?" he inquired politely.

Kyri drew himself up. "Michaelides, Staff Captain, Remini Brigade, Royal Hellenic Army. . . . And may I ask whom I have the doubtful honor of addressing on the eve of Scobiemas?"

The youth's ugly face broke up. "Scobiemas! Of course!"

Sergeant Devenish coughed. "Said his name was Alexander—Alexander *something*, sir. And he said he had papers to prove it."

"My identity card is buried nearby," snapped Kyri. "When we heard the firing we thought you might be *Andartes*—do you understand?"

The youth grinned. "All too well, I do, very sensible!" Then he stopped grinning. "Would you be so good as to dig it up for me, then?"

Kyriakos nodded. "Of course."

"They're both armed, sir," said Sergeant Devenish quickly. "And I haven't had a chance to disarm them."

"Yes?" The youth was staring at Fred again. "Well, in these parts that would also be very sensible. . . . And that's why you're still 'reaching for the sky' as they say, is it?" He nodded. "But I think we can dispense with that precaution now, Sergeant Devenish."

"Sir?" The doubt in Sergeant Devenish's voice keep Fred's arms up.

"It's all right, Sergeant." Another nod. "You were quite right to be careful, they do look a dodgy pair, I agree."

"We spotted them on the hillside. And I think they spotted us, too."

"That was careless of you! So?"

"They were lurking behind this rock, sir." Doubt and anger filled the sergeant's voice.

"We weren't 'lurking,'" said Kyriakos. "We were just taking the shortcut to the village. And then we heard the firing. So we took cover."

"Ah!" Another nod. "But may one ask why you were going to the village, Captain Michaelides?"

Fred had been waiting for his chance. "Captain Michaelides was taking me to see Delphi. But our jeep broke down two or three miles back." Not knowing the youth's name and rank inhibited him. "You are . . . who?"

"Audley, David Audley, West Sussex Dragoons." The youth grinned. "Lieutenant—strictly expendable cannon fodder . . . *Hughie!*"

"Mr. Audley, sir?" It was the little wireless operator who answered.

"Hughie, be a good fellow and tell Sunray that everything's okay here. Tell him that Charlie Three was defective. But also tell him that we're bringing in two innocent bystanders for him to meet, got that?"

"Right-o, Mr. Audley." The little man shambled away, uncomplaining although the sweat shone on his face. "*'ullo, Sunray— 'ullo, Sunray! Charlie One to Sunray.*"

"Do please lower your arms, gentlemen . . . And Captain Michaelides." Lieutenant Audley nodded at Kyriakos, and then carried the nod to Sergeant Devenish. "It's all right, Sergeant, I can vouch for Captain Fattorini personally, don't worry!"

Kyriakos looked questioningly at Fred. "You've met before?" As he observed Fred's incomprehension he stopped and transferred the question back to the ugly dragoon.

"No. But the face is familiar." Audley grinned once more at Fred, hugging his secret knowledge to himself as warmly as his sheepskin jacket. "Right, Captain Frederick Armstrong Fattorini? Border Armstrong—which side, Captain Fattorini?"

Who the hell was he? "Scottish, of course." Who the hell *was* he?

"Could have been either. But in your case, Scottish." Audley nodded his delight at Kyriakos. "Border family, English and Scottish, but all brigands of the worst sort. No surprise meeting one here—all brigands here—right, Captain Michaelides?"

Kyriakos stared at him for a moment, and then knelt down to retrieve his buried identity while Fred frowned at the dragoon, trying to place him at one remove from actual acquaintance.

Kyri stood up again, with his papers and his torn-off epaulets in his hand. "Do you wish to see—" But then the expression of idiotic pleasure on the youth's face stopped him even before the youth waved his offering away.

"Good Lord, no!" The pleasure almost transformed the dragoon's ugliness into beauty as he continued to grin at Fred. *"Thought* I knew that face—*no* bloody mistaking it, even without the name." He stopped suddenly as he remembered his sergeant, who was still holding the owner of the face at unmoving gunpoint. "It's okay, Sar' Devenish, you can relax. I can vouch for this officer, even though I've never met him in my life, right?"

The Thompson remained pointing at them. "Sir?" The dragoon's happiness tortured the question from his careful sergeant.

"It's all right." The youth nodded positively at Sergeant Devenish. "I've played rugger with this officer's brother, Sar' Devenish. Same name . . . *not* a lot of Fattorinis in the British Army . . . but also same *face*." He took the nod to Fred. "I've seen blood pour out of a Roman nose just like that one—*Matthew* Fattorini's blood, from *his* nose—a family nose, that is, Sar' Devenish. Three peas from the same pod—Matthew, Mark, and *Fred* . . . God knows what happened to 'Luke' and 'John,' if they were baptizing 'em out of the New Testament!" Another grin. "Lower your arms, Captain Fat-O'Rhiney!"

The Thompson still didn't move. "And the Greek . . . officer, sir?" The sergeant's voice was still doubtful.

"Captain Michaelides," said Fred. "And as it happens, my father's name was John. And I have an uncle named Luke."

"Yes?" The dragoon looked from Fred to the sergeant, and then back again. "Well, I'm sure Captain Michaelides is . . . whoever he says he is, in Captain Fattorini's company." He spoke lightly, quite unaware that he was unnecessarily humiliating a good NCO. "How are things on the ridge, then?"

"Everything's under control." The sergeant breathed in through his nostrils as he lowered his gun. "No one has tried to

21

come up the path after we put a burst over their heads . . . as ordered."

"Well, thank God something went according to plan!" The dragoon nodded at the sergeant. "So you came over this side because there seemed to be a problem here, is that it?"

"Yes, sir." The sergeant clenched his jaw. "I left Corporal Weekes in charge."

"Uh-huh." Another casual nod. "Well, you just trot on back there—there's no problem here now. And you can take Hughie with you. His set's not on the blink. *Hughie!*"

"I 'eard, Mr. Audley, I 'eard!" The little man groaned audibly. "Fuckin' mountains! Up yer go, down yer go . . . up yer go, down yer go!" He trudged off in the sergeant's wake, mumbling and cursing repetitively under his breath.

Audley watched him go. "The trouble with Driver Hewitt . . . apart from the fact that he's a perfectly d-d-d—*awful* driver . . . or *one* of the many troubles with him . . . is that he comes from East Anglia, where everything is p-p-pancake flat!"

The little man swung around, almost unbalancing under the weight of the set on his back. "I 'eard that, Mr. Audley."

"Go on, Hughie, go on! The unwonted exercise will strengthen your legs!" Audley turned back to Fred. "Now, let's go back and explain ourselves, shall we?"

Kyriakos rolled his eyes at Fred as Audley set off downhill. "Who is this eccentric friend of yours, old man?"

Fred blinked. "No friend of *mine*, Captain Michaelides. But it would seem he's acquainted with my little brother Matthew, luckily for us." He stared at the large departing figure, whose long legs had already taken him far down the slope. "But Matt's with the Guards, on the German frontier by now."

"And he's from an armored unit—that badge I do not recognize. But I wouldn't have thought you have a tank large enough for him." Kyriakos stared in the same direction, at Lieutenant Audley's back.

"Must be some obscure yeomanry regiment." Fred accepted his own Royal Engineers' disdain for the rest of the British Army, from Matt's snooty Guards to Audley's mindless ex-horsemen from the local hunt. But that reminded him unbearably of how young Matt was, with Mark still missing over Northern Italy. "If he played rugger with Matt, he must have been at school with him." He tried to put Northern Italy and the RAF out of his mind. "That's probably it."

"But you never met him?"

"No. But we each went to different schools—it was one of Father's conceits. That way, we didn't compete with each other's

22

reputation. Mark and Matt were much cleverer than I was, and Matt was a better sportsman than Mark. And . . . I rather suspect Father reckoned we'd make three different sets of influential friends, to help business along in the future." He turned to smile at Kyriakos, but then he saw that the expression on the Greek's face was not one of polite curiosity. "Why do you ask? What's the matter, Kyri?"

Kyriakos pointed. "We must go! See, he is summoning us—"

Fred caught the Greek's arm. "You bloody answer me, Kyri! Why?"

"Why?" Kyriakos shrugged. "I have a feeling about him, that's all." He pulled at Fred's grip. "We must go."

"A feeling?" Fred looked down towards the track again, where the big dragoon subaltern was even now chivying his drivers into attempting to turn their vehicles round in what was quite obviously an inadequate space for the 15-cwt, if not the jeep. "He's a baby, Kyri. And he isn't too smart when dealing with NCOs who know more about his business that he does, even if they can't pronounce my name. I've seen a hundred like him, a thousand . . . all babes-in-arms, all cannon fodder—" He stopped suddenly as he remembered that that was Audley's own description of himself.

"His business, yes!" The tone in Kyriakos's voice drew his attention away from the balls-up on the track, where the jeep had been turned successfully, only to be blocked by the broadside truck. "But what business is that, would you guess? What business has your army, breaking the truce here?"

"God knows!" Fred's eye was drawn irresistibly back to the confusion on the track, where Audley now had his men trying to lift the truck bodily, after its own turning-circle had baffled him. "I doubt whether he knows, whatever it is, anyway."

"That may be. But I wouldn't stake my life on it." Kyriakos was also watching the truck. "A baby he may be . . . but I recall fighting German babies in Italy who were not so childish when it came to killing. And, as you say, that sergeant of his knew his business. And he was a very *cautious* man, I think, not a *trusting* man, would you say?" The Greek pulled at Fred's grip again. "I have seen his breed before. But not in the *British* army—no, not before in *your* army Captain Fattorini."

What Fred saw was that they were actually turning the truck, with brute force triumphing over ignorance, in the best British Army tradition when there were not Royal Engineers present. But what he thought as he watched was that Captain Michaelides's experience of different armies went back a long way—all the way from the triumph of 1940 to the 1941 debacle,

23

and from victory through defeat and escape to the long, hard slog up Italy, which they had shared. So, compared with Captain Michaelides, he was a baby too, maybe. "What breed would that be, Kyri? And what business?"

Kyriakos didn't reply immediately, even though Fred released his grip. "Who knows?" They were letting the truck do its own work now. "We Greeks have our business to settle, here in Greece." He didn't move. "For which we need you bloody British, most regrettably. At least, until we can involve the Americans in it, I am thinking."

"The Yanks?" Fred heard the incredulity in his voice. "What have they got to do with it?"

"Nothing yet." Kyriakos didn't look at him. "I think we had better move, old man. Because your brother's old school-fellow will be remembering us again very soon. And . . . and I would not have him mistrust us, after having trusted us so foolishly—even though he had us in sights all the time, as he very well knew, eh?"

Fred looked down at the road and understood; because young Mr. What's-his-name—young *Mr. David Audley*, the big baby dragoon—had spoken to his two machine gunners on the vehicles, and they had kept their guns trained up the hillside, by God!

"What you want to think about, old man, is"—Kryi waved deliberately at Audley without looking at Fred—"is . . . why did your great Mr. Winston Churchill come all the way to Greece on Christmas Day—not Scobiemas Day tomorrow, but your real Christmas Day—when we were both so busy, eh?"

And it was so bloody cold! remembered Fred irrelevantly: his Greek baptism had been that bitter wind cutting him to the bone. In fact . . . in fact, he hadn't registered Christmas Day at all—that gunner's party for the children hadn't actually been on Christmas Day, he remembered now. It had been after Boxing Day actually. Because all the bloody days had been just bloody days, one after another.

"He came here because he had *business* here." Kyri waved again. "So when you think about *this* business, maybe you'd better think of *Mister* Winston Churchill's business, okay?"

"Yes, okay!" Fred checked for an instant, and then jumped past the Greek, knowing that he really hadn't the faintest idea what the man was talking about, but also that he didn't like it. This was all bloody politics, and no one in his right mind trusted politicians—the bloody politicians fucked things up, everyone was agreed on that. The bloody politicians had never heard an S-mine go *click* underfoot on the roadside verge, beside a blown bridge, in that single careless moment—or felt all the bones in a good right hand go *crunch* between unyielding metal.

But Audley was waving and beckoning at them. And the real mercy now was that Audley's business was none of his business, even if Kyri wanted him to think about it.

He waved back, suddenly lighthearted. Because the *real* mercy, now that he thought about it, was that Audley's business hadn't been the accidental death of them back there on the hillside. "Hullo, there!"

He jumped down onto the track, quickly composing his happy lack of responsibility into a straight, serious face. Young Mr. Audley's problems (no doubt relating to his "business," whatever it was) rated some small sympathy, but no more than that. Every junior officer had his problems, so what? "Ready to go?"

"You took your time, Captain Fat-O'Rhiney." Audley looked past him.

Cheeky! "You seemed rather busy. I didn't want to disturb you."

"What was all the conversation about?"

But observant as well as cheeky. So it might be as well to approach the question truthfully. "Captain Michaelides was interrogating me about you—how you know who I was. Or at least, how you were prepared to give him the benefit of the doubt because you know Matthew, anyway."

"Oh, yes?" The look was still directed past him, as Kyriakos arrived in the midst of a small avalanche. "I was rather trusting, wasn't I?" Audley opened his mouth. "C-Captain . . . M-M—"

"Kyri, my friends call me, David Audley." Kryiakos came to the young man's rescue quickly. "And you definitely qualify as a friend, I think."

"Kyri-Kyriakos—that's not very friendly!" Each time Audley stumbled, the words came out on the double. "That's as bad as *M-M-Michaelides*, damn it!" He took the third M with a supreme effort. "But . . . g-get into the jeep anyway. Otherwise, my commanding officer will have my g-guts for . . . *garters*, right?"

It was pathetic how the stutter seemed to feed on itself, as the young man's nervousness increased with each failure. But once again, Fred found his sympathy strictly limited.

"Go!" Audley addressed his driver peremptorily. "Get in, get in!" Then he saw the Vickers-Berthier gunner, who was still in the jeep. "Get out. Len! G-go and get in the front, there's a g-good chap, right?"

The machine gunner's face was a perfect picture, although perfectly expressionless, as he conceded his place to Captain Michaelides.

"'Garters' . . . 'David,' is it?" Kyrikos was suddenly his most charming self. "Kyri'—?"

"'Kyri'?" Audley took the abbreviation almost with surprise, and then blinked at Fred. "You know, I don't *really* stutter. It's a purely t-temporary thing, which will go away eventually . . . like a head cold, or a sprained ankle. I have that on the very best authority—a specialist who s-s-sp-sp . . . *specializes* in s-s-s-*impediments* of a s-s-s—*shit!*" He sniffed. "He says it'll go away when I'm no longer scared out of my wits, anyway." Another sniff. "Which is probably true, because I acquired it that way, one sunny afternoon. And it comes and goes quite without rhyme or reason." He nodded at Fred. "My c-commanding officer . . . will no doubt be waiting in eager anticipation to see what I have found . . . even though he'll not be in the best of tempers." Audley spoke carefully as the jeep bucked over a succession of potholes. "See how I didn't stutter, Fred? Fred-Fred-Fred-*Fred!*" Shrug. "Like I s-s—*told* you: no rhyme or r-reason, it just comes and goes. . . . Not like a chap I knew at school who developed his sss—*impediment* solely to hid his inadequacy in Latin word endings, to give him time to to think." Grin. "Like, '*Quieta G-G-Gallia, C-C-Caesar, ut c-c-con-s-s-stit-t-tit-tit* . . .' Used to drive the masters crazy, I tell you!" Wider grin. "Must confess I do use the same w-wheeze on my betters on occasion, when I'm up against it . . . like now, eh?" The grin was transferred, through the next succession of bumps, to Kyriakos, but vanished in that instant. "So what were you *really* doing on that path, Captain M-M-, I beg your pardon, *Kyriakos?*"

"I told you—" Fred started to cut in hotly, but then remembered what Kyriakos had said about the lieutenant and controlled his irritation. "But I told you . . . 'David,' is it? We were going to the village, David."

Audley grimaced at him. "The broken-down jeep, and all that?"

"Yes." Kyriakos's insight continued to caution him, against his inclination. "The broken-down jeep and all that. Osios Konstandinos is the closest place to where we broke down. Captain Michaelides was hoping to commandeer transport there. And if you care to send one of your strom troopers to the main road, our jeep should still be there . . . if the locals haven't found it." Anger, once it started to cool, froze quickly. "And even if they have, then you'll still find the heavier bits of it, maybe."

"Of course, of course!" Audley rallied. "W-what I meant was . . . by *that* route, that *particular* one, I mean." He managed the travesty of a politely inquiring smile.

"Ah, yes, of course!" Kyriakos moved smoothly into the next moment's silence, turning towards Fred as he did so. "What

David means is that the path is not very evidently a promising route to Osios Konstandinos, old boy." He shook his head encouragingly. "You remember where we left the track, up the steep incline? 'Where are we going?' you said. And I replied, 'By the shortest route—and on the other side it is even shorter. It is down a cliff, with steps cut into it'—do you remember?"

Fred nodded. "Yes?" All Kyriakos had said was "This way!" And he hadn't waited for an answer. But no matter. "Yes?"

"This is my country, my 'neck of the woods,' yes?" Kyriakos switched back to Audley, his voice all casual friendliness. "You see, my family has a house by the sea, beyond Itéa—by Galaxídhion, where my grandmother was born. After Delphi we were going on there, to celebrate Scobiemas Day, David." He rolled with the potholes while waving his finger at Audley. "But . . . but what *I* would like to know is . . . is how *you* know the secret back path from Osios Konstandinos, up the steps in the cliff?" The finger and the voice flattered Audley simultaneously. "Do you speak our language? Or our ancient language, perhaps?"

"No." Audley was falling for it, flattered by the implied admiration. "I'm not a classicist. 'A little Latin, and no Greek' is me, I'm ashamed to admit. Or . . . not ashamed . . . But—"

"Wouldn't have done you any good, old boy!" Kyriakos shook his head, sure of his man now. "No one in Osios Konstandinos would have told a stranger about that path—not a khaki stranger any more than a field-gray Jerry. Winston Churchill or Adolf Hitler—or Archibishop Damaskinos himself. My wet nurse was a girl from Osios Konstandinos, that is how *I* know." The black eyebrows furrowed, perfecting the flattery with incomprehension. "So how do *you* know?"

"Oh . . . that's easy, that's . . . nothing at all, actually." The young man was at once smugly pleased and disarmed by such implicit praise. "It's all in the history books, don't you know . . . I mean."

"In the *what*?" Something in the Greek's voice tore Fred's attention away from Audley.

"In the history books. Or *book*, actually—Pemberton's *History of the Greek War of Independence*." A pothole caught Audley unaware as he was trying to be properly modest. "I looked up 'Osios Konstandinos' in the British Library in Athens when I learnt where we were going." The jeep swerved, presenting Fred himself with a momentary glimpse of the Gulf of Corinth, purple flecked with red in the sunset, before a bank of pine trees cut it off. "The Turks razed the village in the Greek War of Independence—1824, that was. Reshid Pasha had got wind that Markos Botsaris was there, apparently." The youth's grin twisted. "It's

27

like history repeating itself, you might say." He caught his tongue, and the grin became a grimace as he realized what he had said. "But with us as the Turks, you see."

"Ah, Reshid Pasha!" Kyriakos glossed over Audley's indiscretion quickly. "He was moving up against Mesólongi hereabouts in 1824, wasn't he? And against your Lord Byron—he was there at the time, wasn't he?"

"Yes." Audley seized Lord Byron eagerly. "It was Byron and Markos Botsaris who were g-g-galvanizing the Missolonghi defenders in '24. And Reshid aimed to trap Botsaris in Osios Konstandinos, by coming in from the sea." He swung round in his seat as Osios Konstandinos surrounded them.

It was just another Greek village, which looked as though it had been sacked and rebuilt at regular intervals, all the way from the Peloponnesian War through a hundred other wars, including Audley's Franks and Turks, and Kyriakos's Turks and Germans, so that it was now a jumble of infinitely reused stone, half a dusty ruin and half a triumph of man over man's inhumanity.

"Here at last, by God!" Audley pointed ahead for the benefit of his driver, of whom he had not taken the slightest notice since commanding him to get going, five uncomfortable miles back. "Go on past the square, as far as you can, there's a good fellow."

"Yes, sir." The driver sounded weary enough to have served in all those ancient wars. "I know where to go, sir."

"You were saying?" Kyriakos encouraged the youth. "Botsaris?"

"Yes." He gave Kyriakos a quick frown, as though he had at last realized that he'd been maneuvered into answering most the questions, instead of asking them. "But you know the story. So why am I telling it?"

"Captain Fattorini doesn't know it though." The Greek was ready for him.

"Well, you tell him, then." The youth's suspicions were clearly roused at last. "After you've answered my last question, that is."

"Your last question?" Kyriakos echoed the words innocently. "What was it?"

The squalid houses on each side of them all seemed to be empty, staring at them with blank eyes. But of course, they weren't empty. And they reminded Fred depressingly of Italy. And yet Italy, at least, was where the real war was: in Italy, at least, a man knew which side he was on.

"You wanted to know how we had met." Fred felt his patience snap. "I don't see what the devil that has to do with you, though."

As Audley started to stutter a reply they came out of the narrow street into what must be the village square. One half of it had been comprehensively demolished, and the other half was full of British military vehicles. A line of sullen-looking prisoners, some in the ragged remains of British battle dress, was backed up against the wall of another of those tiny Byzantine-Greek churches, which looked at though it had been built for a race of midgets. At each end of the line a bored British soldier covered the prisoners with his Sten.

"Go on, go on!" Audley pointed ahead, towards the only unblocked exit, the sudden harshness of his voice hinting that he found this tableau of Liberated Greece no less depressing.

The jeep accelerated, jerking them all this way and that as it bumped over the ruined road surface. Fred caught a glimpse of a group of soldiers between two of the lorries, one in the act of trying to light a dog-end without burning his nose, another urinating on the rear wheel of his lorry. The urinator had full corporal's stripes on his arm.

Discipline was going to hell! thought Fred. Those, for a guess, were Royal Mendips of 12 Brigade, who had been notably reliable in Italy. But now they looked sullen and mutinous.

He turned on Audley savagely. "I've told you why we were up there on that bloody path of yours—but what the devil is happening here?"

"*Doucement, doucement!*" murmured Kyriakos, touching his arm above the elbow. "*Doucement, mon vieux,* eh?"

"It's not my bloody f-f-fault!" protested Audley, his voice lifting. "I've got to explain you both to the brigadier himself—*damn!*" The jeep lurched over fallen stone from another ruined building that half-blocked the road. "He'll want to know. I know how his mind works. And if you don't want to go all the way back to Athens with us while he checks your story—I'm trying to *help* you, damn it!"

"Of course, of course!" Kyriakos soothed them both. "It is all my fault"—he squeezed Fred's arm—"*my* fault, old boy."

The jeep stopped abruptly, having climbed steeply out of Osios Konstandinos, up an apology for a track that only a jeep could have attempted, short of a tracked vehicle. Certainly nothing with either wheels or tracks could ever have penetrated farther than this point, where huge boulders blocked the way, leaving only a narrow path hardly fit for mules . . . although there were buildings of some sort higher up, just visible through a scatter of pines under an uprearing cliff high above them.

"Your fault?" The buildings ahead were roofless and ruined. Half the bloody world was roofless and ruined, thought Fred savagely. Or half of the poor, innocent, impoverished villages of Greece and Italy seemed to be ruined, anyway, as the price of their resistance and liberation, no matter how inaccessible. And as this was Kyri's country that thought suffused him with guilt—guilt all the more irredeemable because he was here because the Greek had invited him home as his guest, for wine and a soft bed if not for some dark-eyed virgin. "It isn't your fault, Kyriakos."

"Oh, but it is, old boy." Kyriakos began to climb out of the jeep. "An Englishman teaching *me* about Markos Botsaris—in Osios Konstandinos!" He straightened up, and then pointed. "Look there! Do you see?"

"What?" Audley followed Kyriakos's instruction first. "Yes, I do! By God—*eagles!*" He pointed. "Do you see them? They said in Athens that there'd be eagles here!"

Fred looked upwards and saw that the bloody birds were still circling above the cliff, knife and fork in claw, and napkins knotted ready.

Kyriakos cleared his throat. "I meant the cliff. The path goes up that gulley, and then across, to where that tree sticks out, under the overhang."

"Yes." Fred couldn't see. But what he could see was that, whatever happened in 1824, one burst from Sergeant Devenish's machine gunners would have turned Osios Konstandinos into a surrender-or-die trap. Except . . . *except* . . . if the sergeant's own position had itself been taken in the rear, by someone coming up that path behind him, on the other side of that impossible cliff. Then that would have ruined the trap, of course.

"They *are* eagles, aren't they?" Audley had retrieved a fine pair of German binoculars from the jeep and was struggling to adjust them.

"You are a bird-watcher too?" Kyri's voice was hollow with disbelief, as it had been with the thirteenth century. "As well as an historian?"

"No." Audley lowered the binoculars quickly. "It's just . . . everybody keeps asking me whether I've seen them, and I'm tired of telling lies, that's all." He grinned at the Greek. "It was the same with the eighty-eights in Normandy. I never could see the bloody things, when everyone else could, don't you know. . . . But that was Botsaris's cliff, was it? Or . . . is it?"

"You were in Normandy?" The Greek frowned as though one so young could not have been allowed to participate in a real war.

"Yes." Audley's mouth opened, and then closed again, wordlessly. "It was very unc-c-c—*unpleasant*, I can tell you. Greece is infinitely more p-p-p—*agreeable*." He grinned unashamedly. "No G-Germans, no eighty-eights, eh?" The grin became disarming. "That's the monastery up there, is it? The one the Turks burnt in '24?"

"Yes." But now Kyriakos was dead serious. "You haven't been here before then?" He blinked. "Somebody told you about the path, did they?"

Audley blinked back at him. "Actually . . . *no* . . . But it's all in Pemberton about the path, and Markos Botsaris. There was a map too." The half grin became a frown. "Why d'you want to know? Are you an historian?"

"No. I am merely a Greek." Kyriakos glanced at Fred. "And once I was also a banker."

Someone was shouting at them, through the trees.

"A . . . *what?*" Audley struggled with this intelligence, against the shout. "A . . . *banker?*"

"Merchant banker," elaborated Kyriakos. But then not even he could ignore the figure that was approaching them, its hobnailed boots cracking on the stony track like caps in a child's pistol.

Audley quailed. "What is it, Mr. Levin?"

"*Sar!*" The RSM somehow contrived to look immaculate, even under a fine coating of dust. "The brigadier and the colonel have both been asking for you, Mr. Audley, *sar!*" He addressed Audley from beneath a quivering Guard's salute, totally ignoring Fred and Kyriakos. "They wish to hear about your prisoners, *sar!*"

"Ah!" Audley managed something between a wave and a clenched-fist gesture, which he rendered even more equivocal by ending up scratching the back of his neck. "Well, they're not exactly . . . *prisoners*, Mr. Levin. But never mind . . ." He trailed off humbly.

"As you wish, Mr. Audley, *sar!*" The RSM pronounced the words like a formula dissolving all but the inescapable links between himself and the author of that parody of a salute. "If-you-will-permit-me-to-return-to-my-duties-then, *sar!*"

"Why . . . yes, of course, Mr. Levin. Do carry on, please."

"*Sar!*" The RSM swept past them down the track. And as sure as God made little apples, he would see where the Mendip corporal had pissed on the rear wheel of that lorry, thought Fred. So there were two stripes lost.

"Well, that was Mr. Levin!" murmured Audley, to no one in particular. "We just don't seem to hit it off. I had a much better relationship with my old troop sar-major in the Wesdragons. But of course, Mr. Levin was a peacetime soldier before the war . . . and my old sar-major ran our local garage at Steeple Horley." He shook his head sadly, as though in another world. "But he's dead, of course . . . and now he's really dead." He stared at Fred suddenly. "Funny to think of that, isn't it? Becoming *really* dead?"

The question caught Fred by surprise. "What d'you mean?"

"He means . . . now that *your* war is nearly finished, then the

31

dead can become properly dead," snapped Kyriakos harshly. "And the survivors can become properly alive at last."

Fred was shocked by the Greek's intensity. "Our . . . war?"

Kyriakos nodded at Audley. "Your war is almost finished—no Germans here—not in Greece anymore. And now, if the truce holds, if you are both lucky, then your war *is* finished. So you will go home"—he switched to Fred—"to your merchant banking"—back to Audley again—"and you to . . . Cambridge, was it? Girls in punts, and the odd lecture?" He showed his teeth in a wolfish grin. "I was up at Cambridge in '39. My father called me home in October—we thought it was just *your* war." The grin became unnaturally fixed. "We thought the Balkan Mercantile Bank and the Aegean Mutual Trust stood to make a lot of money out of you British, one way or another. And now my father is dead, and my two brothers are dead. . . . But my war is not finished—perhaps it is only just beginning. So that makes a difference, yes?"

"Yes." Audley nodded stupidly, like a ventriloquist's dummy. "You've b-b-b . . . bloody *got* it. They're not d-d- *dead* yet, quite? Because you can still join them, right?" He stopped nodding. "You're the first one I've met who knows what I'm talking about—would you believe that?"

Fred felt anger stir, beyond shock and unreality and incomprehension, as they both blocked him out with their private joke, which was no joke at all. But pride refused to let him show how he felt: they each understood too well what the other was saying for him to admit that he didn't measure up to their insight, whatever it was they shared. So he couldn't say anything.

"The Balkan Mutual Trust?" Audley found another joke. "I w-wouldn't have thought that there was m-much m-mutual . . . *trust* . . . anywhere in the b-b-bloody Balkans?"

Kyriakos raised his chin arrogantly. "*Aegean* Mutual Trust, *Balkan* Mercantile Bank, Mr. Audley, *sar!*" He grinned at Audley, under the arrogance. "How about letting us both return to our duties, eh? Like . . . you could talk a jeep out of your adjutant, to take us to Itéa, maybe?" He carefully didn't look at Fred. "How about that, then?"

Audley looked at Fred, nevertheless. "You know each other because your families are both in merchant banking? The Fattorini Brothers, the Mutually Trusting Balkans? But how did you both end up . . . back there, on the path, 'lurking,' was it?"

Kyriakos tossed his head. "As you said, 'Fattorini' isn't a common name in the British Army." He gave Fred a quick glance. "I was with the Canadians last year, and we were stalled on this river, over which your engineers were throwing this Bailey bridge. And I heard someone shout for 'Captain Fattorini' . . .

and my family's bank had acted for the Fattorini bank in Greece ever since the First World War."

Fred nodded. "That's right, ever since *his* father met *my* uncle—Uncle Luke—in Salonika, in the Military Hospital, in 1918. They were two young bankers in adjoining beds, each with Bulgarian bullets in them. So they exchanged addresses."

"And then they did business. Out of which came the first Aegean Mutual Trust." The Greek took his cue. "And last year I saw this appalling mud-covered apparition. But I thought . . . 'Fattorini' isn't a common name in the British Army. So I gave it an address in Athens, where I intended to be."

"Coincidence," agreed Fred. "Just like you swanning up in your jeep back there, Dave Audley, and thinking that 'Fattorini' isn't a common name in the British Army. So when I finally reached Athens—"

"Okay! Okay!" Audley surrendered. "That'll do fine. In fact, it couldn't be better. . . . *And* I'll get you transport. Itéa, was it?"

The youth's sudden confidence pricked Fred's curiosity. "What's so fine about it?"

"Oh . . . it was fine all along, actually." Audley grinned disarmingly.

"It was?" Fred's curiosity outweighed his irritation. "Why?"

"The brigadier will like you, even if my colonel doesn't." The grin twisted. "The brigadier may not go much on coincidences, but he does love rich men. And bankers, *merchant* bankers—one merchant banker, good, *two* merchant bankers—you'll brighten up a bad day for him, I shouldn't wonder, by golly!" He pointed through the trees. "Come on! You're just what I need!" He stepped out ahead of them. "*Two* bloody bankers!"

Kyriakos raised his shoulders eloquently and rolled his eyes at Fred. But then he moved quickly after Audley. "But why, why does he like *rich* men?"

Fred accelerated after them. Five wasted years—three of boredom, one and a half of discomfort and terror, plus an aggregation of odd months of other experiences, including disillusion and, during the last hour, more terror—those years ought to have inured him to anything the army could imagine, for his further education. But Lieutenant Audley and his brigadier were something beyond the ordinary lunacies.

"Rich . . . *men*?" panted Kyriakos, in Audley's wake.

Through the last scatter of trees Fred saw the ruins more clearly and remembered what Kyriakos had said a lifetime earlier: This was the little monastery the Turks had smashed up, presumably in revenge for Markos Botsaris's escape up that cliff just behind it.

"Bankers?" Kyriakos tried again, breathlessly.

This was the sharp end of the operation, the sounds of which they had heard on the other side of that cliff, Fred saw at a glance. Not only were the soldiers here alert, and very different from the smokers and pissers down below, but there was a line of groundsheeted corpses, with their protruding feet indicating their origin: three good pairs of army-issue boots, and then a dozen anonymous pairs, scuffed and pathetic—*no*, there were two feet at the end, encased in jackboots, or something like—

"Bankers?" Audley finally registered the question, but then dismissed it as a figure ducked out from a narrow monastic doorway. "*Amos!* Is the brigadier in there?"

"He is, dear boy." The figure straightened up and became a captain in a Very Famous Regiment who gazed past Audley at Fred and Kyriakos with mild astonishment. "Are these your prisoners? But dear boy, they can't be, they positively *can't* be!" The gaze, with one eyebrow delicately raised, flicked from Fred to Kyriakos, finally coming back to Fred. "He's expecting a couple of desperadoes. . . . But you've got a sapper there, and I know that sappers are notoriously eccentric . . . But this is preposterous, quite preposterous!" He returned to Audley, shaking his head. "He's not at all pleased, I warn you, David, dear boy. I should run away if I were you, that's what I'd do." His voice was quite conversational as he returned to Fred. "I admit that you *look* like one of ours. . . . But are you?"

Before Fred could answer, or even open his mouth, Audley jumped in. "Of course he is! And you're quite wrong, Amos. I'm just about to become quite p-p-p-pop-pop-pop—"

"Pop-popular?" The man's eyes didn't leave Fred. "I doubt it very much. But who am I to keep you from a posting to Burma?" The eyes pinned Fred for another second, and then the languid captain smiled ruefully.

"It is evident that Mr. Audley is not going to introduce us, Captain. So . . . I am Amos de Souza, formerly of the Guards but now fallen upon hard times. But nonetheless at your service, Captain."

The man's smile was as infectious as his good manners were comforting after the horrors of the last hour. "Fattorini, Brigade RE, Captain de Souza. Also fallen on hard times, apparently." He grinned at de Souza. "I wish I knew what was going on. Perhaps you can enlighten me?"

"My dear fellow, I wish I could!" The rueful smile twisted. Then de Souza frowned slightly and cocked his head. "Fattorini . . . not the *banking* Fattorinis, by any chance."

Fred felt that he ought to be able to place the Guards de

34

Souzas, who had plainly been as anglicized over so many generations as the banking Fattorinis, and with blood that was even more blue. But to his shame he couldn't. "Yes, Captain de Souza."

"Ah!" Captain de Souza didn't bother to explain his own secret. Instead he switched to Kyriakos. "And this gentleman?"

"Michaelides, Captain." Kyriakos stopped there.

"Yes?" De Souza waited until he was sure nothing more was coming. "Regular Greek Army? Or National Guard?"

Suddenly Fred was aware of the seconds ticking away, as the Greek failed to rise to what was clearly intended as a provocation. Somewhere nearby Lieutenant Audley's brigadier must be fuming. And down the rocky path the RSM would be approaching those lorries and the slovenly Mendips like the wrath of God. And without looking up, he knew those bloody birds would still be circling, waiting in vain for the meal under those groundsheets that would now be denied them.

"Neither, actually, old boy," Kyriakos drawled, packing all his years of British education into his accent. "Banking too, actually."

"Ah!" Captain de Souza permitted himself a well-bred snigger. "*Now* I understand!" He wagged a finger at Audley. "What a sly fellow you are, bagging a brace of bankers for the brigadier! I really must stop underestimating you, David. You have the precious gift of luck which Napoleon Bonaparte admired so much, in preference to vulgar cleverness." He jerked his head towards the little arched doorway. "Go on, dear boy, go and take your gifts to him without delay. If you cheer him up, we shall all be better off—go on!" He turned from Audley, favoring Fred and Kyriakos with the slightest of bows as he began moving towards the bodies. "And leave me to my ghoulish tasks. Gentlemen, I confide that we may meet again in happier circumstances. . . ."

Fred was torn between following de Souza and watching Audley bend almost double to enter the ruins. But then he remembered Kyriakos.

"Are they all m—?" He bit off the word as the Greek shook his head, following the direction of his friend's gaze instead.

Captain de Souza had thrown back the groundsheet from the body with the jackboots and was stripping it methodically.

"*Mad?*" Fred whispered.

"No!" Kyriakos whispered back without looking at him. "Not mad."

The languid captain from the Very Famous Regiment was examining the corpse's jacket with all the distaste of a man who knew from bitter experience that all *Andartes* were flea ridden

35

and lousy. But his examination was nonetheless careful, pocket by pocket, seam by seam.

"Not mad?" Fred watched de Souza cast the jacket aside and apply himself to one of the boots.

"No!" Kyriakos repeated the word out of the side of his mouth as de Souza unwound a piece of rag and then let the foot fall back to earth while he felt inside the boot.

Yuk—urch! Fred imagined the sweaty clamminess of the inside of that boot. "What's he doing?"

"Isn't it obvious?" murmured Kyriakos, almost contemptuously.

Captain de Souza added the boot to the jacket and pulled at the second boot, and went through the same process, letting the second dirty white foot fall back, jarring the corpse with a false shudder of life.

"Good boots, those." The Greek turned to Fred suddenly. "Do you remember where we last saw boots like that? And a rag instead of socks?"

"No." Fred watched the careful examintion of the second boot before it joined its comrade. But as the slender, fastidious fingers began to unbutton the corpse's fly buttons, he decided that he had had enough of de Souza's duty and could more usefully pick over the contents of Kyriakos's brains. And that concentrated his memory. "Yes. That Russian officer, the liaison fellow we had to put to bed?"

"That's right." Kyriakos returned his attention to the corpse-stripping as he replied, "So . . . now you know, eh?" Something almost approaching a smile, albeit a terrible one, lifted half the Greek's mouth under his mustache. "It's actually very comforting, old boy."

"Comforting?" Against his will and better judgment, Fred's attention was drawn back to de Souza's duty. And although he instantly regretted the impulse, he was hypnotically held by the image that comforted Kyriakos, of Captain de Souza's emptying the trouser pockets first—scrutinizing their pathetic contents and then throwing them on the already checked pile . . . clasp knife, coins, filthy handkerchief—and then ripping at the lining savagely. That was a skill his Guards regiment had never taught him, and those hairy white legs, and the raised shirt above them exposing the dark bush of pubic hair and genitals, had never been included in his Army Training Instructions. "Comforting?"

"Uh-huh." Kyriakos was hardly listening to him: his fascination was absolute as the trousers joined the pile. Instead he murmured something in Greek, which Fred wouldn't have understood even if he had heard it.

"What's that?" He couldn't *not* look now, even if he hadn't wanted to look, as de Souza straddled the body and turned it over, face in the dirt, arms flopping obscenely as gravity shifted their dead weight. "What was that you said?"

"I said . . . 'Go on, do it properly!'" Kyriakos paused as de Souza began to do something so revolting that Fred couldn't believe his eyes. *"Ah, that's right!"*

"God Almighty!" What was almost more revolting than what de Souza was doing was Kyriakos's approbation of the unnatural act.

"Nothing?" Kyriakos exhaled slowly. "Bad luck! But . . . well done, de Souza!" He came back to Fred at last. "You were saying?"

"I wasn't saying anything. I was just feeling sick, that's all."

"Then . . . the more fool, you?" The Greek's eyes were hard. "That's where they hide things, when they have to, old boy."

For the next foul moment, Fred found himself looking at de Souza again. He was stripping off the corpse's shirt now, leaving the whole naked body leprous white, except for its brown hands and arms and ruined, bloody face.

"But . . . but *why*, Kyriakos?" He abandoned the final tableau of Captain de Souza's doing his duty. "For God's sake!"

Kyriakos bit his lip, under his mustache. "My poor Fred!" He let go his lip. "These are professionals, they know what they want. Which is not *killing* their enemies, anymore. They have progressed beyond that, they are not mere soldiers . . . like you and me, do you understand?" The lip drooped one-sidedly. "They are not crude—"

"Crude!" That was a joke he couldn't laugh at.

"Don't be deceived by appearances."

"Appearances?" The repeated word suddenly sounded foolish as he realized that he *had* been deceived. He had taken de Souza for a civilized man and the large young dragoon for a major, and then for a typical subaltern. But neither of them was what he had at first seemed.

"Actually, I really feel quite comforted." Kyriakos stared at him. "I am comforted, comforted and *surprised*—or comforted and much reassured, anyway."

"Reassured?" After six weeks in Greece, never mind all those months in Italy, Fred regarded himself as a veteran, and an expert on war's idiocies. It irritated him to be treated like an innocent. "This has reassured you, has it? About what?"

"That you British are beginning to know your business." Kyriakos gestured to stop his replying. "Oh, yes, I know you came to Greece"—he nodded—"and that proves *someone* knew his business . . . which would be your Mr. Churchill of course. But you did not really anticipate events, did you?"

"I didn't?" Whenever the Greek talked high politics, he always addressed Fred as though he were personally responsible for War Cabinet decisions. But then, as he controlled the temptation to adapt his answer accordingly, he saw the truth of the question. In early December the brigade—indeed, the whole division—had been under orders for Palestine and had actually had to repossess all the equipment it had surrendered on the eve of embarkation. So Greece had plainly been an unforeseen emergency. "No, we didn't. But—" As he spoke, Kyriakos nodded past him, in de Souza's direction again.

"See there, old man."

Much against his will, and fortified only by the thought that de Souza couldn't be doing anything nastier than what he had already done, Fred obeyed the injunction—and instantly regretted his decision.

"Ah . . ." The Greek caught his arm. "He has something—*yes*—he has something, indeed!"

Captain de Souza had been taking a dentist's view of the shattered head, probing inside a gaping bloody mouth with a sliver of bright metal. And until the Greek spoke, all Fred had been thinking was . . . *at least he's not just using his finger now!*

"*Yes!*" Kyri's fingers tightened, then relaxed as de Souza examined what he had found. "So now we know!"

Fred swallowed. "What do we know, Kyri?" But in that instant as he asked his question, he realised that he did indeed know something now, even if it had nothing to do with the beastliness he had been witnessing. Or not directly, anyway. "What do we know?"

Kyriakos caught the change in his voice. "Are you shocked?"

"Not by that." Comparatively, that was the truth.

"You know what he's found then?" Kyriakos misunderstood him.

Fred faced a bitter truth. There had once been a Captain Michaelides he had known, who had been a Greek soldier much beloved by the Canadians with whom he was liaising, who didn't love fools and cowards. And that had been his own Captain Michaelides, devoted to war and wine and women in whichever order the immediate circumstances allowed.

"You lied to me, Kyri." He thought about the new Captain Michaelides, with whom he had made happy contact in Athens, who had seemed exactly the same as the first one, except for the mustache . . . and a slight tendency to talk politics, which had seemed fair enough now that he was in his homeland.

Kyriakos frowned. "I lied to you?"

"Yes." As always, thinking for himself paid dividends . . . even though this payout sickened him as he remembered how very interested Kyriakos had been in the morale of General Scobie's troops, and their feelings about what they were doing in Greece; and although he had never thought about it until now, he didn't know what Captain Michaelides had been doing . . . except that he always knew what was going on, and where (until this last hour or two) the safety line could be drawn.

"Yes?" To his credit, the second Captain Michaelides didn't try to add to his deceptions. "When?"

"Just now." Even as Fred knew he was right, he knew also that he had no right to judge the man in his own poor bloodthirsty, bloodstained, and ruined country. "You said you and I were different from this lot, just another pair of simple soldiers, eh?" He watched the Greek narrowly. "But you know *exactly* what is happening here, don't you?"

Kyriakos stared at him for a moment, then shook his head. "Not . . . not *exactly*!" Then he smiled. "If I knew that, then we wouldn't be here." The smile vanished. "But you're right, of course. I know *what* these men are, if not *who* they are, shall we say?"

This was the moment to ask questions, Fred sensed. "What did Captain de Souza find? Or would you rather let me guess?"

The Greek shrugged, aware that he had lost a friend, but also that his hospitality-invitation to an ally still obligated him. "A happy pill." He let the memory of the shrug do its work. "When you don't want to talk, but you think you may, then you crunch it . . . and then you don't talk ever again."

"Oh . . ." He didn't really know what he would have guessed. But he wouldn't have guessed that. "And that's happiness, is it?"

"Compared with being tortured by experts, yes, it is."

That was nasty. And more than nasty, it was libelous. "But we don't torture our prisoners, Kyri." He could recall having leaned quite heavily on the rare German rearguard prisoner he'd been given who might be expected to know where the booby traps were. But that had been in the nature of give-and-take, and it really only stretched the Geneva Convention somewhat, falling infinitely short of torture. And then an alternative possibility presented itself. "Could be he was expecting to be captured by your lot though, eh?"

"Could be." Kyriakos accepted the insult without taking offense. "Except, old man, he *didn't* crunch the pill, did he, eh?"

Fred resisted the renewed temptation to see what Captain de Souza was doing now. "Obviously no, if that was what Captain de

Souza found." Thinking about the stripped white-hairy-defiled body was bad enough: it didn't need a double check. Indeed, he had no desire either to think about it or discuss it. Nor, come to that, was he particularly keen to face up to the implications of Captain Michaelides's too professional interest and expertise in such matters. But since they could not be ignored, he could hardly leave those matters unresolved. "Didn't do him any good though, did it!"

"No—"

"No. His name was on a bullet, not a pill." Fred was simultaneously pleased and ashamed of passing himself off as a hardened veteran. "So what?"

"Ah!" Kyriakos pounced on him. "But you have missed the point, old man, missed it by a mile." As he spoke, David Audley ducked out from the little doorway again. "By a mile!" He repeated the distance for Audley's benefit. "Would you not agree, Mr. Audley, David."

"How's that again, 'by a mile'?" David blinked at him. "Missed . . . the point? What point?"

"Your Russian friend, old man." Kyriakos gestured towards the line of corpses without disengaging his attention from Audley.

Audley followed the gesture and grimaced, his natural ugliness contorted by whatever Captain de Souza was now doing. But then, as he came back to them, his face composed itself into telltale innocence. "Russian? Well, that's news to me, Captain Michaelides. But . . . *friend*—whoever he was, he was no friend of mine, so far as I am aware." Much too late, the false innocence became polite inquiry. "What point would that be, which Captain Fattorini—or Fat-O'Rhiney—has missed by a mile?"

Kyriakos's white teeth showed below his mustache. "You didn't shoot him. Friend or enemy, you didn't shoot him."

"No?" The innocence increased. "Yes, well, you're right. Because I certainly didn't shoot him, Captain Michaelides. But then I am notoriously incapable of shooting people. Given a large enough gun, in a tank, I can sometimes hit buildings, though. In fact, I once demolished an entire church, you know."

"I didn't mean *you*, old man." Kyriakos gestured dismissively.

"No?" Audley came back quickly, with an edge to his voice. "But . . . well, I can tell you, Captain, that our chaps are damn good, even if I'm not." He nodded at the corpse line, and then frowned at the Greek. "The bastards got three good men with their first burst. But that's because they must have got wind of us. And that's *all* they got—all the rest were *ours*. And our chaps deserve the credit for it, I'd say."

Fred started to warm to the young man, but then remembered

the Greek's warning and that falsely innocent expression. So all Audley was doing was drawing Kyriakos out in his own way, most likely.

"No. Not all." Suddenly Kyriakos spoke mildly, without emphasis. "You chaps didn't shoot your Russian friend. Not unless they shoot other . . . chaps . . . in the back of the neck." He paused. "Which I'm sure they don't, being decent chaps." Mild still. "And certainly not on this occasion." Cold, hard voice suddenly: the voice of Captain Michaelides Mark II. "Because your Russian, friendly or unfriendly to you, old man, *he* was shot by his own side, from behind." If possible, the voice became harder and colder. "These last few weeks I've seen quite a lot of wounds like that, courtesy of *Hellenikos Laikos Apelefteroikos Stratos* . . . and some understandable reprisals by the men I have the honor of trying to command, I'm sorry to say." The voice was ultimately frozen now. "So I know what a man's face looks like when he's been shot in the back of the neck while lying down. So do not argue with me, Lieutenant."

Fred stared at Kyriakos. He had started off watching the young dragoon, to see how he reacted to the Greek's mild disagreement. But then Captain Michaelides Mark II had taken over. And finally, at the last, it hadn't been Captain Michaelides Mark II either: it had been a complete stranger.

For a moment Audley didn't reply, which drew Fred back to him to observe what he felt might well be a mirror image of his own expression, although on a very different face.

"I w-w-wouldn't dream of arguing with you, Captain M-Mmm—" Audley shook his head and scowled as his impediment got the better of him. "You can g-g . . . *go* and argue with the b-b-b—"

"I will do just that, yes." The Greek drew himself up.

"In there." Audley pointed towards the low doorway in the ruins. "He's w-waiting to mmm-meet you both." He tore his attention from the Greek to Fred, and instantly relaxed. "I've told him all about you, and he's jolly keen to make your acquaintance, he says. And"—the boy just managed to avoid looking at Kyriakos again—"and the good news is that I'm to find you some transport, if possible."

"No," said Kyriakos.

They both looked at him.

"I shall go and see the brigadier by myself first." Kyriakos ignored Audley. "I'm sorry, old boy. But that's the way it is. Because this happens to be my country."

He gave Fred a nod, and then ducked into the doorway without another word.

41

"And he's *b-b-bloody* welcome to it, if you ask me," murmured Audley. Then he looked inquiringly at Fred. "Bloody Greek Secret Police!" Then he frowned. "And he's a friend of yours?"

"Yes." It was true. Or it had been true.

"And you really did break down, and all that?"

The innocent look was back. And if Kyriakos hadn't warned him, he would have believed it. But now he didn't believe either of them. "Yes."

Audley breathed in deeply. "Well . . . you've got some funny friends, then. So you'd better watch out, if you ask me, if you're stuck here." He breathed out slowly. "Thank God we're posted elsewhere after this, to where the real war is! Not that we'll see much of it, more's the pity!" He grinned at Fred. "I never thought I'd ever say that, you know!"

Was he being led on? Fred wondered. "What d'you mean, 'the real war'?" If he was, then he'd be safer among questions than answers.

Audley glanced nervously at the doorway. "Well . . . this isn't the *real* war, is it?" The glance came back to Fred, but then went past him, towards whatever Captain de Souza might be doing now, if he was still at work among the bodies behind them; but whether he was or wasn't, Fred wasn't tempted to find out. Yet he felt the presence of the dead at his back nevertheless.

"This isn't war?" He almost felt that he was putting the question on behalf of those nearby who could no longer ask it.

Audley shrugged. "If it is, then it's a different kind of war. And don't ask me what kind." Then he looked past Fred again. "An 'in the back of the neck' war? A most *un*kind war, I'd call that, eh?"

Part Two

The Unkind War

On the Roman frontier, Germany, August 6, 1945

CHAPTER ONE

The moment he set eyes on the driver, Fred was sure that he'd seen him before somewhere, sometime. But then, in the next moment, he knew that it couldn't be so. And it wasn't just one of those tricks that the very anonymity of uniform perversely played on occasion: it was a simple case of wish fulfullment brought on by intense loneliness. For nothing, not even changing boarding schools (and certainly not leaving home itself), was more inner-desolation making than being torn untimely from the bosom of one's own unit, and from longtime friends and comrades. He had started to feel it in the very second that the adjutant had shown him the order, this loneliness. And he had felt himself as utterly forlorn and abandoned as Alexander Selkirk on his desert island among these crowds of noisy, gum-chewing, cigarette-smoking Americans in the leaking, badly repaired airfield building—forlorn and abandoned even after the altogether surprising American Air Force major beside him had plucked him out of the scrum like a long-lost buddy.

"See there—over there!" The American addressed him cheerfully over the butt of his cigar. "There's your man, and there's your transport. And . . . and now that is *some* transport, by Gahd!"

It was also the uniform, of course, thought Fred. The crowds of Yanks debusing from their huge lorries were no different from all those he had seen in Italy—more than half a year now, but it seemed more like half a lifetime; except (and it was a bloody big difference, on second thought) these Yanks were happily loaded down with what looked like loot and were presumably destined for home . . . whereas the Yanks he remembered had been *un*happy, loaded with weaponry and combat gear, and destined for the meat grinder of generals quite notoriously unconcerned with casualty lists, unlike their British opposite numbers.

But . . . *it was the uniform*, of course: one little British soldier, albeit in surprisingly well-pressed and well-fitting battle dress, stood out from among them like a rough-haired terrier among a pack of sleek foxhounds with their tails up after feeding time.

"Yes?" It was the uniform, of course. He felt the forlornness dilute slightly, if not the bewilderment; if anything, the bewilderment increased from the high point it had reached when the major had hailed him by name out of the line of disembarked Dakota passengers while they were still appreciating the feel of solid ground underfoot after that hair-raising landing, and more simply glad to be alive than to be where they wanted to be. "Yes, I see him, Major."

For a moment he lost sight of his man and his transport as a phalanx of huge Americans, more or less in disciplined ranks, cut them off from their objective, en route to flight departure and God's Own Country and Betty Grable. And Fred wasn't outraged by their bulldozing interruption, even though he could hear the Air Force major swearing at them beside him. Because . . . *one day that'll be me—me en route to Mother, Julia, and Uncle Luke, and tea in the Savoy, and a World fit for Heroes inside Armstrong, Fattorini Brothers, by God!*

The thought warmed him even as the soldiers slowed and concertinaed from a more-or-less ordered column into a jostling crowd, and the major continued to blaspheme impotently. *One day, in God's good time, this will be me* . . . but in the meantime, even if this was dark, ruined Germany, and not his own dear sunny Greece, at least it wasn't an embarkation depot en route to a crowded troopship and the dreaded Far Eastern posting of everyone's nightmares. At least he was safe from that now!

"It's all right, Major." He felt that he had to say something, if only by way of common civility, to his rescuer. "I'm in no hurry."

"No?" The major looked at his watch. "Well, I sure as hell am! *Goddamn* army!"

"Well, if you have other duties, I beg you not to wait for me."
What Fred would dearly have loved to have asked was how the
major had come to be waiting for one *goddamn* limey officer—
and a junior one at that—off one particular transport plane, the
very arrival of which must have been problematical, what with
the bad weather and the rerouting. "I saw where my transport
was. It's not going to leave without me."

The major looked at him, and he studied the press of GIs, as
though estimating their chances of ever getting through it
unscathed and without a fight. "You reckon? But . . . hell! I
promised Gus I'd see you safely on your way."

"It's quite all right, Major." Who "Gus" might be was beside the
point, but "on your way" wasn't, Fred decided. All that mattered
was that there was a staff car and a driver out there, beyond this
near-mutinous half of the United States Army. And whether or
not it was intended for Captain Fattorini, Captain Fattorini
intended to have that car. But he stood a better chance of keeping
it if the major wasn't in attendance when he commandeered it.
"I'll tell Gus you put me on my way—I'll make a point of it."

"You will? Great!" The major beamed at him. "Okay, then
. . . And say . . . While you're about it, tell him 'thanks'—for
the pig—okay?"

"'Thanks'—Fred steadied his voice—"for . . . the pig?"

"Dee-licious!" The major made a circle with his thumb and
forefinger. "Tell Gus 'anytime,' okay?" A faint thunder of aircraft
engines penetrated the hubbub. "Tell him, if he's got the pigs,
then I've got the planes. Tell him that, huh?"

Fred returned the nod and watched the major stride away
towards whatever pressing matter had recalled him to his duties.
Then a loud cheer distracted him, turning him back to the United
States Army. The concertina was expanding at last, as whatever
obstacle ahead that compressed it gave way.

It must be mistaken identity, but if it wasn't then he had been
traded in return for a pig, it seemed.

The columns expanded, and accelerated, affording him an
adequate glimpse of what lay beyond it, as he thought of pigs.

"Major!"

Across the suddenly opened space, the driver was saluting him.
He was a little ratty RASC man of indeterminate age—a very
typical RASC driver, except for the smartness of his battle dress.
And that was really why he looked so familiar, of course. But
much more to the point, he was also compounding the American's mistake, that was certain. But with his inferior rank safe
under his trench coat, Fred held to his objective, returning the
salute and dumping his valise at the little man's feet.

"Right! Let's go, then."

The driver ignored the valise, opening the rear door of the car instead.

Fred had intended to get in the front, but the important thing was to get going. So he accepted the offer without demur and sank back into the luxury within—real leather, softly padded and sprung—while the little man banged around, stowing the valise and then bestowing himself just in time as the first spatter of rain, which had followed the Dakota all the way from Austria, pitter-pattered the windshield.

"Sorry I didn't come for you, Major . . . sir." The driver half-twisted towards him. "But . . . the American gentlemen said not to. 'E said I was to stay where I was, an' 'e'd bring you, 'e said, 'e did."

Fred perked up. If the little man was talkative, then he might let slop their present destination; and then, when they had gone far enough, he could be browbeaten elsewhere. "He did?"

"Ah"—they passed a line of trucks, and then swerved too late to avoid a crudely filled crater across half the road—"but I wouldn't 'ave gorn, even if 'e'd arsked me . . . not with all these Yanks around, see?"

All Fred saw was that most of the American drivers were Negroes. "Yes?"

"They'd 'ave 'ad the car, one of 'em would, sure as God made little apples." The little man spoke without rancor.

"Of course." It had been foolish of him to forget for a second that anything left unguarded for more than five seconds was at risk. Soldiers or civilians, it was all the same, they were all thieves; and what they couldn't steal they stripped—like that Bailey bridge transporter in Italy, which had been found the day after minus every removable part, engine, wheels, nuts and bolts, and Bailey bridge. And there was no reason why Germany should be different. But he wanted the little man to go on talking. "They'll steal anything, will they?"

"Lord no, sir!" The little man chuckled throatily. "The Yanks is choosy now. The Jerries, you've got to watch . . . speshly the little kids—they're not scared, see. An' the DPs is worst—they'll 'ave the shirt orf yer back if they takes a fancy to it. But the Yanks"—he tapped the steering wheel—"this is a good vee-chicle, this is. Wot they call a 'collector's piece,' this is."

Fred lifted himself slightly, the better to see ahead through the two arcs cleared by the windshield wipers. The road was empty and flanked by seemingly endless ruins on both sides. But that was more or less what he had expected. The industrial outskirts of the city, which were also adjacent to what would certainly have been a major Luftwaffe airfield, would have been heavily bombed many times. "'A collector's piece'?" Cars didn't interest him, but as he observed the length of the hood and the array of dials on the dashboard, adding them to the luxuriousness of the rear seats and the relatively smooth ride over the much repaired road surface, he also remembered the Air Force major's admiration.

"Ah, that it is." The little man massaged the wheel approvingly, even though he drove perilously close to a huge pile of ruins—a pack of slanted concrete floors—which narrowed the road. "French, this is . . . wot was owned by a famous film star before the war, before Jerry pinched it. Built like a tank, it is—weighs nearer three ton than two. More like a tank than your proper Froggie tanks, wot they made out uv cardboard an' ticky-tack, wot I remember of 'em, huh!"

"Yes?" That the little man could remember French tanks, however libelously, for purposes of comparison, confirmed Fred's estimation of him. There was nothing unusual about his evident contempt for the French, which was common among all those who knew nothing of the incomparable performance of Juin's *Corps Expéditionnaire Français* in the Italian mountains, and almost universal among British soldiers, outside the 8th Army. But this wasn't the moment to put him right. "Is that so?"

"Ah." The little man let the big car demonstrate its excellence over a series of former bomb craters, while Fred began to marvel at the extent of the city's ruins. "Only trouble is . . . it's got a terrible lot of electrics—gearbox an' all. So it needs a proper REME mechanic to keep it on the road." Another throaty chuckle. "But Major M'Crocodile's got hisself a proper REME mechanic to look after it, see—Corporal Briggs, that is—this is the major's speshul car, this is, Corporal Briggs!" The repeated chuckle was like a death rattle in the little man's throat.

"Corporal Briggs?" Obviously there was a story to Corporal Briggs that the little man was bursting to tell. And the more talkative he became, the better.

"Got 'im out of a court-martial, to get 'im for the major, the colonel did—got 'im *orf* an' then got 'im posted to us, see?" The little man turned towards him, ignoring the endless rain-blurred vista of bombed-out ruins through which they were driving. "Proper artful, 'e is—"

"Watch the road, man!" Fred commanded quickly as a pile of rubble came dangerously close. But then, as the driver snapped back to his duty, he moved quickly to rebuild the bridge between them. "Corporal Briggs is artful?"

"Naow, sir, Major, not '*im*." The little man sounded the car's mellifluous two-tone horn as they came to an intersection, and then accelerated across it. "Though 'e is a good mechanic, I'll say that for 'im . . . an' 'e was court-martialed for doin' up Jerry cars an' then floggin' 'em back to the Jerries, see. . . . But *naow*, it's Colonel Colbourne wot's artful . . . but then, o' course he was a lawyer before the war, gettin' murderers orf from bein' 'anged, wot was guilty, an' all that, see?"

"Colonel"—Fred steadied his voice—"Colbourne?" Relief blotted out surprise. "How far is it to Kaiserburg . . . and TRR-two, driver?"

"The Kaiser's Burg?" The little man confirmed the name in correcting it to his own liking. "Not far. If it wasn't pissin' down, we could maybe see it from 'ere, almost." He pointed into the murk ahead. "Right up on top of the Town-us, it is—'igh up, in the woods."

Taunus, Fred remembered, from the only map he had been able to find in Athens. But there had been no *Kaiserburg* on the map. "Yes?" *But at least they were agreed that that was where they were going!* he thought. "I couldn't find it on the map."

"No . . . well, you wouldn't now, would you?" The little man agreed readily. " 'Cause it ain't anywhere, is it? The bleedin' Kaiser's Burg!"

Fred saw an opening. "It's a bad billet, is it?"

The rain slashed across the windshield, and the car bucked in well-bred protest over another crater—*down . . . bump-bump-bump . . . up*—and then ran smoothly again, still flanked by ruins.

"I've known worse." Uncharacteristically, the little man looked on the bright side, in the midst of unseasonable summer weather likely to render even adequate billets depressing.

A hideous thought offered itself to Fred. "We're not under canvas?" He had taken it for granted that the occupying forces would have looked after themselves properly in this desolation. But they were well to the south of the zone earmarked for British military occupation, and the teeming Americans had had plenty of time to move into the best of what had been left standing.

"Under?" They had reached another crossroads in the ruins, but this time the little man had his nose against the windshield as he peered up at a signpost festooned with information, most of it in Military American, but some pathetically civilian, indicating streets that existed only in memory. "What was that, sir?"

For a moment Fred didn't reply. And then the moment lengthened as they continued to drive through the ruins. And there seemed no end to them, and he realized that he was passing through not "ruins," but the ruin of a once-great city, which might never rise again—or not in his lifetime, anyway.

"Under canvas?" His unnaturally prolonged silence animated the little man's memory. "*Naow*, Major, sir—we're snug enough, for the time bein', like, eh?"

Fred closed his eyes and sat back in comfort, trying to blot out the dead city. Or, alive or dead, *it was finished, here*—that was what he must think! Or . . . he was tired and hungry . . . and the terrible inadequacy of memory was that, while he could recall the exact picture of a leg of roast pork, with golden crackling on it, he could not recall the smell and the taste, *the taste of crackling*.

There was a bump, and he opened his eyes again as the big car surged forward. And suddenly, they were in open country—country soaked and dripping, but mercifully untouched by war, after all they had been through. And that was like a blessing, after the anathema of the city: all the worst that the war could do had its limits, leaving the rest quite untouched, outside Plymouth and Bristol and Cassino—leaving places that hadn't had their names on the bombs untouched, as though there had never been a war. "Where are we?"

"Wot?" Now that he was free of the responsibility of threading his way through the ruins of the city and had his right passenger in the back of the car, the little man was free of all responsibility. So it didn't matter what the original question had been, never mind his answer to it.

"Where are we going?" All the more important questions that he wanted to ask—*Who the hell is Colonel Colbourne?* and *What the hell is "TRR-2 Kaiserburg"?* in the unembattled British Army order-of-battle in Occupied Germany—were out of order. *First*, because they were too humiliating to be asked, and *second*, because the little man probably couldn't answer them usefully anyway.

"Wot?" After that stretch of peaceful, unbombed Germany they were passing through a peaceful, utterly unbombed little village. Or, not quite peaceful, because there was a group of American Army vehicles in the center of it now—a big white-starred staff car, and a jeep with its rain-hood up, and a 15-cwt . . . and a large American NCO, with chevrons half the way down his arm, chewing his cigar regardless of the rain.

"Not far now." The little man humored him, like a father with a tired child in the back.

"To Kaiserburg?" Fred felt the big car stretch itself uphill, under the dripping forested slopes of the Taunus Hills.

"The Kaiser's Burg, *yus*." Sniff. "An' a nasty, dirty night it's goin' to be, like it always is when we've got a job on." Another sniff. "Bloody rain!" He twisted towards Fred. "Not like where you've been, eh?"

"No." He answered automatically, as the memory of the crystal clarity of the evening light and the inviting waters of the Bay of Marathon tugged him momentarily away from *when we've got a job on.* "What job?"

"The Kaiser's burg, huh!" The little man appeared not to have heard him. "It's only temp'ry billet, mind you. 'Cause . . . we've bin movin' around down 'ere, amongst the Yanks, like. An' the Colonel, it suits 'im, bein' wot it is, an' 'im bein' wot 'e is—suits *'im* down to the bleedin' ground!" Bigger sniff. "No bleedin' electrics . . . an' we only got water because it's bin pissin' down, so the cisterns is all full." He twisted towards Fred again. "We were in shirtsleeves up north, in May—would you believe it? An' in June, it was a treat. On'y good thing, bein' 'ere *now*, maybe we won't 'ave to come back again . . . 'Cause it'll be perishin' up here, come winter, wot with the wind and the snow. Mr. David sez it'll be comin' all the way from Russia, 'cause there's nothin' in the way to stop it." The head shook reassuringly suddenly. "But we'll be all right, come winter, if only we're still up in the Swartzenburg—with them thick walls, an' all the trees round-about, to keep the 'ome fires burnin'. We'll be snug as a bug while the Jerries is freezin'—serve 'em right!"

"What job?" Fred plunged straight in as the little man drew breath.

"Ah." The little man fiddled maddeningly among the controls, switching switches on and off quickly, until a feeble yellow flow finally illuminated the trees ahead, totally useless in the half-light and the rain. "*Ah!* I did that once, an' all the electrics fused up. . . . Yes, but you could be lucky sir, arrivin' late, like . . . 'cause it wouldn't be fair to send you out . . . always supposing we ever gets there." He pushed his face up against the rain-smeared windshield again, peering into the gathering murk. "All these little roads looks the same to me, this time uv day . . . An' most uv 'em don't go anywhere, anyway."

Fred's heart sank as he identified the familiar whine of the totally useless and incompetent driver, who was accustomed to following the taillights of the lorry in front and believed that maps were for officers only.

"No! I tell a lie!" The little man sat bolt upright as he looked directly into the muzzle of an 88-millimeter gun, his voice joyful with recognition as the car crunched past the enormous tank on which the gun was mounted. "Not far now!"

Fred swiveled in his seat to peer back at the abandoned

monster through the rear window, his irrational fear dissolving slowly.

"That's wot we call our signpost—proper useful it is," confided the little man as the tank disappeared in the rain and the overcast behind them, like a dead dinosaur sinking into its primeval swamp. "Gawd know 'ow 'e got 'ere, up the top. Prob'ly just lost 'is way, like I thought we 'ad. But Mr. David sez 'e was most likely just goin' 'ome through the forest as the crow flies, an' this was where 'is tank run dry. But 'e's a yarner, is Mr. David."

"A . . . yarner?" Something stirred in Fred's memory. "Mr. David?"

"'E tells yarns—make up stories. Wot 'e sez is that everythin's got a story behind it, to account for where it ends up. An' it's the same with people—like for you an' me, sir. We ain't 'ere by *accident*, is wot 'e means, 'e sez . . . We're 'ere because of wot we are, or wot we done." The death rattle was repeated, but happily now because the little man knew where he was at last. "Which in *our* case must've bin somethin' wicked, 'e sez . . . So, 'ave you done somethin' wicked then, sir?" This time the chuckle degenerated into a smoker's cough that racked the man and swerved the car dangerously between ranks of dripping trees on each side of the road.

"Not that I'm aware of, no." Fred searched for something in the cobwebby attic of the past that still eluded him because it was hidden under more recent rubbish. "Mr. David?"

"Yes. Captain—" The yellow headlights caught the loom of something substantial through a thinning screen of trees up ahead. "There we are! Wot did I tell you. 'Not far'—didn't I say it?"

Through the driving rain and the trees the substantial something became long, pale yellow-brown stone walls—crenellated walls, almost medieval, except that they were too low for the siege warfare of those days and far to untimeworn to be anything older than nineteenth-century work.

"Yes." It was a barracks, of course. Now he could even see the two low towers, with their distinctively unmedieval low-pitched tile roofs, on each side of a double gateway, as the car swung off the road and transfixed them momentarily in its headlights—up here, in the middle of nowhere, what else, of course? "It's a barracks, is it?"

"Yes." The wheel spun as the car turned again, and then spun once more as the driver lined up the car on one of the gateways, between the wooden struts of a bridge crossing the barracks ditch. "Yes, you could say that. A *barricks*, that's wot it is—a bleedin' *barricks*, is what it is!"

The car began to accelerate again, somewhat too fast for Fred's peace of mind, given the narrowness of the arched gateway, which he could now see even more clearly in the brief intervals after each sweep of the windshield wipers swept the rain from the glass.

" 'Ere we go, then!" Like so many RASC drivers, the little man evidently belonged to what Fred's first company commander had always called "the school of empirical verification." If a vehicle got through a gap, or crossed a suspect stretch of ground, then that gap was wide enough for it, or that ground was free of mines, as the case might be. " 'Old tight!"

There was a rumble under them as the big car advanced across a plank bridge over a double ditch, and he caught a glimpse of an equestrian statue between the double doorways. It looked more like a Roman emperor than a German kaiser. In fact it looked *exactly* like the statue of Marcus Aurelius he had admired in Rome last year, during his leave in that memorable time-out-of-war before the battle of the Gothic Line—so perhaps it was a kaiser dressed as a caesar, maybe?

But then the statue was gone, and they were squeezing through the gateway, with more familiar sights in the glare of the headlights: canvas-hooded jeeps and 15-cwt trucks lined up, with even more familiar soldiers, caped against the downpour, attending to their unloading—TRR-2 at last!

But . . . *Christ! Because there was a man—a British soldier—standing bold as brass and unashamed under an umbrella! Christ Almighty!*

"Right, there you are, then!" The driver swung the car round the umbrella-carrying soldier, braking so fiercely that Fred's chest thumped sharply against the front seat. "End uv the line, this is, sir." He peered at the car's switches before flicking them off one by one; and then swiveled towards Fred, grinning familiarly as though they were equals who had shared some testing experience. "I'll see you to your bag, sir. Your servant's Trooper Lucy, shared with Mr. David, so you'll not 'ave anythin' to worry about there. 'Avin' Trooper Lucy is like 'avin' a good lady's maid."

Between Marcus Aurelius and the umbrella soldier and Trooper Lucy and the fact that he couldn't find the door handle, Fred cursed impotently under his breath.

"Wot you wanta do is to find the adjutant. An' 'e'll be in 'is office—first on your left as you go through the door right in front, an' round under the little roof wot keeps the rain *orf*—which is that way, see?"

Fred had found the door handle. "Well, thank you—what's your name?"

"Hughie, sir." The little man came quickly to his rescue. "Knock twice, an' ask for Hughie, is what they say." The little man stared at him in the gloom. "You're a sapper, sir—Major Fattorini, sir. Wouldn't that be reg'lar army or 'ostilities only?"

"Territorial." He found himself answering automatically, as a distant but warning bell sounded in his memory. "March, 1939."

"Is that a fact?" The date seemed to meet with the man's approval. "Terriers is orl right, most of 'em. The colonel, 'e's a terrier." He nodded. "You'll be orl right wiv' 'im then, I reckon."

"Indeed?" Fred tightened his grip on the door handle. "Haven't I met you before somewhere? Was it in—?" Before he could finish, a movement at the front of the car took his attention: the soldier with the umbrella appeared to be examining the right door intently.

" 'Scuse me." The little man caught his change of attention, turned towards its direction, and was out of the car like a ferret out of a bag. "That wasn't me! That was there 'fore I sets orf, that was. Someone else done that!" The sound of his voice, raised to a protesting whine, entered the car with a wind-driven spatter of rain.

The umbrella-carrying soldier straightened up to his full height, the wind catching his umbrella and almost pulling it out of his hand. "Hughie, you're an absolute and in-invv— *inveterate* 111— liar. I checked the whole b-bloody car myself before you set out. And there wasn't a mark on it. So now the Croc-Crocodile will have c-cast us b-both into outer d-darkness!"

Oh, God! thought Fred, the mists of half a year's memory clearing instantly in the same instant as the umbrella soldier turned towards him. Then he knew that he must pull himself together and confirm the hideous certainty that confronted him in the headlights.

The full force of the wind and rain hit him as he stepped out of the car. "Hullo, there!" Even as he spoke, he saw that things *were* as bad as they seemed. "David Audley, is it."

"It was them Yanks, Mr. David—it must uv been them," whined the little man. "I 'ad to leave the major's car, jus' for a minnit."

"It is. Or what's left of him." Audley struggled with his umbrella. "Captain Fat-O'Rhiney, well met!" He gave the little man a quick sidelong glance. "Hughie, I told you most particularly *not* to leave the car, remember?" He came back to Fred. "Bad trip, was it?" He gave Fred a friendly grin. "We've been expecting you these last three hours . . . at least, the CO has been."

holding out his hand in friendship. " 'Frederick'? David there says I should address you as 'Fred.' But I can't possibly do that. Because . . . apart from the fact that I once had a cocker spaniel who answered to that name, albeit a most intelligent and affectionate beast . . . because, apart from that, we are accustomed to refer to our sovereign lord and master, the brigadier, as 'Fred' . . . so that would only be to confuse matters quite unbearably." He smiled devilishly. "So henceforth you are 'Freddie'—is that acceptable?"

He had to accept the hand, even though he knew what that hand had done once, and therefore must have done many times. And he also had to answer the man coolly and confidently, if he wasn't to be despised. "Anything, so long as it isn't 'Fatty,' which I had to answer to all the way through prep school, is perfectly acceptable, sir."

" 'Amos,' Freddie. We're all equals here." De Souza's grip was firm and dry and strong—the best sort of handshake. "All, that is, except this young whippersnapper, temporary Captain Audley." The hand relaxed its grip. "Talking of whom . . . have you dealt with those transport problems, young David? Are the drivers properly briefed?"

"All except Hughie, Amos." Audley was quite unabashed. "Yes."

"Well, go and attend to him." Beneath the lazy drawl there was a sharp reef of concern. "I want no mistakes tonight, no unfortunate accidents, like last time. Apart from which . . . I have a strong suspicion that our Fred himself may very well materialize out of the darkness up on the *limes Romanorum* tonight. So we wouldn't want anything less than maximum effort, would we, now? Eh, Captain Audley?"

There was a fractional pause before Audley replied. "It w-wasn't my fault last time. It was Croc who fucked things up, if you ask me, Amos."

"But I'm not asking you, David. I am just making sure that you do not . . . as you put it so delicately . . . 'fuck things up' this time. Right?"

Audley rocked slightly on his heels. "Yes, Amos."

"Thank you, David." Amos de Souza acknowledged the boy's surrender quite deliberately, without mercy. "Now . . . Freddie . . . we're due in the mess in fifteen minutes, and Colonel Colbourne is a stickler for punctuality. But he expected you here earlier, so I'd better wheel you in to him right away, without more ado, right?" He turned back to his desk for a moment, and a tiny beam of lamplight glinted on the rosette on his Military Cross ribbon: MC and bar and the desert ribbon established

Major de Souza as a sharp-end soldier in the past, whatever malignant fate had condemned him to do in Greece in the more recent past, and whatever he was doing in Germany now. Then he looked sideways, without straightening up, towards Audley. "I thought you were going back to your horse lines, dear boy. What's keeping you?"

Audley stood his ground. "I w-w-w-was . . . j-j . . . just thinking, Amos."

"J-just thinking?" De Souza straightened up. "Now, that's half your trouble, young David: 'j-just thinking,' eh?" Then he shook his head. "All right! What have you been j-just thinking, then? Share the wisdom of the ages with us, go on!"

Audley opened his mouth, and then closed it as though he was nerving himself to control his stutter.

Major de Souza turned back to his desk, selecting a thin file from a pile of thicker ones before returning to Audley. "But now you've thought better of it? Which is probably j-just as well. Go—to the horse lines, dear boy. You'll be much safer doing your duty there."

The young man drew a deep breath, which seemed to make him even bigger than he was. "You should tell him about the colonel, Amos."

"Tell him what?"

Another breath. "That he's a loony."

Major de Souza looked at Audley for a long moment, and as the moment lengthened and with bitter experience of his own of adjutants' taking their job seriously, Fred braced himself for an explosion. But the young man stood his ground, to the credit of his courage if not his intelligence, or his obstinacy if not his courage.

De Souza smiled, and shook his head, and finally laughed softly. "David, David, David . . . How many times do I have to tell you, dear boy . . . that we're all loonies here. If we weren't loonies, we wouldn't be here." He favored Fred with a cynical twist of the lip. "So you go back to your horse lines, David . . . and make sure all our transport is ready to move on H hour, like a good dragon. Because we don't want any slipups this time. So . . . *move, Captain Audley!*"

Audley moved. And Fred thought, as the hobnails on the young man's boots scraped and skittered on the stone floor, that he would also have moved after that order from the adjutant. Particularly this adjutant.

"Now then, Freddie"—Major de Souza indicated the open doorway, out of which Audley had vanished—"shall we go then?"

59

Fred let himself be shepherded out of the office, into the gathering gloom of the cloister.

"To your left." But then de Souza closed the door behind him and locked it carefully, turning a key on a chain in a heavy padlock as Fred waited for him. And as he waited, he drew into his nose a faint savory cooking smell, which must have drifted from somewhere round the colonnaded square, because the steady downpour still glinted in the open space in its center, and that would have damped down such smells.

"He's a good boy, is David." De Souza pointed their direction. "Very bright. If he lives, he'll go far, as they say. But quite out of his depth, I'm afraid."

"Yes?" For a man who was supposed to know what he was about, Fred still felt nonplussed.

"Too young, far too young." De Souza led the way. "Fred—*Fred*, our Lord and master—he should never have lumbered us with him. And Colonel Colbourne shouldn't have accepted him." He stopped abruptly outside another door and rapped his knuckles on it. "This is men's work. And boys aren't up to it, no matter how bright they are."

"Come!" A high voice, almost querulous, invited them from the other side of the door.

"A great pity, really." De Souza ignored the voice, staring at Fred in the light of a hurricane lamp hanging on a bracket on one of the pillars of the colonnade. "This'll spoil him. Because he can't really understand what he's doding. He's got a scholarship waiting up at Cambridge. So . . . he's done his regimental bit, in Normandy . . . so they should have let go of him." He grasped the door handle. "A pity, a great pity."

"Wait!" There were so many questions Fred couldn't ask now that he didn't know what to ask. He only knew that he didn't want to go straight into that room.

"What?" De Souza stared at him.

"Come!" The invitation was repeated.

A useless question surfaced. "What is this place?"

"Huh! It's a Roman fort." De Souza didn't seem surprised. "A Roman auxiliary fort on the *limes*, in the Taunus, rebuilt by a rich German in the nineteenth century, in the Kaiser's time. The last unit to occupy this place, before us, was *Cohors IV Britannorum Equitata*, in the second century after the birth of Christ. Which makes us the second British contingent up here, on the Taunus. Which is probably why we're here now, actually." The door handle rattled, and de Souza let go of it, and the door began to open.

"Who's that?" The voice came out of the gap, still high pitched, but irritated now.

"It's Amos, sir." De Souza stood back from the door. "Major Fattorini has just arrived. I've got him with me."

The door opened wide, and de Souza sprang to attention and saluted as it did so. So Fred did the same, but not so smartly, because the colonel was stark naked.

"Whisper-whisper-whisper—*huh!*" The colonel waved a large sponge at them with his saluting hand, dripping water all around him. "What were you whispering about, Amos?"

"I wasn't whispering, sir." De Souza addressed his naked CO with cool deference. "I was merely explaining to Major Fattorini that this is a Roman fort."

"Yes?" Colonel Colbourne lowered his sponge and peered at Fred. "Doesn't he know a Roman fort when he sees one, then?"

"I was explaining that the last British unit to be billeted here was *Cohors IV Equitata.*" De Souza avoided answering this lunatic question with what Fred suspected was well-oiled adroitness.

The colonel dropped Fred in preference for de Souza, raising his left arm and sponging his armpits as he did so. "There's too much whispering going on, Amos. Whenever I come round a corner there are other ranks and NCOs whispering as though they're bargaining with each other—as though they're *selling* things . . . which they probably are. And I don't like it. And I won't have it. Is that understood?"

"Yes, sir." De Souza paused. "I'll tell them to speak up." He paused again. "So that we can hear what they're selling. Right, sir."

"Good." The colonel dropped de Souza this time. "Major Fattorini, I know your aunt . . . aunt-by-marriage, that would be?" He began to sponge the lower part of his body absently. "An Armstrong, your aunt?"

Major de Souza kicked Fred's leg quite painfully under cover of the shadows.

"Yes, sir." The pain concentrated his mind. "My mother is an Armstrong."

"That's right." Colonel Colbourne turned back to de Souza, shifting his weight so that he could sponge between his legs. "I know full well what they're up to. And I know there's precious little we can do about it. Corrupt and corrupted, they are—it's the same with all armies of occupation—even though Mr. Levin and I have handpicked them. And it'll get worse before it gets better—if it ever does get better. But at least we can fire a shot over their heads. . . . So you can post Sergeant Devenish, for a start. And see that it's a Far East posting, too. That'll frighten 'em, by God!"

"No, sir." De Souza stood his ground. "Devenish is a good man."

"Tcha! I know he's a good man, I chose him. But he's also a whisperer. And Alec McCorquodale has compained about him."

"He also speaks tolerable German, sir. We need him."

"Huh! It's because he speaks German that he's up to no good!" Colbourne waved the sponge. "Oh, all right, post someone else. They're all corrupt, so anyone will do." He looked at Fred suddenly. "Lydia Ferguson née Armstrong—your mother's sister?" He sniffed. "A decent, respectable woman . . . but married to a wastrel husband. I handled her divorce. A dirty business, as divorce always is. Give me a good murder any day." He invited Fred into his room with his sponge. "Come in, Freddie, come in!"

Fred thought: *Audley was bloody right!*

And then he thought: *If I have Audley to thank for this posting . . . or whoever it may be . . . then Colonel Colbourne may soon have another murderer to defend before long, by Christ!*

CHAPTER TWO

"**N**ow then, Freddie"—the colonel turned his back on them as he spoke and stepped into a battered hip bath—"if you allow me to complete my ablutions, eh?" He bent down to dunk his sponge in the water.

"Yes, sir." Faced with his commanding officer's white buttocks, Fred chose to study the room instead, although there was little enough to study. It was much the same as the adjutant's office, with its single unnaturally high-up latticed window, and apart from the hip bath its sole contents consisted of a camp bed with the colonel's clothing neatly laid out on it, and a battered metal trunk on which a pressure lamp hissed away softly. So the colonel clearly wasn't a believer in creature comforts, he thought disconsolately.

"So, you're a friend of young Audley's, is that the case?" The colonel gyrated under a cascade of water squeezed from his sponge.

"No, sir." That was not the case in more senses than one at this precise moment. "He was at school with my younger brother, I believe."

"Mmmm. But you are acquainted with him, are you not?" The

63

colonel stepped out of the hip bath onto the cold stone floor without a hint of hesitation, into a large puddle that he must have left when he'd gone to investigate the whisperers outside his door.

"I have met him once." The atmosphere in the room was cold and dank, to match its musty, unoccupied smell. And Fred suspected that it was a cold bath that the colonel was enjoying so inhumanly.

"Just once?" The colonel pointed to the camp bed. "Would you be so good as to hand me that towel?"

"Yes." The towel was rough as sandpaper.

"In Greece? Thank you." The colonel began to towel himself vigorously. "In Greece?"

"Yes." If, as Driver Hewitt and the colonel himself had suggested, Colonel Colbourne had practiced law before the war, then this was a cross-examination, he began to suspect. But why?

"Good." The colonel nodded in de Souza's direction. "Any friend of young Audley's might be one too many for us, eh, Amos?"

For a moment de Souza didn't answer. "Sir?" He paused for a second, almost as though he hadn't heard the question. "Captain Audley does his job well, sir. He's just somewhat younger than the rest of us, that's all."

"Huh!" Colbourne folded his towel carefully and placed it on the edge of his hip bath. "But you are a friend of Colonel Michaelides's, are you not?"

The question came out of the gloom unexpectedly, just as Fred was watching the towel slide down the side of the bath into the water. "Sir—? Yes . . . I am a friend of Colonel Michaelides's." It was a cross-examination. But the cross-examiner knew too damn many answers to his questions already. So it was time to have all his wits around him. And his wits' first requirement was that he must counterquestion. "Are you a friend of Colonel Michaelides's, sir?"

"Eh?" The question took the colonel off balance.

"I said . . . are you a friend of Colonel Michaelides's, sir?" It was easier to study his naked commanding officer now that the he was neither standing in the ill-lit doorway nor presenting his arse and twisting under his sponge. The upwards-directed light distorted his features, but he had a good, well-muscled, hairy body—light heavyweight—with the familiar distribution of tanned and untanned skin that Fred had observed among his own men in Italy and Greece, before they had had time to sunbathe peacefully. So that meant the colonel had put in six years of open-air living, but hadn't enjoyed any Mediterranean service in recent months, to spread that sunburn as uniformly.

Major de Souza gave a little dry cough. "They'll be waiting for us in the mess, sir . . . quite soon."

"Yes." The colonel continued to stare at Fred. "Ah . . . you go on, Amos."

"Sir?"

"I said—" The continued stare began to worry Fred, as it occurred to him that he had unwisely crossed swords with an expert. "You heard me, Amos. *Go on!*"

"Yes." But de Souza didn't move. "I was going to introduce . . . Freddie . . . to the rest of them. That's all."

Fred suddenly knew perfectly what was happening. Adjutants were usually creatures of colonels, quite properly. But adjutants weren't usually majors, and this wasn't any sort of usual unit, so Major de Souza wasn't a usual adjutant. He was a rescuer of junior officers in adversity, from whatever fate-worse-than-death awaited them—whether their name was *Audley* or *Fattorini*. And that might be because it was peacetime, at least here in Germany, and he didn't give a damn; or it might be because he disliked Colonel Colbourne, and still didn't give a damn—for colonels or Germans or ELAS *Andartes* or anyone. Because that was Amos de Souza's pleasure.

"We've got one of your pigs tonight, sir." De Souza's most casual voice was stretched to the breaking point, it was so thin. "And that ham of Otto's too."

"Thank you, Amos." The colonel's quick reply was polite on the surface, but equally stretched beneath. So he also knew what was happening. "And we have work to do tonight. I had not forgotten."

"No. Of course not, sir." Like a good soldier who had fought to his last round, de Souza surrendered quickly to save his life. "With your permission, I'll withdraw, then."

"You do that." The colonel sounded only partially mollified.

"Thank you, sir." De Souza turned away. "I'll see you in the mess shortly then, Freddie. It's just up the colonnade—"

"Thank you, Major de Souza." This time the colonel imposed his will as nakedly as his person. "That will be all for now."

As de Souza withdrew, Fred reviewed his position. The adjutant had bought him time with his obstinacy, but he didn't quite know how to spend it because he had only the haziest idea of the internal politics of this unhappy unit, with its mad commanding officer who was evidently at odds with his own adjutant, never mind young Audley; and in itself that was confusing, because every commanding officer he had ever served under had very soon got rid of those officers whose faces and attitudes didn't fit. But then . . . but then if this *was* somehow the same bunch he'd fallen in with, by sheer bad luck, that day long ago in Greece . . . if it was . . . then he had to start thinking hard and fast, not about them but about himself.

Not good honest soldiers, like we were in Italy, Kyri had reiterated afterwards, carefully glossing over his own change of role. *Those were hunters, old boy—a new breed. And if you'll take my advice, you stay well clear of them, Captain Fattorini, my friend.*

"Well now, Major Fattorini." While Fred had been thinking, Colonel Colbourne had put on his socks, which made him look ridiculous, as he had never quite looked when he was stark bollock naked and unashamed. "'Freddie,' is it? Or 'Fred'?"

"Either will do, sir." Fred watched the colonel pick up his shirt and methodically examine it in the lamplight, as though for lice, before plunging into it.

"I have a message for you, sir . . . actually," he addressed the hooded figure, which was still naked from the waist to the socks. "I am to thank you for the pig." Ever since de Souza had mentioned pigs—*one of your pigs*, indeed—the pig had been squealing in the background of his mind, he realized now. "There was this American officer who met me on the airfield, sir. I'm afraid I didn't get his name." Fred adjusted his voice to his situation: he must seem deferential, but ever so slightly embarrassed. "He was most helpful . . . in getting me through the formalities." That was enough. "But he said . . . he said, I was to thank you for the pig. And . . . whatever you wanted, if you'd got more pigs, then he's got more aircraft . . . sir."

"Hah . . . hmmm!" The colonel pulled down his shirt. "It wasn't a pig, that's damned slander."

"Yes, sir?" Whatever the animal was, it had given him an edge, Fred thought exultantly. "It wasn't a pig?"

"*Fattorini*, eh?" The colonel's eye had fixed on him now. "Merchant bankers, right?" Without unfixing his eye he snatched a tie from his bed. "Armstrong Fattorini Brothers?"

"Yes, sir." This had always been where the cross-examination had been going. But if Colonel Colbourne had conducted Aunt Lydia's divorce, he would undoubtedly know all about Armstrong Fattorini . . . if only to adjust the size of his fee. So what else did he want?

"Armstrong." The colonel examined his underpants critically. "An old Scottish border family of brigands and bandits turned merchant bankers when the old ways became unprofitable—a natural enough progression. Who was it said 'better to found a bank than rob one'?"

The man had done his homework. "Yes, sir."

Colbourne looked up at him, one leg trousered. "Luke Fattorini, or *Sir* Luke, as I should call him now . . . your uncle, he would be, I take it?"

"Yes, sir." The man knew damn well. But somehow the mention of Uncle Luke strengthened his confidence. In times of adversity, ever since father's death, Uncle Luke had always been a powerful and wise ally.

"Clever man." Colbourne sniffed as he began to put on his glittering brown boots. "Influential, too. . . . Dealt with that wastrel Ferguson, Captain the Honorable whatever-he-was—your aunt's husband—*he* thought he had influence in high places . . . and so he did. But your Uncle Luke had *more* influence in *higher* places. And he knew how to use it too. So we took Captain the Honorable for a settlement that made his eyeballs pop, between us . . ." The colonel straightened up and reached for his battle-dress blouse. "Clever man, yes!"

There was a DSO among the colonel's ribbons. But that didn't equal de Souza's double-MC: it could have come up with the rations in the Judge Advocate's department, even when teamed with the desert medal of the 8th Army—there had been more than a few undeserved DSOs wandering around Cairo and Alexandria in the bad old days before Monty, so it was said.

"Yes." The colonel tightened the belt of his blouse. "And you were in Italy, before Greece?"

"Yes, sir." Now he was on safe ground. "Fourth Division."

"A very good division, too." Colbourne looked down suddenly. "How's that hand of yours? Crushed under one of those bridges of yours, was it?"

"It's much better, sir." Praise of the 4th Div had momentarily weakened Fred's critical faculty. But now caution reasserted itself. "I was lucky."

"You were?" The colonel's lack of further interest showed that he didn't know much about the hazards of Bailey bridging. "Did you see many Roman bridges in Italy."

Fred felt his mouth open. "Roman . . . ?"

"Bridges. They built damn good bridges." Colbourne's eyes glittered in the lamplight. "Good military bridges, too—don't you recall Caesar's bridge across the Rhine? Don't you sappers know your history?" The man's face creased into what the lamplight made into a diabolical frown. "And you were up at Oxford before the war, so you must know your *Gallic War*, for heaven's sake!"

"But I read—mathematics, sir." Fred began by snapping back, tired of saying "Yes, sir." But then that fanatical glint warned him, like the glint of metal on a roadside verge that betrayed the mine beneath it. "I did know a chap in Italy, though . . . he was an expert on . . . Roman remains."

"Yes?" Suddenly, and for the first time, he had all Colonel Colbourne's attention. "Who was that, then?"

Fred had to search for the name. "Bradford, sir."

"Bradford?" Frown. "What regiment?"

"No regiment." Now he knew he was on a winner. "He was RAF photographic reconnaissance and interpretation."

"*Ahhh!*" Colbourne beamed at him. "*That* Bradford, of course! How stupid of me! *John* Bradford—Flight Lieutenant . . . Roman centuriation and Etruscan tombs—met him last year. Disciple of O.G.S. Crawford's—next generation of aerial archaeology. Another *clever* fellow—*yes!*"

"Yes, sir." All Fred could recall, and then only vaguely, was the young RAF man's fifty-fifty enthusiasm for German defensive activity at the mouth of the Tiber and the incidental photographs he had acquired that also betrayed the town plan of the abandoned old Roman city of Ostia. "He had some very interesting pictures, I believe."

"Yes. Quite remarkable, his pictures—very fine. Never seen such eloquent testimony of the way the Roman field systems continued." The colonel's voice was animated by something of the RAF intelligence officer's enthusiasm. "Bit too taken up with the Etruscans, for my taste—a rum lot, the Etruscans. Like the damned Greeks." He frowned at Fred suddenly. "I wonder what he's doing now."

"Sir?" For a moment Fred thought that the latest frown was directed at him, and he closed his open mouth smartly. But then he saw that the question was self-directed, and the colonel wasn't really looking at him at all. "You mean Flight Lieutenant Bradford?"

"Ye-ess . . . I wonder whether we could get him up here, come autumn, when the leaves are off the trees." The frown went clear through Fred. "No problem with the equipment—the Yanks can take care of that, even if the RAF can't. It might not produce anything . . . probably wouldn't." The intensity of the pale eyes was most disconcerting. "But if Varus did build a marching camp—just *one* marching camp, mind you—*just one* . . . somewhere on the middle Weser or the Upper Lippe." Nod. "In fact, we could draw an arc from Moguntiacum to Castra Vetera, coming back through Detmold, and try that for a start. . . . And Bradford would be the very man to spot the slightest sign of one—he'd know a Roman marching camp from an Iron Age enclosure at a glance, *at a glance!*" The eyes focused on Fred, with a fierce yellow lamplight glint in then. "Good man, Major Fattorini—Freddie! I hadn't thought of that. Stupid of me, but I hadn't! Air photography, by God! *Should have thought of that, by God!*" He smacked his fist decisively into his other palm. "Yes. I suppose I could ask the RAF. In fact, they've probably got a million pictures of the whole area, full of bomb craters miles from the target. . . . Detmold was quite well-bombed, as I recall—Luftwaffe station not too far away, I think. . . . But it would be easier to borrow a pilot and a plane from the Yanks. They've got the planes and the pilots, yes."

And you've got the pigs, thought Fred, utterly disoriented by this new and irrational turn of an interview that had never made much sense. But then, if the colonel wanted to give him credit for a chance remark, he might as well claim it while he could. "Flight Lieutenant Bradford was an extremely competent interpreter, as I recall, sir."

"Yes, you're absolutely right, Freddie." The colonel seemed to have forgotten that he'd said as much himself, in his enthusiasm. "Good man!" He nodded. "You'll do, you'll do, by God!"

Fred saw his chance at last, in a flash. "Do what, sir?"

"What?" Colbourne was still staring down from a great height inside his brain, at—what was it? *Marching camps? Somewhere on the middle of the Weser upper Lippe?* "What?"

"Do what, sir?" The Weser was a German river. In fact, it was the German river into which the Pied Piper of Hamelin had piped all the rats, before he'd piped away all the children. So the Lippe was probably another German river, another Rhine tributary. But what the bloody hell was a *marching camp*? "You said . . . I'd do." He mustn't lose his temper. Not with his new commanding officer. "I was merely wondering why you wanted an officer of engineers, Colonel Colbourne. My posting orders were not precise on that point."

Colbourne blinked at him, as though at a fool. "They weren't? No . . . well, of course, they wouldn't have been, would they." He gestured towards the door. "But we're late, so let's go. . . . You ask Amos—Major de Souza, whom you've met. Come on, come on."

Fred started to move, but then stopped automatically, to give his commanding officer precedence. Colbourne also started to move, but then stopped and faced him. "Or you could ask young Audley—he'll tell you if you ask him, later tonight. Can't talk shop in the mess . . . but you'll be with him tonight afterwards, and you'll have plenty of time then, I don't doubt. Go on, man, go on!"

Fred gave up and went ahead out into the feeble glow of the hanging lantern, not knowing where he was going and almost without hope, but remembering the ORs' favorite litany as he did so: *Roll on death—demob's bound to be a failure!*

"Left, left, towards the light there"—Colonel Colbourne pointed down the pillared cloister—"but don't believe all he says, eh?"

The pillars were unreal. Only the utter darkness beyond them—a darkness emphasized by the flashed reflection of the occasional raindrop out of the millions that were falling in the open square outside the pillars—only that darkness was real. Colbourne wasn't real either, and Audley was a nightmare from the past . . . and the allegation that this was a Roman fortress set the seal on them both.

"All my officers are mad, quite mad," Colbourne confided, from just behind him.

Kaiserburg, he had been thinking. But now Colonel Colbourne and Captain Audley were in total agreement.

"Quite mad." Colbourne agreed with himself. "In any sort of military sense . . . almost unemployable, in fact."

The Kaiser's Burg, Fred applied himself to his original thought, unwilling to let Colbourne and Audley agree with each other. But perhaps that wasn't *Kaiser Wilhelm's Castle: perhaps it was Castra Caesaris . . . or would it be "Castrum" Caesaris?*

"But as a sapper you'll have no trouble with them." Colbourne touched his arm. "Round the corner, then on your left there."

He was exhausted, and filthy, and he wanted a pee. But if that was the officers' mess, he needed a drink, and a strong one, and a large one even more urgently.

"And then . . . the brigadier wouldn't have asked for you if he didn't think you were suitable, mmm?" The Colonel rumbled question and answer in the back of his throat. "In fact, he said— Ah, Amos! There you are!"

Major de Souza appeared in the wide double doorway. "Gus! You're damned late for dinner. Your pig has been crying out for you—and so has Otto, actually."

"I'm sorry, old boy, I really am." The colonel would have pushed past if Fred hadn't already been trying to get out of the way. "But look here. I want you to get on to the RAF—try Wing Commander Fraser first, at Minden, he'll know who to get on to. . . . You remember him?"

"I remember him." De Souza winced slightly. "But what do you want, Gus?" He rolled an eye at Fred, sympathetically. "Can't it wait?"

"Air photography, Amos. What about that, eh?"

"Air photography?" De Souza abandoned Fred, expressionless now. "What about air photography?"

"It's the answer to all our problems." Colbourne lifted a tumbler off a silver tray that had materialized out of the darkness at his elbow, held by a white-gloved hand on the end of a disembodied white-coated arm, without taking his eyes off Amos. "Got it off Freddie here—he's a friend of John Bradford's. Very clever young man."

"I never doubted it." Amos misunderstood the reference suavely. "But I haven't got any problems, that I am aware of. Except in the matter of demobilization, that is. And who the hell is John Bradford?" He looked sideways quickly. "Otto! Where is Major Fattorini's drink?"

"Herr Major!" The disembodied arm acquired a substantial body—an immaculately white-coated body topped by a beaming red-brick face slashed diagonally by a line holding a black eyepatch in place. "Herr Major! My most profound apologies! What is your pleasure?"

"I didn't mean Freddie, Amos," snapped Colbourne.

"He's not a clever fellow?" Amos simulated surprise. "I rather thought he was. Oxford degree, and all that—and a better one than yours, Gus, actually. . . . Mathematics was it, Freddie? Are you a musician too? They say music goes with maths, don't they?"

Fred was caught once again with his mouth open, midway between the piratical Otto and the baffling proximity of his commanding officer, and Amos de Souza's transformed behavior, and all the questions that had suddenly been directed at him.

"Good God, Amos! Let the poor man order his drink, damn it! First things first—eh, Freddie?" Colbourne seemed oblivious of Amos's scorn. "You order your drink—and you come away with me, Amos, and I'll tell you all about young Bradford . . ." As he trailed off, the colonel raised his head and stared into the encircling lamp-lit gloom in a series of jerky movements, as though he was searching for something. "Where is young David? He's never there when I want him . . . where the devil is he?"

De Souza turned slightly. *"David!"*

A huge presence loomed from behind the one-eyed Otto. "You c-called, Amos?"

"Look after your friend." De Souza returned his attention to the colonel as he spoke. "Get him a drink and introduce him to everyone. . . . Now, Gus, you just tell me all about this John Bradfield of yours . . . and about air photography, right?" He pointed into the gloom.

"Herr Major." One-eyed Otto tried desperately to catch Amos's attention.

"Gently, Otto, gently! Your pig will just have to keep. . . .

71

Gus?" De Souza's hand shrugged off Otto and directed his commanding officer in a flowing double gesture. "Just give us a few minutes."

Mess rules, Fred decided belatedly. Outside wherever the mess happened to be Colonel Colbourne was God Almighty; but one inch over the threshold of the mess he was *primus inter pares*— just another officer, who talked military shop at his peril. And since he made the rules, those were the goddamn rules.

"Don't w-worry, Otto!" Audley wound a great arm round the white-coated pirate familiarly. "Your pig won't run away squealing. More like, his crackling will c-c-crackle even better!"

"Ach! He will crackle all right—he will crackle all through, is what he will do! But where will all his good juices go? Up the fucking chimney, I tell you, Captain David—up the fucking chimney!" One-eyed Otto rounded on Audley angrily.

"Well, I like my meat overdone. Better a burnt sacrifice than one bloody offering, any day."

"So?" Otto almost accepted this reassurance, but then rejected it. "But you are a child, you know no better." He shook his head at Audley. "The war has ruined you: you think you have won . . . but the truth is, you have lost." The shake continued for a moment, and then became a shrug. "We have all lost—that is the truth!"

"No." Audley shook his head back at the man. "*You* have lost— *and* we have lost. But the Yanks and the Russians have won, remember?"

Otto brought both hands—white-gloved hands—in front of him, chest high and clenched. "But they don't have my pig."

"But the colonel won't blame you, Otto—he won't know, will he?" Audley matched Otto's gesture, except that his big hands were unclenched and placatory, as though he was trying to sell the overcooked pig.

"Fuck the colonel! It is *my* pig, and *I* know!" Otto looked up at Audley. "And he was a good one—he deserves *better*, Captain David."

Audley nodded seriously. "Fuck the Colonel—I quite agree: a very *p-p-p-proper* sentiment. But"—suddenly he became aware of Fred and clapped his hand to his mouth, looking from Otto to Fred, and then back again—"b-but, hadn't you better offer *Herr Major* Fattorini a drink, like you were ordered to?"

"*Ach, mein lieber Gott!*" Otto faced Fred, openmouthed. "Sir?"

"What would you like?" Audley moved into the instant of silence.

It took Fred another second to gather his wits. "What have you got?"

Audley grinned. "You name it, we've got it. Except . . . if you've acquired a taste for that dreadful Greek retsina . . . and we're not actually very good on Italian wines, either." He paused. "Bordeaux and Burgundy . . . we have some unconsidered trifles, which are almost settled down now. But we shall be offering them with Otto's pig. And I would personally recommend the Haut Brion, rather than the lighter clarets. But then, I am not a Burgundy man. Otto thinks that is a sign of callow youth, but it's still my opinion, right, Otto?"

Otto spread his hands. "The Haut Brion is superb."

"Ex-Luftwaffe Haut Brion." Audley nodded. "But we've also got some delectable Hocks and Moselles—very refreshing and invigorating. And you can still have the Haut Brion with the pig"—he looked towards Otto—"and with the deer ham before, maybe? Would that be okay, Otto?"

But Otto was staring at Fred. "I think the Herr Major may be thinking of something stronger at this moment."

Christ! The Herr Major was thinking of anything! thought Fred, despairingly.

"Well . . . if it's a sherry, we have it." Another Audley nod. "The most delicate dry sherry—also courtesy of the Luftwaffe . . . and presumably, General Franco."

"We have whiskey." Otto knew his man better. "Ration Red Label and VAT Sixty-nine. Black Label. Single malt—and an Islay malt, which is good. And good gin, Booth's and Gordon's." He stopped suddenly. "And we have also Tennessee whiskey, of Jack Daniel's. And several other American whiskeys. And rum from Puerto Rico and Cuba, as well as Jamaica. But only a little Trinidad rum, I regret."

"Yes. That's because the Crocodile likes it. So you'd better lay off that," agreed Audley hastily. "But brandy, of course. And a whole lot of Russian vodkas, of varying toxicity . . . which I wouldn't actually recommend. And a whole lot of other things— just try us and see, okay?"

Curiosity was great. But thirst was greater. "I'll have a large Black Label—as soon as possible, please." Fred looked around. There were other officers in the gloom, but as Audley wasn't trying to introduce them, he'd better let that go. "You don't travel light then? Alcoholically speaking."

"No, we don't." Audley grinned happily. "We inherited all the contents of the Schwartzenburg cellars, and it was a Luftwaffe headquarters. And we're a very small unit, you see. So the aim is to drink the place dry by New Year's Day, 1946."

Fred started to think, *Audley isn't stuttering.* But then Otto materialized at his elbow with his silver tray again, and a glass on it.

"Thank you." The glass was large and heavy, and there was a lot in it.

"We have no ice. But you would not have wanted that." Otto bowed slightly. "If you'll excuse me, gentlemen?"

"Go on, Otto, go on." Audley waved at the man. "Just make sure you keep the Crocodile's glass full, that's all. I want him in a benign mood this evening."

"Because of the injury to his car?" Otto checked, and nodded. "Yes?"

"Oh, you know, do you? But of course you do!" Audley leaned towards Fred. "All is known to Otto—Otto knows everything. Otto can get you anything. Isn't that true, Otto?"

"Have no fear." Otto raised a white-gloved hand. "The matter has been well attended." He bowed to Audley and backed away into the gloom again.

"Yes, I don't doubt." Audley watched the white coat disappear before turning back to Fred. "Otto likes Hughie—they're thick as thieves. Which, of course, is what they both are. So they recognize the other's worth. Amazing, really, when you think about it."

"Amazing?" Somehow, Fred didn't think Audley was referring to the Otto-Hughie entente, from the way he spoke. "What is?"

"Trinidad rum." Audley nodded. "It's *rather* amazing that Otto very quickly discovered that it's Major McCorquodale's favorite tipple—his Achilles' heel, if you like . . . in so far as a crocodile can have an Achilles' heel. . . . But it's *absolutely* amazing— quite incredible really—that he was then able to conjure up supplies of the stuff, here in Germany." He shook his head. "Trust our Otto!"

"He's the mess waiter?" Fred sipped his whiskey cautiously, aware that there were many other items of information he needed more urgently.

"Oh . . . not really." Audley's unlovely features screwed up conspiratorially. "He's a lot more than that. In fact, he doesn't usually honor us with his presence before dinner . . . unless we're entertaining top brass, anyway." He brought his face close to Fred's ear. "I *rather* suspect that the white coat and gloves have been put on solely for Hughie's benefit, to make sure that Major McCorquodale is well oiled this evening. Because one of his very few virtues is that alcohol makes him mmm-more agreeable. Which gives the lie to one of our glorious leader's favorite Latinisms—*In vino veritas*. . . . Because the veritable Major McCorquodale is most unpleasant, in my experience."

It occurred to Fred that Audley, if not Major McCorquodale, had already drunk deeply. Which was at once surprising, but also somewhat disquieting, if there was some sort of night operation ahead of them, as the colonel had indicated. And with the whiskey warming his empty stomach his surprise and disquiet concentrated his mind on that.

"There's something on tonight, I gather."

"Yes, uh-huh." Audley buried his face in his glass. "There's a kraut hunt tonight, crowning all our recent inquiries. It'll probably end in nothing, or disaster. But at least the weather's on our side."

"The weather?" Fred recalled Audley's umbrella.

"Yes." Audley craned his neck, peering into their ill-lit surroundings from his full height. "You know, we really ought to start eating soon, or Otto's jolly old porker *will* be spoilt . . . and the Crocodile does seem sufficiently well oiled now. . . . But Caesar Augustus is jawing poor old Amos again!" He gave Fred an accusing look. "What on earth did you say to set him off?"

"If I told you, you'd never believe me!"

"Oh, yes, I would! Where Augustus Colbourne is concerned, nothing is unbelievable." Audley caught his tongue. "You're not a friend of his, by any unhappy chance? But no . . . you are a Brigadier Clinton volunteer, aren't you."

That was too much. "I am *not* a volunteer." Fred felt his patience stretch thin. "I've only met your brigadier once, damn it—and it was you who introduced me. So I have you to thank for being here, when I could be sunning myself on a Greek beach, eh?"

"Me?" Audley blinked at him. "No, honestly. . . . I only told him who you were, that time." The boy's mouth twisted nervously. "And I actually told him mostly about Matthew—I'd never met *you* before. . . . And that uncle of yours, who used to come down to the school and give Matthew fivers at half-term and on Foundation Day. And he seemed to know all about *him* the moment I opened my mouth." The mouth turned downwards. "Maybe I did lay it on a bit thick . . . but I thought you wanted to get away, I mean . . . ?"

"I did. And you obviously did." The voices all around them sounded unnaturally loud, and full of alcohol-induced argument and bonhomie. "But I haven't, have I?"

Audley looked crestfallen. "You must have impressed him. And I did warn you that he liked rich bankers, Fred."

"I'm hardly a banker." Fred felt himself weakening. "And I'm certainly not rich."

"Well, you are compared with me. I've just got debts and

mortgages and things." The boy moved from defensive apology to bitter accusation. "So . . . if you don't like it, you can always volunteer for the Far East. And then you can start a branch of Fattorini Brothers out there. . . . It's not *my* fault, anyway."

There was no point in recrimination, thought Fred. And in any case, young Audley was the nearest thing he had to a friend in this madhouse. "No—no, of course, David. I'm sorry. . . . It's just that I really don't know what the hell is going on here tonight" —he smiled— "like, why is the weather on our side, for a start?"

"Oh . . . that's simple." Audley relaxed. "The rain drives the poor devils under cover—whoever we're descending on. And it also damps down the sound of our elephantine approach, so we can creep up on 'em more easily." He returned the smile as a grin. "Although, with the Yanks in attendance tonight, God only knows what'll happen." The grin became almost ingratiating. "But it should be interesting. And as you and I are both in the front line, we shall have a ringside seat, too."

The silver sound of a tinkling bell somewhere out in the courtyard cut Audley off, also momentarily hushing the hubbub of loud conversation of the other officers in the shadowy room, of whom and of which Fred had only been half-aware. Or less than half-aware, he thought quickly, as the hubbub started up again.

"Otto's pig will be quite ruined by now. So there's no need to hurry." Audley raised his glass. "Would you like a refill? I really am a terribly bad host . . . and I haven't introduced you to anyone either, have I? *Otto!*"

"Hauptmann David!" The tray, with two fresh glasses on it, and then the white glove-and-arm-and-coat, appeared as if by magic, in that order. "One Islay malt, one Black Label . . . and the pig, as you say truly, is ruined, dried up, as a corpse in the desert of North Africa."

"You were never in North Africa, Otto." Audley swapped his empty tumbler for a well-filled one. "But you have been eavesdropping, eh?"

"I already know all there is to be known about the *Herr Major*." Otto presented the tray to Fred. "I do not need to eavesdrop."

Fred looked at Audley. "Since when have I been a major?"

"It was on Part Two orders yesterday, Herr Major," said Otto. "Captain Fattorini FA, RE, to T/Major—my congratulations Herr Major, on your well-deserved advancement."

"'Promotion,' Otto." Audley sniffed. "And now, will you kindly encourage the adjutant to get the CO to get us into dinner. Because, whatever the condition of your pig, I'm bloody starving. And we've got work to do tonight, while you're safe and comfy in bed . . . and tucked up with whoever you're tucked up with. So do be a good fellow, eh? Ring the bloody bell again?" Audley delayed for a moment. Then he raised his glass in Fred's direction. "But like the man says, congratulations, *Herr Major!* And . . . like *I* say . . . make the best of it, okay?" He grinned. "'Give strong drink unto him that is ready to perish'—Book of Proverbs, chapter something, verse something else, okay?"

Fred drank, adjusting to his undeserved promotion. Who was he to argue with the British Army, right or wrong? "Thank you, David." And yet, he had never expected to make field rank, however temporarily. And certainly never like this, so equivocally, which made it not quite good enough, however good the Black Label was, on his empty stomach. "But . . . make the best of what?"

"What?" Audley had been looking around, in the hope of dinner, while he had been thinking. "Oh . . . it's not so bad." Using his full height again, Audley continued to look around for movement. "Not if you're like me. . . . No soldier" —he focused on Fred suddenly— "no soldier, by God! Because when it was real soldiering, I was bloody scared most of the time. . . . And when I wasn't scared, I was bored, bored, b-b-ored . . . *bored.*" The focused look became fixed. "But this is different. We're VIPs now—we can do what we bloody like now!" He nodded. "If we tangle with anyone, we pull 'Colonel Colbourne' on 'em. And he pulls 'Brigadier Clinton'—and that rocks 'em back on their heels, I can tell you."

The silver bell tinkled again.

"Yes?" inquired Fred.

"Second bell!" Audley downed the remains of his drink. "First bell, wait for the CO. Second bell, every officer for himself. Mess rules."

"Wait a moment." He would never get a better chance than now, Fred decided, with the young dragoon like this. Because, although Colbourne had instructed him to get an answer to his One Question from Audley, "no shop in the mess" would undoubtedly inhibit him at dinner. And after that he might well be incoherent.

It was about time to cash in on his opportunity, Fred thought, lifting his glass almost to his mouth, and then lowering it. "VIPs . . . doing what, David?"

Audley stared at him for a moment. "Chris, Fred—or is it 'Freddie'?"

Fred didn't want him sidetracked. "Take your pick, David." He lifted the glass again. "Go on?"

"Well" —Audley willed him to drink— "it's . . . it's rather like peeling an onion if you ask me." He thought for another moment. "Fred."

"An onion?" Fred decided that he didn't wholly dislike David Audley. But in the circumstances, he could only reward this with a sip. "Peeling an onion?"

"Yes." Audley glanced into the open doorway, beyond which the rain still glinted in the lamplight as it fell. "Shall we go?"

"In a moment." Another sip. "An onion?"

"Yes." Audley hated him for an instant, fiercely but impotently, trapped by Good Manners and youth. "I mean . . . officially I'm supposed to be researching German tank development." His mouth twisted. "Which is bloody stupid, really . . ."

"Yes?" Knowing that he still had a lot of Black Label, Fred took another sip. "Why?"

"Why?" Another twist downwards, on both sides. "I hate . . . tanks. If I never saw another tank—tank *or* 'Panzerkampf-wagen'—if I never saw another of the bloody great things . . . and the Germans were into *bloody* great things, so far as my researches go, my *ersatz* researches. . . . Because they don't give a damn about that actually." Twist. "Colbourne doesn't, Clinton doesn't. . . . If I never saw another fucking *Panzerkampfwagen* or *Panzerbefehlswagen* or prototype *Pazerjager Tiger Elefant* or what-ever . . . I saw enough German tanks in Normandy to last me a lifetime . . . although there were few enough of them, thank God! Few enough of them . . . and lots and lots of *us*—*us* being bloody cannon-fodder"—twist—"if I never see another one, that'll be too bloody soon!"

"Officially." Fred cut through the whiskey blur quickly. "What d'you really do then?"

"Ah . . . well—" Audley stopped suddenly. "You really don't know?" He frowned. "Didn't Amos tell you? And you were in with Caesar Augustus long enough, for God's sake—didn't he tell you?"

"No." Audley wasn't as drunk as he had seemed, Fred decided. "Nobody has told me anything."

"Then perhaps I'd better not. If my elders and betters—"

"But Colonel Colbourne told me to ask you." Fred barely avoided snapping. "And he also told me 'no shop in the mess.' So if you want your share of Otto's pig before it's cold, David . . ." He lifted his glass tantalizingly. "I can wait."

"It isn't really a pig. It's a wild boar." Audley's voice was no longer slurred, and he was staring at Fred. "He hunts them in the forest with an illegal high-powered hunting rifle. The Germans aren't allowed guns of course, not now. But rules don't apply to Otto, because Colonel Augusts Colbourne likes wild boar for his dinner."

Fred stared back at him without replying, aware both that he was every bit as famished as the young dragoon and that the young dragoon was neither as drunk as he had seemed nor as young, in experience if not years.

"Okay." Audley completed his scrutiny. "Officially we're related to the T-forces—the old SHAEF Target Subdivision. You've heard of them, maybe."

Fred hadn't. "Maybe. But you tell me, David. Just in case I haven't." He smiled. "Now that I'm here."

"Yes." If not drink, then hunger and the prospect of a long night ahead of him had wearied Audley. "German military and technological material and research. All the stuff they were throwing at us latterly—V-ones and V-twos and jet planes—and rocket planes—all the new weapons. But also, and rather more importantly, the stuff they hadn't quite perfected—what's called the next generation." He cocked his head slightly. "'The next generation'?"

Fred waited until it became obvious that Audley expected some sort of reaction. "'The next generation'?" He decided to frown.

"Yes." Audley accepted the frown. "It's a pretty term, isn't it! Here we are, all buddy-buddy and United Nations . . . and a Labor government back home, to welcome us back to a Land Fit for Heroes. But here we are—'we are' meaning *us*, in this instance . . . but the Yanks and the Russians too, just the same . . . here we are, scrabbling for German tidbits with which we can equip the next generation—the call-up class of 1955 conscripts. Or maybe '56—the Crocodile's money is on '56, mathematically. Mine's a bit later, in our mess sweepstakes. The Alligator is betting on 1950. And Amos refuses to bet—he only bets on cards and horses, he says. Because he likes to enjoy his winnings, he says—and he says he won't enjoy ours." He smiled. "But . . . anyway . . . we're not actually responsible to Clinton, and God only knows who he's reporting to. Probably God Himself, is my guess. But I don't know."

It was curious, thought Fred. Because Audley had just said a lot. And yet somehow he hadn't said anything at all.

"Yes." The ghost of Audley's smile lingered. "So officially—*officially*—we're all into our minor specializations: tanks for me, chemical warfare for the Crocodile, radar for the Alligator, communications and cyphers for Amos . . . and so on . . . So you'll probably get nonmetallic mines or something—or whatever the Royal Engineers are into. But all pretty small beer, really. And the Yanks and the Russians don't worry about us too much, because they reckon we're a bunch of drunken amateurs and loonies, trying to avoid boring regimental duty—or Far

Eastern postings, fighting mosquitoes and uncomfortably heroic Japanese, and suchlike. . . . Loonies led by the Chief Lunatic himself, Colonel Augustus Colbourne. Because he's our best cover, by God!"

They were precisely back to the moment when Amos de Souza had first detached him from Audley, in the company office.

Audley nodded, as though he had caught Fred's thought. "He *is* a loony, you know." Nod. "Bloody clever with it, admittedly. Would have been a King's Counsel long since, if there hadn't been a war, for sure by now. Mr. Augustus Colbourne, KC . . . *Sir* Augustus Colbourne—*Mr. Justice* Colbourne—*Lord* Colbourne. Amos says he was absolutely brilliant in court, even as a fledgling barrister. . . . But quite mad, nevertheless."

Fred could only remember the stark naked Colonel Colbourne, variously sunburned and white, and hairy, but utterly unconcerned. But then another memory surfaced. "Where did he get his DSO?"

Audley gave him a sly look. "Oh . . . that was a good one, apparently. Eighth Army, Desert Rats, '42—rallying the ranks at Alam Halfa, or somewhere. Amos says that if he'd been killed doing it, then it might have been a VC—he was only a captain at the time too." The tousled head shook. "Oh, he's brave. But for our purposes, he's mad. Probably got too much sun in the desert, and it fried his brains." The boy shrugged, and then gestured suddenly into the gloom around them. "You know where we are? Eh?"

That certainly was quite mad. "A . . . Roman fort, Amos said."

"A Roman fort, right!" Audley nodded. "The kaiser rebuilt a fort just like this, on the old Roman frontier line—not far from here at the Saalburg, back at the turn of the century, near Bad Homburg. So this German industrialist—one of Krupp's subsidiary suppliers—*he* rebuilt another fort, on another original Roman site also on the *limes*, as they call it. And then he dedicated it to the Emperor Hadrian and Kaiser Wilhelm, right here. So we're in the headquarters building of that fort right now—the 'principia'—which is cold and dark and drafty and generally unpleasant . . . instead of some agreeable American-requisitioned premises, which Colonel Colbourne would certainly get, for the asking. Because he's a great favorite with the Yanks, actually."

Fred recalled his reception. "Because of his . . . pigs?"

"Otto's pigs. And other things." Nod. "And because he insists that we all behave with unfailing politeness to our allies." Smile.

"Also, he has a rich American wife, wooed on the *Queen Mary* before the war."

"He doesn't sound . . . too mad, David."

"No? Well . . . if I tell you that he believes he's the reincarnation of Caesar Augustus—Julius Caesar's nephew, who more or less invented the Roman Empire? The first Roman emperor?" The smile became fixed. "Actually, he's not really interested in Germany, A.D. 1945. It's Roman *Germania*, A.D. 9, that he's concerned with."

He couldn't be serious. "You're not serious? Are you?"

"No." Audley scratched his head. "Just . . . half serious."

"Half serious?" Suddenly Fred remembered Colbourne's irrational enthusiasm for air photography's revelation of the ancient past. "How?"

"How?" Audley looked at him questioningly, and then at the doorway, and then came back to him. "We really ought to be joining the others now, don't you think?"

Fred identified a mixture of hunger and despair in the young man's expression and knew that he shared the first, but not the second. "Of course. But just one thing, David."

"One thing?" A glint of hope now. "What d'you want to know?"

In victory . . . caution. "You said Colonel Colbourne was . . . 'Our best cover,' was it?" He paused for a fraction of a second before popping the vital question again, but now confident that he would get the vital answer.

"Oh, Christ, yes!" Audley forestalled him. "Everybody knows that Gus Colbourne's only interested in one thing! The Yanks know it—the bloody Russkies know it too, I shouldn't wonder. . . . *Every* bugger knows it, for sure! All he's interested in is finding the long-lost site of the battle of the Teutoburg Forest, where the Germans wiped out three Roman legions in the year A.D. 9—where General Varus came unstuck."

"What?" The young man's bitter vehemence caught Fred unprepared in his moment of victory. "Varus?"

"Varus. Publius Quintilius Varus—'*Varus, Fluch auf dich! Redde Legiones!* as Otto says . . . although Varus did have the grace to fall on his sword when all was lost, unlike von Paulus at Stalingrad, Otto also says."

Otto says, like *Amos says*? With his mixture of German and Latin—*Damn you, Varus! Give me back my legions!*—what did it mean? "Now you've lost me, David—Varus?" But then a spark of light, if not light itself, illuminated the incoherence momentarily. "Wasn't he the Roman general who—?" The light flickered. "*That* Varus?"

"*That* Varus, uh-huh." Audley nodded encouragingly. "You know your Roman history, then?"

The light guttered. Any moment now it would go out, leaving him in a blind darkness inkier than before. "No." Everything Audley was saying was insane—*He believes he's a reincarnation of Augustus Caesar. . . . Everybody knows that Gus Colbourne's only interested in one thing. . . . Give me back my legions, Varus!* And yet, on second thought, it wasn't. Because Audley had tried to warn him, and Amos de Souza had echoed the warning in his own way. . . . And finally, Colonel Colbourne himself had rolled their warnings up in his own confided statement, which somehow seemed to confirm everything: *All my officers are mad, quite mad.* "No. But . . ."

"But?" Audley seemed to have forgotten his hunger, together with his stutter and his simulated drunkenness. "Have you read *I, Claudius?*"

"Who?" The sharpness of the young man's sidelong scrutiny sharpened Fred's own wits, so that he instantly regretted the question.

"It's a book—by a chap named Graves. A poet, actually. But it isn't a poetry book. You've heard of *him*?" Audley was suddenly embarrassed.

"Of course I've heard of him. *Robert* Graves." Fred shared the boy's embarrassment. "And I knew about Varus."

"Yes. So it's all in there—in his book, I mean. About the Romans—about Varus getting the chop, eh?" Audley relaxed again. "Sorry! But I keep imagining that you're one of Caesar Augustus's men—another Roman history expert in disguise, leading me on—one of his fellow loonies, recruited by him, like the Alligator. But you're a Clinton recruit, of course—out of our little Greek encounter." The grin became lopsided. "Silly of me. But put it down to hunger. So let's go and eat, then." He pointed the way.

The Alligator, thought Fred. And *The Crocodile*. And Colonel Caesar *Augustus* Colbourne. And now *Publius Quintilius Varus*. It was all too much—just too damn much! "You still haven't told me what we're really doing, David."

"Haven't I? Nor I have! Mmmm . . . that's right—you were just asking me about Gus Colbourne." Audley looked past him and stopped.

"Herr Hauptmann David, I can the meal delay no further." Otto bowed slightly to Fred. "Herr Major."

"No, Otto, not 'I can the meal delay.' It has to be 'I can *delay* the meal,' in that order."

Otto shook his head. "I *cannot* the meal delay, I'm telling you.

The colonel is come now, with Major Amos, at last." He fixed his good eye on Fred apologetically. "They have the United States Air Force hired. And I another pig must provide, in return."

"Okay, Otto. Tell them that Major Fattorini is just finishing his drink, okay?" Audley waited until the German had bowed and scraped out into the darkness before turning back to Fred. "Poor old Otto! Out into the forest again, with his trusty rifle. And he says it isn't so easy now, with other people hunting meat on the quiet. Not to mention dangerous, with all sorts of rough DPs still on the loose out there, he says. . . . But there! Where was I? Colbourne, yes—'Gus' to the Yanks . . . 'der Kaiser' to Otto . . . and 'sir' to us. And 'Caesar Augustus' to himself. . . . Yes, well, what he's up to is no problem. He's hell-bent on finding the actual site of the *Hermannsschlacht*—or the *Varusschlacht*, if you prefer." He grinned at Fred. "The site of the battle in the Teutoburg Forest where Hermann's Germans wiped out Varus' Romans." Audley slipped his hand inside his battle-dress blouse. "What *we're* after is somewhat different." He handed a leather wallet to Fred. "Go on, open it."

It wasn't actually a wallet, it was just wallet-sized: two pieces of scuffed and dog-eared stiffened cardboard, rexine-covered, held together by two snap-open metal rings.

"Our bible," said Audley. "You'll get one of your own. I'm surprised Amos hasn't given you one already. But then, of course it *is* supposed to be Top Secret—not for strangers or other ranks, or any lesser breeds, without the law, huh!"

Something in Audley's voice diverted Fred for an instant.

The young man's mouth had twisted again into its familiar shape, which suggested a mixture of youthful doubt and uncertainty unnaturally aged with wartime cynicism. "I was only thinking that Otto probably has his own private picture gallery. . . . Go on, open it, man!"

It *was* a picture gallery.

For an instant out of time and place and circumstances—out of wet summer and wet Germany and all present insanity—Fred was reminded of all the group photographs he had seen over the years of his life, on the walls of school and college and home. Fading sepia pictures, sharper modern pictures . . . pictures in which his predecessors, or even his ancestors, or even he himself had figured—stiff and unreal, in well-pressed or crumpled civilian suiting; or stiff and unreal, in unmuddied sports gear before the match, with clean rugger ball, or wicket-keeping pads, or with hockey stick, and striped jerseys or immaculate whites; or in the smartest-of-all passing-out battle dress of OCTU, which would not be cherished and remembered by all those in it because not all those in it—*that one grinning foolishly, and that one grimacing, and that one blurred*—not all those were alive now, to grin or grimace, but were rotting in their graves, or off the beaches, or wherever new subalterns rotted, marked or unmarked.

But this was a gallery of *Germans.*

"I always think Otto is the spit and image of Number Seven," said Audley.

Some of them were in uniform, and some of them were in civilian clothes: smart, unsmart, handsome, ugly. . . . But each one was numbered.

"But he can't be, of course."

The numbers had been painted on crudely, across each chest, in white. And since both the "7" and the "17" were unadorned by the Continental mark, those numbers were of British origin, not German.

"If you look closely, you'll see that Number Seven has only got one arm," murmured Audley as Fred lifted the photograph closer to his eye in the uncertain light. "And although Otto's pretty damn clever, he's not quite up to that—growing another arm. . . . And also, if your turn on to the enlargements, the shape of the jaw is different, too."

Fred delayed for a moment as he ran his eye along the double row of mixed German military-civilian personnel, in search of a common denominator. No. 7's right sleeve was indeed empty and pinned under his number across his chest; and for a fact, most of his uniformed comrades were more or less battered—legless or armless, or hideously scarred . . . or merely old.

"Come on." Audley held out his hand. "Amos'll give you your own pictures in due course, Fred."

Fred turned the group picture over, ignoring him. "Just a moment, David."

No. 7, enlarged, certainly wasn't Otto, he could see that. But somebody had done an amazingly good job of enlarging the group faces, he could see that too. It was as John Bradford had said: war had improved photography, as well as methods of navigation and surgery, and mass murder.

"Besides which, Number Seven is dead." Audley sighed. "Quite authentically dead. Which I know, because he was one of mine to research. And I don't make mistakes." The familiar twist met Fred's scrutiny. "We were rather unlucky there, as it happens."

"Unlucky?"

Audley shook his head. "Don't make me go into details before dinner. It might put me off my food. Come on, for Christ's sake, Fred!" He held out his hand for the mock wallet.

Fred folded the wallet up. Obviously there were enlargements of every one of the group, by the thickness of it. But he still kept hold of the collection. "What are they? War criminals?"

"War criminals?" Audley's eyebrows lifted. "Good God, no! Perish the thought! We're not . . . we're not *policemen*, for God's sake!"

"Then what are they? *Who* are they?"

"Well . . ." Audley shrugged. "Really quite decent chaps, so far as I can make out. On the whole, I mean. That is, allowing for the fact that several of 'em were Nazi Party members. And all of 'em are Germans, of course. Or *were* Germans—" He stopped suddenly, cocking an eye at Fred. "You're not one of those chaps who think the only good German is a dead one, are you?"

Fred felt his temper slipping. "What the devil d'you mean?"

"What I say." Audley took the wallet out of his hand. "Because they are—or *were*, in the majority of cases now, unfortunately—a group of officers and gentlemen, and scholars and gentlemen, working out of the Rheinische Landesmuseum at Trier—sort of official, and also semiofficial, like the old *Gesellschaft für nützliche Forschung*." He grinned. "They were . . . a sort of follow-up party to the RAF you might say."

The Society for Useful Research (allowing for Audley's barbarous German pronunciation)? "The . . . RAF?"

"That's right. Christ, you've seen what we've done to Germany, haven't you? That pile of broken bricks on the way from the airfield was the city of Frankfurt—*Frankfurt!* And it's the same everywhere else—or worse. Cologne's worse . . . or 'Colonia Claudia Arts Agrippinensis,' as our beloved commanding officer insists on calling it." Audley drew a deep breath, which became a sigh. "A lot of fine old cities. German cities, I agree, but some of 'em go back a thousand years—or even back to the Romans. But all flattened now." He stared at Fred. "But also cleared and opened up, too. Okay?"

It wasn't *okay*. But Fred was unable to describe what it was.

"Great chance for the archaeologists, after the war, someone thought." Audley nodded. "After Germany had won the war"—slight shrug—"they thought . . . a lot of rebuilding. But they mustn't miss the oportunity to excavate first. So someone had to mark the sites for urgent excavation. They even invented a long German technical term for what they wanted to do . . . which I can't remember now, because I don't actually speak the lingo—'urgent-rescue-excavation,' it translates, more or less. But Amos will tell you, if you ask him, anyway." Nod. "Great scholars, the Germans—*classical* scholars." Audley touched his battle-dress blouse, where he had replaced the wallet. "Several of 'em in our picture. Stoerkel, Zeitzler, Peter von Mellenthin—the late Peter being Number Seven." Audley shook his head slowly. "Enno von Mitzlaff—scholar and soldier . . . Langer, Hagemann . . . and of course, old Professor Schmidt himself—ex–Cambridge and Bristol universities, friend of Mortimer Wheeler." Audley paused. "Dead or 'missing, presumed dead' or still missing . . . but mostly dead, they are."

But not in battle, thought Fred. Because the military wrecks and the elderly citizens in the photograph were plainly not cannon fodder. "How dead?"

"Franz Langer was killed in the bombing. And we think Stoerkel was in Dresden when the RAF took it off the map—that's near enough certain, the Crocodile says." No nod this time, just a stare. "And Enno von Mitzlaff was strung up on piano wire by the Nazis after the Hitler bomb of July twentieth, in spite of all his battle honors—he was one of Rommel's bright young men. . . . And Willi Hagemann—Dr. Hagemann being Number Thirteen . . . he was unlucky, too. He was run over by a Russian staff car just as we were about to pick him up, would you believe it?"

"Unlucky?" There was something very wrong about this litany.

"Yes. Apparently he didn't look where he was going." Audley's expression became curiously blank. "But then, *we* do look where we're going. And we do seem to have the most damnable bad luck too. Our 'useful researches' always seem to end up *un*usefully, I must say!"

Fred remembered Osios Konstandinos. "But they're not all dead?"

"No, not *all* dead, my dear chap." Audley perked up suddenly. "The elusive Number Sixteen isn't dead, we think—'Sweet-Sixteen-and-Never-Been-Kissed'! And we're going for Number Twenty-one—'Key of the Door'—this very night . . . in the wee small hours, when he shouldn't be expecting us. And number twenty-one is rather important, in the scheme of things, I suspect."

"Why?" Fred hit the question button quickly, and therefore naturally; although as he did so, he knew that it was another attempt on The Crucial Question, from what Audley had just let slip. "*Why?*"

"Because he knows Number Sixteen." Audley looked down. "You've finished your drink . . . so now we'll go, right?"

Fred looked down. "Yes—yes, of course."

The rain still slanted down in the courtyard, and the wet smell of earth and darkness mingled with the enveloping sounds of rainwater dripping off roofs and cascading over blocked guttering all around them.

Fred shivered, although it wasn't really cold—although it wasn't really cold through the thickness of battle dress, even remembering how it would be now under the stars on the beach in Greece, this night. Because the cold was inside him now.

"This way." Audley pointed. "And let me do the apologizing."

"Of course." He shivered again, involuntarily. "What's so important about Number Sixteen, David?"

"I rather think that he's the only one we're really interested in." Audley pointed again, towards a bright doorway. "'Sweet Sixteen'—lets hope he lives to be kissed!"

Fred slowed deliberately. "Why do we want him?"

"God only knows!" For the first time Audley touched him, trying to propel him into the light. "Nobody tells me anything—I just do as I'm told."

"But you must have some idea."

"Oh, yes!" Audley grinned at him conspiratorially. "A lot of people hunting Germans these days—it's open season on Nazis, of course."

Fred frowned. "But you said . . . these were decent chaps, David?"

"That's right." The grin widened. "That's what makes it interesting: we seem to be trying to *save* these particular Germans for posterity. The only trouble is . . . they don't seem to want to be saved."

paratroopers used it on D day, in Normandy—it's a clever wheeze, Fred." And then it hadn't been so childish.

He pressed the toy: *click-click-click-click!*

Nothing. Only the sound of the rain.

"Herr Major . . . Haut Brion, '34, please?"

"A good year." *(Audley's mouth was full of deer ham.)* "Eh?"

"The best since '29, Captain David." *(Otto bobbed agreement.)*

"Besides which, it's the best wine we have with us. But if you want to enjoy it, then steer clear of the horseradish." *(The voice was friendly, slightly slurred).* "Alex McCorquodale—Frederick Fattorini, is it?"

"Yes." (The *Crocodile, at last! But he had guessed that from the teeth already.)* "Thanks for the advice . . . Alec."

"It's 'Freddie' actually, Alec." *(Amos de Souza, from down the table.)*

"No, it isn't." *(Audley was still wolfing his deer ham.)*

"Freddie? You wouldn't be Luke Fattorini's boy, by any chance?"

"He's my uncle." Everyone seemed to know Uncle Luke.

"Oh, aye?" *(The Crocodile pointed his big nose like a weapon, sighting Fred down it.)* "Now, it was his elder brother married Angus Armstrong's daughter, eh?"

"Yes." *(His own mouth was full.)* "My . . . father"—*(Chew!)*— "and my mother."

"F-f-fff . . ." *(The sound came from Audley.)* "It's 'Fred,' not F-ff . . . 'Freddie.'"

"What?" *(The big nose changed direction.)* "Ah . . . now, I've a bone to pick with you, young David. Rrrelating to my vehicle."

"Oh?" *(Innocence.)* "Ah . . . yes, Alec. I w-was going to tell you about that. But I had to look after F-F-Fred, you see."

"I do not need telling about it. I know all about it. It was given to that driver of yours, Hewitt—'driver,' huh! And it was given, against my express orders, by that insolent dog of yours, Devenish. What have you to say to that?"

(Pause.) "Sergeant Devenish, you mean, Alec?"

"What?" *(Pause.)* "Man, I do not care if he is a field marshal and has a Civil List pension. I've had enough of his insolence. And now he has ignored my express order. So he must go."

(Pause.) "No."

"No?" *(Incredulity.)* "What the blazes—"

"Alec!" *(Amos de Souza's voice, from down the table.)*

"Amos? Did you hear me?"

"I heard what sounded suspiciously like shop, Alex, is what I heard."

"F-what?" *(Splutter.)* "I was talking about that damned arrogant fellow of Audley's—Devenish, damn it."

"Not 'Audley,' Alec, if you please. Christian names in the mess." *(De Souza's voice was deceptively casual.)* "Really, I shouldn't have to remind *you* of that . . . should I?" *(Pause.)* "And if you wish to discuss a noncommissioned officer, or anyone else . . . this really isn't the time or the place, don't you know . . . eh? And also David isn't the officer with whom you should discuss . . . whoever you want to discuss." *(Pause.)* "I am that officer, as it happens. And I am looking at this moment to enjoy my dinner." *(Pause.)* "Ah! Now here, at last, is Otto! What have you got for us tonight, Otto?"

"Herr Major!" *(Otto had been hovering behind Amos in the candlelight, silver tray in hand, bobbing and weaving like a boxer looking for an opening between the adjutant and the colonel as Amos had delivered his suave reprimand to the Crocodile.)* "It is the steak of the boar, Herr Major: the steak from the—the . . . wildschweinrücken?"

"'Saddle,' Otto." *(The colonel's voice, calm as a cucumber.)*

"Sir!" *(Otto barked out his British "sir" like a British sergeant major.)* "The steak from the saddle of the wild boar, grilled . . . and the red cabbage, with apple and ham, and the spaetzle, yes?"

"He bagged this boar himself, you know—Otto did." *(Audley delivered the information in a loud stage-whisper, in the hubbub of embarrassed conversation that followed the moment of embarrassed silence.)* "In the Teutoburger Wald, up in the north, near our headquarters."

"Yes?" *(He had to think of something to say. The deer ham had been delicious, but the grilled wild boar looked ever better; and now there were vegetables—delicate young peas and mounds of creamed potatoes, yellow with . . . Christ! It was afloat with butter! And apart from hunger, prudence advised silence in this company.)* "Indeed?"

"What was the food in Greece like?" *(The other officer—Philip? Philip the Pedant? Or Philip the Gourmet?)* "It was quite deplorable when I was there in '41. In fact, the one good thing about being comprehensively defeated by the Germans on that occasion was that at least they delivered us from the horrors of Greek cuisine. I only had one halfways decent meal the whole time I was there."

"Yes?" *(Gourmet, for sure: gourmet if that was his chief memory of Greece; and gourmet equally from his reverence with Otto's wildschweinrücken.)* "Everyone's pretty hungry in Greece just now." *(Food was a safe topic, evidently.)* "I was anticipating much the same here, to be honest." *(God! The potatoes were sheer heaven.)*

"Oh, aye." *(Crocodilian chuckle, friendly-sardonic-smug.)* "Well, the natives are on rather short commons, as a matter of fact." *(The Crocodile piled potato on an impaled slice of boar, and then topped the edifice with peas.)* "In fact"—*(more peas)*—"in fact I was talking to one of those AMGOT fellas in Trier the other day— economist fella, fresh out of Whitehall—London University and Whitehall . . . never done an honest day's work in his life, nor heard a shot fired in anger—shitting bricks, he was." *(The Crocodile opened his jaws to full stretch, gold-filled teeth glinting in the candlelight.)*

"What was that, Alec?" *(De Souza again, from down the table; but all hostility forgotten now.)*

"Economist chap, Amos. Colonel's rank . . . but he looked like a tramp in his ill-fitting uniform . . . one of those clever blighters who told us there wouldn't be any food problems, back in March." *(The Crocodile munched happily, glancing round the table as he did so, sure of his audience.)* " 'Gairrman industrial base destroyed by Allied bombing . . . agricultural setup intact. No problem.' " *(Munch, munch, munch.)* " 'Don't want any more tanks, jet planes, U-boats—just a bit of coal. . . . Take over Nazi food distribution system—minus the Nazis of course. Put them all in jail.' " *The Crocodile's knife and fork were busy again, assembling another mountain.)* "All bloody nonsense, of course."

"How so?" *(Fred spoke before he could stop himself.)*

"Huh! Wish fulfillment—the old, old story!" *(In goes the mountain.)* "Industrial base *not* destroyed. . . . If we want the best tanks, the most advanced aircraft, then they could soon start making them for us. . . . Only problem is the transport system, which *has* been blown to smithereens. But that can be restored effectively enough, and quite quickly, given a few competent engineer units, and pioneer battalions—*you* should know that, of all men, Freddie—having done that halfway across Europe, in the wake of extremely efficient demolition by your Gairrman opposite numbers, eh?"

"Yes." *(Very true. But there was heresy here, somewhere.)* "But the bombing—I thought their factories were destroyed?"

"Propaganda. We knocked down their cities—flattened 'em. And latterly the transport system. But the industrial base is still there, most of it. Minus spare parts and fuel, of course . . . but that's mostly a transport problem." *(The Crocodile actually put down his knife for a moment, in order to wag a finger at Fred.)* "But their agriculture's gone to hell, so the farmers are hoarding what they've got . . . which isn't much. And their distribution system was never very efficient. And we've clapped most of the petty civil servants who knew what little there was to know in jail, anyway."

"Nazis, Alec." *(Mouth full of wild boar now, Audley swallowed urgently.)* "Only Nazis, Alec."

"'Nazis, Alec—only Nazis, Alec'? Oh, aye!" *(The Crocodile mimicked Audley exactly.)* "'Wicked bluidy Gairrmans' is it?"

"You should know, Alec." *(Audley wasn't scared of his elders and betters, evidently. And unwisely.)* "You were in Belsen ahead of most of us."

"So I was. But that doesna make me a fool, by God!" *(Pause. And then the finger wagged again, this time at Audley.)* "You know where I was, in the winter of '39?"

(Pause.) "You were in on the poison gas trials in the Sahara, Alec. You've told us." *(The boy's voice fell just short of disrespect.)*

"So I was. And on the anthrax trials, on that wee island—that wee island where no man nor beast will step in our lifetime, and live to tell the tale. So what would that make me, if the Gairrmans had won, eh?"

(Pause.) "A war criminal, Alec. You told us."

"A war criminal. And they would have stretched my neck for it. And me just a slip of a lad, obeying orders." *(Contempt.)* "Nazis!"

"Nazis, yes." *(Amos de Souza, smooth as ever from down the table.)* "Get to your point, Alec."

"My point? Why, I'm there, man: none of ye understand what the Nazis were all about . . . and how the Gairrmans didna understand the man Hitler, until he had them in the palm of his hand—how the Right saw the man as something temporary, which they could cut down to size. And the Left—the Socialists and the Communists both—they didna understand him either: *they* thought he was part of the Right. Whereas in fact he was *sui generis.*"

(Longer pause, while "sui generis" echoed in the dark, above the candlelight in the wet smell, faint-alcoholic-tobacco-soap-and-underarm-sweat-and-khaki smell . . . British Army smell, not so different from Greece—Germany-now smell; but what was different now was that this man was in an altogether different officers' mess from anything Fred had experienced before: it was bloody weird.)

"Alec, my dear fellow . . . regardless of your quaint theories about Hitler himself"—*(now it was Colonel Colbourne himself at last, equal to equal, and slightly cautious)*—"to pursue Amos's point . . . Nazis?"

(Pause.) "Aye, sir—Gus. . . . We've been arresting the wrong men, is what I'm saying—it's bluidy nonsense, is what it is." *(Pause.)* "And I don't mean just us, of course. . . . But it's beginning to be our problem, with nobody to talk to, who can

give us answers." *(Pause.)* "Och . . . I mean, they've been taking in the police inspectors and their sergeants . . . and the wee bluidy postman and the stationmaster and the schoolmaster . . . never mind the mayor and the little civil servants. . . . And I'm fed up and sick and *bluidy* tired of getting 'don't know' from what's left, when I ask what you want me to ask."

"So what are you suggesting, then?"

(Pause.) "What I am suggesting, sirrr—*Gus* . . . is that we do like the Russians and the French have already done. We either shoot them out of hand, if we don't like them, or we leave them where they are, to do our work, which needs to be done." *(Pause.)* "And we get back all the middle-rank servants too, from the camps—all young David's Nazis, who had to join Corporal Hitler's democratically elected Party, or lose their jobs. . . . They're the ones who'll do our work for us now, much better than we can do. And then we can always shoot them afterwards, if someone tells us to do so." *(Pause.)* "Because, having won the war, that's our privilege, right? But in the meantime, we have to make this country work, do you see?"

(Pause.) "We see what you mean, Alec, and we have heard it all before, actually." *(Major Macallister's voice was calm and donnish now that his plate was empty.)* "And . . . I do agree that *our* work would be a lot easier if our people—ours and the Americans'—behaved more pragmatically, as the Russians and the French are doing. . . . I would *agree there*. But—"

"But it isn't our job to run this country." *(Amos de Souza's tone poured oil on troubled waters, in default of imposing "mess rules" on his brother officers in a more generalized gray area of argument.)* "Our job . . . is to obey our orders as best we can, with things as they are."

(Pause.) "And there are still people who can help us, you know, Alec." *(Audley sounded eager and very young suddenly, and ingratiating with it; but that might be to keep the Crocodile away from Sergeant Devenish and Driver Hewitt!)* "I found a super policeman, just the other day. And he said—"

"Shut up, David!" *(Colonel Colbourne's sharp command belied its own "mess rules" friendliness.)* "That's enough."

"You were saying, Alec"—*(De Souza moved in smoothly behind his commanding officer, to obliterate Audley's gaffe)*—"you met this AMGOT fellow, who was shitting bricks. . . . So what did he have to say, then?"

"Eh?" *(The Crocodile struggled with de Souza's direct question for a moment, unable to avoid it.)* "Listen to the rain, man—do ye no hear it?"

(For another moment they all listened to the sound of the rain

splashing distantly over brimming gutters.) "So it's raining?" *(Amos de Souza smiled.)* "According to Gus's American friend, Major Austin, it's raining all the way from here to London—and Land's End in Cornwall. . . . So what?"

"Aye. And that's the sound of Europe starving this winter, man." *(The Crocodile had forgotten his Nazis, and Sergeant Devenish and Driver Hewitt with them. But suddenly he was looking at Fred now.)* "Was it England ye flew from this day, man?"

"What?" *(The memory of the hair-raising flight was equally best forgotten!)* "No. It was . . ." *(Best forgotten!)*

"Oh, aye! From Greece, it was? *(Pause.)* "Are they starving there?" *(Pause.)* "If it goes on raining, and the harvest fails . . . then the Americans will be feeding us by the autumn, aye, and feeding the Gairrmans too, if they're lucky—the Nazis and all the rest, as well as Number Twenty-one in the picture tonight—"

"Alec!" *(Colbourne didn't say "Shut-up!" to Major McCorquodale, but he came close to doing so.)*

"I was in England not long ago, actually." *(A new voice came from down the table, almost as lazy as de Souza's, from one of the faceless officers outside Fred's direct range of vision.)* "In London . . . it was quite dreadfully . . . threadbare, you know. So I thought about Paris. But apparently, it's just as bad there—the fellow at the embassy I spoke to said that you had to bow and scrape to headwaiters to get any sort of decent meal. . . . And as I wasn't going to do that, I ended up going down to our place in the country, where my wife is . . . where I thought I might at least get a square meal—away from the rationing with no bowing and scraping?"

"Oh, aye?" *(The Crocodile leaned forward to fix an insulting eye on the interrupter.)* "And of course, your family does own half of Wiltshire, doesn't it, Johnnie. Or is it Berkshire? So they wouldn't be starving, then."

"Starving?"

"They say"—*(Amos overbore the beginnings of Johnnie's outrage diplomatically, like the good adjutant he was)*—"they do say that the hunting in the shires will be exceptionally good this autumn. Is that true, Johnnie?"

"Is that a fact?" *(The Crocodile got in first.)* "And how do they eat the foxes down in Wiltshire? Do they roast them over a slow fire? I'd have thought fox meat would be a wee bit tough, and stringy. . . . Maybe you should ask Otto how he cooks foxes, man. That is, unless Oscar Wilde knew what he was talking about—'the unspeakable in pursuit of the uneatable,' didn't he say?"

(Christ! The colonel must do something now! Because that was as

naked an insult as might be imagined in this company—not even Amos de Souza's diplomacy could gloss over the Crocodile's deliberate scorn!)

"Eh?" *(Down among the candles and the silver and the glasses "Johnnie" wasn't quite sure he'd heard what the Crocodile had said.)* "Who?"

"My ancestors ate rats," said de Souza. "The rats ate the ship's biscuits—and then they ate the rats. But that was in Nelson's time, in the navy. But they used to say that a biscuit-fed rat was as good as a rabbit. So maybe rabbit-fed fox isn't so bad, perhaps?"

"That's a most interesting proposition, you know." *(The mention of food enlivened Philip Macallister's otherwise dry, academic delivery.)* "Dog, which I ate in Shanghai . . . *dog* is perfectly edible—even potentially delicious. And rat certainly has a long and honorable history of consumption in the extremities of siege warfare." *(Now the voice was gourmet-academic.)* "Human flesh is preferable to both, I'm told. But I've never been reduced to that extremity." *(Horribly the voice was characterized by faint regret, rather than distaste.)* "I believe that sailors ate it often enough in the old days. But as it was usually uncooked, they left no recipes for it."

"Oh, aye?" *(The favorite Crocodilian-Scottish interruption.)* "Well, there'll be Gairrmans able to satisfy your curiosity there, Philip, before this time next year, I shouldna wonder. So dinna give up hope, man."

(Pause—pause elongating into embarrassed and horrified silence as those who had not finished their wild boar suddenly contemplated it with wilder doubt for an instant, and then with distaste.)

"I see." *(Amos coughed politely.)* "What you're saying, Alec . . . is that the Germans will be starving soon, is that all?"

(Fred swallowed his last mouthful of boar, with an effort, feeling it go down insufficiently chewed, to join the deer ham that was churning up in his guts.)

"What I have been saying, Amos"—*(The Crocodile pushed his empty plate away and reached for a toothpick with which to dislodge a morsel of meat from between his teeth)*—"is that the wee foolish men who are supposed to be making policy for us do not know what they are doing. They are starving the Gairrmans by accident, not by design. While the Russians, they have no such problems because they have no romantic notions about their role as conquerors. So with them, the Gairrmans know exactly where they are. . . . Whereas with us—why, man, they know us for the fools we are! So the clever ones among them . . . they are neither scairt of us, nor do they trust us." *(The Crocodile reached for his glass and held it up to the candles' light for an instant, and then drained it in one swallow, knowing that he had the whole table hanging on his next pronouncement.)* "Waiter!" *(He awaited while the one-eyed Otto refilled his glass and then raised it mockingly to the colonel.)* "Which may well be why this unit is having such little success. I'm thinking—eh, Colonel, sirrr? Or may we hope for better luck tonight?"

Click-click-click!
For Christ's sake! thought Fred in a panic. He should have been clicking and he'd clean forgotten!
Click-click-click!
"Fred?"
Utter darkness, all around him. Dripping, utter darkness.
And . . . "This is how it must have been," Audley had said. But what had he meant?
"David?"
A sodden, muted-crunching sound. "Thank God, for that! I thought I'd never find you. I've been straining my ears, but I couldn't bloody well hear a sound. . . . You have been clicking, haven't you?"
"Yes, of course." He still couldn't really see Audley. But somehow the voice created the person.
"It's the rain." Amos de Souza's voice came out of an adjacent area of darkness. "Don't let it confuse your senses."
"It doesn't seem to confuse *you*, I must say," Audley half-grumbled. "But I suppose we should be comforted by that. Or is it just adjutant's quiet, misplaced confidence?"
"Probably. Hullo there, Freddie. Sorry you've been left alone like this. Hope you're not too wet."
"I'm fine. David gave me his umbrella." He could just make out the loom of them now. And de Souza's quiet confidence was somehow comforting. "Is there anything I can do?"
"Yes, there is, actually. David explained what's happening, did he?"
"Ah . . . no, I didn't actually—"
"Why the devil not?" De Souza's tone sharpened.
"Hold on, Amos! I didn't get the chance before dinner—or after. And then we had the devil of a job getting to the start line here, I tell you. So there just wasn't time. Apart from which we should have left him behind, in any case—" Audley caught his complaint. "I don't mean that insultingly, Fred. But we had Caesar Augustus's briefing before you arrived. And I thought you'd rather have a decent night's kip than tag along behind this shambles—"

"Do shut up, David, there's a good fellow." Mild reproof overlaid de Souza's earlier sharpness. "It isn't a shambles."

"Thank God for that! We can't afford another—"

"Shut up . . . Captain Audley." De Souza paused just long enough to make sure that discipline had been reestablished. "Let me assure you that it isn't a shambles, Major. In fact, thanks to the efficiency of our loyal American allies, it seems to be going strictly according to plan at this moment."

A shaded flashlight illuminated the ground between them suddenly in a pale yellow circle. "Don't worry, Major—we're a mile from the objective, and several hundred feet of well-forested undulations. But I want to show you the map. And then Captain Audley can fill you in with the details. . . . Just hold your umbrella up, over us—okay?"

Fred glimpsed a cellophane-covered map, and below it a soiled canvas bag at de Souza's feet on the edge of the yellow circle, as he raised Audley's umbrella over them both.

"We're here." The flashlight seemed to be attached to de Souza's waterproof jacket somehow, leaving him a free hand. "That red circle marked 'A-one.' And next we're moving up to 'A-two'—there."

It was not an issue map. But that didn't matter. What mattered was that he could see the operation at a glance: the objective was an isolated building in thick forest, and there were a number of routes—forest tracks?—converging on it; and each was marked with a series of numbered letters and times that brought different groups to precise points simultaneously on the circumferences of ever-smaller circles, until they reached the center.

"Yes, sir." It all seemed rather elaborate, until he remembered all TRR-2's "bad luck" in the past. And it wasn't for him, as a new recruit, to criticize, anyway. "Nobody's going to get out of there." But then he became aware of the darkness outside their own yellow circle. "Except . . . it is damnably dark."

"Don't worry. Our American friends are bringing up search-lights—'B,' 'D,' and 'F' will illuminate the objective at 0230 hours precisely. Then it'll be brighter than daylight around the whole perimeter. And in case you're wondering how we're going to manage a silent final approach, just don't give it a thought."

"No, yes?" Fred had been worrying about no such thing, but the mention of the American involvement made de Souza's confidence all the more surprising. This was their zone, of course, so presumably they had a right to be involved. But he remembered floundering all-too-noisily in Italian darkness (and Italian mud), hauling equipment across country to several disastrous river-crossing attempts.

"Yes." De Souza chuckled softly. "Dealing with silence will be Major Jake Austin's contribution—you met him this afternoon, off the plane, I believe?" The adjutant bent down to retrieve the canvas bag. "A most efficient officer, Jake. . . . But here, Freddie"—he thrust the bag at Fred—"you hold on to this and follow David here. . . . And David—*you* tell him what's what, eh? Any questions?"

Audley emitted a strangled sound, but then silenced himself.

"You were going to say something, David?" The torch went out, leaving them in blind man's darkness. "Spit it out, man!"

How the hell were they going to find their way to A2? thought Fred despairingly as he hugged the bag. *For Christ's sake, ask that!*

"N-no." Audley trailed off.

"Good. Then I'll see you again at A-two. And do try to be on time for once."

Gradually Fred's night-sight returned, so that he could just make out the large vague shape of Audley as he squeezed the bag's contents. It had an incomprehensibly soft feel to it . . . but it wasn't *entirely* soft. In fact, from its weight it almost certainly contained a weapon of some sort, wrapped in some sort of thick material . . . and also what felt uncommonly like . . . a pair of boots. *A pair of boots?*

There were two slight crack-crunch sounds as de Souza trod on fallen branches in departing. Then the sodden, dripping forest-silence closed in on them—a not-so-quiet silence, to go with the not-quite darkness.

"God, it's miserable, isn't it!" exclaimed Audley. "Although, you know, I don't think it's raining quite so hard, actually. And the American weather chaps said it would be clearing from the west before dawn—that was Jake Austin's final contribution at this afternoon's briefing before he went off to collect you. . . . Do you think it's clearing, Fred?"

Dawn was still a very long way away, thought Fred. "Jake Austin is the pig-fancier, is he?"

"Yes. Good chap, though—jolly efficient, like Amos said. Ex-Mustang pilot . . . but into all sorts of nefarious enterprises now. Shall we go, then?"

He sounded confident! "You know which way to go, then?"

"Oh, yes—sure. . . . You know, it *is* raining less—good show! Actually, I'm blind as a bat at night—it was a great mercy that we couldn't fight tanks in the dark, in the late nastiness. . . . 'Just follow the rear light of the tank in front,' when they wanted to get us somewhere before dawn, out of the laager . . . and I could depend on my driver for that. But at least they didn't expect us to *fight.* Next time round, it'll be done by radar—goggling at screens and pushing little buttons. But with a bit of luck I shalln't be there—I *hope* I'll be too old . . . or doing something safer, somewhere else. . . . Shall we go?"

Next time round? "What's in this bag?"

"The bag? Oh, yes! Battle dress, blouse and trousers, medium size . . . belts, one; gaiters, two; boots Gs, one pair; beret, one. But don't ask me about badges and rank and all that—Amos has a funny sense of humor there, so it could be anything. And he forgot to tell me, anyway."

Christ! "What's it all for, David?"

"Ah . . ." A shielded light showed suddenly. "Sorry about this, but I can't read my wristwatch in the dark. It just doesn't seem to show up, the way it should . . . or maybe I need spectacles, I don't know—*ah!* Okay! We've got a full five minutes in hand, actually. So . . . what's it all for, did you ask? It's quite simple, really: we are about to deceive our loyal American allies, that's all." The light went out.

"How?" *Madness!* "Why?"

"How? Ah . . . well, you remember what we're doing—I did tell you just before dinner. Rather hurriedly, I admit. But I did. Number Twenty-one, and all that, remember?"

"Number Twenty-one? The man in the photograph?"

"That's right: 'Key of the Door,' like in Housey-Housey—a mindless game of quite excruciating boredom, which I shall never forget because we were obliged to play it endlessly while we were in readiness for Normandy. You know it?"

"For Christ's sake, David!" *Steady!* "Number Twenty-one—we're going to pick up Number Twenty-one. Does he have a name?"

"He does. But he won't be using it tonight, and neither will we. For our purposes he's now 'Keys,' Fred. But the name you've got to remember is 'Krausnick,' in any case—'Krausnick,' okay?"

"Is that his real name?"

"Lord, no! Krausnick is an entirely different fellow—a scientific fellow. . . . But he's the one we're *officially* supposed to be picking up tonight, you see. Are you with me?"

It was no good saying no. "Yes. We're pretending to go after a scientist named Krausnick. But we're actually after . . . 'Keys.' And that's the deception?"

"Partly. Because . . . actually, we're not going to get him, of course."

"Keys?"

"No. Krausnick."

"Why not?"

"We don't want him. Or . . . I suppose we *do* want him, actually. But he won't be there anyway. In fact, the truth is, he's probably *nowhere*. Because the last time he was spotted was in Berlin, back in late April, at the very end of things there. So the Russians have probably got him, if he's still alive."

"So why are we after him? Or pretending we are?"

"Ah! Well, he's big-time stuff still, even if he is 'missing, presumed' et cetera. On everyone's 'Most Wanted' list, with his picture in every sheriff's office, Fred, is friend Krausnick."

"A big-time Nazi?"

"Nazi? No . . . or maybe he is—*was*—that, too. But nobody seems to be worrying much about that now—not with scientists, anyway." Audley was shaking his head; Fred couldn't see him doing it, but he was, nevertheless. "Krausnick's a rocket-propulsion expert—one of the Crocodile's alleged specialities. So when we've got the prisoners all lined up, the old Croc will be striding up and down muttering 'Krausnick' loudly, and f-frowning at each of 'em and saying, 'Not that one, not that one,'" and so on. . . . All for the benefit of the Americans, you see?"

It was still no good saying no. At least, not directly. "But this isn't the deception—or only partly?"

"Right." This time it was an invisible nod. "Because they'll be watching us like a hawk. Because they're hell-bent on picking up every rocket expert they can lay their hands on, Fred. Be-cause . . . *because* . . . the word is that the Germans had plans for super rockets which could fizz their way clear across the Atlantic. And you just imagine rockets landing among all those skyscrapers, eh?" Audley allowed him time for a brief catastrophic vision. "In fact . . . if, by any remotest accident, Herr Krausnick *did* turn up in the lineup . . . then they'd probably grab him from us—and apologize afterwards, the old Croc says. But maybe he's doing them an injustice. But . . . *but* . . . the possibility of that happening has wonderfully encouraged their cooperation, at all events. Hence the searchlights. Plus a large number of their military intelligence chaps too, more's the pity! Although, of course, they don't take us too seriously—or not Caesar Augustus, anyway!"

There was method in Colonel Colbourne's madness, decided Fred. But there was also rather too much risk-taking for his taste. "Did we tell them about Krausnick?"

"Lord, no! But we did accidentally let them find out, just to encourage them to help us." Audley's flashlight went on again, illuminating his wristwatch. "We'll have to go soon, Fred."

"Just to deceive them?" Routine Anglo-American military

double-dealing had been par for the house in Italy, Fred remembered. And everyone had tried to fuck up the French, as a matter of routine enmity (although the Frogs had had the last laugh—and his admiration with it). But this was all curiously depressing, nevertheless. "Why?"

The flashlight went out. "We had to tell them *something*—for God's sake, Fred . . . they're not *stupid*. They know we're up to *something*, I mean!"

The depression hardened him. "So what is our deception then, our real deception? Just picking up 'Keys,' instead of Krausnick?"

Audley said nothing for a moment. "Wait and see. We ought to be moving now."

"No." Apart from the hardening, there was the prospect of blundering about in the sodden darkness of the forest. "If I'm going to carry this bloody bag . . . then, apart from what the adjutant said—what he told you to do, David . . . I want to know what's happening, damn it!"

Again, Audley said nothing for a moment. "Oh, . . . very well, then!"

Fred waited for another moment. "Yes?" He lowered the umbrella and found that Audley was substantially right about the weather. Apart from the spattering drips from the thick foliage above, the rain had almost ceased. "And you can have your brolly back now, David."

"I don't need it—you can have it, Fred."

The very last thing Fred wanted to be seen carrying, either by his commanding officer, or by the Americans, was an umbrella. "I don't want it, David, thank you."

"Oh . . . have it your own way!" The umbrella was seized from him with an accuracy that suggested that Audley's night vision wasn't really so bad. "Here—you take this, then."

It was . . . a stick? A walking stick? "Thank you." That wasn't so bad, anyway. "All I want is an answer to my question, David." He felt himself almost pull rank—overinflated majority over overpromoted captaincy—and weakened slightly. "I've had a long day, you know."

"Sure—of course!" Audley accepted the olive branch. "Okay. So . . . we go into this damn place like a dose of salts. . . . It's a house, with some outbuildings. Like stables—or kennels—I don't know. . . . I think it was an old hunting lodge of some sort, in the kaiser's days. When he hunted Otto's boars hereabouts, and suchlike—I don't know. . . . But it's been empty for years, anyway. Because it's in the middle of nowhere, Amos says. Right?"

He had heard briefings like this, from other overpromoted infantry subalterns of tender years, full of the same careless confidence. But now wasn't the time to remember them. "So?"

"So you follow me. With the bag." Audley drew a deep breath, and an overloaded branch above suddenly deluged Fred. "And we'll have Devenish with us by then—he'll be waiting for us at A-two."

Fred's morale lifted slightly, at the thought of Devenish. "And then?"

"Then we wait patiently for H hour. And when that comes, all the pretty searchlights go on, and loud and frightening military noises are made for a moment or two. And then Colonel Augustus addresses his cowering victims—that is, assorted Germans on the run, and hardcase DPs who don't want to go home, and the odd American deserter no doubt. . . . *He*—our Glorious Leader— addresses all of them in his execrable German. Which will only serve to confuse them, undoubtedly. But over the loudspeakers he will address them nevertheless, because he fancies his German. . . . Although I've heard him address one unfortunate group of Teutons for all of quarter of an hour, and none of 'em understood a word he said. . . . But maybe then Amos or the Crocodile will take over—or even the Alligator. And it'll be okay then, because they each *spraken* quite reasonable *Deutsch*."

Audley's own German accent was on a par with his commanding officer's. "But you don't speak it?"

"No. How *did* you guess?" Audley seemed amused. "Just a few necessary phrases, that's all. I'm supposed to be the unit's French speaker—all the rest have more German than me, even Driver Hewitt, I suspect. But then I'm an exception to the TRR-two rule in more ways than one. . . . Shall we go, then?"

Fred stood his ground obstinately. "What happens then?"

"We go in—like I said." Audley was trying to be languid, in the style of his admired Major de Souza. But he couldn't conceal an undercurrent of juvenile excitement that Fred recognized. It was something he could still remember from his own youth: the foolish optimism of young subalterns who knew no better, without which wars would be impossible. But he had lost all that in Italy.

"Like a dose of salts?" Once it was lost, it never came back.

"We go in behind Major de Souza and his warrant officer." Audley caught the mocking edge in the question, and his voice stiffened. "We always operate in pairs, Major Fattorini. I shall be with Jacko Devenish."

That made five, not two. "The four of you, plus me?"

"You are a supernumerary, Major Fattorini. Shall we go?"

"But I'm carrying the bag, Captain Audley." Fred played his ace. "I'll go when you explain that. Not before."

"Oh . . . *okay*, Fred—damn it!" Mercifully, the young man realized when he was being ridiculous. "Amos fingers Number-Twenty-one—'Keys'—for us. And then he and his man cover us while we dress him up as a British soldier. *Savvy?*"

Fred savvied instantly, suddenly aware that he had been halfway there already, with his bag and David's deception of their allies. "We put 'Keys' into this uniform?" He sensed Audley staring at him in the dark. "As one of ours?"

"That . . . that is exactly right." For a moment there was silence between them. "Full marks—join the club, and all that. . . . Like 'God Bless America,' but 'God, don't let's trust the Yanks'—*exactly* right, Fred!"

The sudden bitterness in the young man's voice caught Fred's interest. "You don't like what you're doing, David?"

"Like it? Huh!" Audley paused. "You should hear Sar' Devenish on that subject!"

"He doesn't like it?"

"On the contrary, old boy! *Sergeant* Devenish poached me to rights long ago, when we were in Greece together, when I made the mistake of saying that I didn't much like killing Greeks, when I'd been hired to kill Germans—huh!"

Even more interest. "What did he say?"

"He said: 'Well, Mr. Audley—' I was a humble lieutenant then . . . and I can't do his voice—I've got no ear for mimickry. . . . But anyway, he said: 'Well, Mr. Audley, I don't remember being signed up to do anything but obey orders. And I certainly never expected to do what I liked. Because if I could do what I liked, then I'd be doing my job back in England, and I'd be going home to the wife and the kids every evening. And none of this foolishness.'"

God! A supersaturated branch above gave way, spattering Fred with German rain. *God, this foolishness!*

"So let's go then. We can't afford to waste any more time discussing free will and military n-n-necessity, anyway. So come on, Fred."

After a time Fred began to realize that he'd been *going* and *coming on* almost automatically, in almost total darkness and more by a mixture of sound and instinct. But then, when he lost the sound of Audley's footsteps for an instant, his fear came back.

"David!"

"Come on! We've got to *move* now! We can't be late!"

"David! How d'you know where we're going?"

"Don't worry. Just follow me."

It was no use worrying.

Well . . . at least he could work out the logic of the assault. If there was anyone who could be trusted to do the clever stuff, it would be Amos de Souza—no problem there. . . . And by the same logic, Audley and Devenish were an ideal snatch squad: the young dragon was built like a brick shithouse, and Devenish was a veteran and a hard man, as he himself had reason to remember.

He almost tripped up, on an invisible fallen branch thicker than anything he had encountered before, and saved himself with Audley's stick; and caught the sound of the boy crushing his way ahead, regardless as a tank, and in the surrounding silence, almost as noisy.

Then the noise stopped. "Are you all right, Fred?"

"Yes." Led by the voice, and with all his senses sharpened by the night, he could just see something darker in the darkness of the forest. Or might he just be imagining that he could? "But I can't really see a damn thing."

"I can. So don't worry—just follow me." Audley waited for him to close up again. "We've got to leg it now, too. Because we can't be late for the fun—Amos would never forgive me if I missed the party, you know. Right?"

Fred clenched his teeth, trying to forget the aftermath of those other Italian fun-parties when the dawn had revealed the bodies of the fun-party-goers on the riverbanks, with others bobbing in the shallows among the wrecked pontoons, or caught in the reeds. And the bobbing corpses were usually his men too, because the heavily laden infantry sank to the bottom quickly: they were the ones you trod on, who had drowned quietly in three feet of water, when you went to recover the sodden engineeer bundles later on—*damn! Damn! Damn! Damn!* "Right, David. But I hope you know what you're doing—and where you're going."

But Audley didn't go. Instead his flashlight came on suddenly, blinding him totally.

"Put that damn thing out!" The old night discipline asserted itself.

"It's all right." Audley soothed him quickly. "We're still half a mile from A-two. No one can see us here—and I know exactly where we are, too! *Look.*" Instead of going out, the flashlight beam swept left, and then right, into the forest. *"See?"*

Fred tried to see. "We're in . . . some sort of a ditch?" That was all he could see in the pale yellow light as it moved, directing his eye. There were banks either side, humpy and uneven . . . but banks, nevertheless, with trees on either side, and only the

105

minor debris of fallen branches in the bed of the ditch, ahead of them.

The flashlight went out. "That's right: we're in a ditch. And so long as I don't go up on the bank on either side—which I can feel with my feet . . . and my umbrella . . . because you've got my ashplant now, damn it!—then we're on the right track to A-two . . . *right?*" The tightness of Audley's voice marked the end of his patience. "So now we're going, Fred—'quam celerrime' as my old Latin master used to say—or 'double-quick'—or 'on the double'?"

They went, then. And they went almost, but not quite, 'on the double'—the old sergeant major's double, hallowed on a thousand parade grounds and route marches—but as close to it as the ditch, and the debris in it, and Audley's longer legs, permitted.

(But, dear God Almighty! Damn you, Kyri, for getting me into this mess—damn you! And I could be dining with you in Athens, this very night, but for that, Colonel Michaelides, damn you!)

(Phew! The bloody ditch was almost vertical now!)

And, he could feel the sweat running down his chest.

And, thank God he was nearly at the top now! He could even see, far off on his right, a few distant lights twinkling of what remained of German civilization.

But—a ditch? Since when did ditches climb up almost vertical hillsides in forests?

"David!" The name came out in a hoarse, exhausted wheeze. But then, as he opened his mouth again to repeat it, the sound of an aircraft that had been droning in the back of his consciousness suddenly increased, drowning out his intention and replacing it with the fear that even if he *clicked* now, Audley wouldn't hear him. So instead he felt around with his stick like a blind man, for the guidelines of the improbable ditch on either side of him.

They were still there—there first on one side, and then on the other, as the continuous drone became a steady drumming, and then graduated to a final ear-splitting roar as the plane swept over them finally, far too low for comfort, above the top of this Taunus hill.

Eventually the sound died away. But then, even as it did so, he heard more droning engines. *Click-click-click-click*, he pressed desperately.

Click-click-click came back to him, humiliatingly close, but then *click-click*—two more *clicks*—but farther off and almost drowned by the second approaching aircraft.

Christ! Maybe they weren't so clever at that! thought Fred, clicking again instinctively. *What if there were a couple of mad low-flying Yanks up there, practicing their night flying . . . or maybe helplessly lost and circling the airfield on which he'd landed a few hours back?*

"Hullo there—Fred?" Audley pitched his voice against the crescendo of sound as the second plane swept overhead. "Jolly good!"

"Is it?" There would soon come a point when this young man's version of Amos de Souza's nonchalance irritated him beyond endurance.

"You've still got the bag, I hope?" Audley's cheerful confidence was worse than de Souza's imitation. "That last bit was bloody steep, wasn't it?"

Foul words presented themselves. But already the first aircraft was on its second circuit. "Yes"—he had to shout—"YES!"

"JOLLY GOOD!" Audley waited then, until the first plane had passed over them for the second time. "We're almost there—you heard Sar' Devenish signal?"

"Yes." He couldn't say he hadn't been warned. Audley had warned him that Colonel Colbourne was a lunatic, and Colonel Colbourne had warned him that all his officers were mad. And long ago, Kyri Michaelides had warned him to steer clear of them all. "What sort of ditch is this?"

"What?" As Audley started to speak the drumming of the second aircraft increased. "WHAT?"

This time, impossibly, it was worse. In the black, starless sky the second plane almost touched the treetops just ahead of them, with its red and white lights winking to outline it.

"WHAT . . ."—Audley let the sound disperse before he continued—". . . sort of ditch?"

So he had heard, the first time. "Yes."

"Yes, of course! It's—"

Click-click!

"I didn't have time to tell you." *Click-click-click,* Audley returned. "It's a *Roman* ditch, Fred. Because we're spot-on the old Roman front line, which curves up round Frankfurt—or 'Moguntiacum,' as Caesar Augustus Colbourne is wont to call it—the old Roman *limes,* in Latin. It linked up with their Raetian defenses, on the Danube, with the Antonine Line, on the Main . . . and then north and west through the Upper German lines, to reach the Rhine at 'Confluentes'—which is Coblenz to poor ignorant types like you and me, Fred." Audley's voice had been lifting as he continued, becoming a shout again. *"FRED."*

It was no good replying. With the noise, he could hardly think.

"The Romans dug a ditch, all the way from the Danube to the Rhine"—now as the sound decreased, Audley adjusted to it again—" with lookout posts and forts . . . sort of, like Hadrian's

Wall, but not so good—sort of customs and excise, plus soldiers
. . . Hadrian's Wall?"

"I know what Hadrian's Wall was. Go on, man." The planes
were going away at last, it seemed. But he couldn't be sure. "Go
on?"

But Audley appeared to have been struck dumb by the
mounting silence.

"What's the matter?" After so much noise after so much silence,
Fred cracked it first. And he also heard one of the planes coming
back again. "We're in the Roman ditch, is that it?"

"That's right. Our billet—the fort—is on the same line. Ten or
twelve miles away, as the Roman legionnaire might walk it—
eight or nine, as the crow flies. But twice as much, on the road
tonight. And now we've done about a mile and a half, from A-one,
anyway. . . . With another half mile to do, to the objective.
Which is also on the line."

Click-click! came out of the darkness ahead of them.

"And we should be moving now. Because A-two is damn close
to A-three, I tell you. And the Yanks'll be in position now, I'd
guess."

The circling planes were only a drone, but they were still out
there, higher up, yet not far away. And suddenly Fred knew why.

Click-click-click, Audley answered. "Right, Fred?"

"The planes will be coming back as we close in, I take it? To
drown our approach sound?" Amos de Souza had almost said as
much, he remembered now.

"Spot on, Major! An old trick."

"They'll be awake, of course."

"Oh, sure. And tired and irritable too, because Jake Austin's
been night-flying over them for the last week. So . . . awake, but
not suspicious, supposedly." Audley spoke lightly. "An old trick
. . . an old *British Army* trick . . . first witnessed by Brigadier
Clinton's father in 1918—his father being a lance corporal at the
time, according to Amos. . . . Night-flying noise, to conceal the
real noise of hundreds of British tanks starting up outside Villers-
Bretonneux, near Amiens, on the night of August seventh/eighth,
1918." He sniffed. "Personally . . . it's all bloody stupid, if you
ask me."

For a moment the memory of Brigadier Clinton, in the ruins of
the Osios Konstandinos monastery, almost diverted Fred from
his sudden doubts. But not quite. "You don't like it, David?"

For a moment he could feel Audley staring at him in the
darkness, undecided, but weakening. "Spot on again, Major—if
you must know . . . *yes*. I don't think I like it."

"Why not?"

"Isn't it obvious?" Audley couldn't go back now. "Too bloody complicated by half, if you ask me . . . even apart from our past *debacles* . . . one of which you witnessed, as I recall, Major— back in Greece?"

Fred remembered Osios Konstandinos all too well. "So what do we do, David?"

There was silence for a moment. "We obey orders, like always. But . . . if you'll watch my back tonight, Fred, then I'll try to watch yours, *right*?"

CHAPTER FOUR

Click-click . . . click-click: the sound came out of the darkness ahead of them again, faint but clear against the distant drone of the night-flying aircraft.

"That'll be Devenish at A-two—good for old Jacko!" Audley spoke cheerfully. "With Sergeant Devenish looking after us now, we shalln't come to any harm. . . . Has it occurred to you, Fred, to wonder why we've been for this unpleasant and unnecessary perambulation tonight?"

"It did cross my mind." Perambulation! "But shouldn't we be clicking back, David?"

"In good time. It was bloody Caesar Augustus's idea . . . although the Crocodile probably put him up to it—or maybe the RSM. They all conspire to make me do everything the hard way. If I had a nice German girlfriend, they'd make me sleep with her in a hammock, I suspect."

"Why do they do that?" Not that the question required an answer, thought Fred.

"Oh . . . to keep me 'up to the mark,' Caesar Augustus says. So tonight was my bit of night map-reading, apparently—they knew I'd be bloody lost without Devenish. . . . What they didn't know was that Amos is a decent sort, hah!" Audley chuckled. "He gave me the A-line, which follows the old Roman ditch. And even I couldn't lose that, he reckoned."

It might have been decency. But it might also be that the contents of the bag were too important to be lost, decided Fred.

Click-click!

"The truth is, they just don't like cavalrymen," continued Audley innocently.

"Especially cavalrymen who carry umbrellas?"

"Ah . . . I try not to let them see my brolly, actually. But it is a fine old cavalry tradition, you know—Salamanca and Waterloo. . . . I'm just sorry you've had to suffer with me, is what I mean. They've got nothing against sappers, I'm sure. . . . *Is that you, Jacko?*"

"Sir." The answer was midway between a growl and a grunt, warning them that the sergeant had noted Audley's failure to click his proper recognition signal.

"Don't be so bad-tempered, Jacko." For his part, Audley was quite unabashed by this disapproval. "We're the ones who should be pissed off, having had to blunder about in the rain quite unnecessarily, just because Caesar Augustus—"

"Sir!" Devenish interrupted his officer loudly. "Have you brought Major Fattorini with you?"

"What?" Audley's tone was incredulous. "For Christ's sake, Jacko! Who the hell d'you think I've got? Field Marshal Montgomery? Or Caesar—"

"Sir!" Devenish's voice changed. "Captain Audley is here with Major Fattorini, *sir!*"

"Thank you, Sergeant." Colonel Colbourne spoke out of the farther darkness, beyond Devenish. "I heard."

"Oh, b-b-bugger!" whispered Audley. "Hullo there, sir . . ."

"Captain Audley." The slight weariness in the colonel's voice was more eloquent than anger. "You are two minutes late."

"Sss—" Audley's treacherous tongue tied itself up, and Fred crossed his fingers. "Sir!"

"Yes?" Although that was the correct and complete answer, Colbourne still pursued the boy. So those two lost minutes could hardly be crucial to the success of the operation. And although the boy had only himself to blame, that altered the case somewhat.

"It's pretty dark out there, sir." Fred kept the words level, as a statement rather than an excuse. "The terrain is difficult, too. I had difficulty keeping up with Captain Audley."

Colbourne sniffed. "Thank you, Major. I take it you still have the bag which the adjutant gave you?"

"Yes, sir." He felt himself relax.

"Good." Another sniff. "This operation is meticulously planned. It is not going to go wrong. You will follow Captain Audley and Major de Souza and do exactly what they tell you tonight, Major. Audley will have told you what's happening."

Another sniff came out of the dark, but it came from a different direction and was even more obviously derisive.

"Very well, then—carry on, Captain Audley . . . and no more lost minutes, eh?" Colbourne paused. "Mr. Levin!"

"Sah!" The bark came from the direction of the second sniff.

No one spoke as the colonel withdrew in the direction of the bark, vanishing into the night.

"Phew!" exclaimed Audley. "Thanks, Fred." He breathed out again. "I'll bet it was that bastard Levin who wound him up."

The boy was incorrigible. "The RSM?"

"That's right. *Mister* Levin to the likes of us—Mister Isaac Levin, DCM—ex–Desert Rat, with the emphasis on *rat*. . . . Scourge of subalterns and other ranks . . . but, more to the point, old comrade and chief informer and *éminence grise* to Colonel Augustus Colbourne, DSO—our beloved emperor." Audley produced a sniff of his own. "And 'Busy Izzy' behind his back—don't they call him that, Jacko?"

Devenish cleared his throat. "If you say so, sir."

"Oh, come on, Jacko!" Audley shrugged off his bodyguard's disapproval. "You know they do—come on!"

Another pause. "I . . . have always found Mr. Levin to be a most efficient warrant officer . . . sir."

"Oh, yes? And you have also found yourself disliking him as much as I do—almost as much as we both dislike the Crocodile. . . . The only difference is that Busy Izzy is scared of you, because you know your King's Regs like the back of your hand. So he knows he'll burn his fingers if he tries to lay one of them on you. . . . Whereas he damn well persecutes *me*. In fact, but for Amos he'd have had me tarred and feathered and run out of Schwartzenburg on a rail long ago."

Somehow Fred was beginning to see in the dark, but also in his imagination too, without sight. And so Audley had his mouth open now, but Devenish was tight-lipped, he imagined.

"Major Fattorini's all right. He's one of us, Jacko." Their joint silence sucked Audley on. "Busy Izzy is a circumcised *shit*—and you know it!"

"I'm sure I can't say, sir. . . ." Something goaded Devenish out of his own safe silence, forcing the words out into the open. "They may call Mr. Levin names . . . behind his back . . . for all I know. I expect they do."

A most diplomatic answer, thought Fred. Like any sensible soldier, Devenish was loyal to himself and his own interests first. But more to the point, he was learning something about Audley from this indiscretion. And he needed to know more, if this was the case.

"You don't like Jews then, David?" As he spoke, he remembered that this same problem had also surfaced in Greece, as replacements from the Middle East had percolated through, and there had been officers and other ranks posted from Palestine whose experiences (and consequent anti-Jewish prejudices) had conflicted horribly with all ghastly information coming out of Europe.

"What?" The presumption of Fred's question stripped the copycat-de-Souza casualness from Audley's voice. "What?"

"Time's getting on, sir—" began Sergeant Devenish.

"Shut up, Jacko! What did you say, Major Fattorini? I don't . . . what?"

The boy was angry. So maybe he had jumped to a wrong conclusion. But this wasn't the time to explore the matter further. "I'm sorry, David. Forget it, okay?"

"No!" Audley's outrage cut him off. "Let me just tell you this, Major Fattorini. My best friend in the Wesdragons—he was a 'Jew boy' as they say. . . . And circumcised to prove it—and no church parades for him, lucky blighter—"

"David—"

"—and the bravest of the brave, too—"

"David—"

"—and the brightest: Open Scholar of Magdalen, Oxford, with brains to prove it—I ought to know, by Christ! Because I've seen them—"

"David—"

"Sir—" Devenish tried to get between them.

"—spread all over the top of his fucking turret—brains everywhere, halfway across Normandy! And blood, too—brains over the turret, but blood inside the tank, after he got his head blown off." Audley drew a quick breath. "I tell you, it gives a chap a whole different slant of The Merchant of Venice to find out how much blood a Jew has in him. Because we mopped up and swilled out about half of it." Another breath. "The brains on the turret were easy. . . . But there were about ten million flies—big fat greeny-blue flies . . . and they lived on Ben's blood for a week, until the Germans brewed up his tank—"

"Sir!" Devenish's voice was coolly disciplined. "We've got less than a minute now, before we should move, according to the

113

timetable. And we don't know what the lay of the land is like, between here and A-three."

"What?"

"We shall have to move out in about . . . forty-five seconds, sir." From being disapproving first, then mildly irritated, and finally neutral, Devenish became gently encouraging. "Major de Souza won't like for us to be late at A-three, sir. Because he'll be waiting for us."

"Yes . . . yes, of course." Audley took hold of his voice. "Well . . . any questions, Fred?"

"No, David." The enormity of the lie somehow made it true. But then he realized that he owed it to Audley to make amends more effectively than that. "Or . . . there is one thing that confuses me a bit, actually."

"Yes?" The boy was hauling himself back from his private nightmares now, trying to recapture reality. "You want to know why we always operate in pairs—the Crocodile and Sergeant Wilson? And Caesar Augustus and Busy-Izzy? And . . . the unbeatable Devenish-Audley combination?" The boy was almost back to his old self. "We always come up trumps, don't worry!" Sniff. "But 'two' is logic—and experience, Fred. Ancient British Army logic and experience, actually."

"It is?" Fred had wanted to know no such thing, but he was so enormously relieved to get away from Jews and tanks and voracious flies that he pressed the question willingly. "How's that, then."

"You don't know your Kipling—obviously! Although it's just plain common sense, really—

When from 'ouse to 'ouse you're 'unting,
you must always work in pairs—
It 'alves the gain, but safer you will find—
For a single man gets bottled on them twisty-wisty stairs,
An' a woman comes and clobs 'im from be'ind.

"You take the point, Fred?"

"Yes."

"Yes . . . Although, actually there's no such word as 'clob,' according to the Alligator—not in that form, anyway. He thinks it's late nineteenth-century military slang, probably Anglo-Indian. But I think Kipling just made it up, you know." Audley paused. "However . . . I also think that there may be another reason. For always operating in pairs, I mean. Don't you think so, Jacko?"

"I think it's time to go, sir."

"Thank you, Sar' Devenish. But I will decide when we move out." Audley's tone sharpened momentarily. "As it happens, Fred, the route to A-three will be much easier, if the map and the air photographs can be trusted. . . . So, as I was saying . . . 'Loot' is the title of the poem, you see. And that happens to be the one thing all ranks of this unit are not allowed, in any shape or form—unconsidered trifles, black market . . . black*mail*—the lot. No winking, no blind eyes turned—right, Sar' Devenish?"

"Sir." Devenish filled the word with sullen anger.

"Thank you, Sar' Devenish. So you see, Fred, we don't just watch *over* each other, so as not to get 'clobbed' from 'be'ind'—we also *watch* each other. Right, Sar' Devenish?"

"If you say so, Captain Audley." If Devenish had been a piece of coal, he would be glowing orange-red now. "But don't you think you've said enough, sir?"

"Probably. I usually say too much, I agree. But that's because I am quite unfitted for this dirty business. To a scholar and a gentleman, it just doesn't come naturally, you know."

Fred felt sympathy for the long-suffering Devenish. "Don't you think we should be moving, David?"

Audley answered this betrayal with a moment of silence. "Oh . . . have it your own way, then! No more questions, Major Fattorini? Jolly good, and good huntin' and fishin', and all that—*jolly* good! So let's go, then?"

The going was easier, just as David Audley had predicted. Or maybe, as the last clouds hurried away eastwards (as the American major, still droning away in the distance, had also forecast), it was just that the darkness lightened even as his night vision returned, and he no longer felt so lost and dependent.

Yet that did not make for confidence. There were too many questions out there, unasked and unanswered. Not only unasked, but unaskable, which was worse . . . even infinitely worse, because he had some inkling of what the answers must be, almost certainly now, after young Audley's indiscretions . . . but even before that; and even long before that, from Kyri's warnings long ago.

Kyri . . . who was the antithesis of the ancient Greek virtue of moderation in all things: fatalistically brave, totally cynical and coldly cruel (it had come as a cold-water shock to learn after Osios Konstandinos how Colonel Michaelides was hated and feared by his enemies on the Left) . . . but also a wholly honorable man, unshakably loyal and honest with friends.

And Kyri had said afterwards: *"Don't get mixed up with these people, Fred. They are not for you! Go back home, to your safe green*

115

*England, and be a good Englishman and a good capitalist: make
money . . . and find a good wife—and if you cannot find one in
England, then you come to me . . . understood?—and make good
sons, and better daughters, like my own father did. . . . I have a
little sister, in truth. . . . No! But stay away from this man
Clinton."*

Clinton.

He could see the loom of David Audley ahead of him: Audley
moving fast and confidently on those great long legs of his, to
make up time lost carelessly and obstinately, half in protest at
this dirty business.

The brigadier had been a surprise—almost a shock—in the
ruined monastery of Osios Konstandinos, after David Audley and
Amos de Souza, so that even now it wasn't difficult to remember
him. A surprise not because of the searching questions beneath
his surface apologies after Colonel Michaelides had finished with
him.

Clinton—a brigadier, but not quite a gentleman, was it?

"Major, sir!" Devenish's voice came from just behind him,
urging him on.

"Yes, of course!" Fred realized that the memory of Brigadier
Frederick Clinton had slowed him down in the bottom of Audley's
Roman ditch. "I'm sorry!" He started to move again.

"That's all right, sir." There was room for Devenish to come up
beside him now. "You don't want to worry about Mr. Audley—
Captain Audley, as I should say—you don't need to worry about
him, sir."

At first Fred found himself worrying that Audley should hear
Devenish's confidence. Then he realized that the young dragoon
was already well ahead of them. "No, Sergeant Devenish?"

"No, sir." The man's voice was perfectly pitched not to carry
beyond them. But much more arresting than that, it was
confiding. "He's a good officer." Devenish bit his tongue on that,
as though momentarily undecided about continuing. "It's just he
talks too much, that's all."

That was true. And it was also true that Devenish did not share
that fault. "Why does he do that, Mr. Devenish?"

No reply. So whatever message the man had wished to impart
had been imparted. But that wasn't really good enough. But then
again, getting more out of the man wouldn't be easy. "I suppose
he is very young." Fred pretended to speak to himself. "He's much
younger than the other officers. . . ."

No reply. So what had sparked that curious confidence in
defense of the young Audley? Was it just loyalty? And yet, after

praising the boy as "a good officer," Devenish had plainly suggested that he'd been talking nonsense.

"Yes, sir." Devenish agreed suddenly. "He is that."

"Of course." Fred matched the agreement encouragingly. It was nothing less than the truth, after all. Apart from Colbourne himself, who had to be forty if he was a day, neither McCorquodale nor Macallister would ever see thirty again; and such other officers as he had noticed in the gloom of the mess and across the candlelit dining table had all been older than he himself was; and at a guess, he had five or six years over Audley himself. And those years, lengthened by the rigors of war, made for self-confidence. "So I expect he's a bit nervous, eh?"

"Yes, sir." No delay this time. "I'm sure you're right, sir. Nervous is what he is. He had a bad time in Normandy. And—"

"Fred! Are you there?"

Damn! Just as Devenish had been about to open up! "We're here, David."

"Thank Christ for that! I thought I'd lost you for a moment!" Audley's voice came down to a whisper. "We're almost there, I think. Jacko, if you'd go forward now. And two clicks if Major de Souza is in place, okay?"

"Sir!" Devenish lifted his own whisper against the drone of American engines.

Audley waited until they were alone. "What were you two gassing about?"

"Nothing, really." Had Audley broken up their conversation deliberately? "I was just asking a few questions."

"Did you get any answers?"

It sounded an innocent question, but Fred didn't think it was. "Not really, no."

"No . . . you wouldn't." Audley sounded relieved now. "He's a good man, is our Jacko. The best, actually. But he doesn't say much. Even the egregious Crocodile can only claim *dumb* insolence." He chuckled to himself suddenly.

Fred echoed the chuckle, and not altogether falsely because of the sameness-with-difference of the two men's opinions of each other. "Whereas your insolence will never be dumb, David?"

Another nervous chuckle. "Oh . . . I'm only deliberately rude to the Old Croc. With everyone else it's just accidental, Fred." Pause. "What were the jolly questions, then?"

"Questions?" Below the boy's superficially innocent curiosity, Fred sensed wariness and suspicion—the same disturbing state of mind, in fact, which he now realized lay hidden beneath the eccentric chitchat of all ranks of TRR-2 whom he had met so far, from the colonel downwards. But perhaps that was the occupa-

117

tional disease of their "dirty business," against which Kyri had warned him.

"What do you want to know?" Silence always goaded Audley into trying again.

"Ah . . ." *Why doesn't Devenish* click-click *and save me, damn it!* "Well . . . there was your umbrella, for a start, David."

"My . . . ?"

"Umbrella." Fred's wits quickened. "An old cavalry tradition, you said?"

"Oh . . ." Audley sounded disappointed. "Yes . . ."

Fred knew he was on a winner. "Waterloo, was it?"

"Yes." The boy sighed. "But actually, it started in the Peninsular War. Lots of cavalry officers had umbrellas. And then Wellington stopped it in 1814, when they crossed the Pyrenees into France—he said it was unmilitary. . . . Although General Picton always carried an umbrella . . . and it came back in '15, at Waterloo." Audley paused. But then history became too strong for the future historian. "I had an ancestor in the cavalry down there, in Spain. He was actually killed at Salamanca, charging with Le Marchant, you know. Bought into the King's Own—the third—from the West Sussex Yeomanry, my old regiment—" Audley stopped suddenly, again. "Yes . . . well, Sergeant Devenish wouldn't have given you anything on *umbrellas*—I can well understand that."

"He doesn't approve of them." Still no *click-click!* "Like the Duke of Wellington?"

"Only more so. And what else did you ask of him?"

There would be a time for real questions, but now wasn't that time. And young Audley wasn't the man, in spite of his inclination towards indiscretion. It was de Souza he needed for real questions. But what other unimportant questions were there?

A single drop of rainwater, diffused through the network of overhanging branches above him, hit Fred on the tip of his nose. And that was the answer, of course.

"When it was pissing down, earlier"—he felt his voice lifting from a whisper to a conversational level as the sound of the aircraft engines rose—"you said, 'This is how it would have been,' David." What was good about this utterly unimportant question, apart from the certainty that Devenish wouldn't have had the answer to it, was that it actually had been irritating him, this last hour. "What did you mean by that?"

"Oh . . . that's not me, really—that's Caesar Augustus."

Click-click! "Colonel Colbourne?"

"Yes." Audley ignored the signal. "He says it every time it

pisses down, Fred: 'This is what it was like in A.D. 9' is what he means."

Click-click! "Ah . . ." A.D. 9? *Fuck* A.D. 9! "Was that Sergeant Devenish, David?"

"Yes." But Audley didn't move. "He reckons it was probably raining then, up in the Teutoburger Wald, when poor old Varus was trying to march his three legions through it—with all their transport and such. . . . Because it was pretty much a peace-time march, apparently. Just showing the Roman flag—showing the Eagles—to the conquered German tribes. . . . Three full legions, plus auxiliary regiments, plus the usual camp followers, and NAAFI wagons and all that, and the Roman ABCA people— education wallahs, peddling the Roman Way of Life to the troops and the German natives. . . . When, of course, the German natives were leading him astray, into ambush, and sharpening their assegais and licking their lips—poor old Varus! Up to his knees in German mud, with millions of German trees around him—and thousands of bloodthirsty Germans, too—"

Click-click!

"David! Isn't that Sergeant Devenish?"

"—and the rain pissing down!" Audley caught himself at last. "So it is, yes"—*click-click-click!*—"so we'd better be going. But . . ."

But he still wasn't going. "But what?"

"Illusion and reality—that's what, old boy." Audley touched his arm, out of the darkness, pushing him in the desired directon. "Illusion and reality . . . *also like now, I very much fear!*"

"What?" Fred let himself be steered, but then slowed down.

"Oh . . . we're not about to be massacred, like Varus—don't worry!" Audley's hand dropped away as he moved. "But if I pick up Amos's signals aright, then we just *may* be more into illusion than reality just now, is what I mean."

That was worrying—and worrying because Audley wasn't passing on his juvenile ideas now. He was parroting Major de Souza's fears, which would be well-matured by knowledge and experience and judgment—

"Captain Audley?" For some unfathomable reason de Souza's whisper out of the dark reassured Fred that things couldn't be as bad as he had just feared. "David? Freddie?"

"Sir!" Audley said.

"David"—with that calm voice, there were people in the half-dark, and there was subdued activity all around them suddenly— "this is Major Hunter, of the United States Army, with me."

"Hullo there, Captain Audley!" Deep, familiar American whisper, oddly comforting.

"Oh!" For an instant Audley was taken aback by the presence of the United States Army. But then he rallied. "Hi there, Major!"

"Major." Fred wondered what the collective noun for "majors" might be. "Majors" were the army's alpha and omega: the last and highest rank for some (including all "hostilities only" officers such as himself), but the "field rank" beginning of promotion to higher command, and fame and fortune, for the generals of the next generation.

"Major." Major Hunter couldn't see Major Fattorini, so neither of them knew what sort of major he was up against.

"Slight change of orders, David. But nothing to worry about." Wisely, Amos did not introduce Sergeant Devenish. "Major Hunter will be accompanying us. But I shall be looking after him. So you just watch out for Krausnick, eh?"

"Right-o, Amos," Audley answered lightly. "G-g-gettin' to be quite a crowd of us. But the more, the merrier!"

"Now, Major . . . as I was saying . . . we are going for the back entrance, which is in the angle of the wall, partly concealed by some bushes, so far as we can make out from the photograph . . ." De Souza's words faded as he turned away to address the American, against the continuous background drone of the planes.

"Shit!" Audley caught Fred's arm again. "Nothing to worry about!"

"No?" As the young man put his head close, Fred picked up the familiar winter's-night smells of front-line Italy: wet uniform, sweat and alcohol, to which—less familiarly, amongst the British anyway—this evening's dinner had added an un-British whiff of garlic.

"The Yanks suspect we're up to something . . . or rather, they don't suspect—*they know!*" The grip tightened. "Surprise, surprise!"

"But I thought you already expected that, David?" Jollying-along depressed young engineer subalterns was another Italian memory: it came quite naturally to him to do the same for Audley. "Isn't all this"—he almost said *"nonsense"*—"all this elaborate business a sort of smoke screen?"

"Oh, sure! But there's so much bloody smoke about now that *I* can't see, either. Not that I ever can see much." The boy's tone was bitter. "The trouble with the bloody army is that you never really know what you're doing. I haven't known for years . . . or since last year, anyway." He sighed. "I thought I was liberating Europe and winning the war. But I wasn't doing that at all, you know."

It's just he talks too much! So much the better! "Then what were you doing?"

"Jesus Christ! You may well ask! God only knows! Or . . . He probably doesn't—only Brigadier Frederick J. Clinton knows—" Audley bit his tongue. "Do you really know what *you* are doing, Major Frederick Fattorini? I'll bloody bet you don't, by God!"

Audley's voice had been rising as he spoke. But it didn't matter, because the engine noise had been rising at the same time, from that steady drone to a drumming that Fred recognized for the first time. There was a pair of good old Dakotas out there, circling one behind the other in the darkness, separated by the diameter of their circles; and he had already survived one Dakota crash, outside Bari, in which the pilot had ploughed neatly through two lines of poplars and an olive grove, losing more and more of the aircraft at each obstacle—wingtips, wings and engines, and at the last even tail planes—until only the fuselage had remained when it came to a halt, with its human cargo bruised and bloody, but unbowed. Good old Dakota!

And . . . *what the hell was Audley complaining about? He'd survived the war, when a million—or ten million—better men hadn't! Christ—what more did he want!*

He could see the Dakota's lights now, dead ahead through a gap in the trees, and almost level with him—God Almighty!—almost *below* him as it roared up from the plain below the hills, so that he felt himself willing the pilot to pull the stick: *Pull the stick, man! Get the nose up—up, for Christ's sake!*

With an earsplitting crash of sound, which made him duck instinctively, the Dakota was on them—and over them, and gone, sucking its noise after it.

"God Almighty!" he murmured—or not murmured, he realized, but shouted.

"No. Not God Almighty, Fred," Audley shouted back at him, "that'll be Our Jake—Jake Austin. . . . He likes low-flying, does Our Jake!"

"Ready, David?" De Souza was almost shouting too, now: the sound of the second Dakota was increasing it's turn. *"Let's go, then!"*

Suddenly everyone was moving, and it was all familiar: the shadow shapes, and the nearer sounds of heavy footfalls and the *chink-chink* of equipment—sounds that he couldn't really hear, except in his memory—all brought back the recent past, and he felt his blood pump as he became part of the movement forward and thought the old familiar prayer—*Sweet Jesus Christ! Let it not be me tonight!*

Then his heart lifted, and it was like—it was *exactly* like—

121

waking from that old black examination nightmare, in which the terrible fear of total lack of knowledge and inevitable failing always enveloped him—waking to the sweet realization that it was all long in the past, and over and done with. That he'd taken the exam long ago, and passed it . . . *and now this wasn't Italy, but Germany with the war over and done with and finished forever, with no mines and booby traps on the riverbank, and no machine guns and shells waiting to seek him out in the darkness ahead!*

He giggled to himself with pure joy at the thought. He had been tired, and that was why his memory had played cruel tricks on him—tiredness notoriously distorted rational thought. But now he wasn't tired at all. Which was funny, although not half as funny as the thought of Audley's going into action umbrella in hand, just like his dragoon ancestor—that *was* funny—

Thump!

He half-checked, but then knew he couldn't stop.

Thump.

But then he identified the mortar sound instinctively out of all the other sounds, and automatically threw himself full length on the ground, and Sergeant Devenish tripped over him.

For a confused moment they were a tangle of arms and legs and equipment and breathless grunting. Then they pushed clear of each other, scrabbling for recovery just as the first parachute flare burst into unearthly brightness far above them.

"F——" Devenish started to swear, but then stopped. "Sir?"

Fred found himself staring up at the unearthly, flickering light as it descended beneath its trail of smoke. It was odd how quickly one's own side's flares seemed to come down, compared with the agonizing slowness of the enemy's, which always took forever, as though they were suspended on invisible wires.

"Are you all right, sir?" inquired Devenish doubtfully.

The second flare ignited high above simultaneously with another *thump*-pause-*thump* of two more going up from somewhere on their left.

"Yes." Fred remembered, from his long-distant subaltern past, a grizzled major of engineers admonishing him: *"You are a perfect idiot, Mr. Fattorini—insofar as perfection is attainable!"* "Thank you, Sergeant Devenish." Well . . . now he was a major, too! So even closer to perfection, by God! "I tripped over a treeroot."

"Yes, sir—so you did!" Devenish was on his feet and already moving—"Don't forget the bag, sir."

The bloody bag! "Go on, Sergeant, go on! I'm coming." With no dignity left to salvage, Fred hated himself and Devenish equally as he grabbed the bag and launched himself in the sergeant's wake, desperate not to be left behind.

Another engine sound, very different from that of the departing planes, startled him from somewhere away in the forest on his left. Almost simultaneously, even as the light from the second flare faded and another ignited, much brighter light burst alive ahead, silhouetting moving figures sharply in the final fringe of trees—trees that themselves seemed to move against a background of fiercely illuminated buildings in the clearing beyond them.

The most distant figure stopped suddenly, raised its arm, and dropped to one knee. Almost magically, the other figures followed suit, moving left and right behind convenient tree trunks and sinking out of sight.

"Come on, come on, come on!" Audley stage-whispered irritably. "What's the old bugger waiting for? Let's get on with it!"

So this was Audley beside him, with Devenish just ahead to the right; and the American in his distinctive pot helmet had dropped down to Amos de Souza's left. Of all the figures, de Souza's was the only one in the open, and the other big silhouette, which he had assumed to be Audley's, must be the major's accompanying escort, whom he had not yet encountered.

"What are we waiting for?" Audley's nervousness infected him. "David?"

Two new silhouettes intruded from the rear left, half-crouching and half-walking, and distinctively American both by their helmets and the rich flow of invective that they trailed. More Americans?

One of the Americans was unreeling a line. The other offered something to Major de Souza. And as he did so, a sudden crackling noise, unnaturally loud—a fish-fried-in-batter sound, multiplied a thousand fold—overlaid the roar of the searchlight generators.

Another flare ignited, high up in the now-impenetrable blackness above, making all the shadows around them dance madly as a loud and hopelessly distorted gibberish of words started up against the 'fish-frying-tonight' crackling.

"Oh, bloody wonderful!" exclaimed Audley. "Makes you wonder how we won the war!"

"Do shut up, David, there's a good fellow." By one of life's mischances the crackling had stopped just as the young dragoon had started speaking, so that his opinions were as clearly audible as Major de Souza's flattening rebuke.

"Sorry, sir." Yet against all odds, Audley didn't sound flattened. "But . . . Amos . . . if that's Caesar Augustus calling on the Germans to surrender"—the boy started to shout as the crackling began again—"they're not going to—"

"Shut up, David!" De Souza waved away the nearest American, who was offering him a megaphone, and stood up and looked around him.

"Major Hunter?" He addressed the American officer beside him almost conversationally, without urgency. "If you would be so good as to follow Sergeant Huggins, after me. . . . Shall we go then?"

That was the way to do it, of course, when it had to be done. Matter-of-fact and prosaic and quietly confident . . . not with young Audley's edge-of-disaster nervous tension, right or wrong. When it was done right, it always sounded the same, whatever happened afterwards.

Always the same! Fred felt disembodied then, as he always had done in the past, when whatever was going to happen wasn't going to happen to him—*not this time—next time, maybe, but not this time!*

All the different silhouettes rose. Even the two recent Americans stood up, after their recent useless journey, although they didn't move forward with the rest. For a moment they were ahead of him, and then he was beyond them, running forwards by the majority decision through the last trees, into the open.

But . . . *it wasn't the same, nevertheless!* he reassured himself. Those were not real Germans out there, in that false daylight—*if this was another nightmare, it was a different bloody nightmare, for a different bloody exam!*

He saw the cluster of buildings clearly, at last.

Just a bunch of alien buildings, shuttered at ground level, blank-windowed above, without any sign of life in them.

(In Italy, they said, most of the Germans will be up above, with a clear field of fire, and ready to drop grenades on you if you reach the outside walls; and the civilians will be in the cellar, if there is one, if they're still there, hoping that you won't toss a grenade down among them, just in case!)

They were coming in from the back. He was running behind Devenish now, towards a tangle of bushes, out of which rose a black-leafed tree—no, those weren't black leaves . . . it was a holly tree—a black holly tree without berries, because it was a long way for Christmas.

Scobiemas!

They were converging on the bushes, towards a gap—towards a back door in the gap—and de Souza was trying the door, trying it once, almost perfunctorily, as though he didn't expect it to open, then springing back from it to one side, to let the big soldier behind him get at it.

The soldier backed up, and Fred saw that he was a giant. Not only was de Souza insignificant beside him, but even David Audley was diminished, at his shoulder; and for a moment out of time, he watched the giant balance himself before delivering the full force of the heel of his boot accurately alongside the door handle.

The door splintered inwards with a tremendous concussion, and he saw a sliver of wood cartwheel into the light, and then disappear as Audley ducked to avoid it; and then, in the same slow-motion timelessness, he saw the giant—sergeant's stripes, rain-darkened leather jerkin—swing sideways almost gracefully to let de Souza go in ahead of him, as any gentleman might do who had opened a door for his lady.

Then time speeded up, making up for lost time. De Souza moved, and then the American major tried to move, and so did Audley. But both of them were shouldered aside unceremoniously as de Souza's sergeant reversed his original swing in order to follow closely behind his officer. The American cannoned off the bigger man into Audley, who staggered back against Devenish, who stepped back smartly and trod heavily on Fred's foot.

"Ouch!" Fred saw Devenish's submachine gun, which was an Italian Beretta with a solid-walnut stock—an officer's customized model now rendered even more useful with a flashlight neatly taped to its delicate barrel—then he felt the pain of Devenish's full weight.

"Sorry, *sir!*" Devenish plunged into the doorway behind the American.

Fred wished that he had a Beretta and a flashlight instead of a canvas bag. And it was odd, he thought, that the sergeant—Sergeant Huggins?—hadn't gone in first, ahead of de Souza. But then, of course, it wasn't odd, because de Souza wasn't the sort of man to go anywhere second. And then he was comforted by everyone else's eagerness to enter the doorway ahead of him, in whatever order of precedence. Because he was the bag carrier, and he was certainly not about to draw the revolver that he had signed for so very recently. Because, at the best of times, nobody ever hit the desired target with a revolver, outside Hollywood. And there were too many men ahead of him, anyway. And one of them was Devenish—which was somehow quite extraordinarily comforting.

Now there were flashing lights in the darkness.

Keep well back, Fattorini! he admonished himself. *You're just the man with the bag!*

A foul stench suddenly enveloped him, even as different flashlights gyrated in a passageway, with doors on each side being methodically kicked open ahead of him, to the sound of shouting and screaming as de Souza and Sergeant Huggins worked their way down the passage; and over this panicky rape-and-pillage noise he heard de Souza's voice, uncharacteristically loud, but also still calm and controlled, repeating the same words—

"Stay where you are! You are surrounded! Remain where you are—do not leave this room! Anyone trying to leave this building will be shot! You are surrounded—that is a final warning!"

De Souza's German was quite beautiful. It was far beyond Higher Certificate (distinction) German, such as his own—it was colloquial.

But this smell.

As Devenish passed one of the open doors, just ahead of him, a figure appeared in the doorway, half-naked and half-draped in what looked like a Roman toga.

"Get fucking back!" Devenish propelled the man back into the room with his free hand. *"You heard the British officer!"*

The smell wafted round Fred as he passed the doorway. And the last six years had vastly increased his dictionary of smells, from childish memories of roast beef and chicken, and the tobacco richness of Uncle Luke's library, and the linseed-oil-and-sweat changing-room odors of school and university; and now he had barrack-room smells, and cordite, and a thousand army smells, all the way from trenches full of shit to the sweeter-rottener stench of flyblown meat, human and animal, insufficiently buried . . . apart from all the good smells, from most recent memory, of spices and thyme and lavender, and olive oil frying on an open fire on crystal-clear Greek evenings. But this was something new.

Another door crashed open ahead of him.

"Stay where you are! You are surrounded."

"Are you all right, sir?" Devenish addressed him solicitously.

"Yes, sergeant." This was a different smell—compounded of—what? But there was a more urgent question: "Are we going according to plan?"

"Oh, yes, sir." Devenish leaned back towards him conspiratorially, while his flashlight illuminated the American major's back two yards ahead. "This is just going through the motions, sir. This is just the usual rubbish down here." The torch jerked left and right as he spoke, but on the last jerk uncovered a totally naked woman in the doorway ahead. "Jesus Christ—*sir!*"

Not a woman, but an emaciated child, with thick-painted red mouth smudged and spread pathetically beyond her lips, and bony shoulders above inadequate breasts; and (what was far worse) a frightful welcoming smile on those lips, below wide, terrified eyes.

126

"Hullo, Tommie."

Devenish's free hand was already on its way, fingers spread so wide that they took her from collarbone to collarbone. *"Get out of the road, you silly little bitch!"* He spun her back into the darkness. "Sorry about that, sir . . . But we're going up the stairs."

"Cap-itan!" Another half-naked figure loomed in the doorway behind an ingratiating voice. "I am Polish officer—officer of dragoons—"

"Get back!" This time Devenish swung the machine pistol menacingly to cut off the appeal. "You can be a general in the fucking Polish army, for all I care!" The sergeant recovered himself as the sounds inside the room died down. "I'm sorry about that, sir—*You bloody lot—don't you move a fucking eyebrow!*—but we have to get on, sir! Up the stairs!"

"Yes, Sergeant Devenish." But he was already addressing Devenish's back as he spoke.

We're going up the stairs.

But the smell was still with him: a sour-sweat, old-clothes-and-cabbage, unwashed-wet-undried, peculiar smell—just as all the other undifferentiated human smells had been peculiar, each with its unforgettable nuance.

Then they were out into the open suddenly, through the final door, with a staircase doubling round on his left, with Devenish already swinging round onto it, leading him on, with the crash of boots ahead of them on the wooden stairs.

And—

They knew where they were going! They had known long before they had smashed down the back door. "This is just going through the motions, sir!" and all that had been for the American major—*they knew where they were going!*

He accelerated after Devenish, with the canvas bag flying out behind him spinning off the wall on one side, and then off the banisters on the other.

And they were the real assault group, too! That was obvious now, not simply because no else had burst in ahead of them, from the front of the building, but for a crowd of other good reasons that should have occurred to him: from the composition of the group—Amos de Souza as its brains, and Sergeant Huggins, David Audley, and Sergeant Devenish as its brawn—to the simple clinching detail that *he was carrying the bag.*

"Whoa there, sir!" Devenish restrained his headlong progress at the top of the stairs, his flashlight beam arcing over an ancient collection of trophies of the chase fixed high up on the wall above them: moth-eaten antlered stag's heads and yellow-tusked boars drooling cobwebs from gaping dusty mouths. "Steady now! Let the dog see the rabbit, then!"

Crash! Huggins had put his boot through another door, just down this new passage to the right, that explosion announced.

Boom! This time the concussion reverberated from behind and beneath them, echoing through the building just as Amos began his formula ahead down the passage: Colonel Colbourne's assault on the main door below had commenced belatedly, even as they were deep inside the building.

Boom! It sounded as though they were using a battering ram.

"If you'd just like to come this way a bit, out of the road, sir." Devenish addressed him politely. "They'll be coming up behind us—Major Macallister's party. But they'll be going the other way, like."

Boom-CRASH! The main door had come off its hinges in one piece, it sounded like. But Fred's attention was drawn to his left in the same instant by Devenish's flashlight, to a collection of tattered white-faced ghosts that was milling in the other passage, crying out in terror.

"GET BACK THERE!" Devenish roared, blinding the leading ghost even as the hallway below filled with the noise of Major Macallister's party.

Crash! Another door splintered ahead of them! "This way—up the stairs!" Major Macallister's shout from below reminded Fred unbearably of his old games master, with its half-hectoring, half-encouraging note only a hair's breadth from falsetto. "Captain Hornyanski—are you with me? Sergeant Little—see to the American officer!"

So Major Macallister had his attendant American too. Fred looked quickly up their own passage, where flashlight beams were flashing in between the silhouettes of moving figures. Was this good honest allied cooperation, or well-founded allied mistrust? Much more likely the latter!

"Just hold it, sir." Devenish restrained him again. "Any moment now—*get back there!*"

With the heavy clump of Major Macallister and his minions on the stair below him, Fred resisted the urge to move. But looking to the left, he saw that the flock of ghosts were shrinking back into their own darkness under the combined threat of Devenish's gun, the major's shout, and that metal-studded tread, and he felt a pang of sympathy for them. Whatever they were, innocent or guilty, they were the conquered—and *vae victis—the conquered had no rights!*

Crash! Another door caved in.

Fred abandoned the ghosts, with the mtallic taste of power in his mouth and the old excuse in his brain, which he remembered all too well from Italy and Greece: *We didn't start this—and we didn't make the rules . . . so hard fucking luck, then!*

128

"Come on, sir—this way!" Even with the sound of Major Macallister at his back, Fred also remembered the snappy reply from the ferret-faced drunken gunner captain to that anodyne disclaimer: *"Then what's the difference between us and your average Jerry, then? So . . . they obey their orders, right?" Hick! "And we"—hic!—"we obey orders too!"*

"For Christ's sake, sir! *Come on!*

Fred let himself be pulled, with all the commotion of Major Macallister meeting the ghosts behind him, beyond the first and second doors down the passage. And then Devenish was pushing past him into the third door, without deference, leaving him no choice but to follow.

Once again, the concentrated sweaty-clothes-and-cabbage smell assailed him, stronger in the confined space of the room than outside, even before he could sort out its contents in the combined light of Devenish's and Audley's flashlight. And then for a moment Audley and Devenish seemed themselves to be the main contents, well-armed, well-fed, and well-washed in the center of their stage, and dominating the room's occupants huddled in its furthest corner.

There were five of them, he saw. All males—and somehow it was a merciful relief that there wasn't another naked painted-and-smudged child like down below—all males, in varying states of disheveled undress and standing in the midst of the wreckage of their bedding—old army blankets and stained mattresses.

"Right then! Let's be having you, then!" Devenish's voice took on something of the tones of any sergeant major addressing an awkward squad of recruits, mixing resignation and brutality in equal parts, with only the merest angostura dash of encouragement.

The huddle shuffled uncertainly within itself, those more at the back resisting the efforts of those more at the front to replace them, terrified by the sound of the words without understanding any single one of them.

"Get them up against the wall, Sar' Devenish, if you please." Audley's voice, by contrast, was conversational, edged with fastidious distaste.

"Sir!" Devenish took a step forward, his boot crunching on something breakable and already broken in the darkness below him. "Get in line there! Hands high—up—up! Come on, you buggers! In line—in line!" The jerk of his gun galvanized the huddle into feverish activity, if not actual obedience, with those who didn't understand hampering those who got the message.

"Come on!" Patience exhausted, Devenish took another step forward, jabbing at the disobedient minority of the group with the combined flashlight beam and muzzle of his gun to encourage them to imitate the majority. "Against the wall! Hands up—up—up—*UP!*"

All this flurry of activity seemed to stir up the smell, so that it was pungent in Fred's nostrils, and bitter tasting in his mouth. It was as though their fears were increasing their smell, adding the sweat of terror to all their other odors, like foxes hounded to no ecape by hounds.

"Faces to the wall—if you please, Sar' Devenish." Audley pronounced the words carefully, one after another, as though he was concerned not to stutter.

"Sir!" For an instant Devenish said nothing, as he struggled with the problem of obtaining obedience. "*ABOUT—TURN!*"

The farthest man on the right turned immediately to face the wall. And then the man next to him turned after him, as though by osmotic action.

"Go on! Face to the wall!" Devenish jabbed at the next man, and as he followed suit, at the next, down the line, until they were presented with a line of backs, in creased shirts and dirty vests overlapping crumpled trousers or hairy legs until the last in the line conformed.

"*Yrrch!*" Audley's flashlight beam fell away, momentarily sweeping over the room, over the blankets and mattresses and across scuffed suitcases and an ammunition box on which a bottle with an encrusted candle in its mouth was set. Then it came up again, and an untidily furled umbrella stabbed along its line, towards the obedient man on the right. "That one, Sar' Devenish, thank you."

"Sir!" Devenish stepped forward again. "*YOU THERE!*" But then, to Fred's surprise, he jabbed the man next to Audley's choice in the small of the back with his gun. "*AND YOU—AND YOU*"—he touched each man in turn, down the line—"*OUT!*"

The marked men lowered their arms uneasily, almost unwillingly, half-turning towards their persecutor.

"*NOT YOU!*" Devenish addressed the obedient man, who was also lowering his arms now. "*YOU STAND FAST!*"

The obedient man's hands shot up again, higher than ever.

"*The rest of you*"—Devenish's voice came down to ordinary harshness—"*out you go, then!*"

And out they went then, shepherded past Fred by Devenish, with Audley's flashlight beam playing on them, one after another, and Devenish bringing up the rear.

"Major Fattorini!" Audley addressed Fred for the first time since they had broken into the place. "Empty out the bag—on the floor, please." He indicated a patch of bare floorboards, on the edge of one of the filthy mattresses.

Fred loosened the drawstring and upended the bag into the circle of yellow light, shaking it as its contents tangled up.

An army boot—a tangle of unfolding battle-dress uniform: trousers mixed up with blouse, and beret falling with them, accelerated by gaiters and belt, and another boot . . . but inhibited by something else, which had become entangled in them.

He shook the bag again.

Christ! It was a Sten! And complete with its magazine!

"Don't worry about that, old boy—it's got no firing pin." Audley stirred the uniforms with the tip of his umbrella, flipping out one arm from the blouse. "A corporal, by God!" The corporal's chevrons showed. "So it's *'Corporal* Keys' then!" Pause. "Right then, Sar' Devenish—get on with it if you please."

"Sir!" Devenish grabbed the man by his shoulder, swinging him round. "Right then, you bugger! You get your clothes off— and you get into that British uniform down there . . . *understood?*"

The man stood still, his arms only half-lowered, gaping into the light uncomprehendingly in a moment of silence within the room, which somehow separated them from the more general world of noise outside it—a confused commotion of bangs and crashes and shouting, and boots stamping.

"Whooff!" The man broke their private moment with the pain of receiving the butt of Devenish's submachine gun in the pit of his stomach, which bent him double, and then he muttered in agonized German.

"Stop it!" The umbrella rapped Devenish across the shoulder sharply. "That's not the way—" Audley caught his anger too late as the German quickly started to disprove him by stripping his clothes off even before he had undoubled himself from the pain of the blow, throwing off the unbuttoned shirt and then ripping at his trouser buttons.

"Sir?" Devenish pivoted slightly between his target and Audley, but remained still balanced, ready to deliver more encouragement.

Now the shapeless trousers had joined the shirt, revealing spidery thin hairy legs and genitals pathetically wizened in adversity, when fear outranked every other feeling.

"No matter." All the shame and embarrassment was Audley's from his voice. "Just get on with it."

"Sir!" The answering growl started with Audley, but continued over the German who was already busy proving that he understood English by fumbling with the unfamiliar khaki uniform with clumsy fingers.

"Christ O'Reilly!" exclaimed Devenish in sudden exasperation, thrusting his submachine gun into Fred's empty hand. "Take hold of this, sir—and keep the light on the bugger, right?" He threw himself down on his knees in front of the man, slapping the hands away, and addressed himself to the fly buttons urgently. "Stand still, damn you!"

Fred watched, fascinated, as Devenish pulled and pushed and buttoned and tightened the man into the uniform, cursing and blinding in a continuous monologue undertone as he did so—

"Christ O'Reilly, hold still! If I hadn't been born unlucky, I wouldn't be here—hold still! Where's the other boot, then? I had a good wife, and good kids, and I left 'em all—lift your foot then, for fuck's sake—and a good job in a safe reserved occupation—where's the sodding gaiter?—but I was born stupid, as well as unlucky, wasn't I! . . . That's the bloody left one—where's the bloody right one? . . . Oh, no! I wanted to be a soldier, didn't I! Could have been building aeroplanes, I could—sleeping between sheets every night, drawing good money—give us your bloody arm then—what am I doing, then? I'm fucking dressing fucking Jerries in the middle of the fucking night, is what I'm doing!"

Finally he stood back and surveyed his handiwork for a moment, before stepping forward again to readjust the beret, tugging it round and down savagely until the cap badge was at the regulation level above the German's left eye.

"I beg your pardon, sir!" He glanced at Audley, and then bent down and came up with the Sten. "Best I can do, in the circumstances. Everything's a size too big, but I've laced the boots up tight, and the belt too. So he's not going to come apart right away, any road." He plucked the Beretta out of Fred's grasp with his free hand and held up the Sten with the other. "Shall I give it to him, sir?"

"Thank you, Sar' Devenish, yes." Audley spoke with curious formality as he moved to get a better view. "Yes-esss . . . he doesn't look exactly like the spearhead of the British Liberation Army. But I've seen worse. And it's a dark night." He sighed.

"Huh!" Devenish grunted throatily and thrust the Sten towards the German. "Here you are, Jerry—take hold of this then!"

The ersatz Corporal Keys stared at them uncomprehendingly, breathing heavily as though he'd been running to keep up with a forced march that had left him behind. And suddenly Fred felt for him, in his incomprehension.

"Please?" He spoke in English. "What is this?"

"Go on, Jerry—take it." From the slight change in Devenish's voice, from rough to gruff, there was also some human understanding. "We're going to get you away from here, is what we're going to do, understand?"

The German took the gun unwillingly, looking at Audley as he did so.

"Not like that!" Devenish's harsher voice came back as the German accepted the weapon. "Hold it properly, not like a bleeding lavatory brush!"

"Please?" The German fumbled with the Sten, as though it was too hot to hold, blinking at them. "But . . ." Then he took hold of it and himself, squaring his shoulders. "But I do *not* understand, I am telling you, sir—*Captain!*"

"Of course not." Audley accepted the appeal. But then he nodded to Devenish. "Jacko, get outside and see what's happening. . . . Look for Major de Souza." In the half-light of their flashlights, he lifted his arm (with his umbrella hooked over it now) to consult his wristwatch, shining his own beam directly onto it. "We're two minutes over schedule. So he should be in the offing out there now, right?"

Fred realized that he had lost track of time altogether, ever since they had first moved out of the safe darkness of the forest into the naked light and confusion of the assault on the hunting lodge. There were, as always, two separate times—the fast time of pleasure and happiness, and the slow, elongated time of pain and fear, which seemed to last forever. And they had been in the stretched concertina of it, within this room, with six hundred seconds to every minute.

"Now, then"—Audley addressed the German with that curiously formal voice of his—"the sergeant is right, of course—as always. We are going to get you out of here, sir. Which is for your own good and safety—you have my word on that. Do you understand?"

What Fred understood was that, with Audley's flashlight shining straight into the man's eyes, never mind that British officer's promise, the German could understand nothing at all—and least of all because of that strangely deferential "sir" that Audley had thrown in. Better by far, at this stage, to have stuck to Devenish's approach.

"No!" The German dropped one hand from the Sten to shield his eyes. "Please—"

"Sir!" Devenish barked the word from the doorway. "Major de Souza is here, sir—now! He is with the American officer, and he says to tell you that he has a prisoner for us to escort to the assembly area . . . *sir!*" The bark increased to a stentorian military shout, raised to reach the other side of any parade ground.

"Thank you, Sar' Devenish." Audley matched Devenish's shout. "The corporal and I have processed everyone from here. So we'll take the major's prisoner!" Then his torch came back to the German. "We have to go, sir—now! So . . . you are a British NCO—noncommissioned officer. . . . You are 'Corporal Keys,' if anyone asks you who you are—'Corporal Keys'?" He stepped forward and caught the German by the arm. "Come on, sir—we must *go*—"

"No!" The German resisted him, pulling away. *"No!"*

"What the devil?" The beam of Audley's flashlight gyrated over the room, across sharp angles and damp-stained walls, down to the tangle of blankets in which a uniformed corporal in the British Army was now rummaging desperately.

"My spectacles! My spectacles!" The corporal was on his knees beside the ammunition box, scrabbling desperately with searching fingers in the blanket folds. "Without my spectacles . . . *I cannot see!"* The search stopped suddenly. "I have them! *Grüss Gott!"* The German held something up high, fumbling with it.

"Don't put them on!" Audley's voice cut through the man's action decisively. *"You mustn't look like yourself, sir—we can't risk that! Put them in your pocket. Don't put them on—that's an order!"*

A light came in from the doorway, silhouetting Audley and the German before blinding Fred himself.

"Sir . . ." The slight pause encompassed Devenish's surprise on finding Fred among the probably flea-ridden bedding. "If you please, sir?"

"Right, Sar' Devenish." Audley started to move. "Major Fattorini, Corporal Keys—*MOVE!"*

Fred moved all the faster, to be free of the bedding before he inherited its inhabitants, pushing Corporal Keys ahead of him all the more unmercifully.

The corridor outside was crowded with people. And there was David Audley, using his size and weight to shoulder his way through them, bulldozing an opening down the passage to the entrance hall, with its antlered trophies and cobweb-drooling heads at the top of the staircase.

And there was Major Macallister too—or was it the Crocodile?—with British and American soldiers in attendance, and a crowd of ghosts dressed and half-dressed, but all outraged and protesting their innocence as Audley smashed through them regardless.

God! It was like Paddy's Market on quarter day!

Except that he caught sight of Major de Souza suddenly, at the head of the stairs with the hint of a smile on his face, holding back all the criminals and deserters, and displaced persons, and homeless bombed-out refugees who had found this roof over their heads, when there were so few roofs anywhere to be found unbombed in Germany; and alongside Major de Souza, larger and wider, and built like a brick shithouse, was Sergeant Huggins, with one meat-plate hand grasping the shoulder of one of the ghosts—a terrified ghost, draped in a field-grey blanket.

Audley reached the de Souza-Huggins block, and Huggins released his prisoner to him, and Sergeant Devenish accepted the prisoner, pushing him down the stairway just ahead of Corporal Keys and Major Fattorini. Audley's incongruous umbrella was lashing out ahead of them, to clear the way for the snatch squad; and Fred could hear Sergeant Devenish swearing as they cut into the maelstrom of the hunting lodge with British and American uniforms like currants and sultanas in a swirling suet pudding of civilians.

The black opening of the main doorway gaped ahead of them, at the foot of the stairway where the main door had come off its hinges. But Audley wasn't going that way. He was turning back round the last carved banister, to lead them again towards the passage to the rear entrance, through which they had come. That had been the way in, so now that was the way out—*right?*

Right!

And . . . *right*, because Devenish was urging their new prisoner in that direction, relying on Major Fattorini to encourage Corporal Keys, with his useless Sten and clumping oversize boots. And whatever blurred images of chaos and panic were left to Corporal Keys without his spectacles, whatever they were, they didn't matter. What mattered was that their way was not impeded. Either the inhabitants of the rooms in the passage were still inside them, or they'd been chivied out to join the terrified crowd in the entrance hall. All that mattered now was that the passage was empty . . .

Or almost empty. For there in the doorway ahead of them, caught in the beam of someone's flashlight just inside it and silhouetted against the fierce mock daylight of the searchlights outside, was an American soldier, rain-caped and armed.

"Make way there!" Audley's voice was loud and offensively British. "Out of the way, soldier!"

Corporal Keys bridled just ahead of Fred, as though unwilling to take part in the charade at this last and most important moment, so Fred gave him a brutal shove to get him moving again, conscious at last that he was a full and paid-up member of the TRR-2.

"Get on, you bugger!" Devenish, ahead of Corporal Keys, admonished their newer prisoner angrily—that poor confused devil had also balked momentarily, like Corporal Keys, at the prospect of finally exchanging his smelly freedom for the bright uncertainty of captivity beyond the doorway.

The American soldier stood aside, blank-faced and holding his carbine close to his chest, and Fred caught an incongruous whiff of eau de cologne as he pushed by the man, as distinctive against all the doss-house smells as the perfume of roses in a midden. And then they were outside, in the open chiaroscuro of night-and-searchlights.

For a moment the bushes on each side of the doorway protected Fred's eyes from the harshness of the searchlights, but after two or three strides the delicate tracery of leaves was gone, and he was suddenly blind in the full glare, transfixed by it as though it was focused on him only.

An earsplitting explosion overwhelmed the rest of the shout, seeming to come from all around them in the millisecond of its concussion, but then galvanizing Fred to grab instinctively at Corporal Keys, to pull him down onto the wet ground.

The next elongated fraction of time was filled with the aftermath of the explosion, beyond rational thought. Then, in the midst of its confusing echoes, as he began to think and hear again, Fred knew that the explosion hadn't harmed them, and that they must get moving again.

But now there was another sound. Where there had been a continuing babel of noise behind him, coming out of the passage from the entrance hall, now there was a terrible mixture of shrieks, which together became a thin wailing—*God! He had heard that wail before, in Italy. It was the appalling distillation of maimed surviving flesh-and-blood on the edge of a bomb's impact in a cellar crowded with human beings!*

He raised himself slightly, above the body of Corporal Keys, which he had pulled down with him. First, the pitiless continuing glare of the searchlight blinded him; then Audley was on his knees ahead of him, cutting off the beam.

"Get up—for Christ's sake, get up!" Audley was up now, gesturing at him. "Get him up, Fred!"

Fred felt the wet earth under his hand, and the cold damp through his trousers at his knees as he levered himself up.

"Jacko! Help him!" shouted Audley.

Fred was suddenly aware of Corporal Keys beside him, and that only Corporal Keys mattered. But when he grasped the German's arm, it was a dead weight, tensed against him. The man was hugging the ground almost literally, for the illusion of protection it gave him when everything else around him had gone mad.

Sergeant Devenish appeared out of nowhere, on the other side of the German.

"Come on now, sir—let's do like the officer says then, shall we?" The sergeant addressed the German in a voice quite different from any he had ever used before in Fred's hearing: unhurried, gentle, almost as though wheedling a frightened child. But without the slightest effect, nevertheless.

"Right, then." Devenish spoke the two words to himself, and then his chest expanded. "Take my weapon, if you'd be so good, sir"—he thrust his gun into Fred's hands a second time across the inert body—*"LET'S BE HAVING YOU THEN, YOU BUGGER!"*

Whether it was the effect of the sudden transition from gentleness to roaring anger, or the grasping hand on the collar with every ounce of the sergeant's muscle power in the lift, or both, Fred never knew. But in the next second Corporal Keys was on his knees, and in the second after that he was moving, even before his legs were fully straightened, with one of Devenish's hands still grasping the collar, and the other pulling his battle-dress blouse.

"Fred!" Audley gesticulated as he came alongside Devenish. "The other one—bring him!"

Fred followed the direction of the boy's hand. Major de Souza's prisoner, who had been lately Sergeant Devenish's, was now all alone in the open and in the glare of the searchlights, hunched under his blanket and imprisoned by the same fear that had rooted Corporal Keys to the ground.

"Right!" He heard his forced acknowledgment of the boy's order, and he felt angry with himself for the inadequacy of his performance so far, for which the excuse of six peaceful months in Greece was no bloody excuse at all—*damn, damn, and damn!*

The prisoner was no more than half a dozen yards away—the prisoner who, for a guess, didn't matter a damn, compared with Corporal Keys—*damn, damn, and damn!* But at least he'd get this right, damn it!

"Come on!" The wretched fellow had rolled sideways, into a twitching blanket-covered ball, even as he covered the distance between them. But Audley's much admired Sergeant Devenish was his model now, even though he couldn't match either of the sergeant's voices. "Get up!"

A bare foot, emaciated and filthy white in the unnatural light, kicked out from under the blanket.

"Damn you—*GET UP!*" Fred seized an edge of the blanket and ripped it aside. "*DAMN*—" But then the Devenish words died on his lips as he saw the blood, black as ink, bubbling out of the

137

man's mouth and streaming to join the great spreading wound on his chest.

God!

The man was trying to say something, but he was gargling and choking as he tried to speak, and he wasn't even looking at Fred— he was arching his back and looking up into the dark sky, at nobody and nothing as he died.

"Fred—*Fred?*" He heard Audley's voice in the distance. "What the devil are you playing at?"

Audley's voice was one sound. And he could still hear the slaughterhouse-din muted from the wrecked building behind him. And there was the roar of generators powering the false daylight, which blackened the man's blood as his eyes rolled upwards and the breath rattled finally in his throat.

"*Christ!*" exclaimed Audley, above him.

That, among the other words of the ancient formula, was what Father de Vere had said over his dying sappers in Italy, Fred remembered. So, with no more time left, it would have to do for this poor unknown, who had just joined them. And anyway, the exact words didn't matter, Father de Vere always said.

He straightened up. "Come on, David."

Audley looked at him. "What—"

"Let's go." For the first time he felt their roles reverse, and age and rank take precedence, together with self-preservation. "He's dead. So he won't mind." That last consideration hardened him: they were both still alive, but in the open, where it wasn't safe. "Come on!"

Without waiting for Audley, he ran towards the safety of the trees.

Part Three

A Free Man

In the Teutoburg Forest, Germany, August 7, 1945

CHAPTER ONE

As they drove northwards, Fred slept the sleep of exhaustion. But unmercifully, it was not dreamless. Rather, it was full of images—sharp images, but disjointed and unconnected, of things and people . . . and even words.

Or a word—

Wildschweinrücken.

In Audley's jeep, at first, he slept almost upright and very uncomfortably, with his chin down on his breast, so that his neck stretched and stretched as his head rolled first one side, and then the other, over every pothole. And there were hundred of potholes—thousands, millions, billions—an infinity of potholes, into which Audley deliberately and maliciously drove, out of the last vestiges of night, into a gray, cloud-swept day.

Wildschweinrücken.

There were, at irregular intervals, villages untouched by war. Then there were towns: towns of rubble, with tall chimneys standing up out of the ruins . . . *buildings burned, because they were not built not to burn . . . but chimneys were built for fire, so they didn't burn—that was the rule!*

And then there were long stretches of flattened open country-side, so often like, and yet unlike, bits of the English countryside he remembered, out of another world, in August—another August, long forgotten.

He had taken the men, one day in that other August long ago, to a farm, where they were harvesting. And . . . it was wheat—stiff, heavy-eared wheat, deep yellow-gold—but also with a fine crop of thistles in it, which made the men swear, those who had never before taken hold of a wheat sheaf, let alone a handful of thistles. They were mostly conscripts, with a leavening of regulars and territorials such as himself, but they were also all sappers, and proud of it.

Bridges, endless bridges! And the bridge over the Volturno was more than just a bridge: it was the eighth bloody wonder of the bloody world! And I saw Leese—Jolly Polly Leese!—drive on at one end, past irate, gesticulating military police, and approach a column of tanks that had lumbered onto the other end—the far distant end—towards him. . . . And he was driving himself too, Jolly Polly! And he'd had to back up all the way, while the MPs were tearing their hair, because the first tank commander wasn't going to back up for anyone, not even God Almighty himself, let alone the commander of the 8th Army—not for Jolly Polly, not for anyone! But at least he'd still been jolly at the end of it.

Wildschweinrücken! And then a nightmare wild boar's head poking out of a wall, with its glaring red pig-eyes but its tusks dripping black blood.

Harvesting! How the men had hated stooking! Men who fancied their skills with metal and wood—anything was grist to a sapper—but they couldn't stand up two wheat sheaves, one against another, in the stubble. While they were turning round to grab another sheaf, the first two had fallen over—to the loud contempt of the farm laborer driving the tractor, and the little gnarled man sitting high up on the binder behind him—*"Garn! Can't yer do it, then? It's too 'ard for yer, is it? Too much like 'ard work, like, is it?"*

Christ! There were no tractors in the fields of Germany now! And there were no men, either; only women, bent down in the

corn—the thin fields of a poor harvest—among the flattened crop,
beaten down by the rain.

And . . . *was it the Crocodile or the Alligator who had said that
they'd all be starving soon?*

Somewhere along the way, beside a copse of silver birches
standing up tall and thin, in the middle of nowhere, with his
tongue furry-thick in his mouth, and his eyes gummed together
. . . they had stopped.

And young Audley's face had been brown-gray. Brown with the
outdoor soldier's tan, but gray with weariness, and lined like an
old man's, with that ugly sneer of his . . . which wasn't really a
sneer, but the defensive mask of a youth's uncertainty among his
confident elders—was that it?

"What's happening?" His own exhaustion harshened the question. "What are we stopping for?"

Audley's features twitched. "This is where we're meeting up
with the others, old boy—the bloody baggage train, and the camp
followers . . . *tirones*, as Caesar Augustus calls them. But . . .
chiefly Otto, and his German auxiliaries, rather than the QM and
his acolytes—they *have* to follow us, being allegedly part of the
British army. But Otto . . . everyone's nightmare is that he will
suddenly fade away and go native—maybe even decamp to the
Russian Zone, to do even better business, maybe."

Fred blinked. "The Russian Zone?"

"Uh-huh." Audley nodded. "It's not far away, you know. North-
south, that's a long way; but west-east . . . that's not really so
far, if you know the right highways." Another nod. "Of course,
you've got to be able to handle them—the Russkies. But they're
quite extraordinarily amenable to the right stimulus, apparently." Another nod. Then a shrug. "Same with the French—they're
really buddy-buddy with the Germans. That is, with the Germans
who know their business, and what's what. . . . The French are
what they call 'pragmatic,' you see, Fred. *Pragmatique*—is that
the word?"

Fred frowned. "What?"

Audley's expression changed as he looked down the line of
vehicles that had been parked nose-to-tail under the silver
birches, alongside which the northbound convoy had come to
rest.

"Captain Audley!" What Audley had actually been looking at
was a figure that had issued out of the parallel lines, who was
striding towards them now. "Captain Audley, *sah!*"

"Mr. Levin"—Audley blinked—"I d-d-don't think you've h-had

the p-p-p . . . *opportunity* . . . of properly meeting Major Fat-torini, who was with us during last night's adventure?"

"Sah!" RSM Levin was at once very Jewish, but also a very British Army RSM: compact and immaculate and confident, and in his prime: Joshua, strong in battle but with a hint of Joseph, with Pharaoh's civil service at his command. "With your permission . . . *sah!*"

"Mr. Levin?" Simultaneously (although also informed by what Audley had said in the past), Fred didn't like RSM Levin, but was also a little afraid of him.

"With your permission, sah." Levin fixed him for an instant, and then dismissed him. "Captain Audley is to report to the colonel, sir"—the basilisk eye came back to Fred—"and you are to travel with Driver Hewitt, as of now, in alternative transport . . . *sah!*"

"Thank you, Mr. L-L-L . . ." Audley curled his tongue round the consonant impotently, nodding his head like an idiot.

"Thank you, Mr. Levin." Fred wondered, and not for the first time, whether Audley's impediment was nervous or deliberate. But more than that, he knew that he must put Mr. Levin firmly in his place now, or he would be lost forever. "When I've finished with Captain Audley . . . then I shall expect Driver Hewitt to find me . . . here—here, right?"

RSM Levin's square blue-black chin came up aggressively, almost arrogantly, with the thin lips above it tight, as though he well understood the nature of this deliberate challenge to his authority. "Sah! But, if I may—"

"Thank you, Mr. Levin." Fred concentrated his failing courage on the RSM's well-shaved chin, aware that his own chin was undoubtedly stubbly, and even Audley's ugly boxer's-face had its own juvenile fuzz too.

And that poor dead bastard, from last night. The black frothy blood had dribbled down through several days' razorless growth, blond and colorless as the pale eyelashes and eyebrows above the glazing dead eyes in that final moment of truth.

"Thank you, Mr. Levin." As he repeated the words he concentrated on Audley. "Now, David—as you were saying?"

"Y-Yes . . ." Audley blinked and wrinkled his nose nervously, contriving to remind Fred of nothing so much as an enormous and terrified rabbit as the RSM stood his ground beside him.

"With respect, sah—" There was no respect in the RSM's tone, only cold certainty. But then he stopped.

"*Hullo there!*" Amos de Souza's voice came sweetly to the ear as the distant trumpets of any relieving force to a doomed garrison.

"Morning, Freddie, David . . . Mr. Levin. Is there some sort of problem?"

"No." In turning towards his rescuer Fred was careful not to show relief. "No problem at all. Mr. Levin was just relaying information about my transport, that's all."

It was curious—now he could remember exactly the end of his dream: how the men had always hated stooking until the very end, when there was only a narrow strip of uncut corn left in the center of the field, because then they could stop stooking and pick up sticks, and chase the poor terrified rabbits that had been driven back and back until forced at the last to break cover or be cut to bloody ribbons by the binder's knife-blades. . . . Only this time, in his dream, there had not been rabbits, but wild boars in the corn; and also, striding through the stubble, there had come not the farmer, but Colonel Colbourne and RSM Levin, both dressed in civilian tweeds, yet with their medals at the breast.

"That's all. . . . Thank you, Mr. Levin. I shall look for Driver Hewitt as soon as I've finished talking to Captain Audley . . . and the adjutant."

No one enlarged on that for a moment. Then the RSM saluted de Souza smartly and strode away, stiff-backed. And for another moment, no one enlarged on that, either.

"Phew!" murmured Audley finally.

"Oh, yes . . ." De Souza looked from one to the other, more philosophically than expecting a straight answer. "So what mischief have you two been up to, then? Not annoying Mr. Levin, I hope?"

"G-Good Lord, no!" Audley relaxed like a schoolboy. "P-p-p . . . *perish* the thought, Amos!" Then he straightened up belatedly. "Actually, Amos—"

"The truth, please." De Souza shook his head. "Come on, young David—I have to run this Fred Karno's outfit . . . one way or another—the truth, please."

"Of course!" Audley was plainly delighted by this unwise admission of weakness. "I was just going to tell you—"

"Yes, Amos." Fred overruled the boy sharply. "I was. And I'm sorry."

"Yes?" De Souza raised a hand to silence Audley, without looking at him. "What happened?"

"Nothing, really." Also without looking at the young man Fred understood the problem the boy represented: brains and over-promoted youthful arrogance, and immaturity, plus a tongue like a cowbell, would not endear him to an RSM with no other subalterns to bully. "I rather think the RSM was pulling rank . . . or pushing it, if you like." He shrugged. "But I was tired, so

145

when he pushed, I pushed back, I'm afraid." As always, honesty eased his conscience. "It wasn't necessary. But I did—and I'm sorry, Amos."

"Yes . . . you will be—huh!" There was no sympathy in Audley's murmur. "Busy Izzy's a bad enemy—as I can testify from bitter experience, by golly!"

"Shut up, David." De Souza didn't bother to look at Audley. "That's fair enough, Freddie—take no notice of that. Levin's a good man."

But that wasn't all, Fred sensed. "He is?"

"Actually, yes." De Souza accepted his doubt. "He knows his duty, and he does it."

That still wasn't all. So Fred waited for more.

De Souza nodded. "He was with the CO in the desert. Hence his DCM. That was at Alam Halfa. When things weren't so good."

From de Souza that was no small accolade, that understatement. But it still wasn't what the major wanted to say. And that whetted Fred's appetite even more. "Yes?"

"All your service has been in Italy, hasn't it?" Beneath the innocent inquiry there was a curious hesitancy, almost embarrassment. "And in Greece, of course—as we all know!"

What the hell did that mean? Of course they all bloody well knew!

"For God's sake, Amos!" Having been hopping and twitching and chafing on the sideline, like a reserve in a losing game, Audley exploded suddenly. "Levin's a swine, for God's sake! So—"

"*Shut up, David!*" De Souza's snarl was as uncharacteristic as his hesitancy, with its suddenly undisguised anger glowing red now.

"Sorry!" From trying to push himself into the action, Audley shrank into himself. "Amos, I didn't m-m-mean—"

"*Shut up—*" De Souza caught his anger quickly. "I know you didn't mean to interrupt me. You just wanted to hear the sound of your own voice, that's all." He disengaged himself from Audley. "As I was attempting to say, Freddie . . . we were pulled out of Greece pretty soon after you happened to cross our path, and we ended up more or less attached to Eighth Corps in their final advance. Between Hanover and Hamburg, we were. . . . And you've heard of the concentration camps, obviously—eh?"

"Yes." He sensed de Souza wanted him to say more than that. "Of course we did. We heard they were . . . pretty disgusting."

"Pretty disgusting?" De Souza stared at him. "Yes . . . well, let's just say they were worse than anything you care to imagine and leave it at that, shall we?" He drew breath. "And Mr. Levin had the back luck to run into this particular camp, at Bergen-

Belsen, near Celle, where most of the poor devils were Jews, you see. There were others there: resistance prisoners from all over, and quite a few Russians . . . and Germans, too—politicals and the like. And even the odd Englishman and American, by courtesy of the Gestapo. But most of them were Jews. And as young David here has no doubt reminded you so tactfully, Mr. Levin is a Jew." He cocked his head slightly. "An acting warrant officer, Class I, late Queen's Own South London Rifles. Holder of the Distinguished Conduct Medal. Religion, Jewish. Do you see?"

"Yes." All this time, though really without consciously thinking about it, Fred had been conditioned by Amos de Souza's languid Brigade of Guards drawl, pink complexion, and pale-brown hair. But however English and C of E he was now, his ancestors could well have been Portuguese immigrants, as Jewish as the original Italian Fattorinis. "I see, yes."

"Do you?" De Souza's mouth twisted slightly. "Our much esteemed brigadier, whom you did of course meet so briefly in Greece . . . *he* has ordered us to cultivate a proper soldierly sense of detachment, if not proportion, now that it has fallen to us to obtain particular Germans, safe and sound and in mint condition for his collection. But that is more difficult for some than for others . . . so I would appreciate it if you exercised a certain tolerance—toleration?—with regard to Mr. Levin's irascibility, Freddie . . . d'you see?"

Fred nodded. "Yes, sir. Point taken."

"Excellent." De Souza smiled at last. "*Now* . . . what I have done in your case, Freddie . . . so that you can maybe make up for lost hours of sleep on the way north, to our home billet, is to give you both Captain Audley's private transport *and* Captain Audley's favorite driver, whom you know—who collected you at the airfield, indeed. Driver Hewitt, no less. . . . And *you*, young David, for your sins . . . *you* will reinforce Corporal Keys's escort, when the CO is finished with you—okay?" De Souza shared his gentle smile between them. "Whilst I . . . *I* will attend to the undoubted disagreement which is almost certainly even now developing between Mr. Levin and Herr Schild over the contents of Herr Schild's three-tonner"—the last words were delivered over de Souza's shoulder as he departed—"and you may both wish me the best of British luck, for I shall need it."

Fred watched the adjutant's departing back (which, irritatingly, was still immaculately pressed, battle-dress blouse pleats and trousers separated by a newly blancoed belt with glittering brasses, in spite of their wet and disastrous night and an uncomfortable morning). Then he heard Audley stuttering beside him.

"What?" He had to be ready for the boy's recriminations.

"I s-said 'b-b-b-*bullshit.*'" Audley got it out at last.

"What?" It irked him that Audley presumed to criticize a better man.

"*Bullshit!*" Having mastered the word once, the boy repeated it vehemently. "He was rotting you—about Busy Izzy . . . *bullshitting you,* Amos was—Amos, of all people! God! It makes me sick, I tell you!"

"Why should he do that?" All Fred wanted to do now was to find Driver Hewitt, not explore David Audley's juvenile prejudices.

"God knows! Guilt, most likely."

"Guilt?" In spite of his preoccupation with trying to spot his driver among the vehicles, Fred caught up the word. "Guilt?"

"Oh, yes—guilt." Audley nodded. "There's a lot of it about, since they found the camps. But it takes different forms with different people. We had some chaps who just wanted to shoot up the Germans indiscriminately—not just the SS and Gestapo, but anything that moved. Made 'em feel better, apparently. But Amos isn't that sort, of course."

Fred frowned. "But he's not . . . Jewish?"

"Amos? Good Lord, no! Amos is RC—high-class old Catholic. Talks about '*taking mahss,*' and all that." Audley grinned momentarily, but then erased the grin quickly. "With some of them—like the Crocodile—it's guilt because they know they're actually anti-Semitic themselves, basically. So they have to take a hard line now, because they've a sneaking suspicion that if God had made them German they might have ended up with two lightning flashes on their collars. But with Amos . . . with him I think it's the feeling that we ought to have done something more positive to stop it. Or maybe he thinks the pope should have done something—I don't know. . . . But he did once say—to the Old Croc, he said it, too—'We are to blame. Perhaps even more that the Germans themselves.' I heard him say it."

It was a novel concept of war guilt, thought Fred. "How are we to blame, David?"

"God knows! He clammed up after that. So you'd better ask him, old boy." Audley shrugged. "But what *I* know is that Busy Izzy was a bad tempered, officious, bullying, d-d-double c-c-c-crossing, twenty-four-carat *shit* long before we crossed the Rhine—long before he and the CO went into Belsen, not to put too fine a point on it." He fixed an eye on Fred suddenly. "And don't get any ideas about *me* being anti-Semitic. Because I'm bloody not!" The brutal chin lifted. "My regiment had Jews in it—including a damn good fullback named Isaacs, who got his silly head blown off in Normandy, as I told you—didn't I?" Audley blinked at him, and then shook his own unblown-off head and bared his teeth. "I did! But that doesn't mean I have to be nice to *Mister* Levin . . . who is one of God's—or Jehovah's—Gadarene swine."

Fred felt tired. And . . . although he conceded within himself that young Audley was an intriguing youth, in spite of all his defects (which must certainly be a sore trial to Amos de Souza) . . . far too tired now to argue the toss, about the Jews and the Germans, never mind RSM Levin, anyway.

"Oughtn't I to be finding Driver Hewitt, David?" He took the coward's way out, disdaining to remind the boy that he himself, although C of E, came from an old Jewish family too.

"Yes. Perhaps you ought." Audley looked around, reaching up to his full height from his normally slightly-hunched stance . . . which must, thought Fred, offend RSM Levin every time he glimpsed it. "And I ought to be finding Caesar Augustus, too, I suppose." The big chest expanded, and Audley's height increased another inch with it. *"HUGHIE! Where are you!"*

Silence. High above the line of vehicles Fred saw the silver birch leaves shiver in a breath of wind against the gray sky.

"He's out there somewhere—brewing tea and smoking his eternal dog-end . . . and probably watching us." Audley's chest expanded again.

"DRIVER HEWITT! LET'S BE HAVING YOU!"

More silence. Then—

"SIR!" The answer came as a muted cry of recognition.

Audley sniffed. "He's even now dodging round the back somewhere, so he can pretend he's been looking for you. Wait and see!"

Fred followed Audley's glance and saw a diminutive figure straighten up at the farthest end of the line of vehicles.

"Sir! Mr. Audley—Captain Audley—coming!"

Fred observed the figure critically, recalling Driver Hewitt's well-pressed turnout at the airfield. "He seems remarkably . . . smart." In fact when he thought about it, he had never seen such a well-pressed and blancoed and polished RASC driver.

"Oh, yes"—Audley drew breath—"you can thank Mr. Levin for that, if for nothing else. . . . Where the hell have you been, Hugie?"

Driver Hewitt came to attention. "Attending to your vehicle, Mr. Audley—*Captain* Audley—*sir!*" Hewitt rolled an eye at Fred. "Or . . . Major Fat—Fatto—Fattor*ini's* vehicle . . . sir!"

"Oh, yes." Audley hunched up again. "Well, then . . . you look after both of them now, right?"

"Both of them?" The eye rolled back at Audley.

149

"Yes." Audley sighed. "For Christ's sake, Hughie. You know that I intend to take that little car back to England somehow. So I want it all in one piece, remember?" He bent over the little man, driving home his point with a single raised finger that stopped one inch from Hewitt's nose. "Any damage to it will result in reciprocal damage to *you*, Hughie—right?" Then he straightened up, grinning at Fred with a suddenly disarming youthfulness. "Not to mention any damage to Major Fattorini. . . . You are to ensure, rather, that he has a few hours' undisturbed rest, en route to Schwarzenburg. Those are the adjutant's exact orders. Because he hasn't had a proper kip since he left the isles of Greece, where burning Sappho loved and sung"—he swung back towards Hewitt as he spoke—*"right?"*

"Sir!" Driver Hewitt's wizened monkey-face remained impassive, but he infused the acknowledgment with the weariness of the old soldier long accustomed to being patronized and talked down to by young officers who didn't know any better, but who were nonetheless useful to him.

"Good." Such implicit wisdom was lost on Audley. "Well, Fred . . . I suppose I must go to receive my wigging from the headmaster. And you'd better wish me something better than the best of British luck now. Because I expect Busy Izzy has sneaked to him about us both by now. . . . So I expect it's the Fourteenth Army for me—*Burma*, here I come!"

They both watched the young dragoon depart, slouched for the first few steps—*however had he fitted all those long bones into a tank?* wondered Fred; *but at least he wasn't still carrying his umbrella to judgment!*—and then suddenly he straightened up as though he felt their eyes on him—*shoulders back! Swing those arms! Go take your medicine, David Audley!*

Driver Hewitt chuckled throatily beside him, below him. And then checked the chuckle, turning it into a controlled cough, and swallowed the sound and the phlegm together.

"What was that, Hewitt?" In any sort of conventional unit, Driver Hewitt's considered opinions wouldn't have mattered. But this was not any sort of conventional unit, and it was quite outside his military experience. For a start, it seemed to have more chiefs than Indians . . . or, as a private soldier of the Royal Army Service Corps, Driver Hewitt was an exception of the rule that had promoted both Audley and himself, anyway. "What was that you said?"

Driver Hewitt swallowed again, suggesting to Fred that in the absence of Major Fattorini he would have cleared his throat and spat. "Nothing, *sir!*"

The little man's sudden diplomacy, in contradiction to his

chuckle and when taken with his lack of promotion, convinced Fred that he needed Driver Hewitt on his side, if not Colonel Colbourne and RSM Levin, if he was ever to discover what was happening. But also (what he had on his side, which he surely didn't have with the colonel and the RSM) he had a moment's choice—whether to pull rank, because presumably, he could make Hewitt's life hell now, or ingratiate himself (as he had never done before with an Other Rank; but he had never been in this peculiar situation before).

"He's a caution, Mr. Audley is! Or . . . *Captain* Audley, as I should say now . . . *sir!*" Hewitt confided in him suddenly.

"A caution?" Fred took Driver Hewitt's gift of confidence in him as an Understanding Officer as his cue, breaking all his established rules. "Come on, Hughie—now is he 'a caution,' eh?"

The Hewitt eye rolled at him again, but this time appraising him much more shrewdly for a moment, and then blanking out. "You 'ad some trouble last night, after I put you orf in the middle of nowhere—yes, sir?"

Men like Hewitt always knew everything, so there was no harm in admitting the truth. "We took a prisoner, though."

"So you did! An' I saw Jacko Devenish wiv 'im, wiv a blanket over 'is 'ead—fair enough!" Hewitt agreed quickly. "But I also 'eard tell there was a man shot down right in front uv you—ain't that the truth—so you lost one of 'em again?"

Not quite everything, then. "Again?"

"Aye! Jus' like the last time!" Hewitt looked up at him unblinkingly. "An' Mr. Audley got a rollicking for that, too. . . . Though it weren't 'is fault, as I can testify. 'Cause I were there that time, sir."

There was one hell of a lot he didn't know about Colonel Colbourne's operations, thought Fred bitterly. But then he remembered Greece, and the indirect road to Delphi. "Do you mean . . . in Greece, Hughie?"

"In Greece?" Driver Hewitt looked around shiftily, as though he had momentarily forgotten where he was. "Yes, in Greece, that would be, like you said." When the look reached Fred again it had become one of pristine innocence. "But we ought to be goin' now—if you want to get your 'ead down, like Mr. Audley an' the adjutant wants you to, eh?"

This wasn't the moment to push his luck, Fred decided. Not only because Driver Hewitt wasn't quite ready to be pushed, but also because there were engines revving up along the double line of transport that had gathered here, coming both from the hunting lodge and the Roman fort. Colonel Colbourne's command was now united and in retreat, out of the American Zone and into somewhere safer, which that engine noise indicated.

151

"Of course!" He stretched his shoulders and yawned theatrically. But then, as he did so, he also saw his opening instinctively: either from self-interest or inclination, Driver Hewitt was David Audley's man, so that was his way in. "But . . . you're sure there's nothing we can do to help Captain Audley?"

"Captain Audley?" Driver Hewitt glanced down the line. "Cor! You don't need to worry about '*im*! 'E's as artful as a cartload uv monkeys when 'e's up against it . . . an' . . . *'e's also a friend uv the brigadier's—Brigadier Clinton hisself!*" Driver Hewitt accompanied that last confidence with a shameless theatrical wink as he started to follow his own finger. " 'E was born to be 'anged— not *posted!*"

Well . . . there was the truth, pure and unvarnished as only an RASC driver could impart it, thought Fred. The anomaly of young Audley's presence here, among his elders and betters, could be explained as simply as that: *he had influence!* "Come on, then!" Driver Hewitt gestured urgently and disappeared in a gap between two of the vehicles.

Fred skipped after him smartly into the gap as he observed the reason for the little man's urgency approaching in the distance: Colonel Colbourne was waving a finger at Captain Audley, who for once seemed to be keeping his mouth shut, with the RSM just behind him. And he felt a slight pang of conscience as he did so, but then allowed himself to be consoled by Driver Hewitt's judgment of the young man's ability to defend himself, added to the boy's special relationship with Brigadier Clinton. And besides, as a new boy himself, what could he do, anyway?

More engines started up—and Hewitt was beckoning him into another gap—and there, sure enough, was another argument in progress. He glimpsed Major McCorquodale addressing an imperturbable Amos de Souza while, so it seemed, shaking his fist at Otto Schild, at the adjutant's shoulder, and a Schild now British from the waist down, in battle-dress trousers, boots, and gaiters, and German from waist up, in a badgeless Wehrmacht jacket and forage cap. Better to avoid that encounter, too!

On the furthest side of the two lines of vehicles, under the dripping branches (and presumably, discreetly avoiding both those disagreements) there were several other officers, whom he vaguely remembered from the night before, and two or three NCOs beside their transport.

"Mornin', Freddie" and "Hullo there, Freddie"—they seemed to know him better than he knew them; and the NCOs straightened up as he passed them; and the smartness of everyone's turnout made him feel crumpled and shabby. What was not least tatalizing about this unit was its mixture of extreme eccentricity

and positively regimental smartness. Even little Hewitt, marching stiff and straight ahead of him now, as though on a parade
ground, was blancoed and polished and well-pressed—and that,
with an RASC old sweat, was a commentary on Mr. Levin's
standards that aroused admiration and incredulity equally.

" 'Ere we are!" Hewitt presented Captain Audley's vehicle
without a hint of apology. "It don't look much. But it's what they
call in the motor trade 'a nice little runner.' "

What struck Fred first was the question of how Captain Audley
ever fitted himself into such a small car; although, to be fair, the
fact that it was parked in long summer grass that almost came up
to its windows, and between two monstrous ten-tonners that
diminished it further, belittled it cruelly.

"It's what Jerry called the People's Car." Driver Hewitt patted
the little car's sloping hood through the grass. "Before the war
'itler promised 'em they'd all 'ave one like this—an' took their
money. But uv course 'e didn't divvy up—'e just took their money
an' scarpered with it. An' what you've probably seen is the army
version, what they called a *kooblewaggon*, wiv no top to it"—he
looked up at Fred—"like, it was their jeep, wot the Yanks give
us." He returned to the car, patting its sloping roof affectionately.
"But this is the real thing, like a proper car. An' Major M'Crocodile sez this is one uv the very first wot they built, the Jerries
did"—pat-pat—"wiv a lovely little air-cooled engine in the back,
'orizontally opposed, what starts up a treat, no matter 'ow 'ot or
'ow cold it is . . . A little bloody marvel, is what this is. If you
can get inside it, that is. We 'ave to take a shoe 'orn to get Mr.
David in it, if there's anyone in the back there—wiv 'is knees up
under 'is chin. But 'e likes it, all same, 'e does."

Fred bent down to look inside. "He does?"

"But we ain't takin' anyone in the back." Driver Hewitt
reassured him quickly. "That's Mr. David's—Captain Audley's—
kit in there. An' yours too—all cleaned an' pressed by Trooper
Lucy last night, while you were busy—don't you worry, sir!" Now
he looked Fred up and down critically. "An' if we get time, along
the road, we can maybe change you up before"—he blinked, the
wizened features contorting suddenly—"*before* we gets to the
Schwartzenburg for dinner, like, tonight." He looked away, up
and down the lines, along where the men who had greeted them
earlier were now mounting up, high above them. " 'Cause we've
got a long drive ahead uv us, round about . . . if they 'aven't
repaired that bridge what's fallen down, by the viaduct at
München-what's-it, on the river there?" He came back to Fred. "If
you'd get in then, right?" He opened the car door, pulling it
against the tall grass.

There was a curious odor inside the tiny vehicle, like nothing he could put an origin to, which made him sniff interrogatively as he searched for its source.

"You don't want to worry about that smell." Driver Hewitt got in much more easily behind the wheel. "That was from last night, when Otto was making 'is deliveries in it. I think 'e may 'ave 'ad somethink that was startin' to go *orf* a bit, maybe." Hewitt sniffed himself. "But then a lot of 'is meat, it ain't right until it's been 'ung a few days—like pheasants an' rabbits an' such. They 'ave to be goin' *orf* before they're just right—*here we go!*"

The engine whirred somewhere behind them, firing immediately against the roar of the lorries' engines, and the blue clouds ahead of them.

"There! What did I say?" Hewitt squirmed in his seat. "You little beauty, you!" He turned to Fred. "Got enough room, then?"

It was all too much. Too much after yesterday, too much after yesterday evening . . . and far, far too much after last night. And even too much after what had been left of last night, running into this morning . . . which was also too much. "Yes."

Somebody banged on the roof, half an inch from his head.

Driver Hewitt shouted unintelligibly in answer, and Fred glimpsed a figure passing on up the line beyond them.

"*Aarrgh!*" Driver Hewitt turned to him again. "Good to be movin' again—that's what I like! An' 'specially now!"

"Why especially now?" The little man's relief invited the question.

"We bin up to somethink dodgy, don'tcha know?" Hewitt's hand rotated the gear lever in anticipation. "Don'tcha know?"

What Fred knew was that Driver Hewitt knew a lot more than he did, even now. And what he didn't know he was well placed to guess at. But he needed leading on, all the same. "We're still in the American Zone, are we?"

"Too bloody right!" The lorry ahead shuddered for a moment, and then lurched forward. "Come on, you big bugger, come on!"

That confirmed his suspicions. "You've been down here before, have you?"

"Too bloody right!" Driver Hewitt advanced the little car in the wake of the lorry. "We've bin all over—up an' down, in an' out—we've bin there! Arsk no questions, an' I'll tell you no lies. *That's* where we bin." A half-grown bush sprang up behind the lorry, and Hewitt swung the wheel to avoid it. "But now we're runnin', an' it'll be back roads, wiv no questions arsked at roadblocks by soddin' great Yank MPs swingin' their truncheons likes they own the place. I 'ates them . . . almost as much as I 'ates the Redcaps, what never done an honest day's work in their lives, let alone a day's soldierin'. But the Major—Major Amos—'e knows 'ow to deal wiv the Redcaps. They don't bother *'im* none." The little man pronounced his accolade with relish. Only then he shook his head. "But the Yanks is different, I tell you." Another shake. "Wouldn't want *them* pokin' around."

"Poking around . . . where?"

Hewitt nodded towards the ten-tonner that bumped up and down over the ruined road surface ahead of them. "Inside there, for a start—inside that 'ippo."

"Ippo?" Hewitt might, or might not, know all about "Corporal Keys." But Fred hadn't seen the German get into the lorry.

"Leyland 'ippo—one uv the new ones they was bringing over last year, the Mark Two. For long-distance 'eavy work, like." Driver Hewitt lapsed suddenly into uncharacteristic professionalism. "The Mark One 'ad an open cab. So you got boiled or froze in it—or drownded. But that's a Mark Two—'fact, it's a Two A—see them dual tires on the back? Six-in-line soddin' diesel, what I never liked. But we've got some proper mechanics, thank Gawd! Not to mention Major Kenworthy, 'oo's a bloody marvel wiv any sort of engine. . . . An' it's 'im as filled it up this time, I shouldn't wonder—see 'ow 'eavy it's loaded. . . . 'Cause 'e was out the night before last wiv some 'eavy liftin' gear, too. So 'e's got somethink dodgy in there, too."

Fred sorted Major Kenworthy out from the dozen or so officers to whom he had been finally and briefly introduced after dinner. The hunting and fishing major had been . . . Carver-Hart— Johnnie Carver-Hart? And there had been a thin-faced, darkhaired KRRC major . . . but he had been Liddell? And then a roly-poly-faced one—but he had been Ingrams, with an oak-leaf mention on his European ribbon.

"Major Kenworthy?" Everything Audley had let slip suggested that Colonel Colbourne's Band of Brothers were collectors of men, even before last night's raid. But one didn't need a Leyland Hippo Mark 2A to transport human cargo.

"Wiv the spectales," explained Hewitt simply. "Now . . . can I arsk you somethink, if I may?"

"Ah!" Small, bespectacled, and donnish-looking—and with no regimental or corps identification: Major Kenworthy! "What? Yes, of course." He looked at Hewitt expectantly. "Ask away, Hewitt."

"Ah . . ." The little engine in the back whirred as Hewitt shifted down, as the lorry ahead of them labored up a slight incline in the midst of another tract of birches. "What's 'reciprocal'? An' 'oo's Sappho—Sappho was it? The one that loves an' sings, anyway?"

A wave of tiredness engulfed Fred momentarily. But he mustn't sleep yet. "'Reciprocal' means . . . 'equal'—'equal in return,' you might say." He struggled for another moment to find a better definition, but then decided against it. "And Sappho is . . . or was . . . a Greek poet, Hewitt. A female one."

"A lady poet—a girl, is that?" The little man persisted.

"Yes." The problem of defining Sappho further sorely taxed him. "At least . . . she was a girl a long time ago—two or three thousand years ago. And she preferred women to men then, actually, Hewitt."

"*Aarrgh!* I *knew* it!" The little man breathed out in relief.

"Knew what?" The lorry reared up dangerously ahead. "Steady, man!"

"I knew 'e didn't know no girls in Greece—Mr. David didn't." Hewitt braked sharply. "'E didn't 'ave no time, see—I didn't think."

"No?"

"*Naow!* An' 'e wouldn't 'ave known what to do, anyway—'e don't know nothink about girls, except in 'is books . . . so 'e's shy wiv them, see." Hewitt screwed up his face sideways at Fred. "We 'ad some Queen Alexandra's nurses come to the Schwartzenburg one night, what 'ad lost their way. So they was in for dinner, an' one uv 'em was sittin' next to 'im—a real cracker. . . . See, I was waiterin' that night, 'cause Otto was short'anded. . . . An' 'e 'adn't a word to say for hisself—would you believe it?—not a word!"

"No?" The idea of David Audley wordless in any circumstances was hard to accept. But there was more to this surprising confidence than that. "Indeed?" He nodded encouragingly.

"*Aarrgh!* But that don't mean 'e don't need watchin'—no!" Hewitt warmed to his subject without needing any stimulus. "More like, 'e needs *more* watching—'specially now, see."

"'Specially now—" Fred echoed him automatically, "is that so?"

"Oh, yes." Hewitt nodded back. "You bin in Greece. But there's still *men* in Greece. Not like 'ere—'ere all the men's POWs now. We got millions of 'em. An' the Yanks got millions. An' the Russians 'as got millions of 'em, Gawd 'elp 'em!" He grinned unsympathetically. "*An' we've got all the girls!*"

Fred felt a frown was required. "But . . . I thought there were strict regulations against fraternization, Hewitt? In fact, there are—"

"Reg'lations." The little man chuckled. "Cor! I ain't never 'eard of any reg'lation that 'ud keep soldiers orf of women—'specially when the women are 'ungry . . . an' 'ungry for food, as well as

for men—an' for soap, an' for fags, wot they can buy food wiv."
This time the repeated chuckle was mirthless. "You want to talk
to Otto, Major Fattorini, sir. A bar of soap, an' a packet of Players
or Luckies . . . an' a nice bar of chocolate or an 'ershey bar . . .
an' you can take yer pick. An' this is only the beginnin', too. We
'aven't bin 'ere but a few months—they ain't bin *really* 'ungry an'
cold yet. But that'll come, you see—that'll come!"

He had seen it already in Italy of course, thought Fred. But that
had at least been under pressure of war, and battle and murder
and sudden death, which was a pretty bloody good excuse as well
as an explanation. But . . . but now he was being naive and
childish—and something more (or worse) than that after his own
Athenian experience, courtesy of Colonel Kyriakos Michaelides.

Well! But—

"*Aarrgh!* I can 'ear what you're thinkin'!" Driver Hewitt caught
him cruelly. " 'E's an *orrficer*—an' a captain, too! An' a gentleman—an' a scholar, maybe?"

"No." Hewitt had picked up that phrase from Audley himself
most likely, if not from Amos de Souza. "I wasn't thinking that at
all, actually."

"No?" Newly promoted majors of engineers answering stiffly
didn't disconcert Driver Hewitt one bit. "Well, I bet a pound a
pinch uv—a pinch uv *snuff*—that you wasn't thinking uv old
Greek lady poets, sir—right on?"

"No . . . no, I wasn't, Hughie." Fred decided simultaneously
that he would lie to Driver Hewitt while ingratiating himself
with that diminutive. "I was just thinking that everything David
Audley has told me about you is true, actually. And he's a
gentleman and a scholar, as you say."

"Oh, yes?" Hewitt liked that, quite evidently. Because, of
course, it signaled that he had another officer and gentleman in
the bag. And yet also that didn't perhaps do Driver Hewitt
absolute justice, either. " 'E's a caution, is wot I knows."

"Yes." The problem was, they were on delicate ground now.
Or . . . not on ground at all . . . but very thin ice, over deep
cold water. "You've been with Captain Audley long, have you?"

"Since last year, sir." The ice creaked with that warningly
repeated "sir." "Just about this time, it was—August."

August was Normandy, near enough. "In France, that would
be?"

This time Hewitt didn't reply instantly. "Beg pardon, sir?"

In Normandy, August 1944, Audley would have been how old—
nineteen? With maybe two years military service, and a qualified
tank commander . . . and maybe never kissed a girl, other than
his mother (who wasn't a girl) and his sister (if he had a sister;

157

but who still didn't qualify, anyway); and now he was in Germany, anno Domini 1945 (or A.U.C. whatever-it-was), where girls were to be had from Otto Schild for a bar of soap and a packet of Players Medium Navy Cut and a bar of ration chocolate (all three together? Or individually? He wasn't sure of the rate of exchange yet, anyway)—

"Fraternization reg'lations don't apply to *us,* sir." Hewitt changed the subject quite out of the blue. "Or . . . not to the orfficers of this unit. They 'ave the right to . . . to *in*terrogate former enemy persons, *oo*soever an' *where*soever"—the precision as well as the emphasis of the wording indicated its official source—"as may be necessary in the course uv their duties—their duties"—the little man's memory betrayed him for a second— " 'aving the appropriate orders an' authority thereto, all signed an' sealed, like—" Hewitt gave up the unequal struggle there, aware that he was obviously extemporizing the incantation now, and that Major Fattorini must know he was, and he changed gear and accelerated.

So he wasn't going to get any more about Audley, Fred understood. Even, he had already got more than he had any right to expect. But then . . . *who the hell cared about David Audley? That wasn't what he'd been after at all!*

"I think I'll try and get some sleep now." He stretched his legs as best he could, knowing that there was too much in the back of the little car to permit any more room; but at least he wasn't right next to that *whirring* engine! "Wake me up when we get to . . . wherever it is . . . okay?"

"Right!" Hewitt settled back comfortably himself, like the old soldier he was.

Out of the corner of his eye, Fred saw the trees—delicately leafed birch branches and dark, uncompromising evergreens, rocket-stiff—swim past, against a gray sky.

One last try, perhaps.

"What's Major Kenworthy got in the Hippo then, d'you think?" He tried to sound sleepy and not-very-interested.

Once again, no instant reply. "I'm sure I can't say, sir." Pause. "Major Kenworthy . . . 'e likes gadgets, an' bits an' bobs of machinery—'eavy stuff."

Heavy stuff.

People were *light stuff.* You didn't need a Hippo to carry off people. Although . . . *that poor devil, last night, when he was dead . . . he'd seemed heavy, even though there was nothing of him, really. But then the dead were always heavy—heavy and awkward, as though they objected to going and were set on causing*

*as much trouble as they could to the living, if it was the last thing
they did . . . which of course it was.*

Kenworthy: that was his ten-tonner—his Leyland Hippo Mark
2A—making heavy weather of every dip and undulation, with the
weight of its contents. . . .

Kenworthy, Liddell, Ingrams, Carver-Hart, Simpson—*Simpkins?*—Simpkins . . . McCrocodile—*M'Corquodale, damn it!* And
then Macallister—*not Macalligator, mustn't say that!*—and then
Colbourne, de Souza, and Audley (that was easy, like learning the
dates of the kings and queens of England, which mathematicians
always had trouble with, by some perverse illogic: 1066–1087;
1087–1100; 1100–1135 . . . the Normans were easy, and the
Stuarts and the Hanoverians too, later . . . 1714–1727; 1727–
1760—*"George the Third remarked with a smile/ There are seven-
teen-sixty yards in a mile"*—but the Plantagenets and the Wars of
the Roses lot were confusing . . . not like Colbourne, de Souza,
and Audley!)

*Mustn't dream again. Must just go out like a light and sleep, with
no silly nightmares. Must remember that the war's almost over—
almost over—almost over and over and over—over here, if not out
there . . . and I'm over here, and not out there—ignoble thought!
Ignoble, sensible thought—sensible, ignoble thought—sensible, sensible thought.*

*Huge, amorphous nightmare: yawning great lorry, heavy-loaded
with inadequately secured Bailey bridge components, bouncing up
and down and shifting, because the silly bloody driver was exceeding
the speed restriction—must slow down, get off the road—get off the
road!*

Fred shook himself awake, with his mouth full of foul, leathery
tongue and empty-stomach taste, quite absurdly sorry for himself, and yet also ashamed of his overimagined horrors. Because
this wasn't Italy, the home of all Bailey bridges . . . *this was
Germany, of course!*

And it was doubly Germany, because there were trees everywhere—tall trees, rising up on every side, and ahead, as they
swung round a hairpin corner, with the engine whirring at his
back.

And no bloody great lorry, either. As they *whirred* round the
bend he saw the open road ahead, rising steeply—just a foul
dream—

What?

He sat bolt upright, and hit his head on the roof of the car—
ouch!

"How long have I been asleep?" He addressed the driver thickly, only realizing gratefully in the next second it was still Driver Hewitt in broad daylight, and not some grinning stranger whom he'd never met and couldn't remember.

"You've 'ad a right good sleep—quiet as a baby." Hewitt grinned at him encouragingly. "Your 'ead did knock against the side a bit . . . but it didn't seem to worry you none"—they came to the end of the straight stretch and Hewitt spun the wheel again, twisting the little car round another hairpin—"so I didn't think to wake you."

Fred squinted ahead, at another stretch of trees heavy with summer, and an open road still climbing ahead. And then turned quickly to peer out of the divided rear-window behind them.

They drew away from the corner, and the road behind was as empty as the road in front. "Where's the convoy?" His voice was still thick with sleep: he could hear it outside himself, beyond the eternal *whirring* of the engine, but without any other sound.

"Oh, we lost that—about ten miles back, before Detmold," replied Hewitt cheerfully. "I laid back for a bit, round Paderborn. The proper road's no good there jus' now . . . I think they're repairin' a bridge what's fallen down. . . . An' then I went like the clappers, an' I took the wrong turnin'. . . . But you don't need to worry none."

"I—what?" Words failed him.

"They knows the way." Hewitt agreed with himself. "They drove it enough times, so they oughta know it. An' we're spot on, like."

"Spot on?" He had control of his tongue and his senses at last. "Spot on *where*?"

Driver Hewitt spun the wheel again, with the same maddening nonchalance. "Up on top of the Two-toe-burger-*vald*—as they likes to call it. The Two-toe . . . *burg* . . . Woods, is what you and I'd say, though." The little man pointed. "See there?"

Something had flashed past Hewitt, outside the car just beyond the edge of the road in the trees as he spoke, diverting Fred's attention. It was a sculptured bust on a shaft of stone, it looked like. But it was gone before he could be sure.

"What the hell—?" He turned in the direction the little man had indicated, and the question stifled itself. But the trees were in the way. And there was another long tree-lined avenue ahead of them, but this time it wasn't empty. The rising avenue was blocked at its highest point by an immense monument, pillared and domed, and then surmounted by the gigantic statue of a warrior brandishing his sword far above the treetops.

"Hewitt"—the monument rose up higher and higher as they

approached it—"what the hell is that?" It wasn't actually the question he started to ask, but the thing was so enormous that it crowded out his original intention.

"Don't rightly know—don'tcha know, then?" For his part, the little man seemed to be quite unimpressed by the view, some of which was already disappearing above them through the restriction of the windshild. Rather, he seemed to be looking for somewhere to park in the wide empty circle round the monument's base. "One of the colonel's old Romans, would it be?"

Fred rubbed his eyes as the car came to a stop. He wasn't still dreaming, but he wished he were. And his mouth tasted of old unwashed socks.

"Ah! There 'e is!" Hewitt relaxed suddenly. Then he turned to Fred. "Orf you go then—look lively, now! The brigadier—'e don't like to be kept waitin', y'know."

CHAPTER TWO

Brigadier Clinton looked down on him from the top of a flight of steps leading up to a doorway in the monument, as from a great height.

"You look a bit rough, Major," he observed, unkindly but accurately.

Fred looked up at the Brigadier. "Yes, sir."

This, he thought, *is where I came in, continued from the Eve of Scobiemas last February, when we last met. Nothing much has changed since then, because I was looking pretty rough then—and I didn't know what the hell was happening then either, come to think of it!*

"As a matter of fact, I feel a bit rough, too." He brought down his saluting hand, which had at least done its job more smartly than his legs had performed on the way from the car, one foot having gone to sleep, inflicting agonizing pins and needles on him, while the muscles behind the opposite knee had contracted with some form of partial paralysis during the journey.

Then the thought expanded: *Rough I may be, but I never asked to be a rough major in this godforsaken place! So you must want Major Frederick Fattorni—must need him—far more than Captain*

Frederick Fattorini ever wanted or needed (or even expected) to exchange three perfectly respectable pips for this questionable crown.

He found himself glancing down sideways at his shoulder strap and rubbing his chin simultaneously. He not only hadn't had time to have that questionable crown replace those honest pips, but he also hadn't had time to shave, the rasp of stubble under his hand reminded him. And farther down, if there had ever been decent creases in this uniform, last night's rain and today's journey had obliterated them; and there was a muddy patch on the half-paralyzed knee, to remind him of how he had knelt beside a dying man—a man who had died for this man Clinton?

He looked up at the brigadier again. "It was a fairly rough night, actually, sir. One way or another."

"Yes. So I gather." The pale blue eyes fixed on him intently. "But also a successful one."

What was wrong with that voice? Fred now found himself absurdly rethinking the same nagging question that had quite uselessly weakened his concentration six months before, in the ruined monastery of Osios Konstandinos. The man's setting had changed (although the war had reached even this unlikely place: the stonework above was pitted and pockmarked with bullets or shell splinters, and the steps were littered with fragments), but that voice was the same—the same and somehow *wrong* . . . but how?

Absurd! "Yes, sir?" He heard Jacko Devenish's far more accurate and embittered formula—*If you say so, sir—I'm sure I don't know!*—inside his head. But majors couldn't say that to brigadiers on such short acquaintance, if ever, he decided.

The brigadier smiled an unsmiling smile at him, which his thin lips were ideally designed to do. "You don't really know what is happening, do you, Major?" He began to descend the steps, his boots crunching noisily on the stone fragments. "Or do you?" He stopped suddenly, still above Fred. "What do you think—and how much do you know? Tell me, eh?"

Fred envied Jacko Devenish, whose certain reply to such a dirty question would have been that neither had he joined up to think, nor did his rank entitle him to do so. But those escapes were not open to officers of field rank.

"Come on, Major!" The brigadier crunched down the last few steps. "Don't disappoint me."

Close up, he was surprisingly young—at least, for a brigadier. Mid-thirties, at a guess, no more. But much more than that— *much more*, thought Fred with a cold inward certainty—he was a damned, bloody dangerous character, who'd shop his mother without a second thought, and then buy drinks in the mess afterwards to celebrate.

"I was just thinking, sir—" Oddly enough, that certainty steadied him. But then again, not oddly at all: it was uncertainty that was unsteadying. The only thing that was odd was that he hadn't been more frightened at Osios Konstandinos. But then he had had Kyri with him, of course. And he had only been an innocent bystander, too.

"That's what I want you to do—go on!"

What was wrong with the voice was that it had no origins. It wasn't public school and Sandhurst (as he had a right to expect), or Oxbridge or BBC or Home Counties or Scottish or soft Irish (Welsh was not to be expected)—*it was from nowhere, by God!*

"I didn't mean that." He mustn't think anymore about that voice: it would only unsettle him again. "I was thinking about what a friend of mine once said—not so long ago, actually." As he smiled at the brigadier he felt his unwashed, unshaven face crinkle with the effort. "He advised me against getting mixed up with units like this one. He said I should stick to bridge building . . . and mine clearance and bomb disposal. Because that would be healthier for me, he said."

The brigadier looked at him expressionlessly for a long moment. Then quite unexpectedly the eyes disengaged, staring past him. *"YOU THERE!"*

The sound of the door of the People's Car opening was quickly succeeded by a boot-stamping sound. Driver Hewitt had to be actually standing to attention, that sound suggested, unlikely as it seemed.

"SIR?" The little man's reply came as a falsetto pig-squeal. "ME, SIR?"

The Brigadier drew a breath. *"CAN YOU SEE ANYONE ELSE HERE, DRIVER HEWITT?"*

"SIR!" The boots stamped again.

"Now . . ." The brigadier smiled his smile at Fred again, stepping forward as he did so until he was alongside him, and then draping a friendly arm across his shoulders. "We shall walk a little way, and—and *kindly* don't pull away from me, Major . . . I have no contagious or infectious disease, I do assure you—*relax*, if you please."

"No, sir." If the brigadier had struck him, Fred would have been less astonished, so that it took a considerable effort of will to simulate even partial relaxation. "Yes, sir."

"'Freddie' is how my inmates address me"—the brigadier steered Fred with an iron hand—"and that is what you call me in the mess tonight, when we meet again—do you understand, Major?"

"Yes, sir." Fred had the impression that he wasn't being steered back towards the car, but obliquely to it. "But . . . that will maybe be a bit confusing."

"Confusing?" The brigadier's head came closer. "How so?"

Fred swallowed. "There's a move . . . to call me 'Freddie,' sir."

"There is?" The pale eyes were terrifying at close quarters. "But your diminutive is 'Fred.' So whose idea was that, eh? One of Colebourne's little jokes, I suppose, eh?"

"I . . ." Words failed him.

"Don't worry. We'll correct that." The iron hand actually patted him. "In fact . . . we'll make a joke of it ourselves. And you can practice laughing right now—so *laugh!*"

It was so unarguably an order that Fred instinctively tried to obey—the more so as Brigadier Clinton was himself obeying the order.

Another pat. "That is, without doubt, the poorest parody of laughter I have ever seen, Major Fattorini. Do you actually obey orders so inadequately?"

Fred tried again, but stopped as he saw not laughter, but hysteria grinning at him from out of the trees ahead. "I was laughing inside actually, sir—Freddie?"

"That's better!" The brigadier dropped his arm suddenly and swung around. *"WHAT ARE YOU DOING, STANDING THERE LIKE AN IDIOT, HEWITT?"*

"Sir?" Pause. *"SIR!"*

The brigadier took several steps towards the rigid little man. "You were told to bring Major Fattorini here, and then proceed to Schwartzenburg Castle. Can't you obey a simple order, man?"

Silence.

"Well?"

"Sir . . . I—" Another pause. "Yes, sir!"

"Well, then—what are you waiting for?" *GET MOVING!"*

"SIR!" Pause (salute!)—stamp (about turn!). Driver Hewitt was now actually attempting to get into the People's Car while at attention, which was not physically possible. But he was doing his best, certainly.

The engine whirred instantly, and the little car jerked nervously several times before turning in a wide circle round the monument and disappearing behind it in a cloud of blue exhaust fumes.

The brigadier's eye returned to Fred. "I think we'll share another joke now, Major—just to see Driver Hewitt on his way properly, eh?"

A joke at attention—or at ease? wondered Fred as he laughed

165

obediently. But somehow that made it easier anyway, as the People's Car appeared again, at a speed that only just enabled it to straighten out in time to retreat down the avenue.

"So!" Brigadier Clinton waited until the avenue was clear. "Driver Hewitt is insatiably inquisitive, and garrulous with it. . . . So that is one job well done, at least." He looked up at the monument. "Do I need to explain?"

There was a long Latin inscription carved into stonework between two of the square pillars, Fred saw. "No, not really."

Clinton himself seemed to be more interested in the carved inscription than in his reply, which goaded Fred towards a smart and undiplomatic answer. "I assume he'll tell everyone from Otto Schild upwards that you've recruited another spy inside TRR-two."

"Another spy?" The brigadier still appeared to be fascinated by the inscription.

"He said Audley was a special friend of yours. Not that it's done the boy any good with the colonel and the RSM. But I suppose I can live with that."

"You can? No . . . it wouldn't I suppose. . . ." Then the brigadier's lips moved soundlessly. So perhaps he was attempting to translate the Latin, but was finding it rather too difficult, Fred thought nastily.

"Is he your spy? Unlike me." Nastiness encouraged cheekiness.

"No . . . at least, not yet, anyway." The brigadier paused. "Now . . . *'florentissimum imperium'*—that's rather good, that superlative."

It was time to join the Latin lesson, Fred decided. *"'Arminius'"*—he began to read the inscription aloud—*"liberator haud dubie Germaniae.'"* The meaning registered suddenly. "Of course! How stupid of me! This is Hermann's monument, isn't it." He stepped back to look up at the colossus. "The German who defeated the Romans—Varus in the Teutoburg Forest, and all that!"

"Yes. That's right." The brigadier looked up too, nodding as he did so. "The Germans themselves killed him in the end, of course—a successful Twentieth July Plot, you might say. . . . But you're right. This is *'Arminius liberator'*—'Herman, without doubt the liberator of Germany . . . who . . .' *'lacessierit'* is a bit difficult . . . 'provoked' isn't right. Although he certainly was provoking. What it ought to mean is 'resisted,' even more than 'hurt.' So let's say 'resisted'—'resisted the Roman people, not in their early days, like other kings and leaders, but at the very height of their power'—*'florentissimum imperium'*: I like that!— 'at the very height of their power, with mixed fortune in battle,

but in war undefeated'!" The brigadier nodded again. "Hmmm
. . . not bad. Tacitus, of course—from his *Annals*. In fact, quite
graceful, really." He looked at Fred. "The German translation's
underneath—'Armin, ohne Zweifel Deutschlands Befreier'—or
am I insulting a properly educated mathematician twice over
now? I suppose I am, at that!"

Thank you, Hermann! thought Fred gratefully. "No. My Latin's
damned rusty." Somehow the brigadier had reduced himself to a
human dimension. "And . . . so this is the Teutoburg Forest, of
course—where the battle took place, by God!"

"Yes. And no." The brigadier agreed and disagreed. "This is the
'Hermannsdenkmal'—and this is the Teutoburger Wald, *haud
dubie* as Tacitus would say. But whether this is the site of the
Hermannsschlact, or the *Varusschlact* . . . nobody knows. There
are dozens of other possible sites, and the German scholars have
been arguing over them for years. Not that it's of the slightest
historical importance—the site. As opposed to the fact."

Fred saw his opening. "It is to Colonel Colbourne, I rather got
the idea." Even, he was tempted irresistibly to presume on his
"friendship." "In fact, I think he's going to organize the RAF—or
the USAF—to conduct a photographic reconnaissance for him in
the near future." He grinned hopefully. "And isn't this why"—he
felt the grin freeze on his lips as he saw the brigadier's face and
instantly amended what he had been about to say—"actually, it
isn't a half bad idea. Because air photography's going to revolu-
tionize archaeology, these next few years, so I'm told . . ." The
spreading cold reached his heart, and he trailed off, bitterly
aware that he'd made the same mistake as the Liberator of
Germany above him in pushing his luck—*proeliis* bloody *ambi-
guus*—like a fool, only in his case, by talking too much, like David
Audley.

"You take Colonel Colbourne for a clown, do you, Major?"

"No, sir." Ordinarily he would have stopped there. But with
this man, it was no good trying to say nothing. Now, because he
had already talked too much, he *had* to talk more. "Or, at
least . . . so far as the battle of the Teutoburg Forest is concerned . . . yes, I do." Instinct reinforced reason. "But successful
barristers aren't clowns . . . unless they want people to think
they are"—that was an insight that hadn't even occurred to him
until this instant—"and—" Another insight hit him between the
eyes, even more belatedly: a man such as this wasn't going to
employ clowns to do his work. But he couldn't say *that*—least of
all when he still didn't know what the work really was.

"And?"

Fred rejected *"and he was a DSO"* because a DSO could mean
everything or nothing very much. And the brigadier himself had

a DSO among his ribbons, anyway. But the brigadier would never let him get away now. "Not after what I saw last night."

"Hmm . . ." The brigadier didn't move a muscle. "And just what *did* you see last night, Major?"

Those last half dozen words had been a mistake. But once a man felt impelled to talk, then he inevitably made mistakes, even when he told the simple truth. In fact, even more so when he told the truth. So the brigadier had caught him with an old trick—*so to hell with the brigadier!*

"I saw a man killed—an innocent man." *Sod* Brigadier Clinton—and all the rest of them! "I watched him die, actually."

"Innocent?" The brigadier's head moved very slightly. "You knew him then?"

"I never saw him before in my life." Steady! "But I believe he was chosen at random. Unlike 'Corporal Keys.'"

"Then he was killed at random. And you must have seen a good many men killed at random, Major."

"In the war, yes. But—"

"This is war—" The brigadier caught his reply midair. "But I'm not going to argue philosophy with you. What else did you see?"

The man was right. And he was also making the rules, anyway. "I thought I was in the middle of an overelaborate, unnecessary, bodged-up . . . nonsense. But now I'm no so sure." Actually, they were back to original point-of contact, before the brigadier had become "friendly." But he knew better now. "Do you want first thoughts, or second thoughts?"

"I want the truth."

Fred almost laughed. But then stopped an inch—or was it a mile?—short of it. Because he had had his ration of mistakes. "We want to take a man, from the American Zone—out from under their noses. And a man they probably wanted too . . . I don't know . . . but probably." He stopped there, not quite sure of himself. "No, not probably. They helped us, and they were going to double-cross us. Only we double-crossed them. Right?"

"That pleases you?"

"Yes. Rather to my surprise, it does, actually."

"Because your Greek friends have been double-crossing you, in Greece?" There was the very smallest nuance of surprise in the brigadier's expression. "Notably your friend, Colonel Michaelides?"

That was mean, no matter how accurate. But at least it cleared the way for what Brigadier Clinton really wanted in that "truth" of his. "Partly that, I suppose. . . . But also partly because its comforting to be part of a double-cross which is itself double-crossed, but which still has a fail-safe extra built into it."

Suddenly he knew what he wanted to say. "It's rather like what happened to us in Italy once, along one particular stretch of road where we kept losing men—from booby traps."

Brigadier Clinton stared at him. "Go on, Major."

Good men, Fred remembered. But at least that had been the name of the game. "There was this German, German sapper officer. . . . And their sappers were *good*, you know—"

"I know." Clinton stopped him sharply. "They were *all* good, damn it! Don't teach me to suck eggs, Major Fattorini. I've been sucking German eggs for eight years now. So I know the taste of them better than you do. *Go on!*"

"Yes, sir." *Eight* years? But that was . . . *1937*?

"There was this German sapper . . . who was good with booby traps. You were telling me?" Clinton spaced each word from the other carefully.

"Yes, sir." He would think about 1937 later. "At least, I think it was just this one man. Because when he set his booby trap, he always booby-trapped the actual trap. But he knew we'd tumble to that, so he used to rig an extra time fuse under the first trap, which was quite independent of the second one, which he set not too obviously, so that a good trained sapper would spot *that* one first. And then, of course, our chap would lift them in reverse order, and . . . *bang*!" He shrugged. "He was quite a character, I should think."

The brigadier's pale blue eyes were intent. "You don't hate him, though?"

"Hate him?" Silly question—strangely silly question! "Christ, yes! I hated his guts! If I'd caught him I'd have made him walk back along the other side of the road, along the verge we hadn't cleared!" Silly question? "Then he stopped playing games with us—maybe he was trying something new and his hand slipped . . . is what I've always *hoped*. . . . But we were fair game: it was him against us, with the extra traps—the riflemen who set off the first traps were your random victims, Brigadier. It was *us* he was after—" He blinked suddenly, aware that he had almost lost the thread of his own anecdote. "What I mean is . . . it's a nice change to be setting the trap, not having to defuse the bloody thing. We never got a chance to do that in Italy." Now he was aware that his mouth was twitching, too. "And fortunately . . . *very* fortunately . . . I moved to Bailey bridges before his successor arrived. Because I might have been caught by the next particular variation."

"Yes." The intentness misted up suddenly. "But it was a bridge that got you in the end, wasn't it? The Volturno bridge was it— the eighth wonder of the world?"

Fred was conscious of his hand for the first time that day. "You know a lot about me." He amended the question to a statement as he spoke.

"I know *everything* about you, Major. Except how your hand is today. How is it?"

"It's okay. Almost as good as new." Thinking about the damn thing always made it ache. "It does most things adequately."

"You've learnt to point with your left hand?"

The bastard really *did* know everything, right down to that one particular crooked index finger. "I use my right hand to point round corners, actually. It does that very well."

"Good." Clinton accepted the tart reply without offense. "I have an acquaintance in the gunners who maintains that all sapper officers are mad. Would you agreed with that?"

It sounded like an exam question. "I have an acquaintance—no, a friend—who says that gunners are people who have just enough maths to pass School Certificate, just enough. If they were cleverer, they'd have become sappers. But they aren't—" *Damn!* he thought suddenly, as he realized that he'd missed the correct answer—the required answer? Was there time—

"Actually, he didn't say 'mad'—he said 'stark staring mad.'" Clinton smiled his terrible thin-lipped smile again.

But that was obliging of him, thought Fred: it offered that second chance on a plate. "Then I have the necessary qualification for joining this unit, obviously. Apart from my banking connection, that is. . . . Everyone's been telling me, ever since I arrived, that everyone else is stark staring mad—or stark *raving* mad. Everyone from Colonel Colbourne himself downwards . . ." He had gone too far?

"Downwards to young Audley? Your fellow spy?"

Something inhibited Fred from shopping young Audley, whose own big mouth caused him enough trouble as it was. "Captain Audley is an exception to the rule, I rather think."

"'In more ways than one'?" Clinton quoted the young man's words cruelly. "He's certainly poor, I grant you. But that comes of having a father addicted to fast women and slow horses before the war, which has mortgaged him to the hilt. Although we can't blame him for that, poor boy. Any more than we can praise *you* for your great expectations, Major."

For the first time Fred crossed the man's stare with one of his own with a sense of steel sliding against steel, even though he knew it was anger and not courage that animated him. "Oh, no?"

"Oh, *yes*, Major. I also know *all* about Captain Audley. And all about Colonel Augustus Colbourne. *And* all his other officers. Which I should know, because each one of them has been handpicked by me—each one, including you, Major." He paused. "Or perhaps not *quite* all. And there's the rub."

The coldness of those final words utterly extinguished Fred's anger. From fancying himself as a duelist he saw himself for the rabbit he was.

"Now—straight questions and short answers, Major. You've talked to young Audley. And you've traveled with Driver Hewitt. And neither of them possesses the gift of silence . . . though Audley's still young enough to learn, I hope. But between them they must have told you what they think TRR-two is doing, eh?"

Kyriakos had given him the answer to that one, long ago and long before Audley or Hewitt had talked. "You are manhunters."

"Don't say 'you,' say 'we.' What sort of men do we hunt?"

"Germans." But then what the devil were they doing in Greece on the Eve of Scobiemas? So that answer wasn't quite adequate. And then he remembered the group picture Audley had shown him—and much more vividly, "Corporal Keys's" inability with a simple uniform. "Civilians, scientists?" But then he remembered the heavily laden lorry. "But also machinery too—equipment." But then he thought also of what Audley had said. "But that may be a cover. Is it?"

"Partially. But now wholly. And in fact, our chief cover has been Colonel Colbourne's celebrated obsession with him"— Clinton pointed upwards—"and with the final resting place of General Quintilius Varus and the men of the Seventeenth, Eighteenth, and Nineteenth Roman Legions . . . whose bones are most likely scattered over many square miles of the Teutoburger Wald."

"And they—the Americans—actually believed that?"

"For a time, perhaps. They, the Americans. And also they, the French. And they, the Russians, Major. Because it happens to be a genuine obsession of Colbourne's—an obsession in an otherwise extremely clever and well-balanced man. And one shared by a great many otherwise clever and well-balanced German professors and scholars down the years, also. But there's nothing strange in obsessions, Major—a lot of us have them. And at least Colbourne's is an innocent one, which doesn't hurt anyone."

Coming from such a cold fish, that was a surprisingly warm defense. Or maybe there was more to Brigadier Clinton than met the eye? "It just makes them—*us*—a laughingstock? But that was what you wanted, of course!"

"Yes." Clinton looked up at Hermann for a moment, who was safely frozen in stone, before coming back to Fred. "Except that it didn't require Augustus Colbourne's private obsession to make a laughingstock of us. Us, the British. Because we were that already, in this particular field of operations."

Lucky Hermann! "We were?"

"And not just among our loyal allies. Among the Germans too, perhaps among them, above all . . . our defeated enemies, Major. The only difference is that their laughter must be bitter as well as incredulous, watching us make such fools of ourselves."

That was what the Crocodile had said. But he hadn't really understood it then, and he didn't now. "What d'you mean?"

"Yes, of course." Clinton cocked an eye at him. "You've been too busy disporting yourself happily on Vouliagmeni beach with Colonel Michaelides's cast-off mistresses." The eye became knowing. *I know all about you, Major*, it reminded him. "Well, we haven't much time for that in Germany. Because we've been discovering just how clever the Germans really were, Major, you see."

"I never thought they weren't clever, sir."

"I don't mean German sappers." Clinton paused. "Although they did have some new plastic explosive which might have surprised you unpleasantly. . . . But then they were way ahead of us in so many fields—synthetics and optics and radar and rocketry, and aircraft design—I'm told that even their aircraft-testing technology was years ahead of ours. . . . In fact, I don't think some of our chaps really understand what they're looking at half the time—like a bunch of savages trying to make sense of a screwdriver. And that isn't the end of it. And don't, *pray don't*, say to me now, as one very senior officer did quite recently, '*By George, Freddie! If half you say is true, then we ought to have lost the jolly old war! But we didn't now, did we!*'"

"I wasn't about to say such a thing, sir." Fred hastily amended his thoughts. "I was going to say . . . but we are *here*, anyway." He remembered the lorry again.

"Huh!" For the first time Brigadier Clinton emitted something like the sort of explosive sound brigadiers usually made in Fred's experience of them. "That is the other half of it, Major Fattorini. Too late and too little, as well as too incompetently, is our story. I can't call it a policy—it would be bad enough if it was an actual policy. . . . But there isn't any policy, so far as I can discover. So we're actually ten times worse than even the Americans, at picking up German technology and the men who can explain it to us. And they're slower than the Russians, the Americans are . . . because the Yanks have some Jewish officers, and some Jews in their State Department, who are at least decently concerned about shaking hands with Nazis who haven't yet even had time to wash the blood off theirs—*that* is at least understandable. . . . Or it would be if the Russians weren't making deals with every-one they can lay *their* hands on—which is easy enough for them,

because their deal is 'Work for us, and we'll look after you, and
your family, and no questions asked . . . or we'll shoot the lot of
you . . . except your daughter, who is pretty.' In which case, it
isn't *too* difficult to reach a sensible decision. . . . And the
French—*they* have an even better sales story: 'Come and live in
France, where it is warmer, and much more *civilized* . . . and
serve your time with us, like a soldier in *La Légion étrangère*, also
with no questions asked, but with better pay and better food, and
finally become a Frenchman like us!' And who would refuse *that*
offer, in Germany in 1945? Would you, Major—if you were
hungry, and had a Nazi record as long as my arm?"

After that "huh" . . . that was the longest and most uncharacteristic speech Fred had heard from any senior office, anywhere,
in all his years in uniform. But then this brigadier's experience of
Germans went back longer than most, he remembered: he had
been sucking German eggs since . . . 1937?

So he could afford to jump the obvious answer. "So what are *we*
doing then, sir?"

"You may well ask, Major, you may well ask!" Clinton stared at
Hermann's inscription this time: *Arminius liberator haud dubie
Germaniae.* So Fred waited patiently to be liberated in his turn.

"We started out . . . trying to pick up certain of the pieces,
much too late . . . amongst other things. But now we're living
on borrowed time, I fear—even after last night's famous victory."
Clinton continued to study the inscription.

Fred waited again, until his patience exhausted itself. "How so,
sir?"

Clinton turned quickly, to his surprise. "Don't be downcast,
Major. Last night did go according to plan . . . except for your
poor devil."

Fred thought for a moment. "And he was set up as a target?"

"Not a target, as such." Clinton shook his head. "But there was
a risk, I cannot deny that. But in this instance I did not expect it.
And . . . there was always the chance that they would miss."

Fred didn't know quite how much of that to believe. "Who
would miss?"

"The Russians, Major." Clinton nodded, as though this had
been the expected answer. "The Americans didn't need to,
because they had the men on the spot to take what they wanted.
And to be fair, their well-developed sense of self-interest . . . or
patriotism, as it used to be called . . . is not yet so ruthless.
Even though I seem to recall that it was an American who first
said 'Our country, right or wrong' . . . yes, it was. But not here,
not now, and not yet, I think. And the French . . . *they* are
undoubtedly capable of anything, since the very mention of
'France' obviates the need for moral debate. . . . But in this

instance they are safely out of the picture—they're much too busy pursuing their own very successful enterprises." He nodded, at first almost to himself, but finally at Fred. "You see, Major, there have been a great many people—and *interests* . . . and commercial interests as well as national, too—concerned with acquiring the details of German technical and industrial and scientific development. And with getting their hands on it before anyone else. Which you can call 'loot' if you like . . . or 'spoils of war,' but strictly speaking it's 'reparations.' And it's really the only worthwhile reparation that's to be had here—*knowledge*." He paused deliberately, as though to let the word sink in. "Oh . . . I know the Russians are carrying off whole factories. And you can't really blame them for that. And in spite of what the bomber fellows say, because they claim to have destroyed everything, there's still a lot to carry off. In fact, there'll still be a lot *after* they've had their pick. . . . So there is equipment. But it's the research that really matters. And some of it's so damned far in advance of anything we've done that we need the researchers themselves to go with it, to explain it. Do you see?"

"The savages need help with the screwdrivers?"

"Huh!" Clinton repeated his brigadierial growl. "The trouble is, some of *our* savages don't believe in the existence of the screwdriver: they think it's some sort of blunt chisel. And some of our chiefs don't want to know. Or they can't bring themselves to talk to the screwdriver makers, anyway, either because of their stupidity, or because of their tender consciences."

"Because the screwdriver makers are Nazis?" The unpleasant truth beneath the imagery made Fred uneasy in spite of the brigadier's earlier honest recognition of it. "Is that so wicked—not to want to do business with Nazis?"

Clinton's coldest stare returned. "Are you about to lecture me on the nature of Fascism, Major? And what our attitude should be?"

"No, sir. But—"

"I should hope not. Because I've forgotten more about that subject than you are ever likely to know." The stare continued. "So what were you going to say?"

Fred felt himself backed into a corner. The wide circle round the Hermann monument was silent and empty behind him, and the forest was silent and empty behind that—empty even of birds, judging by its silence. And the whole of Germany might be ruined and empty behind the forest. But he was nevertheless in a corner. And the bugger of it was that he hadn't even had the chance of taking Kyri's good advice. He had simply had the soldier's choice of no choice at all. And Devenish had summed that up for him.

The thought of Kyri reminded him of Audley's words in Greece. "It's a new kind of war. And I can't say that I like it. I suppose I expected it to be different, that's all. But now I shall have to get used to it, just like I did with the other kind."

Clinton considered that nonanswer in a silence that lengthened uncomfortaby out of time. "Well, I suppose that's as much as I have any right to expect from you. Although you are almost entirely wrong, Major, as it happens."

"I am?" After that silence the man's not-unkind tone surprised him. "Almost?"

"Yes. It's exactly the same war, in essence. And you must *never* get used to it—*never, never, never*, Major." The stare became uncompromising. "You must hate it with all your heart—always, no matter how long you have to soldier in it." This time the silence was mercifully shorter. "Do you know where I was eight years ago?"

Eight years ago? *1937!* "In 1937, sir?"

"*You* were in the middle of your first long vacation from Oxford, Major—August 1937. You were staying with friends, first in New York, then in New England. Then you went out West— you stayed at Jackson Hole, in Wyoming, and climbed up into the Grand Tetons, with a boy named Bill—William T. Schuster, August 1937, remember?" Clinton paused momentarily. "Agreed?"

"Yes." That August he had been with Uncle Luke's Wall Street friends. And the following August he had been at his first TA camp, on Salisbury Plain. But then the man would surely know that too—and the extent of his knowledge was terrifying! "Yes, sir."

"*I* was in Spain, on the Northern Front—the Basque campaign. Near a place called Barruelo."

It wasn't so much surprising that the man had been in Spain, which would certainly have been professionally interesting to any soldier, as that he was swapping his past for nothing in exchange. And for some reason, this information was also frightening. But he mustn't betray his fear. "On which side?"

"The Nationalists'—the full-blown Fascist one." The reply came matter-of-fact, without excuse. "I was a stretcher carrier with the Navarrese—the Sixth—next to Bastico's Italians. And I used to lie on my back and watch the German planes make mincemeat of the Russian Ratas. The Russians had supplied old stuff, and the Condor boys were trying out their latest ME-109s, so it wasn't really a fair fight. But I didn't stay to see the finish of it, after the Italians broke their promise and handed over their prisoners to Franco to be murdered. I got myself conveniently

175

killed in action—'missing, presumed'—so that I could join the Republican side, in Barcelona. Because the only fellow in the British battalion of the International Brigade—the Fifteenth, that was . . . the only fellow who might have recognized me had conveniently got himself killed on the Ebro. So . . . in answer to your most intelligent question, Major . . . I am a hero of *both* sides. Which I can admit to you now because both sides know it now. But fortunately, they didn't know it then, of course."

"Of course." Fred stopped worrying. After that put-down he really had nothing to lose. "Which side did you prefer?"

"Ah . . . now *that* is a good question, actually." The academic mildness of Clinton's reaction piled surprise on surprise. "In a way, it is perhaps *the* question . . . although for most people now, at this exact moment in history, it may seem not a question at all, but an insult. . . . But . . . *mmm*—I have often thought about that. Although perhaps not in quite the same way . . ." He trailed off, for a moment. *"Mmm* . . . if the worst ever could theoretically come—or have come—to the worst . . ." The brigadier trailed off again. "The truth is that . . . *I really don't know, Fred!"* Clinton bestowed the diminutive on him with such transparent sincerity that Fred found himself leapfrogging contempt (which usually came after relief when senior officers betrayed their fallibility) and coming up against that old unjumpable mixture of respect and sympathy and understanding, which always evoked loyalty!

But—damn it!—he mustn't give way to that! Not so easily, and on such short acquaintance! Not with this man of all men!

"The truth is that there were decent men on both sides. There was even an Italian colonel—Farina, I think his name was. . . . Armado? Guiseppe? Gian-Carlo? I can't remember. . . . But he was a decent man—an *honorable* man, in the old sense: he hated what he was doing in Spain, and he resigned in protest in the end. And there were a lot of good men in the International Brigade too, who thought they were good *Communists* . . . although they wouldn't have lasted ten minutes if their side had won—and some of them didn't last much longer than that as it was: if it wasn't a Fascist bullet in the front, it was one in the back for them, when no one was looking!" Clinton drew a huge reminiscent sigh, and then looked directly at Fred, with the pale-blue clouded. "So . . . *no,* in answer to your question—same in Spain, same in Germany, you've got to remember." Nod. "When it starts . . . there aren't just good men on one side and bad men on the other. There are good men on both edges of the middle. And some of them are stupid, but some of them are quite clever . . . but just not quite clever enough. And of course, a lot of them are quite ordinary, also. And then, as one side or the other starts to win, and to show its true colors, they don't know what to do. But by then it's too late, and they haven't anywhere else to go, because they're *inside* the thing by then. They can't run, then: it's Bergen-Belsen or Siberia, or a firing squad for them—and their families. So what do they do then, eh?"

Having asked two silly questions of his own in succession and got far more than he'd bargained for in reply, Fred decided that he would treat this one as rhetorical and say nothing.

"The very brave ones resist, and take the consequences." Clinton accepted his silence. "And there aren't many of them around in Germany now, take my word for it. Or in Spain, although Spain's not quite so bad. But in Soviet Russia . . . there are *none*." He stared through Fred. "And the not-so-brave ones and the confused ones . . . *some* of them try to hide—to lie low, in the hope of better times one day. But you need both cleverness and luck for that, as well as hope." The stare focused on him suddenly. "But your average chap . . . as it might be you or me, my lad—you or me . . . *he* gets swallowed up by the thing—*The Beast!* Because that's the Nature of the Beast, you see. You get involved with it, for whatever reason . . . because of your job, or your family, or at worst your ambition—or even by accident, or by pure bad luck. Or you can even become part of it out of patriotism, or for religious reasons—there was a lot of that in Spain, believe me. Or even for idealism—for any number of reasons. . . . I once worked with a British officer who thought Oswald Mosley had all the right ideas but the wrong friends—*he* died at Dunkirk, fighting the Nazis. But it was damned close-run thing with him, and he was just lucky—lucky being an Englishman—it was 'Our county, right or wrong' with him, so he landed up on the right side by accident of birth, you might say." The terrible mirthless smile returned. "Up until August '38 he always half suspected that I was a damned Red. But then Stalin made his pact with Hitler, and he gave me the benefit of the doubt after that. And in a queer way he was quite right of course—as well as being quite wrong. Quite wrong, that is, because I'm not a patriot, Major. You may choose to insult me in any way you like, but I'd be obliged if you would avoid making that mistake."

They had got past 1937, to reach 1940. But now they seemed to have returned to 1939. But the truth was that Fred didn't know where he was, except that he wasn't in the real world of 1945 anymore.

"The best news I ever heard was the German-Soviet Pact in '39." Clinton was so wrapped up in his own *un*patriotism that he missed Fred's quiet desperation. "Both the Beasts of Spain were suddenly on the same side, which I'd never hoped for in my wildest dreams." He turned away from Fred and Hermann both, to look out into a gap between the trees, over the dull gray-green German landscape. "Of course, I was younger then, and I didn't realize how far the rot had gone in France. And I thought the Americans would be pulled in sooner than they were, so that we'd be back to 1918 before long. . . . Foolish! Foolish! The old idiocy of making pictures of what I wanted to see!" He swung back to Fred unexpectedly, catching him with his mouth open. "But *you* went to America in 1937, *and not to Spain as some of your friends wanted you to do?* Now . . . why was that, Major? New York instead of Barcelona. And the Grand Tetons instead of the Ebro—why?"

Why?

There had been a ferment then, not just in Oxford, but with the word coming from Cambridge and elsewhere, as that summer term had ended. But then Uncle Luke had appeared out of nowhere, with his membership at Vincent's Club and held in surprising esteem there, on the basis of some great and unexpected Oxford sporting triumph over The Other Place in the distant past, which was still remembered by the steward as a famous victory.

"Actually, it was my uncle—Uncle Luke." At such short notice, and with his back to Hermann, Fred could only present the truth by way of an explanation. "He'd got an invitation from the Schusters for me." But that wasn't the whole truth; and he owed that to himself too in retrospect, as well as Uncle Luke. "We talked a bit about Spain, actually." But when it came to the crunch, he couldn't bring himself to go further than that. "I don't really remember much of it." He could only shrug now. "But . . . he's a persuasive old devil."

"He told you to keep your powder dry. He said it took five minutes to put cannon fodder into the line, but nine months to train an infantryman who wasn't a danger to others as well as himself—and eighteen months for second lieutenant. By which time the war would be over. So if you wished for a useful death as well as a glorious one, you might as well join the OTC, and then the TA, and get your degree meanwhile. And then there'd be plenty for you to die for, wearing the right uniform at the right time, in the right place."

That was exactly what Uncle Luke had said. But Brigadier Frederick Clinton couldn't have been there in Vincent's that night, either as himself or as a fly on the wall, because he had been in Spain. So that pointed to an almost certainty, because there had been only one other person there halfways sober enough to recall those words so accurately. "You've talked to him, obviously? Uncle Luke, I mean? About me?"

"Talked to him? My dear Fred . . . your 'Uncle Luke' and I go back longer than the odd talk about *you*! Don't you know that the Fattorini Brothers have useful Spanish contacts—just as they have a hand in Colonel Michaelides's Balkan Mercantile Bank, and the so-called Aegean Mutual Trust?" Clinton stopped as he saw Fred's face. "You must forgive me. I'm sorry."

"Don't be." Feeling foolish in a retrospect stretching back to the late 1930s might well be a burden the brigadier could bear now. But his own failure to put two and two together was of a much more recent date, and its taste was bitter. "I think—"

"*No!* I spoke out of turn. And that was unpardonable—quite unpardonable." After sharply pulling rank with that first interruption, Clinton seemed almost embarrassed. "Besides which . . . I would not have you think ill of your Uncle Luke, of all men."

"I don't." A small revenge offered itself. "You couldn't make me do that . . . sir."

"Good! I'm relieved to hear it." Clinton's confidence and authority returned instantly. He sounded more relieved by Fred's sound judgment than by the news that there was nothing to forgive.

"But I am a little surprised that you didn't mention him the first time we met, though." Fred decided to push his luck. "You gave me quite a hard time in Greece, I seem to remember. 'Gallivanting in hostile territory without a thought'—was that it? And you never said you knew my uncle."

"No." Clinton gave him a hard look. "Your Uncle Luke is a remarkable man in his way, Major. A *good* man, even."

That was no answer. "I know that he's a good banker." The lack of answer had been contemptuous. But that somehow goaded him into wondering where else the old firm had "useful contacts." Rome, certainly. . . . But . . . Berlin? And Moscow? "And you like bankers—I know that, too."

"Who told you that?"

"Does it matter?" What mattered suddenly was that all the ramifications of the Fattorini Brothers in general, and the brigadier's longtime friendship with Sir Luke Fattorini in particular, accounted for the involvement of the unfortunate ci-devant Captain Frederick Fattorini in this murky business, thought Fred. Or, when added to the pure mischance of his own friendship with Kyri, it did. . . . Except that, even there Uncle Luke and the old firm were at the heart of the accident too. So . . . was he never to have free will—even to be a victim?

"It was that young blackguard Audley!" Clinton came up with his own correct answer. "I'll bet it was!"

"Does it matter?" Fred came to the point of decision not so much to save Audley as to assert and save himself. "You're quite right, of course—about Uncle Luke, I mean." He paused for a fraction of a second. "But you're also wrong."

The possibility that he could be wrong about anything that he didn't already know of brought the brigadier up short. "What d'you mean, Major?"

That had saved Audley. Now he had to save himself. "He *did* talk to me in Vincent's—he was afraid I might go to Spain, of course."

"With Sebastian Cavendish, yes?" Clinton asserted his own knowledge cruelly. "Who was killed on the Ebro, uselessly."

"With Bassie Cavendish." There would have been a time when he would have hit the bastard for that, brigadier or not. "And I regretted *not* going for a long time after that. Almost . . . almost until very recently, actually. And then I remembered something else Uncle Luke said . . . which, in a way, you've also said now, you see."

The brigadier plainly didn't see. (So Uncle Luke's memory of that night in Vincent's hadn't been quite word-perfect, then!) But this time Clinton had the wit not to interrupt.

"I didn't much like what was happening in Greece, sir. Not even after I'd realized that the Communists had always planned it that way . . . only, they hadn't bargained on us fighting them. But . . . but anyway, they'd planned to make a clean sweep of the other side. And then the middle wouldn't have any choice. And I didn't much like that, either."

(He had said to Kyri: *"What's the difference between you and them?"* And Kyri had replied: *"Not a lot, my dear chap. Only . . . I am personally responsible for whatever I do, and I cannot say to God therefore that 'I was only obeying orders' when I come before Him—that is really the only difference."*)

Only, he couldn't say *that* to the brigadier. But what could he say, then? And by God, it would have to be good, now!

And the brigadier was still waiting, too.

"We had a fellow posted to us from Northern Italy . . . or it might have been Austria, I don't know." He fought for time. "But he was more or less in disgrace, about half a step from a court-martial. And he got pissed out of his mind one night. . . ." He could see that time was running out. "He said that we'd been sending prisoners back east—all sorts of odds and sods of Russians, and Ukrainians and assorted Slavs . . . old men, and

180

women and children, too. . . . And they were committing sui-
cide, some of them . . ." He trailed away helplessly.

"What else did he say?" The brigadier urged him on.

"He fell under the table then. So we put him to bed." Fred
could still remember Captain Smith's drunken misery as they'd
tried to make him comfortable. And his endless questions—
"What would you have done, Fattorini?"

"Very sensible. And when he'd sobered up . . . what did he
say, then?"

"He wouldn't talk. And he was posted again shortly after that,
in any case." He met the brigadier's stare. "To Burma, actually."

"Yes. Also very sensible." The terrible smile returned. "Traditional, too."

"Traditional?" The last tradition he had encountered had been
Audley's umbrella.

"Yes." The smile twitched hideously. "In Nelson's day, when
there were signs of indiscipline, they always used to ship out
those who knew about it as far away as possible, and as quickly
as possible. Nothing like a long sea voyage to isolate contagion."
The brigadier pointed suddenly at a smaller statue alongside the
path, to a carved stone trophy of Roman equipment presumably
symbolizing loot from the ruin of Varus' army: armor, shields,
sword, eagle standard, and helmet hanging on a central shaft.
"The Romans weren't so kind: they favored decimation—crucify
every tenth man, regardless."

There was no escaping the man's meaning. "Is that a threat?"

"If you think it is . . . then it is." Clinton studied the trophy.
"The Germans took three legionary eagles in the Teutonburger
fight. And the Romans wasted a lot of effort trying to get 'em
back, as a matter of prestige. But they only recovered two. And
I'll bet Gus Colbourne would give his pension for the missing
one." He turned on his heel to study a matching trophy on the
other side of the pathway. "Conventional war, for most people—
for the young anyway—is a group activity, transacted by a
majority vote. The generals—the generals *and* the politicians—
they just want bodies to do as they are told. For the rest . . . if
the bodies are willing, then their job is to carry each other on to
quite remarkable feats of heroism and self-sacrifice, equally in
victory and defeat, in the execution of their orders." He looked
from one trophy to the other, as though comparing them. "All
that is required additionally is a sense of comradeship and duty
and proper training and decent leadership—decent leadership
particularly in the lower ranks . . . and patriotism, of course—
however misconceived—if possible. And then custom and practice—*that's* very important. Because the Germans and the Rus-

181

sians both regarded soldiering as something quite natural and inevitable. The Germans particularly . . . but the Russians too, in spite of grossly inadequate training and deplorable leadership. . . . Both of them performed miracles because of that, added to patriotism. Whereas the British and the Americans really have no military tradition—no military *inclination*. No self-respecting Englishman—or Welshman . . . with the Scots and the Irish I'm not so sure . . . but *in general*, no self-respecting Briton or American would dream of taking the King's shilling, or Uncle Sam's dollar, unless he was starving or otherwise unemployable. But in wartime, by a majority vote and with certain of those additions, you can still do a great deal with them. And of course, in the First World War, thanks to greater ignorance and consequently greater patriotism, miracles *were* done with them, too." He turned to Fred at last. "But all that is in *war* . . . and all you temporary hostilities-emergency-only soldiers believe that you've more or less won *this* war, so now you can go home—is that it?"

That was exactly it, thought Fred. But short of a direct order, he was not about to admit it. And indeed, even with a direct order he would plead incomprehension, ignorance, and stupidity if pressed.

"Well, I have news for you, Major." Mercifully, it was another rhetorical question. "We are still in a state of official war, even though the exceedingly formidable Japanese are far away. So, under the Rules of War—and probably the Geneva Convention too, for all I know—I can have you court-martialed for having a tender conscience and disobeying any legitimate order. Or in the appropriate circumstances, I can shoot you myself and almost certainly get away with it. Whereas, if *you* shoot *me* you will be shot yourself—at least, you will unless you can get Colonel Augustus Colbourne to defend you, anyway." Again the terrible smile. "But that is unlikely, partly because *he* won't . . . but mostly because *I* will get you first, you see."

Actually, thought Fred, he really could plead incomprehension, ignorance, and stupidity honestly now. "Sir?"

"Apart from all of which we haven't won the war. Even, most regrettably, we haven't beaten the Germans. Because the Russians have done that for us, unfortunately. Although that does not oblige us to be grateful, because they didn't do it either for us or from choice. What they intended is that *we* should ruin each other—the democrats and the fascists both—and then *they* could pick up the pieces, as they foolishly hoped they would do in Spain. But Hitler and European geography dictated differently.

182

So don't 'but' me with foolish gratitude for Our Glorious Russian Allies, eh?"

Fred had not been about to do that, either. But also, he was not about to say anything, either.

"But then you wouldn't, would you?" Clinton pressed the question with a disconcerting certainty, as though everything he had said had been perfectly understood and the answer was no more than a marriage-vow formality.

"No. As it happens, I wouldn't." The marriage image persisted oddly in Fred's mind. On the face of it he was agreeing with the brigadier's scorn for those who confused the heroism and achievement of the Russians against a common enemy with selfless friendship for their Western allies. But his recent exposure to the influence of Colonel Michaelides and the drunken misery of Captain Smith of the Intelligence Corps (who was probably sweltering in his Burmese jungle by now) had only confirmed a process started long before by Uncle Luke at Vincent's. But there was also something seriously affirmative about that negative. It was like saying *"I do"* rather than *"I wouldn't."* It was like saying *"I, Frederick, temporary major, take thee, Frederick, to be my lawful wedded brigadier . . . for better, for worse . . . and to obey, if not to love, honor and cherish!* So he couldn't leave it there. "But what makes you so sure that I wouldn't?"

The brigadier liked the question: it almost softened his gaze. "I know everything about you, Major Fattorini—don't you remember? You wouldn't be here now if I didn't—and neither would I."

That was a challenge, as well as a statement. "Everything?"

"Try me and see."

That was a nasty one. Because Clinton had already thrown in Bassie and Cavandish and Bill Schuster . . . so he could eliminate Uncle Luke from the reckoning. And after that he hardly knew where to begin—or even whether it would be good for his peace of mind. Because, equally, he could eliminate Kyri from the trial: Colonel Michaelides and Brigadier Clinton would undoubtedly have talked together—and understood exactly what the other was saying, because they talked the same language, if not the same mother tongue.

"Let's see . . ." Clinton cut through his irresolution. "Smith, *Nigel John*, major, 'I,' Corps, Rangoon?" He paused deliberately to let the cut slice deeper. "Of course, he was only a captain when you put him to be in Athens. But he also wasn't as drunk as you thought he was . . . although he was genuinely miserable, and also quite mutinous, I would agree." This time he nodded. "Which was why I had him shipped out east afterwards, instead of bringing him here instead of you, actually." Another nod. "Oh, yes—he was a double-check on you. Which was necessary because of your reactions to Greece, in spite of your Greek friend's recommendation. Because, as you yourself said, you 'didn't much like that,' did you?"

There was treachery! thought Fred again. But what could he expect, now that former allies were enemies, and (after last night) even present allies had to be double-crossed?

"But don't think badly of Colonel Michaelides." Clinton read his face with disconcerting accuracy. "He tried hard to preserve you from me. But unconvincingly, I'm afraid. He said you were an honorable man, thinking that that would put me off. Because in his own way, he is also an honorable man—just like your Uncle Luke. Although *Luke* didn't try to put me off."

There was no end to the villainy of friends and relations, it seemed. "He gave me to you, did he?" It rankled equally that Nigel Smith hadn't been as drunk as he had seemed on that memorably argumentative evening—and that he himself hadn't been as sober, maybe. So brother officers couldn't be trusted either, and he'd never again know for sure where he was with any of them—friends, relations, and equals . . . not for sure, as he had been able to know on that road to the north in Italy, with that long-lost German engineer brother, who had at least been a trustworthy enemy. "He gave me to you?"

"That he most certainly did not!" No almost-softness now; cold authority *now*. "He said you might be difficult. But he said that, as a good Fattorini, you would listen to a fair offer. And that if you made a bargain, you would keep your side of it."

Again a nasty one. And it was nasty both because brigadiers didn't usually make offers to subordinates, and also because good Fattorinis *always* mistrusted fair offers. And since Uncle Luke knew that rule better than he did, the very statement was a warning.

"I keep telling you, I know all about you. So . . . if you don't believe me . . . then I challenge you to test me." Short of an answer, Clinton tried another tack. "Are you afraid of losing?"

Fred saw the trap just in time. "I'm not afraid. But if I lose, then I lose. But if I win, I lose. So I just don't fancy playing, that's all."

"That's a pity. Because I was hoping you would ask me what it was that your Uncle Luke said, which you remembered just now . . . which *I* didn't remind you of. Because that's the point now."

What Fred remembered at once was that at the time the brigadier hadn't seemed to understand what he'd said then. But not it seemed that he himself hadn't read the man correctly at all when it came to the very heart of the matter. "Very well, what did he say?"

"He said that it wasn't your body the Reds wanted in Spain—it was your soul they wanted, for future use." Clinton nodded. And then stopped nodding. "But I don't want your soul, you see, Major."

That was exactly what Uncle Luke said. "I wouldn't give it to you if you wanted it." As he spoke Fred decided that *wouldn't* should be *couldn't*. "Wouldn't . . . and couldn't."

"I'm glad to hear it. Because for what I have in mind I need men whose souls are their own." He watched Fred for a moment. "That surprises you?"

It was no good denying what his face must be betraying in him. "It surprises me that we're discussing my soul. Or anyone else's soul."

"Not in King's Regulations—*souls*? Nothing about 'Free Will' in the Manual of Military Law?" The man's lack of emotion went with his placeless, classless, accent. "No mention of '*Souls G.S., officers, for the use of,*' or '*Souls G.S., other ranks*'—made out of coarser material, of course—'*if damaged or lost on active service, report to chaplain for replacement*'?" There wasn't the slightest hint of humor, either. "No . . . it was the word your uncle used. And as it happens, also the one Colonel Michaelides chose; although in his case it had a more narrowly religious connotation, I suspect. For myself, I might have selected a different one. But since you evidently understand what it means, then I shall use it to describe our bargain—very good?"

All the Fattorini warning bells rang simultaneously again. "On which side of this bargain is my soul supposed to be weighed—yours or mine?"

"On which side?" Clinton seemed almost surprised. "Why—on both sides, of course. And on neither side. Your soul—if there are such things, and if you have one—your soul *is* the scales on which your actions must be weighed. Isn't that what souls are for?"

Damn the man! "My actions?" *Damn the man!*

"That's right. On these terms, you come to me freely. And you freely obey my orders. But you yourself take absolute responsibility for whatever you do, just as I take absolute responsibility for giving you the order to do it. So . . . in effect, as of now, and probably for the first time in your life . . . *you are a free man, Major!*

Fred had never felt more unfree in his life. "It seems a rather one-sided bargain. If I have to take the responsibility for—"

"Not at all! If you believe you have a soul, then you must admit the possibility that I have one also. And you can't have my soul in order to excuse yourself, that's all."

There was something very dodgy about this bargain. But there was also a much more urgent question. "And what if I disagree with your orders?"

"Then you must question them. I have no use for unquestioning obedience: that is for slaves—and well-trained animals."

"And soldiers."

"And soldiers. But you are no longer a soldier."

"I'm not?" Fred looked down on himself, past his tarnished brasses and crumpled and muddy battle-dress trousers to his disgracefully dirty boots. It was true that he looked unsoldierly: he hadn't looked as disheveled as this since Italy. Or at least, since Osios Konstandinos. "Aren't I?"

"You still wear the uniform. But that's only because it suits the time and the place. And me, of course. Civilians don't have much clout here in Germany. But that will change very soon. And when it does, then you will change."

Fred looked up again. Things were already changing, but they were doing so far too fast, from a taken-for-granted present to an indefinite future that threatened to stretch even beyond the war's far-off-and-bloody end in Japan some time next year, if they were lucky.

"So there are no King's Regulations between us now," Clinton continued before he could speak. "And no Rules of War or Geneva Conventions either. Nothing but our bargain, freely entered into on both sides—'bargain' is also your uncle's word. But the exact word doesn't matter so long as we both understand its meaning."

"But . . . I'm not sure that I do understand it." Fred's voice sounded thick to his ears. "Whatever the word may be."

"In what respect do you not?"

Fred cleared his throat. "The war must end soon."

"Very soon." Clinton shook his head. "But *our* war will not end soon."

Our war? "I have a Release Number which says mine will."

"You have no Release Number anymore—as of this moment."

This time he wasn't going to say that he didn't understand. "But . . . you said I am 'a free man.' How do I exercise my freedom?"

"Very simply." Clinton undid the top button of his battle-dress blouse and drew a long buff-colored envelope from his inside pocket. "This is my side of the bargain, Major. It contains a special release from His Majesty's service, properly signed and officially stamped. Your demobilization papers, in fact—go on, Major—take it!"

Fred's right hand refused to move. Instead he felt his good
fingers clench into a palm that was unaccountably sweating.

"Go on, take it." Clinton sounded almost dismissive. "Have you
got a pen?"

"A pen?" The envelope seemed to hang in the air between them.

"It's undated. So if there comes a day when you cannot obey
my orders, then all you have to do is date it from that day. All my
officers have a similar document—except young David Audley of
course."

Of course? The words repeated themselves stupidly inside
Fred's brain. But then, young Audley had said he was an
exception to all the rules, of course.

"The King hasn't had his money's worth out of that boy yet.
And neither have I." Clinton paused. "But for the rest . . . I have
no uses for any man who has no use for me. For my work I need
free men, nothing else will serve. Otherwise I cannot do the work
and neither can they. And also, I should very soon become a
mirror image of my enemy. And then the work would not be
worth doing."

The envelope was still in midair. And Fred was remembering
that old feeble joke, which he'd first heard in 1939, on Salisbury
Plain, and thereafter at intervals, through bitter Italian winters
and the last time in a gun pit within sight of the Acropolis in
Athens on Christmas Day (the real Christmas Day, not Scobiemas)—

*"There was this squaddie, see . . . an' 'e'd 'ad enough . . . an' 'e
reckoned to work 'is ticket by pretendin' 'e was a loony—"*

("He's mad," David Audley had said; and "All my officers are
mad," Colonel Colbourne had replied.)

*"—so ev'ryfink 'e touches, or picks up . . . 'e sez, 'No! That's not
it!' Like it might be 'is rifle or 'is boots or 'is bleedin mess tin—'e sez,
'No! That's not it.' . . . Until, in the end, after the doc 'ad seen 'im,
an' the padre an' all, they reckoned that 'e really was a loony—"*

(And also, hadn't Clinton himself said: "All sappers are mad"?)

*"—so they give 'im 'is discharge. An' as 'e grabs it, 'e sez: 'Gor'
blimey! THAT'S IT!' "*

It had never been very funny, that joke—and not least because
it had always been told and retold in situations of extreme
unfunniness. But it had never been more unfunny than now, as he
stretched out and accepted the long-dreamed-of manumission.

"Why do I need a pen?" He heard himself reject his freedom
even as he touched it, as though from far away.

"It's August seventh today." The brigadier rebuttoned his
blouse with his newly freed hand. "You can date it from today if
you wish. Although Major de Souza will have to process it and

arrange transport. But that will only be a formality, for he has all the necessary Army Instructions to hand."

The bloody man was so bloody sure of himself that Fred was tempted for a fraction of a second to put him to the test. But then he remembered that his pen was dry, and he'd lost his indelible pencil. And it would be no joke to face Amos de Souza, who possessed the same document, even as a joke, anyway—any more than he could face Uncle Luke if it hadn't been, damn him—*damn him, and damn them all!*

He transferred the envelope to his good left hand and began to fumble with his own top button, forcing his clumsy promoted second finger to do its new work in default of its useless superior.

"So"—it pleased him absurdly that his bad hand obeyed him faultlessly with the brigadier watching it—"what are my first orders then . . . Freddie?"

The brigadier stopped watching his hand and met his eyes. But now, at least, he was truly ready for that steel to rasp down his own. Which was wonderfully more exciting than anything that had happened to him for a very long time.

"Good." Clinton seemed to take his victory for granted, without pleasure. "But they're not simple ones. You may not like them."

Fred felt the weight of the envelope inside his blouse, against his heart. "That doesn't surprise me one bit." All he had to do was to think of that weight as *freedom*—then he could accept it. Because freedom ought to be heavier than servitude. "Who are you hunting now?"

Clinton's stare became blank. "What makes you think I'm hunting anyone?"

Fred knew he was right. "Kyri—Colonel Michaelides—he said you were a manhunter. Isn't that what TRR-two has been doing: hunting Germans?"

"Yes." Clinton paused. "But I am not hunting a German now, Major. It's an Englishman I want now, I'm sorry to say."

Part Four

The Price of Freedom

In the Teutoburg Forest, Germany, August 8, 1945

CHAPTER ONE

Down in the castle courtyard below, someone started singing in a high, sweet voice, quite destroying Fred's concentration in an instant.

> *"Als die Römer frech geworden,*
> *Zogen sie nach Deutschlands Norden,*
> *Vorne beim Trompetenschwall*
> *Ritt der Generalfeldmarschall,*
> *Herr Quintilius Varus—"*

For a moment the very sweetness of the sound, rendered crystal clear in the morning air by some acoustic accident even within his bedroom, deceived him. Then the meaning of the words registered.

> *"Doch in Teuboburger Walde*
> *Hu, wie pfiff der Wind so kalte;*
> *Raben flogen durch die Luft,*
> *Und es war ein Moderduft*
> *Wie von Blut und Leichen!"*

That was quite enough, thought Fred vengefully, throwing back the sheet and starting towards the window across the bare boards.

> *"Protzlich aus des Waldes Düster*
> *Brachen krampfhaft die Cherusker*
> *Mitt Gott für Fürst und Vaterland—"*

Far below him, foreshortened by the angle of sight, there was a German soldier—or anyway, a man in field-gray overalls and a German steel helmet—washing the brigadier's Humber Snipe as he sang. But as Fred opened his own mouth there was a sharp knock on the door behind him.

"Come in!" He turned from the window quickly.

"Mornin', sir." The soldier who had swept up all his clothes and equipment the night before appeared in the doorway. "Trooper Leighton—*char* up, sir. An' your bath'll be ready in ten minutes—I 'ave to bring the 'ot water up, 'cause the pipes broke on this floor, so I'm your *bheesti*, sir."

> *"Weh! das war sin grosses Morden!*
> *Sie erschlugen die Kohorten—"*

"I'll take the major's tea, Lucy." David Audley appeared from behind the man, fully dressed and with a cup of tea already in one hand. "You go and fill his bath." He grinned at Fred. "Blood-thirsty, isn't it! 'Woe! There was a great killing!' Morning, Fred."

Although he very carefully hadn't drunk too much the night before, there was a small knot of pain just above Fred's left eye. "Where's my uniform? Where are my clothes?" he snapped at the trooper.

"Get the major's things first, Lucy." Audley supplemented the question unnecessarily as he lifted the steaming mug out of the man's hand. *"Juldi!"* He grinned again as the man scuttled away. "Lucy started his army service as a band boy in India, so he prefers to be addressed in Urdu. But you don't need to worry about your stuff—it'll be superb. Caesar Augustus insists on nothing less. He says that a Guards turnout impresses the Germans—or 'the Cherusci,' *die Cherusker*— as he calls them. One of Hermann's tribes, that is. And the Redcaps too, when they catch us 'fraternizing.' Saves trouble, he says."

Fred frowned. The almost-falsetto song was even now recounting the massacre of the Roman Army by the Cherusci in grisly and ill-omened detail, and somehow Audley's early-morning cheerfulness made it worse.

"You're not late, don't worry. It's just that I'm an early bird." Audley misread his expression as he handed over the cup. "I've only dropped in to apologize if I disturbed you in the night."

"Disturbed me?" He took a gulp of the scalding tea, and it instantly started to perform its daily miracle. "You didn't disturb me, David."

"Oh, good!" Audley blinked. "It's just . . . I'm next door . . . and I shout in my sleep, so I'm told. I have these nightmares about a tank I once briefly occupied which was absolutely full of flies—big, fat greeny-black ones. But I don't have 'em so often now. They're going away—like my stutter. It's the th-therapeutic effect of the soft life we now lead, the MO says. But I think it's the absence of tanks from my life. I *never* liked them, you know." He took two long steps past Fred and leaned out of the window. "SHUT UP, OTTO! 'FLUCH AUF DICH' TO YOU, TOO—YOU BLOODY CHERUSKER! SHUT UP!" He turned back, grinning widely again. "He always sings his Teutoburger song when he's washing the cars, and it really gets on my nerves. I think he only does it to remind us that victorious armies can come unstuck in Germany if they don't watch out, too. He's a caution, is our Otto! A man of many parts."

Fred looked down into the courtyard, where the silenced Otto had moved on to Major McCorquodale's French limousine. "He sings as though he's lost two of them."

"Lost two of them?" Audley followed his glance. "Oh, I see! Yes, the Crocodile did say something about 'castrati' singing when he first heard him. But the way old Otto gets on with the local girls suggests quite the opposite, if Hughie is to be believed."

"Yes? And where did we get him from—did you tell me?" The golden elixir of British Army life had quite dissolved the pain over his eye, and he felt suddenly benevolent towards the young dragoon. Besides which, of course, there was the boy's pristine innocence.

"Do you know, I'm not quite sure." Audley sounded a little surprised with himself. "I think he just turned up one day and made himself useful. Maybe he brought one of his wild boars with him—that would certainly have been a passport to acceptance in this mess!" He thought for a moment. "But you'll have to ask Amos, or Hughie. One of 'em's sure to know, if the other doesn't."

Amos de Souza, thought Fred with a pang of doubt verging so closely on disbelief that it was painful. If he had to stake his life on one officer in this unit, he would have hazarded it cheerfully on Major de Souza. But in spite of his instinct—and in spite of the night before last, which would have added circumstantial proof to that instinct until Brigadier Clinton had reinterpreted those events for him—in spite of all that, Major de Souza's name was on the brigadier's list, and high up too—second only to that of Colonel 'Caesar Augustus' Colbourne himself.

Damn and damn and damn and damn! he thought, remembering his own troubled sleep. This was going to be bad, one way or another if Clinton was right and if Otto Schild had sung a true song:

> *Yet, in the Teutoburg Forest*
> *Cold blew the wind,*
> *And the ravens flew above.*
> *There was an air of doom,*
> *As of blood and corpses . . .*

"You'll catch cold if you stand there in the window. This isn't Greece, you know." Audley swung his arms. "God knows what it'll be like in winter! Always supposing the Crocodile hasn't got me posted to a tank landing-craft for the invasion of Malaya!"

Fred realized that he had shivered. "Oh, I don't think there's much chance of that, David." He forced a reassuring grin. Audley was a loyal young man as well as a clever one, if Clinton's judgment could be relied on; and it was an irony that he was the only unfree man among them. But . . . (and brave too, Clinton had said: "foolishly and suicidally brave, according to his CO"; but that was no more than had been expected of very young officers, wasn't it?) . . . *but* . . . it was no real consolation, among all these other veteran officers, to have to rely on the least veteran, and most callow and awkward, if push came to shove today.

"You don't?" After searching Fred's grin for a long moment, Audley seized on his reassurance eagerly. But then the look became calculating. "And you *are* a friend of the brigadier's, aren't you! And a bloody dark horse, therefore—at least, according to Hughie, anyway!"

Poor boy! "I wouldn't put too much store on that—" A dull thump at the door stopped him from continuing to qualify his statement. "Come in!"

There was a scuffling noise outside before the door opened, to reveal Trooper Leighton piled high up with Fred's belongings.

"Put it all down, Lucy, put it all down!" Audley started to unload the man quickly of his variously well-pressed or well-blancoed and well-polished cargo. "Put it all down—and get out, man—*juldi, juldi!*"

Trooper Leighton gave Fred an agonized glance. "Your bath,

194

sir. Major M'Crocodile's servant took all the 'ot water while my back was turned."

"It doesn't matter." Fred was grateful for having been saved from contradicting the rumor Clinton wanted spreading. "I prefer to wash in cold water. Just bring me enough hot for shaving."

"Thank you, sir."

"No?" Audley closed the door on the man. "Why not?"

The battle dress was as immaculate as Audley had promised, Fred saw with relief. And for good measure, his major's crowns were there on the straps, too. "What?" This was hardly the moment to tell Audley that, according to Hughie, Captain Audley himself was a good friend of the brigadier's. Because Audley would know that that was a distorted version of the truth. "What?"

"Ah!" The boy's downcast expression vanished suddenly. "It's that bomb, of course!" He grinned hugely. "Saved by a bomb—that's me!"

"Yes." Half the conversation over dinner had been about the amazing new bomb that had been dropped in Japan the previous day—or, at least that part of the evening that had not been devoted to a long and acrimonious argument about the origin of the recipe for the delicately spiced meatballs that had formed the meal's *pièce de résistance* . . . which the Crocodile had maintained was Berlin, while the Alligator had originated them in Hamburg; and which, in Otto Schild's unexpected absence, had never finally been resolved. "Yes, I think you can rely on the atomic bomb, David."

Audley nodded happily. "That's what old Kenworthy said. Bloody marvelous!"

"Kenworthy?" Fred's memory of the little bespectacled major was of sullen silence and heavy drinking. "But he didn't say anything."

"It was after you left." Audley nodded again. "He perked up then for a bit, before he was sick—before Lucy and Hughie carried him away and tucked him up." Nod. "But he said the Japs would be waving the white flag within a week. Or if they didn't, it didn't matter. Because then there wouldn't be any Japs left, so it came to the same thing. And that we'd all be going home." This time Audley shrugged his immense shoulders. "But that was just before he threw up—which was just after he said *he* was going home tomorrow. Which is today of course. . . . But I don't think he will."

Fred looked across the room to his valise, and to the zip-fastened pocket in it with the lock, the key to which hung around his neck with his identity discs. Because his own envelope was there, with his wallet and all the things he had taken out of his pockets last night. "Why not?"

"He was very drunk, drunker than I've ever seen him. So I don't think he'll be able to walk," explained Audley innocently. "But he certainly *talked* last night—before he returned his Hamburger or Berliner meatballs to us, *coram populo*. Which was all the more spectacular because that isn't like him either. . . . Besides which he's not due for release until next year, by my calculations."

"What did he say?" It was unfortunate that Audley was the one officer he couldn't ask about the efficacy of the long brown envelope in practice, and whether it had ever been opened and given a date before.

"Oh . . . he said this bomb was the real thing—not just like the Tallboys our gallant boys in blue dropped on the Bielefeld viaduct just down the road, which brought it down even though they missed it by *miles*." The boy's eyes widened as he exaggerated the RAF's incompetence. "He said it almost certainly isn't very *big*. . . . But that doesn't matter, because it doesn't work like an ordinary bomb. It's quite different from all the stuff we've dropped on Germany. In fact, he says that there's no limit to its destructive power, and that the Jap scientists would know that themselves. So the one the Yanks dropped on wherever it was is probably just a little demonstration job. Some demo!"

It was plain that Audley wasn't a scientist. But then, of course, he wasn't: he was a historian potentially, and an unwilling ex-tank commander and temporary captain actually, at this moment. "What does Major Kenworthy do? Refresh my memory, David? He collects machinery? But what was he . . . before the war?"

"What he really does . . . don't ask me! He never talks to me, or anyone else, much. But he is damn good with his machinery, certainly." The boy was still so entranced with the end of the war that the words tumbled out of him. "What he *was* . . . I think was a physics lecturer at Manchester, or Birmingham or somewhere. But he kept talking about his friends in the Cavendish Laboratory at Cambridge last night. Is there a Cavendish Laboratory at Cambridge? It's all Greek to me, I tell you!"

"Yes." It was almost Greek to Fred, too. But there was a hint of Teutoburger *Blut and Leichen* about it also, with his mathematician's war-weakened recollections of the bright boys of the Cavendish in mind as well as what Clinton had said yesterday.

"Well, whatever it is, it's got my vote if it'll end the war before the Crocodile sets his teeth into me!" Audley peered out of the window again. "Ah! Good old Otto's finally got round to my little car. So you won't have to be ashamed of it if we use it today." He came back to Fred. "You know you're with me today? Everyone else can pursue their private interests or do their paperwork . . . or scratch their balls, contemplate their navels, and generally recover from yesterday's journey and last night's excesses. But Jacko Devenish, and Hughie, and I—*and you, Fred*—for our sins, we four have to report to Amos bright and early, directly after brekker." He returned his attention suddenly to the scene below. "PUT YOUR BACK INTO IT, MAN! GET THAT MUD OUT FROM UNDER THOSE MUDGUARDS! Yes . . . but then, of course, you'll know all about that already . . . won't you, Fred!"

Driver Hewitt had done his work well, and quickly, too. Because even before Clinton had arrived in the mess to contribute his own brief but masterly performance, which had only hinted at an old and special relationship between them, his fellow officers had eyed him differently. So now it was not to be wondered that this young man was fishing. That, and not his self-revealing apology, was the reason for this visit, of course.

"THAT'S BETTER!" The boy's pretended lack of interest in Fred's advance knowledge of the day's operations was not badly done for one of such tender years.

"Why should I know that?" What made the lie easier was the certainty that Audley wouldn't like the truth any more than he himself had done, when the time came for it—if the time came for it.

"Oh, come on! Aren't you Our Freddie's long-lost brother? Don't disappoint me—" Audley stopped as he registered Fred's frown, and his own expression changed from youthful, falsely innocent ugliness to an honest ugliness older than his years. "No, of course, that's not how the game is played, is it!" He sighed. "And to think that I've been blaming myself for taking you away from your Greek fleshpots, because of my glowing references to the Fattorini family that day in the monastery! When in fact you were old acquaintances—" He stopped again, and all expression blanked from his face, reminding Fred oddly of Clinton himself. "In fact, now I come to think of that particular day in all its beauty . . . that Greek bandit you were with—*he* certainly wasn't there by accident, was he!" A hint of belated satisfaction reanimated the boy's face. "So, of course, *you* weren't, either— were you. So I've been slow, slow as usual!"

It was exactly as the brigadier had said: there was always a danger in making pictures from inadequate evidence and misinterpreted facts. So this boy, although he was no fool, was doing that now. But there was nothing he could do about it yet.

197

"My shaving water will be getting cold, David." He steeled himself against the boy's enmity with the promise of a future explanation—one day, if not today. And also, hadn't Audley himself been playing games, with his story of those flyblown nightmares? "And I'd also like my breakfast."

"Yes." Audley was himself again as he started to turn towards the door. "Well, I can recommend the breakfast here. It's quite outrageously Old English, with mounds of bacon and eggs, and fried bread and bangers. And tomatoes and mushrooms too, if Otto's obeyed the Alligator's orders." He almost left, but then leaned back through the gap in the door. "But you'll pardon me if I hope your shaving water is stone-cold, eh?"

Fred stared at the finally closed door, in further agreement with the brigadier. The boy had something about him, in spite of all his defects, in spite of his mixture of arrogance and uncertainty—the mixture that so outrageously loosened his tongue, leading him always to say too much. But what was it, exactly?

He reached into his valise for the scuffed and worn toilet bag that was the only thing he had left of those original gifts from his mother on the eve-of-war so long ago to reach this final eve-of-peace that was dawning amidst Japanese ruin far away. The writing case had long gone, and those three slim volumes of Plato's *Apology* and *Crito* and *Phaedo* with it—somewhere in Italy they were, with the Bible he'd always meant to read, but somehow never had.

What was it?

"*Audley?*" The brigadier had said. "*Yes, he is an exception, and not just in the matter of loyalty. Because all the others were handpicked by me. Just as you yourself have been handpicked finally, Major. And if you and I fail now . . . then it will be back to the beginning again. But much less confidently.*"

But as he lifted the bag, he didn't want to think about that now. He had thought of that long enough already, across the candlelight of those same plundered silver candlesticks of the first night that had reappeared on the table last night. And he had continued to think about it during the night, while sleep eluded him, and then again on waking, before Otto Schild had sung his song "*Yet, in the Teutoburg Forest, the cold wind blew.*"

A cold wind also blew in the brigadier's list—

> *Colbourne,*
> *de Souza,*
> *The Crocodile,*
> *The Alligator,*
> *Carver-Hart,*
> *Kenworthy.*

He didn't want to think of any of them now, but they wouldn't let him go. *"All the others have been eliminated. And the very devil of it is, that I can't believe that any of those men would betray me either. But that only means that I'm making a mistake, that I'm making pictures which I want to see, Fattorini—Fred. . . . So now we have to play for high stakes. Because I need all these men for the future, when the stakes may become even higher—because all of them are marked for promotion."*

But not Audley, of course!

The bathroom was huge, and its plumbing was antediluvian as well as foreign. This wasn't the servants' floor, but it was obviously for the less important guests. (Although he wasn't a less important guest in Schwartzenburg Castle; he was just a late-comer—later than *Colbourne, de Souza, The Crocodile, The Alligator, Johnnie Carver-Hart, Professor Kenworthy and Uncle Tom Cobbley and all, right the way down to Lieutenant (temporary Captain) David Audley.)*

Audley had been wrong about the water: Trooper Leighton had done his best with it, so that the shaving water in its antique silver bucket was more than warm, and even the bathwater was tepid.

Audley—

He stopped there, staring at himself in the mirror with the lather on his face and a new blade in his razor, as a new thought occurred to him.

"But . . . Audley, yes. I took him on last year, in France. And only temporarily, to repay a debt and because there was no one else I could get who spoke fluent French at short notice . . . which he does do, although with a perfectly execrable accent. . . . It was his godfather who gave him to me, to save his getting killed, like all the other subalterns in his regiment were doing, in the bocage there. And I nearly got myself killed, actually—in a quite different operation from this, mark you . . . out of which I picked up several other useful men who are now obligated to me—Sergeant Devenish and Driver Hewitt among them, as it happens. But that's another story. The irony now is that Audley is the only one we can trust . . . because I didn't pick him!"

He saw another story in the mirror suddenly, in his own eyes. *"Of course, afterwards I checked him all the way back—as I have checked you. And the others, so I thought. But no matter! He did well in France. So . . . I kept him on. Because he's also going to be a useful man one day, when he matures. Because inside that great hulking overgrown subaltern's body there just may be that extra thing that we need, and which is going to be in short supply in our business after the war, I fear."*

There was also another story there, Fred saw much too late, but which Audley had seen before him, albeit only just. A story of two officers on a Greek hillside, the English one (or the Anglo-Scottish-Italian one!) innocently and accidentally, but the Greek-Cypriot bravely and deliberately in the execution of his duty— was that it? And if there was . . . then was there more than that, with no blind chance dictating events, all the way back to Frederick Clinton and Uncle Luke long ago? Was that it? Had Kyriakos deliberately tested him under stress, to bring him to Osios Konstandinos at Clinton's bidding?

He rasped the razor across his cheek, suddenly certain that he was hungry for more than his Old English breakfast. But he wouldn't think of that now: he would think of David Audley—

"But he's too young for this. It's always a mistake to give a man's work to boys—even lucky ones, like our young David. Because he lost several of his nine lives in Normandy, before I ever caught up with him. And then I took several more of them, through my own stupidity, I'm sorry to say. So, although you can use him now—and trust him—I'd be obliged if you could return him to me intact if you can, Major!

Fred examined his face carefully for missed stubble. With his uniform so well-pressed, and everything else so well-polished and blancoed, he needed to look his best this day.

"But his survival isn't tomorrow's objective, Major. And neither is yours. Because what I now need above all else is a name."

He made his way back to the room, blindly and automatically, and put on his wristwatch first, while still stark naked, as he always did when he had been able to wash properly first. And then he put on the clean change of clothes that Trooper Leighton had brought with the same thought he also always had when that added luxury had been available: that, if possible, one should always go into action with clean underwear.

"What I want is the name of the traitor in my camp, and nothing else. And then I want him alive. Because we've got work to do now."

In the final analysis, thought Fred as he turned his shoulder to the long mirror on the wall to admire his new badge of rank, if he failed, or if he found the work uncongenial, he could use that envelope with major's crowns on his shoulders, anyway!

"Listen, Fred. Something happened yesterday a long way from here, in Japan—at a place called Hiroshima."

CHAPTER TWO

Audley looked round again, and then consulted his watch for the umpteenth time.

"What are you looking for, David?" Except for the People's Car and the jeep containing Sergeant Devenish and Driver Hewitt, the courtyard of Schwartzenburg Castle was quite empty. "We're late already."

"Only two minutes. And I know the way to the Exernsteine."

"Yes, so the adjutant said." Fred watched the boy curiously. "But we're still late, according to his schedule. So what are you waiting for?"

"I just thought our prisoner might turn up—'Corporal Keys.' I havn't laid eyes on him since we handed him over. But he might still be on the premises, damn it!" Audley frowned up at the blank rows of windows above him. "Isn't he the object of our peregrinations today?"

Peregrinations? And the boy was still fishing, too. But in his heart Fred couldn't blame him. "The instrument, but not the object. Get in the car, David—that's an order." He stretched his own orders slightly. "You'll see him soon enough, now that he's been promoted."

"What?" Audley's mouth opened comically.

"Get in the car." *Poor boy! How many lives have you got left, then?*

"Get in the car, and all shall be revealed, David." He had to stop there because Audley had closed his mouth quickly and was already folding himself up into the little car.

"You don't mind me driving?" The engine whirred behind them reliably. "I'm actually not a very good driver. I think driving's *boring*. But on this occasion . . . I do know the car, and the way." Audley looked at him with eager expectation as the People's Car shot through the castle gateway with half an inch to spare on its passenger's side.

"Yes—no!" Fred shuddered as they barely missed the line of larger transports, which included Major Kenworthy's monster, parked under the castle walls—a line complete with an armed sentry now, he noted.

"You were saying?" Audley couldn't contain his curiosity. "Where's the prisoner, then?"

"Watch the road, David."

"Yes—damn it, I *am* watching it." Audley peered into his mirror. "It's all right, our escort is right behind us. You were saying—about Field Marshal Keys?"

"He's done better for himself than that." Fred began to tire of the riddle game. "As of last night he became a free man."

"*Ah* . . ." Audley swung the little car onto the main road. "Now . . . I *thought* there weren't many extra precautions last night, when I took my evening constitutional and had a look round. Because I only got challenged on the horse lines, by the transport—not anywhere in the castle at all!" He nodded sagely at the road. "And that did strike me as . . . *rather* odd, after our earlier failures."

Clinton was right. "Did you meet anybody . . . on your peregrinations?"

"Meet anybody? They were all pissed, more or less, if you ask me—celebrating the end of the jolly old war! And so was I, a bit. . . . No. Only Amos and Busy Izzy doing their accustomed rounds, checking up on the wine cellar and such, of course—and the state of the duty officer's liver, I shouldn't wonder. . . . But he's *gone*, you say? Our first real and undoubted success— Number Twenty-one—'the Key of the Door'—?" He stopped suddenly, and then thumped the wheel, causing the little car to shake and swerve slightly. "But *of course* he's gone! How stupid of me!"

"Why?" If the boy wanted to talk, who was he to stop him?

"Number Twenty-one! What does the key do?" Audley ac-

celerated. "Why, he opens the door to reveal Number Sixteen—
'Sweet-Sixteen-and-Never-Been-Kissed'!" Then he looked at Fred
quickly. "And Clinton trusted him? But obviously he did, the foxy
old swine! And of course, Number Twenty-one had a bloody
convincing tale to tell, too. Not just 'Come home, and all is
forgiven,' but 'Come home . . . or someone will put a bullet
through you, like they did to my ersatz self last night'!" He
thumped the wheel again, with the same disconcerting effect.
"And by God, that would certainly convince me! Because . . .
letting him go—after all the trouble we had taking him. . . . Oh!
He's a lusty old blackbird is Our Freddie!"

Clinton was right—the boy was sharp.

"God! I wish he'd let *me* go!" Audley sighed. "Only then you
wouldn't see my tail for dust, though!"

"Maybe he will, if you're good, David."

"Some hope! It's nineteen bloody forty-seven for me—if I'm
lucky." Suddenly the car slowed, and so abruptly that Fred was
instantly afraid that the jeep behind would collide with them.
But when he looked over his shoulder he saw that Driver Hewitt
was prudently keeping his distance.

"What's the matter?"

"Nothing's the matter. But I just remembered that you were
going to reveal all. And you haven't actually said very much, have
you?"

Fred let the unspoilt German countryside slide past them for a
few moments while he collected his thoughts. But then, in spite of
his orders, he was tempted to take another route to his own
destination.

"What do you think you've been doing?" It would be interesting to find out how much this clever boy had worked out. "Not
just since I've been around—before that?"

"What have *I* been doing, or *we*?" Audley slowed even more,
down almost to walking pace, craning his neck forward.

"Why are you slowing down?"

"There's a checkpoint hereabouts. It won't hold us up, because
they know me perfectly well. . . . That's funny."

"What's funny?"

"The MPs are there—but they're not checking, see?" Audley
followed his own curiosity for a moment. "There's a DP camp
nearby they keep watch on . . . but it looks like anyone can use
this road today." He sniffed and shrugged. "Oh, well . . . I told
you, anyway: officially, we hunt for items of interest. Though, as
far as I'm concerned, it's a bit bloody late to find out just how
good old Jerry's tanks were. But I go through the motions, as my
old troop sergeant used to say"—he acclerated—"God rest his

black and shriveled soul, like his black and shriveled body." He gave Fred a sidelong look. "You know how you come out of a brewed-up Cromwell? About the size of a bloody chimpanzee, actually."

"But what have you actually been doing?"

"Ah . . . well, among other things, I've done a bit of scouting round the Teutoburg Forest, to see if any Roman artifacts have turned up here and there in the last few years, with the bombing and all that, as per my orders." Audley sat back as comfortably as he could in the confined space. "Not that there is anything here. Because the Romans never settled here—or hereabouts. They just got massacred. And the local lads . . . alias the Cherusci and the Chauci and the Chatti, who were the German equivalent of the Sioux and the Black Feet and other Red Indians . . . *they* all carried off the loot, rejoicing, just like the Indians did after General Custer had stood his Last Stand. So there wouldn't be anything, would there?" Another shrug. "All the good Roman stuff will have surfaced over on the other side of the Rhine."

"Don't play games with me, David."

"I'm not playing games. It's the truth, Fred." Knowing at last that he was playing some sort of game, Audley played it innocently and well. "Those Germans in the picture I showed you—the picture I showed you when I thought you didn't know what was happening—*they* operated in Roman Germany, not here. But when we arrived back there in March, after we were pulled out of that Greek raid of ours, we did fuck-all most of the time. At least, *I* did. Because I was on transport. And every time I got hold of a decent car, some senior bastard took it off me. Like the egregious Crocodile did with my French car, for example. Which is why I ended up with this little dodge-'em—" He caught his tongue quickly as he felt Major Fattorini stiffen beside him. "All right, all right, *all right*! So . . . we were after the Jerries in the picture. Is that what you want me to say?"

"You could start in Greece, David."

"*In Greece?* God, that was the scene of our first *debacle*." Audley swung the wheel to avoid an old woman in black who was pulling a cart round a heap of rubble regardless of him. They were on the edge of a ruined town now. "But you were there yourself, damn it!"

"But what were we after?" The lying "we" had a distinctly bitter taste. But he had to keep the upper hand.

Audley took a breath. "I don't see why I should tell you what you already know—and better than I do, too."

"Tell me, all the same. If you want the rest of it, David."

"Oh . . . *shit!*" But the boy craned his neck again as they turned out of the ruins. "That's another one? I think the MPs are all on strike today."

"Tell me!"

"Okay, okay! Clinton was trying to bring out one of his own men, is what I think *now*. Although all I knew then was that we had to get him alive, and we didn't." He looked at Fred. "Is that it?"

"It is." After the stick, it was time for a carrot. "And that put him back almost three months, David."

"It did?" Audley seized on the information eagerly. "We first got that picture in . . . May, yes? That would be about three months."

"And what do the people in it have in common?" He couldn't resist the extra question.

"Oh . . . that's easy." The prospect of more answers dissolved Audley's caution.

"Yes?"

"Not bloody Roman remains, for a start!" Audley crashed the gears down joyfully as the car began to climb.

"No?"

"No!" Audley tossed his head. "Colonel 'Caesar Augustus' Colbourne may be a loony. But Our Freddie isn't into Roman history—no!"

Fred waited, half expectantly, but also somewhat irritated. Maybe it was the boy's recent military experience, when he had been forced to listen to other people's stupidities in obedient subaltern silence, that now invariably tempted him to hear his own voice saying clever things. But whatever the reason, if he were to remain a useful member of TRR-2 in the future, he would have to learn to hide his bright light more prudently.

"I got it wrong first, actually." Audley steered the little car regardlessly across a succession of potholes in the track that had succeeded the road surface. "Not understanding about Greece, of course."

"You did?"

"Yes." The mockery bounced off Audley's arrogance. "I thought, 'Cushy billet those Jerrie have got for themselves'—pottering round the ruins of all the old German cities. *Roman* cities, rather: *Confluentes, Moguntiacum, Colonia Ara Agrippinesnium.* Picking up this and that after the fires had cooled down, and after their ARP people had carted off the bodies, and *long* after the jolly old RAF had departed—a *real* cushy billet!" He pulled the car to a halt off the track under a stand of great beech trees through which a bright green meadow was visible, falling away on their right. "Very *German* of course, all the same. Great scholarship as

205

well as great military prowess—*too* damn great military prowess for my liking. But great scholars too, they are. And they've always been fascinated with classical history—hence all the famous stuff in their museums. And hence that Roman fort we were billeted in, and the one the kaiser rebuilt on the same line . . . and that bloody great statue in the woods not far from here. . . . So it was a damn good cover, as well as a cushy billet—but cover for *what*, eh?" Audley stared at him for an instant, then began to unwind himself out of his seat.

Fred followed suit, staring through the trees as he stretched his legs. Not far ahead there seemed to be a great gray cliff rising up from the grass of a wide forest clearing.

"*Nazis*, I thought." Audley towered over the car. "Bloody Nazis taking cover in a nice, respectable job, hoping that we wouldn't look for them in Roman Germany, dressed in scholars' gowns. At least, that would be their second line of defense, anyway, if we did trace them. Because it was pretty clear they'd all dispersed and gone underground long before we appeared on the scene. Which meant they knew they had something to hide." Audley pointed towards the cliff. "Shall we walk? The RV is just down the track from here, by the rocks"—he looked at his watch—"but we're still in good time."

Fred fell into slow step beside him.

"But then we started to uncover facts as well as names and dates. And then it didn't seem to work so well, my theory. Because some of them really were pretty distinguished scholars and *not* Nazis at all. Like old Professor Schmidt, for example. And Langer, who was at Oxford. Although he wasn't a classicist, or an archaeologist. He was a very smart scientist, so I discovered—quite by accident. . . . And Enno von Mitzlaff—he *was* an archaeologist, young and up-and-coming. And then he was a damn good soldier, until he lost his arm in the desert. But he wasn't a Nazi—he *certainly* wasn't a Nazi, by God!"

Audley was looking at the cliff now. And yet, it wasn't a cliff. It was an extraordinary limestone outcrop . . . or rather, a series of outcrops, some rising up like great blunt fingers into the gray morning sky above the forest.

"But then it looked like *none* of them were Nazis. And they'd been on the job for years, some of them. In fact, it all really started before the war, as a sort of Romano-German encyclopedia, and the bomb-damage rescue-and-recovery part of it was almost an afterthought, even though it became their main work eventually." Audley continued to stare at the rocks. "You know that this was a place of pilgrimage in medieval times? Some bright religious entrepreneur had a replica of the holy places in

Jerusalem carved into the caves at the bottom. And he may even
have hired a Byzantine sculptor to do the job—possibly a POW
from the Crusades. Or a local man who'd been out East, maybe.
Because it isn't straight Romanesque carving. . . . And then he
fleeced the pilgrims, I expect. . . . But Caesar Augustus says it
goes a back a long way before that as a holy place—all the way to
the pagan times of his Cherusci, Chauci, and Chatti, who
worshiped rocks and trees. And he may actually be right, because
my old Latin master, who is a proper old pagan . . . only *he*
doesn't worship rocks and trees, it's Plato and rugger with
him . . . *he* says it's an old Christian trick to set up shop on other
gods' shrines—"

"They weren't Nazis?" He still wasn't sure whether Audley
digressed deliberately or out of habit. "So what were they?"

"Ah . . . no, they weren't Nazis. But I still had this strange
feeling that it was a cover of some sort." The boy gave him an
uncharacteristically shy sidelong look. "It was really the old Croc
who put me straight, in what passes for one of his more civilized
moments. Accidentally, of course . . . if I'm right, that is?"

"Go on, David."

"Yes . . . well, it was when he was rabbiting on about his
favorite subject one night—the Germans, and what we're doing
to them . . . and what we *should* be doing to them, and all that.
And someone—the Alligator most likely, because he likes baiting
the Croc—*he* said that it was no more difficult than sorting
apples: you kept the good ones and threw away the bad ones. And
the Croc says, quick as a flash, 'Och, but what is a *guid
Gairrman?*'" Audley grinned hugely as he exaggerated McCorquodale's slight burr. "'It's nae guid simply saying it's those that
fought with us against the wee man Hitlerrr. Because there's
many a guid decent man that disliked the both—an' the more so
when yon bluidy bastard in the Kremlin comes into the picture,
as he was bound to do soonerrr or laterrr!'" The smile vanished.
"And he's right, of course."

Right, of course! And so Major McCorquodale seemed then to
be Brigadier Clinton's man to the life, too. *But Major McCorquodale was on the brigadier's list, too!*

"And I was right also, in a way . . . even when I was wrong."
The look on Fred's face halted Audley. "Wasn't I? Am I?"

Fred controlled his disquiet. "Right about what?"

"They were taking cover. Only not just from us—but also from
the Nazis." The boy lifted his hand. "From *both of us*, is what I
mean, Fred."

"Why?" The boy wasn't just clever: he was too damn clever.
"Why did they have to hide?"

Audley stared at him. "They weren't nonentities. Old Schmidt was a very well-respected academic. And von Mellenthin was a biologist, or a biochemist or something—in the Croc's field. Which includes his celebrated anthrax trials. And Langer would have been a top man in poison gasses. . . . And the word is that the Yanks have found some bloody terrifying new gas the Germans were making, down south somewhere—tons of it." He shivered. "And . . . these chaps . . . they didn't want to help Hitler brew the stuff up, to use on *us*. But they also didn't want to help *us* . . . to maybe brew it up ourselves, and then serve it back on their own people, if things came to the crunch—if all Hitler's other secret weapons started to bite." He looked at Fred questioningly. "Am I right?"

"So why did they run, at the last?" He had to find out how much else the boy had worked out. "After we'd won?"

"It wasn't at the last." Audley blinked. "That threw me for a bit. But then I found out all about Colonel von Mitzlaff—he was mine because he was panzer specialist. And also not a scientist: just a poor damned archaeologist who was put into a tank, like I'm a poor damned would-be historian who suffered the same fate"—now a grimace—"only his tanks had better guns and better armor than mine did, Fred."

"But you were a lot luckier, in the end." The memory of what Audley had said about von Mitzlaff's fate after the Hitler bomb plot harshened his voice.

"Not luckier. Just braver." A muscle moved in Audley's cheek. "But . . . unlucky too, yes. But he also broke the rules, too—I think."

"What rules?"

"What rules?" Audley looked past him towards the vehicles on the brow of the track behind them, at Devenish and Hewitt. "Should I get those two under cover somewhere, do you think?"

Softly now! thought Fred. "It wasn't in their orders this time, was it?"

"No." Audley turned his attention to the rocks again, then to a wide lake out of which the farthest of them rose precipitously, and finally across the broad meadow to the dark, encircling woods. "But I don't like this place. I never have."

Fred looked at his own watch. They still had plenty of time. "Why not? You've been here before?"

"Oh, yes. It's one of Caesar Augustus's favorite spots. He brought me here a couple of times to help with his measurements."

Professor Schmidt's rules could wait for a moment. "Measurements for what?"

"He wants to drain the lake." Audley pointed. "See how the land falls away? It could be done with the right equipment." He gave Fred a lopsided grin. "In my innocence, I did rather think that was why he'd recruited you, before I learnt better: as an officer of engineers, to advise on lake drainage, you see."

"Why does he want to do that?"

"Oh . . . it's all to do with 'saltus Teutoburgiensis'—how Tacitus described the Varus disaster. 'Saltus' meaning 'forest pass' or 'glade' or some such."

"He thinks the battle was *here*, you mean?"

"No, not exactly. Because it wasn't actually a battle. In any sort of proper battle the Romans would have licked the pants off the Germans. It was more like a series of cumulative ambushes over miles and miles of trackless bloody woods"—Audley pointed again, but over the lake—"in dozens of hillsides like this, and ravines. More like the way the Afghans cut up the British army in the Khyber Pass, only with dense forest, rather than mountains. But he thinks it might have ended here . . . the big tribal celebration in a place consecrated to the gods, with the prisoners as sacrificial offerings. Because, apparently, they didn't only nail 'em up on trees and burn 'em in wicker baskets, like in Britain— they also trod 'em in water under hurdles, and cast 'em off high places onto sharpened stakes." The boy dropped his hand and sighed. "Cheers him up no end, the Exernsteine does. But then, as I told you, he's mad as a hatter. Because I think he may be right. Only . . . that makes this place pretty nasty, in my reckoning. All those poor bloody Roman POWs being crucified and roasted and drowned and spiked here—d'you see?"

Fred stared for a moment at the oiled metal-gray sheen on the water of the lake, on which the brooding sky and the gray rocks were reflected. Then he shook his head. "Tell me about Professor Schmidt's rules, David."

"Yes." Audley roused himself too. "Old Schmidt was my main job, you see."

"Because he was a historian?"

"That's right, I guess. But I don't really know whether he had any rules. Only . . . he got these chaps together, all nice and safely, before the war. And the proper scientists among them all had something to contribute to his achaeology, it seems. Like, new methods of dating material, and soil analysis, and suchlike— 'scientific archaeology' was what he called it—some long German words. And they kept their heads down and did their work and minded their own business—always very busy, they were. Like, they were good Germans. But they were always safely in the remote past.

"But then Enno von Mitzlaff turned up in '42, invalided out of the Wehrmacht, and looking for work—see?"

"Because he was an archaeologist?"

"He was. And also he was old Schmidt's godson. So maybe the old man just wanted to save him, too. Only, unfortunately, he wouldn't stay saved—he probably knew more of what was going on elsewhere."

So the boy didn't know everything, then. "And he got involved in the plot against Hitler, of course—you said?"

"Yes. And then the fat was in the fire." Audley nodded. "Maybe Schmidt or one of the others was also in on it. I don't somehow think so, but I don't know yet for sure. Only, it didn't matter anyway, because the Gestapo was in a vengeful mood by then—I got this from a fairly senior policeman in Bonn, whom we haven't quite got round to sacking yet . . . But he says that old Schmidt put the police and the Gestapo off as long as he could." There was a bleak look in Audley's eyes. "Schmidt was too old and fat to run himself. But he did his best for the others—which is really what has made our job so difficult, I suppose. . . . But he was a brave man too, like his godson. One of the Crocodile's 'guid decent men,' I'd say."

It was like receiving a delayed message of a friend's death in Burma: it had all happened months ago, while he'd still been trudging through Italian mud, so it was too late for tears. "And then?"

"There was a big fire in Schmidt's office, in which all his records were conveniently destroyed—all the names of personnel, as well as the marvelous new scientific techniques they'd pioneered. Which, from an archaeological point of view, was a great tragedy. So Schmidt added a convenient heart attack to it. Not a fatal one, but enough to delay the investigation somewhat. So by the time this smart Gestapo *obergruppenführer* finally tumbled to the fact that the fire hadn't been caused by a British incendiary bomb, and the heart attack wasn't genuine, all the other birds had flown."

And I was probably on the beach at Vouliagmeni, thought Fred. "And Schmidt?"

"He knew the form, when the game was up and the savages were closing in—just like old Varus did. Only swords are out of fashion now, so he shot himself with an old Webley revolver he'd taken off a British officer in *his* war, in 1917. So no piano wire for him, just like no wicker basket or high rocks for Varus." Audley looked at his watch again. "But the policeman did also give me more than he gave the *obergruppenführer*, whom he insists he didn't like." Another shrug. "Or it may be he just saw which way the wind was blowing by then. Or it could even be the Gestapo was too busy shooting ordinary defeatists by then, I don't know. But that wasn't what was really important."

"What was that?"

"He gave us a cross-bearing on where Zeitzler might be holed up—*Ernst Zeitzler*, alias Corporal Keys. Because Zeitzler was another genuine archaeologist. And his particular specialization was—guess what?—the study of the Roman frontier. Which was why we moved down to the unspeakable Kaiserburg, of course . . . although it was Amos who finally tracked him down, I must admit. So I can't claim all the credit, even though I deserve most of it."

Typical Audley! "And Zeitzler is Number Sixteen's best friend?" Now they were very close to the bone, as well as the appointed hour. "Why didn't you tell me all this the night before last?"

"The night before last?" Audley's memory seemed momentarily to desert him.

"Yes." There was only one thing remaining. "You had your orders, David. You were supposed to tell me what was happening."

Audley made one of his ugliest faces. "I get so many orders. And . . . hell! First, you were late—and then we were pretty damn busy, blundering around in the dark . . . then superintending the death of some poor bloody totally *inoffensive* German—or Pole, or Ukrainian DP—I don't know, damn it!" The boy's square chin lifted, and he looked down on Fred from the height of his extra inches, and then looked around as though he really didn't give a damn.

Good boy! But that didn't change anything. "And . . . ?"

The chin came down slowly, and Audley relaxed slightly, as though he was reassured by what he had seen. "And I didn't enjoy that very much, actually."

That wouldn't do. "And I asked you a question, David. So answer it, please."

The sharpness of his tone reclaimed Audley's attention. And his face did the rest. "Christ, Fred! I know we met in Greece that time, and I know old Matthew—" The wide mouth opened and shut on *Matthew*, like some great ugly deep-sea fish's jaws trawling the seabed. And then it opened again and closed obstinately. "But we've had a lot of bad luck, you know. And I don't really know you, now do I?"

Good boy! Because that was as eloquent as anything else Audley might have said to prove that his mouth wasn't always

211

too big. "And who the hell was I? When you've had all the bad luck you've had, all the way from Greece, even?"

Still nothing. So more than that: so Clinton was right about Audley's being old for his years when it came to the crunch. So now was the moment of truth.

"Yes, David, you are quite right." He nodded without disengaging Audley's eyes. "There is a traitor in the camp. And if you didn't know it for sure before, then you know it now."

Audley studied him for a moment. Then he slowly nodded his acceptance of all those words implied. "So you really *are* the brigadier's inside man?"

"Yes." More than Audley's acceptance, this was his own acceptance of that loyalty for the working day, whatever came after. "I am Clinton's man. And so are you, David—no matter what. Because we have to know who the traitor is. Nothing less will do. So this is a trap, today."

Audley continued to stare at him. And it was also slightly comical to see the boy's hand move up uncertainty to his webbing holster, and then drop down to wipe the palm on his leg beside it.

"Oh . . . *shit!*" Then Audley looked quickly across the meadow, and finally towards the vehicles up the track, where Sergeant Devenish had been walking up and down and Driver Hewitt had been leaning on the jeep, smoking one of his inexhaustible supply of dog-ends, neither able to communicate with the other. "What about *them?*"

He had got it all, in that one brief exchange: all Clinton's logic about the sufficiency of the bait, all his certainty about the traitor's hard-driven determination to take Number 16 from them now, at the last, with all his murderous delaying tactics finally stretched beyond safety, and Major Fattorini here to make the final contact. So perhaps it wasn't unreasonable that his trust even in his own men should weaken with these final certainties.

"They're all right. They're both Clinton's men from way back, David." He remembered that Audley too was in some sense Clinton's man from way back, before TRR-2 had been called into existence. "From France, anyway."

"I know *that*, damn it!" Audley made a face and shook his head simultaneously. "Hughie's been babying me halfway across Europe—I should know *that*. Devenish too." The ugly features twisted as he glanced back up the track again for a moment. "How does it go: 'He was my servant, and the better man'?"

Fred floundered momentarily in his turn. "Then . . . . what do you mean?"

From being questioning, the look became haughty. "I mean, you've just told me exactly how the land lies. And I can accept that . . . because it explains a lot of things—a lot of things I haven't quite understood. All the way from Greece, like you've just said—a whole lot of things, yes!" From being haughty, the look blanked out into nothing. "But how much do *they* know, my men?"

It only irked Fred for a second that he had misread the original question. But then he understood that Audley was still a subaltern at heart, and a well-taught one. So it was no shame on him that he should think of his own subordinates before he risked their lives in some madcap venture. And yet, by the same token, it was time that he got his priorities right. "D'you think anyone's going to catch Sergeant Devenish with his trousers down?" The memory of Devenish on the ridge above Osios Konstandinos, and Kyri's estimation of the man, gave him confidence. "You let him take his chances now, David. Just as we're about to take ours, okay?"

"Mmm . . ." Audley had been looking round even before he had finished condemning the other ranks to their destined fate, taking in the rocks, and the lake and the encircling forest with what must be a tank commander's eyes, which was all the experience he had from that other August, a year ago. But with nothing to see, he had to come back to Fred. "So who is the traitor then, eh?" He fumbled again with his webbing holster, unbuttoning the flap, then rubbing his hand down his leg again, as though his palm were already sweating. "But of course, you don't know, do you? Otherwise we wouldn't be baiting the jolly old mousetrap, of course!" He squinted up the track, past the vehicles. "And I don't even see the cheese yet, anyway." The squint cleared as he came back to Fred once more. "*Not* the Crocodile—*that* would not only be too good to be true, it would also be too confusing. Because no one can be such an absolute *shit*, and also a traitor: that just wouldn't be fair! And the old Croc—he just *isn't* . . . is he? Or not compared with the unspeakable Johnnie—the fifth horseman of the Apocalypse—not *him*, surely—surely?"

"No?" He had to make light of it, just as Audley was trying to do, and for the very same sound military reason: because, to give it its proper due would be to make it something beyond bearing. "Why not, David?"

"Too unbelievable, Fred." The boy came back like lightning. "And therefore too clever for comfort." Nod. "So . . . who— *who?*" He frowned finally, turning the nod into a doubtful shake. "It doesn't make sense, you know."

"Why not?"

"Because everyone's been so damned carefully chosen by Clinton, that's why." The shake continued for a moment, then

213

Audley grinned. "Except me, of course. I was wished on him by my godfather last year, more or less as a favor, when he was suddenly short of a French-speaker. So I'm still here only on trial . . . or more like sufferance. But the others . . . he *chose* 'em. And then he checked 'em back to the cradle, so the story goes. No one forced 'em on him—and there's no bloody 'old boys' network' from school and university with him, either. Or 'the jolly old regiment,' come to that—*definitely* not the Clinton style."

"No?" Anything about Brigadier Clinton interested Fred mightily. "You once said he likes . . . bankers, was it?"

"He likes people with enough money not to be tempted by it. Doesn't matter where it comes from—landed-gentry money, like Johnnie Carver-Hart's, or a whiskey distillery, like the Croc's . . . 'McCorquodale's Highland Cream'—which is apparently so awful that it accounts for the Croc's own preference for rum . . . and Kenworthy made his fortune from writing physics textbooks, so they say."

"But where does Clinton come from, himself? Do you know that?"

"Don't you know?" Audley cocked an eye at him. "No . . . well, nobody knows the answer to that. No regimental background that anyone can discover—or the right school or university. *Definitely* not Eton and Sandhurst, or Eton and Trinity. More like some little grammar school somewhere, my godfather thinks. And then into the army by some back door, straight to the General List—'a self-made man,' you might call him."

A self-made man, Fred thought of Clinton as he repeated the thought to himself: *no class and no past . . . but also with no burden of preconceived and inbred prejudices or illusions, for or against those he had chosen?*

"But now he's come a cropper, and no mistake!" Audley spoke as though to himself. "Because if one of us—or one of *them*—has been on the other side all these months . . . *Christ!* That could mean his whole method of selection is up the bloody spout—if his Tenth Legion turns sour on him! Because—" He stopped suddenly. "Oh, God—*no!*"

"What?" Fred stopped just as quickly as he saw the boy's immense shoulders sag. Then he realized that Audley was looking directly past him, across the meadow by the rocks and the lake. And in that very instant, the shoulders straightened again and Audley raised his arm in greeting.

"HULLO THERE!" Audley bellowed into the silence of the Teutoburg Forest. "Don't you think you ought to turn round and have a look?"

Fred had to make himself turn, in the desolate knowledge that all this time Audley had been looking past him at someone else behind him, in the open meadow. And now, that this victory, even if they came out of it to tell the tale, would be a bitter one.

"HULLO THERE, AMOS!" Audley lowered his arm. "Amos, Fred? *Amos?*"

As he stared, Fred didn't want to believe it either. "Why not Amos?"

The silence came back for an instant. "I don't believe it." Audley blinked at him. "Last night—no, the night before—it was Amos who made the plan to get Zeitzler out. He could have had him hit just as easily, as those grenades went off . . . or whatever they were—time charges, were they? But if that was a diversion, he could have done it, anyway." Audley blinked again, glancing quickly across the meadow again before coming back to him. "And even now . . . it still doesn't make sense."

Fred watched Amos de Souza still ignore them as he completed his scrutiny of the lake, then the meadow, and finally the towering Exernsteine rocks. "Why not?"

Audley thought for a moment, watching the same charade. "If they're going to kill Number Sixteen . . . it doesn't need to be done here. They can do that perfectly well with him back in the orderly room at Schwartzenburg, with Amos minding his own business, Fred. Even if he let Zeitzler go, to get at Number Sixteen . . . he's throwing it all away by coming here now, isn't he? *Isn't he?*"

Once again, Clinton had been right; for his years, the boy was very quick. But because of his years, he still wasn't quick enough. And now, at the last, Fred needed him to understand fully what was at stake. "But what if they didn't want him dead, David—Number Sixteen? What if all the other things that have 'gone wrong,' all the way from Greece, were just to delay us, so that they could get to Number Sixteen first? But now we're too close to him, in spite of all they've done?"

The boy goggled at him, trying to catch up with insufficient understanding of what the whole race had been about, and failing miserably.

"We don't really need Number Sixteen now, David." He had to tell the truth, because there was no time to prevaricate. "We never did need him, thanks to his own conscience. And thanks to your old Professor Schmidt, too."

"Why not?" Failure to understand only made the boy angry.

"It's the Russians who need him. And especially after yesterday."

"Yesterday?" Audley frowned at him.

"All that marvelous German research, David—remember?" At

the last he couldn't sweeten the pill. "Everything they did was better than what we did, David: better weapons than ours— better guns, better guidance systems, and better radar. . . . And their jet planes years ahead of ours . . . and rockets beyond anything we'd ever imagined. And the chemical weapons they didn't use only because they thought we'd got them too?" Now he was straying perhaps too far into what Clinton had finally told him, as they had come to the final crunch under Hermann the Liberator's statue yesterday. So he must stop before he went further. "But *we* dropped that new bomb on Japan two days ago. The Germans didn't drop it on *us*, David." Now, also, he had to look away. Because now Amos de Souza had finished his survey and was advancing towards them.

Audley caught his glance. "So . . . they got it wrong? The atomic bomb?"

"They got it wrong." There was just time to agree. "Because the one man who could have pointed them in the right direction wasn't there to correct them. And the Russians have known that ever since von Mitzlaff joined Schmidt's group—or even before he did, maybe. Because we got that information out of Russia, David: there was a man in Russia who warned us about Number Sixteen." He looked away again, and Amos de Souza was very close now. "Only he got the warning out at the cost of his own life, at Osios Konstandinos. Because you already had a traitor in the Tenth Legion." Time ran out for them also in that second of time. "*Major de Souza*—Amos! I didn't think you were scheduled to join us here? What's the problem?"

"I'm not here—at least, not officially, Major Fattorini." De Souza stared past him. "You've got your two men up there, have you, David? Devenish and Hewitt?"

"Yes, Amos," Audley answered quickly. "As per your own orders, actually. . . . So what's the problem, then?"

De Souza swung on his heel, through a full circle before coming back to Audley. "Perhaps no problem, dear boy." Then he passed Audley by, to concentrate on Fred. "Your rendezvouz is in five minutes' time, Major?"

They both knew that perfectly well. "Yes, Amos."

"Yes." The concentration became fiercer: this was a very different Amos de Souza from any of its predecessors. "And you're quite happy about all this"—De Souza gestured around him— "here?"

"Why shouldn't I be?" But he had to play the game until the last throw of the dice, so he looked at his watch. "Five minutes as of now, yes. But you're not meant to be here, actually. So . . . is something wrong, then?"

De Souza looked round once again, uneasily, until he reached RSM Levin at his back, standing stiff as a board behind his adjutant, exuding blanket disapproval of everything and everyone. "Mr. Levin . . . you wanted to get those two men up there under cover, off the road—so do it, then. They're lounging around as if they were at a vicarage tea party!"

"*Sah!*" The RSM straightened up an inch beyond his usual ramrod self.

"Let me do that, Amos"—Audley moved ahead of the RSM, half-apologetically—"they're my chaps, after all."

"You stand fast, Captain Audley." De Souza immobilized Audley. "Mr. Levin—*if* you please!"

"*Sah!*" The RSM stepped out smartly, always as though on parade.

"Amos, what the hell?" Audley exploded mutinously.

"Shut up, David." De Souza quelled him flatly as he watched the RSM's progress towards Devenish and Hewitt.

"What d'you mean, 'shut up'?" Audley only remained quelled for that single moment before erupting again. "Your own orders—"

"The devil with my own orders!" snapped de Souza. "But if you want an order, then I'll give you one now: you go down by the end of the lake, where you can see round the rocks, and keep a sharp eye on the woods there. And if you see anything move, you come back and tell me. Understood?"

The boy rolled an eye at Fred, while his right hand massaged his leg nervously on the edge of his webbing holster. "W-w-w—"

"Did you not hear my order, Captain Audley?" De Souza's voice had lost its sharpness: now it was menacingly soft.

Fred remembered his own orders. "Do as the adjutant says, David."

Audley seemed to struggle with himself for an instant, then the hand stopped massaging and slapped the leg irritably. "Oh . . . *shit!* Mine not to reason why again! Okay, okay!" He swung on his heel, shaking his head and growling to himself as he stamped heavily away, kicking angrily at tufts of grass as he went like a schoolboy. It was good acting if it was an act, thought Fred. And now he must match it with one of his own.

"What the blazes are you playing at, Amos?" In fact, he only needed to imagine himself in the real military world to strike the right note of outrage. "This is my show, not yours."

"Yes." De Souza looked around again. "This place gives me the shivers, you know. Always has done, and always will." He sniffed. "Maybe Colbourne's right." He looked Fred in the eye. "A bad place for honest soldiers, maybe?"

The flesh up Fred's back crawled with a million tiny insect-feet because of this shared insight. "What are you doing here?"

"My duty, I hope." The sardonic glint was back, with the old self-mocking Amos voice. "David was right, of course—I'm disobeying my orders as well as complicating yours and his." He turned lazily to watch Audley placekicking another piece of grass. "He often is right, actually. But it does him no good. But . . . he's a good lad . . . maybe."

"Maybe?" The curious emphasis de Souza had placed on the word startled him.

"Yes." De Souza came back to him. "Aren't you happier for my presence, then?"

"Why should I be happier?"

De Souza nodded. "After the night before last?"

"The night before last?" He didn't have to think hard to recall those beastly images. But he had to remember who he was supposed to be. "We got our man the night before last. And the other side got the wrong one."

"Did they?" De Souza stared up the path. "I wonder, now."

Fred followed the man's stare. The RSM had dismissed Audley's men and was now standing alone at the top of the track, studying the circumference of his world in a series of jerky movements as though his head were fixed immovably on his neck.

"Almost everything we've done in the past hasn't gone right," said de Souza softly. "We've found men who couldn't help us much, and we've lost the ones who could. But this time we were very clever, and we got our man. But what I've been thinking is . . . perhaps that was what someone intended we should do. And that makes you very vulnerable in this place this morning—if it's true. So today I have taken certain extra precautions, without orders."

A cold hand squeezed Fred's guts. "Is that why—" But then the sharp *snap-crunch* of the RSM's hobnailed boots on the broken road surface silenced him.

"*Sah!*" Having stamped himself to attention, the RSM scorned any further explanation of a completed order.

"Thank you, Mr. Levin." De Souza accepted this information.

"*Arrgh-hmm!*" The RSM cleared his throat formally, but did not withdraw.

"Yes, Mr. Levin?" De Souza interpreted this signal interrogatively.

"Sah! There are two persons now approaching in the distance—*civilian* persons—upon the roadway, from the direction of Detmold. German civilians, I take them to be, by their dress."

Faint disapproval crept into the RSM's voice, as though tatter-demalion natives really had no right to disturb the British Liberation Army in its lawful business in the Teutoberger Wald this gray August morning. "They appear to be in no hurry . . . *sah.*"

Fred looked up the path. From where the RSM had stood he would have had a good clear view.

"*Arrgh-hmm!*" The RSM cleared his throat again. "Shall I now attend to Captain Audley . . . sah?"

"Attend?" Fred's attention snapped back to De Souza. "What d'you mean 'attend'?"

"Do that, Mr. Levin." De Souza nodded. "Disarm him and bring him up here."

"*Sah!*" The RSM stamped a backward pace before moving forward again.

"What the blazes . . . ?" Fred didn't need to act any part.

"Merely a precaution." De Souza raised a soothing hand. "You can rely on the RSM to be as civil as the circumstances permit. He has his orders. And young David is used to obeying him. . . . And there'll be a gun on him now if he isn't quite what we've taken him to be, all these months."

Fred stared at the RSM's fast-receding ramrod back. Typically, the RSM carried an issue-Sten, rather than a more exotic foreign weapon.

"I hope I'm wrong, Major Fattorini. But if I'm not . . . then it has to be someone inside the unit," murmured de Souza. "I've known something wasn't right . . . oh, for a long time, I suppose." He sighed. "But . . . it goes against the grain, rather. Because they are all Clinton's picked men, after all."

The cold hand inside Fred squeezed even harder. If Audley was *right* about Amos de Souza . . . then things were going *wrong* before they had a chance to do so in the way Clinton had intended them to do, and in a manner that neither of them had foreseen. But he still couldn't be sure of that, so he must still play the game.

"All except Audley." He turned deliberately back to de Souza.

"All except Audley." But de Souza echoed him without nodding. "Except that I don't think he's our man, actually. Even though he fits well enough—and he's a smart boy, I would agree."

"He fits . . . well enough?" Watching de Souza was more important than watching the boy's humiliation. "All the way from Greece, you mean?"

"Yes. And he's a bit too thick with the man Schild, who is really a most equivocal character." De Souza's voice tightened. "And whose whereabouts I do not at this precise moment know, as it happens."

"But . . . isn't Otto Schild the colonel's man?" A faint echo of Schild's Teutoburg song came nastily to mind.

"In a sense, yes. But he's also not what he seems, the RSM says."

"I thought he was . . . a butcher—a civilian butcher?"

"A butcher, maybe. But Mr. Levin thinks not a civilian one."

Colbourne, thought Fred. *And this was his place—the Exernsteine!* "Where is the colonel this morning?"

De Souza's lip curled slightly. "He's seeing a man about a plane—an RAF spotter plane, at Gutersloh—to try and spot Roman marching camps east and southeast of here. Which I gather was your idea, Major?" The lip tightened. "I lent him my driver, as a matter of fact. Just to make sure."

Everything was going wrong, one way or the other. And . . . the other officers—M'Corquodale? Kenworthy?"

De Souza looked past him suddenly, up the track again. "Don't worry, Major. The RSM has this place well staked out, by arrangement with the Military Police and our local Fusilier battalion. So your civilians have got in easily enough. But they won't get out unless you are accompanying them, believe me." He straightened up perceptibly. "And now here they are, anyway. So I take it you'd rather I withdrew somewhat, while you have your little chat? Would that make you feel more at ease?"

Not de Souza? Fred could no longer make his mind up there; only, although he experienced a certain amount of satisfaction about that, it was instantly swallowed up by the realization that, if he was innocent, then Amos had nevertheless very likely ruined Clinton's plans with his overintelligent innocence, by scaring off whoever *wasn't* innocent with his unscheduled precautions.

"That might be advisable, Amos." His mind raced ahead, trying to predict how their unknown traitor might adjust to this new situation. In such a last resort, all that was left was an ambush on the way back to Schwartzenburg Castle, which had always been a dangerous possibility in the back of Clinton's mind. "The sooner we're away from here, the better."

Amos de Souza nodded. "I couldn't agree more." He glanced around quickly. "This is a damn stupid spot for a meeting. I don't know what's got into the brigadier today—it isn't like him . . ." He came back to Fred and nodded again. "But don't worry. Because Mr. Levin and I will watch your backs here as best we can. And Mr. Levin has arranged a sufficient escort to pick you up just down the road to take Number Sixteen back safely after that."

"Yes?" That was the final irony: Amos had thought everything through, to amend his superiors' defective planning. And *not de Souza* was certain now, since he would hardly have needed to do as much, even apart from this otherwise risky warning, if he had been the traitor. "Well . . . thank you."

"Okay." Amos looked over this shoulder, at the fast-approaching figures of David Audley and the RSM. "And Audley?"

Audley's outraged voice arrived before Fred could answer. *"Fred—"*

"Hold on, David." He was simultaneously aware of the two Germans hovering discreetly, and of the RSM behind Audley, just as discreetly trying to hide whatever he had used to disarm the boy. And of Audley himself, his ugly features aflame with anger and humiliation.

"But Fred—" The outrage became almost plaintive.

"Shut up, David." At least Audley's face wasn't white with fear, as his own might have been: it was ugly with rage! "Thank you, Amos—Mr. Levin. . . . But you stay here, David."

"Right-o." Amos accepted his dismissal with a good grace. "Come on, Mr. Levin, let's admire the view for a moment, eh?"

Audley watched them for another moment, his mouth working. Then he returned to Fred. "B-b-*bloody* Mr. L-L-*Levin* . . . has t-taken my fff—"

"Yes, I know." Fred had had just enough warning to nip the stuttering fuse before it became an explosive shout, so that he could turn towards the Germans. *"Herr Zeitzler—"* No! That was wrong! *"Professor Zeitzler"*—he felt underrehearsed in matters of greeting—"good morning, sir!"

Professor Zeitzler was less humiliatingly dressed (or, as he had been, half-dressed, undressed, and then uniformed) than the night before last. But he was still tall and very thin, and even with his spectacles safely on his nose he was still very far from happy.

"Herr Major." The eyes behind the spectacles were wide with uncertainty; which was reasonable enough in the circumstances, even if "Herr Major" had been a captain the last time they'd met.

"I'm glad you were able to come, sir." Somehow, it wasn't hard to be polite to the man. He was, after all, "a decent chap" (in Audley's own words, from long ago). Yet it wasn't just that—or even because, if the man had never been an ally, he had also never truly been an enemy. It was just that he was what he looked like—just another middle-aged academic pacifist in a mad world, fallen among soldiers. And that made it easier to pity him, even as Fred turned at last to the cause of all the trouble. "And you, sir."

"Herr Major." The Cause of All the Trouble gave him a formal little bow. But with it there was a look of understanding and resignation that turned Fred's pity back on himself.

"But . . . there were to be two officers only." Professor Zeitzler's expression was less fearful now, after such politeness. "It was promised, sir—only yourself, and the . . . the large young officer."

"An added precaution." *Sod you!* thought Fred with sudden brutality. *You've done your job now—it's only Number 16 that matters now!* So he concentrated on Number 16. "There are dangers, you understand, sir."

"I understand." Number 16 didn't nod, but there was a strained grayness in his complexion and a wariness in his eyes that had nothing to do with any of the more recent privations of defeat. Fred had seen such masks before, on the faces of infantrymen who had been too long in the line.

"But it is not as was arranged—not as was *promised*." Zeitzler looked at his friend as he emphasized the word before coming back to Fred. "A word of honor was given—by a senior British officer. And I—"

"Hush, Ernst." Number 16 cut Zeitzler off softly. "If a word was given, then it was given. If it is to be broken . . . then it will be broken. We have already talked of that possibility. And I have made my choice, just as this officer has done." As he spoke, the man never for one instant took his eyes off Fred; and although not one of his words was stressed more than another, their challenge was plain enough.

So here was the first test, thought Fred. *And it was as searching as the brigadier had warned him it would be, by God!*

"You are free to go, sir. If you wish to do so." The enormity of the lie thickened his tongue inside his mouth as he committed himself finally to the acceptance of the truth about himself, which Clinton had apparently known before he did. "My superior's word of honor is the same as mine."

Again that terrible hint of pity, almost sardonic now. "Then I ask your pardon—shall I do that?"

Did he know? Or had he mistaken those half-strangled words for honest outrage? Fred questioned himself desperately for an instant. "I think you'd do better to remember what happened the night before last, sir." He flicked a glance at Zeitzler. "I'm sure your friend has told you about that?"

"Indeed he has." Still the man studied him. "The Russians want me, just as you want me. So they do not want you to have

me . . . even though all these desires are foolish, of course—
foolish beyond belief! For I am too much behind the times now.
And especially since yesterday's news, yesterday's terrible news,
Herr Major." He nodded. "Yes, I have heard of what has
happened in Japan: it was on the wireless last night."

Fred swallowed. "That's not for me to comment on, sir. I am
here merely to make you an offer. Which you have the right to
refuse." He submitted to the man's scrutiny for another long
moment. "We have no demands to make on you. We merely wish
to take you into protective custody for a time." The closer he got
to something like the truth, the better he felt, and the firmer
became the voice—his own voice—that he heard. "In due course,
when we judge it to be safe, we will arrange for you to be
accepted by the university of your choice. Or any other establish-
ment"—he had got it exactly right—"in Germany, or in England.
But there is another consideration to be made in that choice, it's
only fair to add, sir."

"Another consideration?"

"It will be easier to protect you in England for the time being.
You will be safer with us there, sir."

"Ach so! Yes . . ." Number 16 saw clear through that instantly.
"You have your own nuclear research to think of now that the
war is won—of course!" At last he nodded, but without any hint
of a properly cynical smile. "But . . . if I told you that *my*
research is now into the scientific dating of ancient remains and
artifacts, in which I have been engaged these last six years—
would that be acceptable?"

"Of course, sir." Clinton's exact forecast of this very question,
and his research into its correct answer, kindled Fred's confidence into flame: *"He has no family. Otherwise we'd have got to
him much sooner—or the Russians would have done. And most of
his friends are dead too, now. All except one, you see, eh?"* But he
mustn't look at Zeitzler yet. "We've got quite a few of our own old
Roman cities which have been . . . cleared by bombing, for
archaeology. Canterbury, Bath . . . and London, of course." He
turned casually to Zeitzler. "And we still have Hadrian's Wall for
you, Professor . . . which is much the same as your 'limes,' isn't
it?"

Zeitzler's mouth opened incredulously.

"And naturally the invitation includes you, Professor Zeitzler."
He nodded at Corporal Keys. "Dr. Crawford of our Ordnance
Survey has been one of your admirers ever since he published
your 'limes' articles in *Antiquity* ten years ago. He will be
honored to arrange for your reception"—back to Number 16—
"and yours too, sir."

ANTHONY PRICE

The two Germans looked at each other, just about as non-plussed as Clinton had said they might be, and he found himself admiring the brigadier's cunning. Because, although finding this man had apparently been TRR-2's longtime original objective, entrusted to Clinton by the War Cabinet itself, Clinton's own intention had been to build up an intelligence team of his own on which he could absolutely rely in this new kind of war that he—and David Audley, too—had foreseen, even before that bomb had dropped. And Clinton had used the hunt for Number 16 to gather his chosen men, and to test their efficiency in the field, and to establish his reputation for the future with them. But now, to achieve all that, he also had to use Number 16 as bait to flush out the traitor whom the Russians had infiltrated into TRR-2. Now that the bomb had dropped, better a dead Number 16 than a compromised TRR-2!

"There won't be any problem, sir." The saving grace was that although Clinton wanted their traitor, he still also wanted Number 16 as planned. And that was probably why he'd got on so well with Uncle Luke. *Unforeseen complications,* Uncle Luke always said, *always provide matching opportunities for greater profits if you look at them in the right way!* "You will both be very welcome, I assure you, sir." And . . . *"I want him to come willingly, Fred,"* Clinton had said. *"One volunteer is worth a hundred pressed men. Because, once he's with us by choice . . . there'll be physicists from Cambridge to pick his brains and tempt him back to his old discipline. Because with work as well as women, you only love truly once—everything else is a delusion, Major. So whatever he believes, he's still a nuclear physicist, not an archaeologist."*

"Welcome?" The eyes were not so much pitying now as very tired.

"Yes, sir." Fred continued on what he knew to be closest to the truth. "Our people know all about Professor Schmidt, and what he tried to do. There is . . . a certain sympathy for his intention—at least, among some of our scientists." He tried to blot out the rest of what Clinton had said: that, with the British just beginning to follow their allies in de-Nazifying dyed-in-the-wool Nazis who were useful, there really wouldn't be any trouble getting these two into Britain, willing or unwilling. "So you will be welcome—and free to continue your archaeology."

Number 16 continued to stare at him. But it was Zeitzler who broke the silence. "Heinrich . . . *glaubst du es ihm.*"

"W——?" For an instant Fred couldn't decide whether to pretend he hadn't understood the German words.

"It doesn't matter." Number 16 held them both for an equal

224

instant. "All that matters now, Ernst, is that if it is a lie, then it is a most persuasive one in our present circumstances. For we are undoubtedly caught between the Red Devil and the very deep blue British sea, I fear. But as I said last night, death by drowning is preferable to hellfire." The weary eyes softened. "Yet, as I also said last night . . . I will not impose my fate on you, old friend."

Zeitzler's mouth twitched downwards as he glanced left and right, from his old trusted friend to his new untrusted *ersatz* British friend. But his eyes glittered behind his spectacles, as though at the enticing prospect of all those built-over Romano-British cities, which had been well cleared by German bombs to open them up to archaeologists as they had not been open for a thousand years. "Do we have a choice?"

Fred so much hated the truth, which Zeitzler had reached at last, that he turned away from it in distaste, first towards Audley, and then to where Amos de Souza stood apart from them; and Amos, he saw, was directing the RSM's attention to the menacing woods around them, and to the lake and the rocks; while on young Audley's face there was a mirror image of his own feelings, uglified and brutalized by the face that God had given to the boy, which he couldn't help.

"No—you are right, as always!" Number 16 accepted Number 21's answer as untainted by self-interest, with heartrending innocence. "Then we accept your offer, Herr Major. We are at your disposal, without any compulsion—we accept the word of a British officer. Which is, of course, as strong as that of a German officer."

Shit! thought Fred, cutting off Audley's face from the reckoning. "Major de Souza! If you please!"

Major de Souza disengaged himself from his contemplation of the Exernsteine Rocks. "Major Fattorini?"

"We're ready to move now. Would you ask the RSM to alert Sergeant Devenish?" He worked at the formality of command. Because of de Souza, he no longer knew quite what would happen once they were on the road back to Schwartzenburg Castle, or thereafter. But the game had to be played to the last ball and the final whistle, regardless.

"Mr. Levin!" De Souza twisted on his heel, so that he was backing away from the woods. "Ready?"

"*Sah!*" The RSM snapped to even greater attention than before, first stiff as a board in preparation for obedience to orders, and then falling in behind the adjutant, while he attached an extension to his Sten's barrel in a series of jerky, regimental movements.

"Right." De Souza snapped open his webbing holster, lifting

his arm high to clear his pistol from it. "As of now we assume the worst of all possible worlds until we're in the clear." His glance passed Audley, to fix on Fred himself. "Right, Major?"

Thump.

De Souza jerked forward suddenly, arching his back and dropping his pistol, as his legs buckled beneath him.

"Steady, now!" As the RSM barked the words, de Souza continued forwards and downwards, unbalanced, as though fighting an irresistible blow from behind, until he finally sank onto his knees, almost in an attitude of prayer.

"Steady now!" The RSM swung the curiously long-barreled Sten left and right, right and left, taking them all in with it, but ending up with the muzzle pointing at Fred's stomach.

An unintelligible groan came from de Souza, who was still on his knees, swaying in agony. And then Fred watched, hypnotized with frozen horror, as the adjutant began to reach forward towards his fallen pistol.

"Don't"—the bulbous silencing attachment on the end of the RSM's Sten continued to point at Fred as he spoke—*"don't* make me do it, Major de Souza, sir. Don't make me do it, I beg you!"

De Souza rocked slightly, but continued to stretch out slowly towards the pistol with a hand that shook uncontrollably, as though its overstretched arm was already bearing an invisible weight too great for it.

"Amos!" Audley's voice cracked. *"Amos—"*

Thump! This time the bullet crumpled de Souza instantly, throwing him sideways, half on his back, with his legs kicking out like a poleaxed steer.

"That was a pity." The RSM spoke slowly, his words all the more menacing for the hint of genuine regret in them. "Because it was not necessary as well as useless."

"You . . . b-b-b-*bastard*!" Young Audley's stutter was shrill with rage. "In the b-b-back, you fucking bastard!"

"You want it in the front, Mr. Audley?" The RSM took the boy's acting rank from him contemptuously. "I can oblige you now if you wish." He made an unhurried adjustment to the submachine gun. "I can cut you in two before you can take another step, Mr. Audley. And I will if I have to, if you want to be a hero too, like the adjutant."

Fred's mind began to race. They had their man now, albeit at a terrible and unnecessary cost. But now, also, they had to survive to tell the tale. So this was no moment for subaltern heroics. "Stand still, David." He looked up the track quickly. "And shut up."

"No good, sir. I have sent Sergeant Devenish and Driver Hewitt away." The RSM caught the look. "They are now both guarding the road junction until I come to relieve them. And we shall not be leaving by that route."

"I see." It was no good trying to play games with the man when he was as quick as that. So what could he do? "There are forest tracks, are there, Mr. Levin?" All he could do was to play for time. "And no Fusilier pickets guarding them, I take it?" But even as he spoke, the truth of what he was saying soured the words in his mouth: who better than the RSM, in his unique controlling position between the officers and the men, to *know* everything, and to *order* everything as he wished in seeming to carry out the orders of the adjutant and the commanding officer?

Christ! And of course to betray everything, being above suspicion himself!

"As you say, Major Fattorini, sir." Levin saw through his ploy and shifted his attention to the two Germans, while carefully stepping back to distance himself farther from Fred, and even more from the temporarily silenced Audley, whose fuse was still more dangerously short, in spite of that recent warning. "Listen to me, you two—right?"

That was curious, thought Fred with a detachment of his own that was also curious. In contrast to his deference to his officers, who were now his enemies to be shot down like dogs at need, the RSM's attitude to these Germans, who were his prize, was uncompromisingly harsh.

"In a little while, you-will-be-coming-with-me—do-you-understand?" Levin spaced his words, as though he were addressing British Army recruits of limited intelligence.

Number 16 drew himself up. "And if we do not choose to come with you?"

"Then I'll shoot you where you stand." The RSM pronounced this threatened sentence of death almost with relish. "Don't you make any mistake about that."

"I make no mistake. But your Russian masters would not like us dead, I think, yes?" Number 16 didn't look at Fred, but he was playing the same delaying game now, hope against despair.

"My Russian—?" The RSM stopped suddenly. And then he nodded towards what had been Major Amos de Souza without taking Fred or David Audley out of his reckoning. "You see that, do you?"

"I see a dead man." The German's chin came up. "I see a *brave* man, yes?"

"Aye. And a good one, too." Levin matched the German's measured insult with cold malevolence. "Worth ten of you, you bugger. So don't bandy words with me."

"Heinrich—"

"Hush, Ernst!" Number 16 cut off Zeitzler. "You have made yourself very plain, sir. But I also wish to make myself plain. For I wish to speak with my friend. And I do not think you will prevent me doing so."

"No?" Levin had moved as the German spoke, circling cautiously to keep everyone in view as best he could, while also flicking a quick glance at the woods across the meadow.

"No. For I do not think your Russian masters have paid you for a dead man. But I am not yet sure that I wish to be bought, you see."

"No?" Levin's lips compressed into a thin line, with a fleck of white at one corner. Without looking down, he kicked de Souza's fallen pistol farther away. Then he drew a deep breath and glanced towards the woods again. "No?"

He was expecting company, thought Fred despairingly. And *. . . there were no Fusilier pickets in those woods, of course!*

Number 16 nodded. "So . . . I will talk with my friend. For, believe me or not as you will . . . *I* will decide what *I* shall do—not *you*—and not your masters . . . do you understand?"

For a sick fraction of time Fred thought Levin was going to make good his threat, and he tensed himself to attempt the impossible. But then the long, black silenced barrel came round to cover him.

"Don't make me do it, sir!" The barrel passed him, to point at Audley. "Steady, Mr. Audley—*Captain* Audley." There was something close to contempt in the RSM's warning. "You were going to be the example, not the major, Mr. Audley . . . so you're already on borrowed time, *Mister* Audley."

"David!" Fred held the boy back. "Mr. Levin—"

"That's enough, sir." Levin looked at Number 16 quickly. "Very well, then! If you want to talk to your friend . . . it won't make no difference. But you talk in English to him, right? And you remember . . . if I can't have you alive, then I'll have you dead, right?" The long, black barrel jerked slightly. "Go on, then—*talk, then!*"

"Heinrich—"

Fred fought the lethargy of helplessness and hopelessness: *Number 16 had to give in . . . and once he had done that, when Mr. Levin's friends had arrived, then Major Fattorini and Captain Audley were surplus to requirements—useless even as hostages, after de Souza's death.*

"Mr. Levin!" He felt life within him fight against logic: in killing de Souza, Levin had burnt his boats, and there was no deal left to him. But he had to fight against logic. *But how?*

"Steady, sir." Levin didn't even look at him; Levin knew the score just as well as he did.

"Mr. Levin . . . this doesn't make sense." His tongue was thick in his mouth, hindering the words.

"No, sir." Still Levin didn't look at him. "I don't suppose it does, to you, sir. And I am sorry for that, believe me, sir. But that's the way of it."

The man's politeness clogged his brain. And more than such insane politeness, there was bitterness and regret and loss; and he wanted to use them all to save himself, but he didn't know how to do it because he didn't understand what was happening to him. "Mr. Levin . . . *why*, Mr. Levin?"

"Sah!" For an instant Levin became his old self again. *"Sah."*

"Heinrich, now there is no choice, truly! We must go with him." He heard Zeitzler argue common sense and survival in the distance.

"Mr. Levin." Fred tried to receive different messages simultaneously. "What—"

"This is not how I wished it to be, *sah*."

"There is always a choice, Ernst. Do you not remember—"

"It was Mr. Audley who was to be the example, sah—not the major." Levin drew a huge breath. *"Never* the major." The long silenced barrel swung slightly and then steadied on the young dragoon beside Fred, who stood swaying and twitching, almost beyond reason and sense, waiting to be loosed.

"But Ernst—"

"Steady, David!" *Survival was what mattered now!* "You are taking us prisoner now, are you, Mr. Levin?"

Another deep breath. "If I can, then I will." Levin took in the words again, almost desperately. "Because there is a message I wish Colonel Colbourne to receive . . . if you would be so good as to deliver it . . . *sah?*"

"Yes, Mr. Levin?" Fred steadied the question, so as not to grasp at his own life too humiliatingly, even as he welcomed it and despised himself for his cowardice. "What is your message?"

"Heinrich—" Suddenly Zeitzler leaped into incomprehensible German.

"In English, you bugger!" Levin snarled the order. *"What was that?"*

For a moment they were inside a huge silence. "Do you promise my friend's life? And the lives of these British officers?" Number 16 issued his demand in a flat and uncompromising voice, almost urgently.

The RSM stared at Fred. "Yes."

"On your honor?" The German stretched his arrogance insultingly, leaving "for what that may be worth" unspoken, transcending insult. "Is that your word?"

"Yes." Still the RSM stared at Fred, with a dead blankness as treacherous as Clinton's, which scorned forgiveness, accepting only final responsibility, true or false.

"Don't believe him!" Audley snarled. "Tell him to go to hell! Tell him—"

"Shut up!" Fred preempted the RSM. "Shut up!" was what everyone said to Audley. "Don't get yourself killed, sir."

"Very well, then. I accept. We will go with you."

Still that stare. So, their only hope left was that message to Colonel Colbourne. "Yes, Mr. Levin? What is it that you want me to tell the CO?"

"Yes." The man focused on him. "Tell Colonel Colbourne that I have joined another army now—now that his army has won its war. . . . *His* army." Levin's own concentration outranked his own. "Tell him to remember Bum-Titty Bay, at Haifa, after El Alamein—tell him *that*, Major."

Bum-Titty Bay? At . . . *Haifa*—? He couldn't understand that.

"Tell him that, Major—Bum-Titty Bay? Then maybe he'll understand." Levin fixed him for an instant, and then dismissed him as he looked away, through Number 16 and Zeitzler, towards the meadow and the woods. *"Tell him that."*

Bum-Titty Bay? The faint obscenity of it, which he still couldn't place, delayed him for a moment, even as he was drawn towards the woods, as RSM relaxed slightly.

Christ! The woods were no longer empty. Christ. There were men— men in uniform—the whole bloody Russian army—Christ!

"Time to go, sir." Levin's voice, which had been close to conversational as he transmitted his final message for Colonel Colbourne, became suddenly quite matter-of-fact, beyond argument. "So . . . no trouble now, if you please, sir?" Almost as it could never have been in any other age of the world, Regimental Sergeant Major Levin's voice pleaded with Major Fattorini not to take issue with him: not to go against Number 16's acceptance, or Professor Zeitzler's advice—never mind any foolishness *Captain* Audley might be tempted to, now that Major de Souza's own foolishness had been demonstrated.

"Time to—"

As Fred stared at RSM Levin, accepting the inevitable, the RSM seemed to toss his head.

Fred felt his mouth open, without knowing what he was going to say, as he saw what he had never seen before, had never imagined seeing, as the movement continued, and the bright red spot over the RSM's eye flowered, and the RSM's side-hair lifted, and his beret

*with it, and blood and brains, and beret and side-hair, exploded with
it, outwards with the killing bullet.*

The *crack* of the bullet overtook the nod, and the RSM's eyes
rolled with the impact, and the black barrel of the Sten whirled
upwards as the man fell away from them.

"*Fred!*" Audley pointed at the advancing figures in the meadow,
and then threw himself towards the fallen weapon.

Christ! thought Fred, as the figures began to run. "Shoot,
David!" he shouted, clawing at his own holster feverishly as he
did so. But then he saw the two Germans frozen behind him, like
waxwork figures. "*Run, for God's sake!*" he screamed at them. But
they didn't seem to understand, and it came to him in a moment
of exasperation that not all Germans were the world's natural
soldiers: that these were only ordinary middle-aged men confused by madness.

But at last Audley had the RSM's Sten. There came a succession of increasingly loud *thump*s as the boy discharged it wildly,
more or less in the right direction, just as the enemy opened fire
with an honest earsplitting, rattling *bang-crack-bang-crack* that
deafened him as it echoed and reechoed over the valley around
him.

"*Run!*" He directed the shout at Zeitzler, in the vague hope that
the German had a more recent memory of murder, even while he
saw Audley savagely trying to recock the RSM's Sten. "*Shoot,
David!*"

Audley looked up at him, apologetically. "Oh . . . *fuck!*" He
made a face at Fred. "I never was very good with these things. So
you'd better run too, Fred, I think." He turned towards the
Russians, raising the submachine gun to them. "*Come on, you
bastards!*"

Fred managed to extract his own revolver at last, turning it and
himself to the enemy, in despair of anything better.

It wasn't the whole Russian Army, of course. It was no more
than half a dozen men; and none of them were in any recogniz-
able uniform—that one abortive fusillade of Audley's seemed to
have spread them out, left and right, sorting the brave men from
the cowards; but the brave men were too bloody close for comfort
now, all the same.

He managed to get an inadequate finger to the trigger. But it
pulled the pistol down, and then the remaining fingers couldn't
hold the weapon steady as he fired at the nearest of the Russians,
who was trying to take a steady aim, but not at him.

Bang!

The pistol bucked, just as the Russian fired. And then Fred fired
again, and again, with the same terrible clumsiness, as uselessly

as before; and saw the man steady himself again, this time bringing up his weapon deliberately, even as David Audley ran forward towards him, brandishing the Sten and screaming like a Highlander, beyond reason.

Taking his cue from the Russian's action, Fred clamped his good left hand to his right wrist to attempt a steadier aim just as the Russian turned to meet the boy's insane charge. But before he could squeeze the trigger the man crumpled and fell, and Audley's scream turned into a shout of triumph as he bounded over the final yards and threw himself on his unresisting victim, flailing at him with the Sten.

The Russian's sudden fall confused Fred for a second. Then it came to him in a flash that the sniper who had killed Levin was finding new targets, and hope blazed within him as he squeezed off his next shot quite deliberately at the nearest surviving Russian, knowing that he would miss, and that he now had only three rounds left; and saw the man flinch at the sound of the bullet, and then turn towards him instinctively, steadying his own automatic pistol and turning himself into a statue for an instant, just as his comrade had done.

Shoot, prayed Fred to the invisible sniper as he jinked sideways, *shoot, for Christ's sake!*

The Russian fired, and God only knew where the bullet went. But then one of his comrades was shouting at him—and Audley was shouting, too. And as Fred brought up his own pistol again both the Russians started to run—*but not towards him, away from him—what?*

He observed Audley on knees beside his victim. The boy had recovered the man's pistol and was emptying it wildly at the retreating enemy, shouting his wild dragoon war cry. And then he swiveled and waved at him, pointing past him—

"JACKO! TALLYHO! TALLYHO! AFTER THE BASTARDS!"

Fred turned, seeing not just Sergeant Devenish. Sergeant Devenish was in the lead, but with him there were half a dozen Fusiliers—more now, with the jaunty red-and-white hackles in their berets bobbing as they came out of the trees on either side of the track, rifles at the high port.

And—*oh, God, no!*

"GO ON! GO ON!" Audley's voice cracked, but with triumph as the line of Fusiliers reached him. *"TALLYHO! GO ON, JACKO!"*

The boy was oblivious to everything else around him, and not least to the two civilian figures on the ground, the one on his knees cradling the other in his arms—two nondescript civilians, patched and shabby—*oh, God! Which was which?*

His knees felt oddly stiff as he covered the dozen yards, past the bodies of Amos de Souza and the RSM. *None of this was how it was meant to be,* he thought. *Not Amos, not the RSM, and not—*

"Ernst?" Number 16 held Number 21 close to him: *Sweet-Sixteen-and-never-been-kissed* held *The Key-to-the-door/Corporal Keys,* and the blood dribbled out of the corner of Number 21's mouth, and down his chin onto his tightly knotted tie and frayed shirt collar, just as it had done the night before last, only bright red now, not black.

"*Ernst!*" Suddenly Number 16 looked up at Fred, his face gray with anguish. "When they fired, *he stood in front of me!* Do you hear me? He stood in front of me! Why would he do that? Why did he have to do *that?*"

Number 21 opened his eyes suddenly, and looked directly at Fred also.

"*Ernst—*"

Number 21 arched his back, and the breath rattled in his throat and finally went out of him in a rush of blood from his mouth.

"Oh, my God!" Audley's voice came from just behind him. "Which one—*ahh!*" As the boy saw the expression on Fred's face his lip drooped apologetically. "Sorry. But . . . well?"

Something behind Fred took his attention, and Fred's with it. And there suddenly on the path was Driver Hewitt, blinking nervously and fidgeting with the seams of his battle-dress trousers with callused thumbs.

"Yes, Hughie?" Audley accepted the diversion gratefully.

Driver Hewitt took in the Germans without emotion, but then rolled his eye over the scatter of bodies beyond. "Cor bleedin' 'ell!" The eyes blinked, and the wizened monkey face screwed up. Then Driver Hewitt remembered his officers again and gave Audley an oddly philosophic sidelong glance. "You bin lucky again then, Mr. Audley, ain'tcha?"

The boy had followed the little driver's glance, but seemed unable to tear himself away from it. For a moment silence flowed around them, but then there came a distant rattle of small-arms fire out of the woods, and a flock of birds rose from the trees on the crest of the ridge.

Audley sighed. "Yes, Hughie—I suppose we could say I bin lucky again." He turned to the little man at last. "What d'you want, Hughie?"

Driver Hewitt screwed up his face again. "Nothin' really, sir, Mr. Audley—Captain Audley . . . Except, it's Mr. Schild, sir—Otto, like, sir?"

"Otto Schild?" Audley frowned at him. "What about him?"

" 'E's back with the vehicle, sir. 'E . . . wants to give hisself up, 'e says."

Audley studied the man. "What are you talking about, Hewitt?"

"Yes, sir. . . . Well . . . like, 'e's got this 'untin' rifle of 'is with 'im, wot 'e shoots 'is pigs with. Only"—Driver Hewitt drew a deep breath—" 'e says 'e's shot Mr. Levin with it this time. After Mr. Levin shot the major. An 'e was only obeyin' orders, anyways . . . *sir.*" The words tumbled out in three quick bursts. "Only . . . 'e thinks it'ud be better for 'im if you was to take 'im into custody now, just in case"—the little man cocked an eye back down the path—" 'cause there's a lotta Redcaps comin' up the road now. . . . So I put 'im in your car, sir."

Audley look at Fred. "He was only obeying orders? Whose orders, Major Fattorini?"

They both knew. "Not mine, Captain Audley." But now he had to take command. "Driver Hewitt, you will keep your mouth closed about this. Unless you want a Far East posting, that is."

"I ain't seen *nuthink*, sir—"

"Shut up, Driver Hewitt. Just go back and tell the Redcaps to call an ambulance. And bring a groundsheet to cover Major de Souza. And . . . we will attend to Herr Schild."

"Right, sir—Major, sir." Hewitt swayed for a moment, and then gave Fred an old-fashioned narrow glance. Then he took in the Germans, with Number 16 cradling Number 21 in tears, like Niobe. "But wot about *them*, sir? The Jerries?"

Fred felt Audley's eyes on him. But he also remembered Clinton's cold, uncompromising stare, and his greed. "You leave them to us, Hewitt."

"Yes, sir." Hewitt assessed him momentarily, with a hint of even more old-fashioned understanding, which accepted the insanity of all wars down the ages in which the innocent were always slaughtered. "That Otto—'e always 'ad a good word for the major . . . But 'e never *liked* the RSM, sir."

Part Five

War Without End

Somewhere in England, August 1945

"There are three forms to sign, sir." The RAF flight lieutenant presented his clipboard to Fred. "Actually, it's the same form in triplicate, but we've run out of carbon paper."

Fred accepted the clipboard and the stub of indelible pencil. It was interesting, he observed, that Number 16 had lost his false cover name as well as his number now that he was in England and was his real self at last.

"As you can see, we have already signed on our dotted lines." The flight lieutenant pointed to two signatures, and then to an open space. "You sign *there*, sir. And then you keep one copy, to return to your adjutant. And I keep one, as station movements officer—"

"And I will have the third." The civilian intercepted the clipboard.

The papers fluttered madly on the board as a gust of unseasonable August wind swept over the dead flat Cambridgeshire airfield. It was the same wind that the pilot of the plane had welcomed, that had come all the way from Russia over the equally flat North German plain to help them across the North

Sea. But now it made him shiver, when taken with that mention of his adjutant and the mean disinheriting look in the civilian's eye.

"Thank you, sir." The flight lieutenant's good manners were deliberately directed at Fred as he finally recovered his board. "That discharges your responsibility for your prisoner."

"He's not a prisoner," snapped Fred.

"No, sir?" The flight lieutenant glanced at the shabby figure beside Fred. "Well, anyway, he's ours now, sir."

"Mine," growled the civilian. "You will come this way." The words addressed to Number 16, were not quite an order, but they certainly weren't a request.

Number 16 looked at Fred. For a moment he seemed to be on the verge of speaking, but in the end nothing came out. And that was just about how Fred himself felt: there was so much to say, both about what had happened and what looked like was happening now, that there was really nothing to say by way of explanation and excuse.

"Good-bye, sir." He couldn't bring himself to add "and good luck." But in any case, the civilian was gesturing impatiently. And to be fair, maybe he was properly nervous in wide-open spaces. "I think you'd better go, sir."

"Yes." Number 16 stared at him. "Good-bye, Major."

Fred watched the two men start down the runway, past a line of Dakotas, towards a low huddle of Nissen huts, the civilian purposeful and guardsman straight—policeman straight?—and Number 16 trying to keep up with him, but walking as though his feet hurt, or his shoes didn't fit. And it continued to feel strange to feel sorry for a German so soon after he had hated them all indiscriminately, and even stranger to feel guilt also. But . . . *vae victis*, as the Romans said—as Colonel Colbourne might have said?

"You don't want to worry," murmured the flight lieutenant. "He's only a policeman of some sort. And there's a couple of long-haired types waiting for your prisoner, down in the end hut here—they're the real reception committee."

"He's not my prisoner, damn it."

"Sorry!" The flight lieutenant grinned disarmingly. "And you're right, of course. Because they're certainly not policemen, is what I mean. In fact, they look more like boffins of some sort, from Cambridge just down the road. So he's getting the proper VIP treatment." He grinned at Fred again and pointed. "And so are you, Major: top brass on *your* reception committee. And you better not keep 'em waiting, because your return flight's due off at fifteen hundred hours. So cheerio then, Major."

Fred saw Brigadier Clinton standing on the edge of the tarmac, with another officer beside him and the full length of the runway stretching beyond them. But he couldn't identify the other man as anyone he'd seen on that night in the Kaiserburg on the *limes,* or in the Schwartzenburg afterwards, or anywhere on the Teutoburg Forest these last few days.

"Thank you, Flight Lieutenant—" But the wind blew his thanks away, and the young man had already gone with it, on the wings of his own signed responsibility, prudently leaving Fred and Number 16 each to their reception committees and their respective fates.

Belatedly, Fred felt that he ought to be experiencing some sense of occasion and couldn't quite believe that he had overlooked it, after all he'd dared to imagine. *Because this was his homecoming at long last—even if it was suddenly in the middle of England, not the welcoming white cliffs of Dover seen from a smelly troopship, which he'd always longed for.*

But Brigadier Clinton was waving at him, acknowledging his presence. And that was the reality of his homecoming, and he had to bow to it and march towards it.

"Fred, my dear fellow!"

"Sir." The answer came easily. But already he felt different chains binding him, very different from the old military ones to which he had become accustomed when his soul had not been his own. "I've just handed . . . Number 16 . . . over"—to a brigadier, in the presence of an anonymous major of artillery, his salute was automatic, even though it felt foolish—"as per Major M'Corquodale's orders, in the absence of Colonel Colbourne."

"Well . . . thank God for that, then!" Clinton tossed his head, and then nodded at the gunner. "This is Colonel Stocker, Fred. Give your release to him . . . and then we can be done with playing Housey-Housey, thank God!"

Fred looked directly at the major-who-was-no-longer-a-major, who had a pale desk-bound face that didn't fit his Royal Artillery badges and his double deck of medal ribbons. And for an instant the scrap of paper fluttered in the wind between them. "Sir!"

"Major Fattorini." The new colonel's mask relaxed slightly, into a curiously old-maidish smile. "How are things with TRR-two?"

Fred didn't know how to answer that. "Sir?"

The smile tightened, but the eyes above didn't change. "How have they taken what happened? How is M'Corquodale coping?"

Fred amended his first confused impressions radically. Gunners (even if they weren't sappers) were rarely old maids. But more than that, this was a dyed-in-the-wool Clinton-follower.

And that called for extra caution. "Major M'Corquodale had things well in hand when I left this morning, sir."

"Oh, yes?" The gunner colonel cocked his head slightly. "And in the absence of Colonel Colbourne—as you put it so diplomatically—what is your official story? About what happened when you finally made contact with Number Sixteen?"

So that was the way the land lay. "One of our civilian contacts was bringing in a German for questioning, sir." He carefully didn't look at Clinton. "But we had some serious trouble with an armed band of Ukrainian DPs and Russian deserters who were holed up in the forest. And that was when the adjutant and the RSM unfortunately became casualties. And one of our German contacts was caught in the cross fire. And we have one other German civilian in custody, pending further inquiries."

"And that is your story?" The gunner also didn't look at Clinton. "And you're sticking to it?"

"Yes. Until I'm told otherwise." Fred went so far as to touch his battle-dress blouse, over his heart and his envelope. "Or until I'm demobilized back to civvy street, sir—whichever comes first."

"I told you, Tommy." Clinton seemed to speak from far away. "He is a sapper . . . and he comes from a long line of close-mouthed merchant bankers. And that's a damnable mixture."

"Yes. Thank you, Freddie." The scrutiny still remained. "And if I told you that I've already talked face-to-face with Colonel Colbourne, Major? And if I added my considered opinion that you made a pretty fair balls-up of your first assignment with TRR-two—what would you say then, Major?"

With his envelope safe in his pocket and his feet on English ground, Fred decided that he had nothing to lose, and maybe a lot to gain. "I'd say that's a fair enough opinion—from someone who wasn't there, sir." That just about burnt his boats, and his return ticket to Germany with it, he judged. "And then I'd say that maybe I'm due for demob sooner than I'd expected. But now that I'm in England again at last . . . that won't be too difficult, sir."

"Indeed?" The gunner smiled his deceptive smile again as he turned at last to Clinton. "All right, Freddie: I give you the best with this officer. Or . . . I'll grant you *him*, if not young Audley."

Even without understanding what the man meant, Fred wasn't going to let that pass now. "I'd also say that Captain Audley is a promising young officer, whatever Colonel Colbourne may say."

"You would?" The gunner nodded slowly. "Very well. So now I will say several things, Major. *First*, Colonel Colbourne will not be returning to Germany. *Second*, as of this moment I am in command of TRR-two, and when I need your advice I shall ask for it."

Fred stiffened automatically and held his tongue.

"*Third* . . . I need to promote a new senior NCO or warrant officer, in place of the late and unlamented Mr. Levin. So who do you want, then?" Colonel Stocker closed his mouth on the question, but then opened it again as Fred's own mouth opened wordlessly. "Actually, that wasn't quite in the right order. I should have said . . . *third*, you are my new adjutant and second-in-command de facto. Which makes the new RSM—or new senior warrant officer anyway, to run the show—*fourth*. So who do you want?"

"Who do I want?" Fred repeated the words almost automatically. But then they suddenly became a statement of fact, requiring nothing except an adjutant's instant decision. "Sergeant Devenish, sir."

"Why Sergeant Devenish?"

Fred toyed momentarily with Devenish's conventional virtue of knowing how the army worked, allied to his initiative when it came to the crucial matter of disobeying suspect orders, which had helped to save his life recently. "I think I know which side he's on, Colonel Stocker."

"Yes . . . that sounds reasonable." Stocker glanced to Clinton nevertheless. "Although, I shall want him properly checked out now, Freddie."

"*Mmm* . . ." The sound deepened in Clinton's throat. "Of course—yes!"

"Agreed, then." Stocker nodded. But then cocked his head again. "But who looks after young Audley? He has a way of getting into scrapes, I gather."

The burden of his new duties began to weigh on Fred before he'd accustomed himself to them. "You still want him, do you?"

The head stayed cocked. "Don't you, Major?"

Fred thought about David Audley as he had never quite done before, not as someone too young for this sort of work, but as someone whom they'd caught young and could train for it before he was set in his ways. "There is a driver who is . . . attached to him. But we can't promote him."

"Yes, Hewitt is *un*promotable, I agree." Stocker nodded thoughtfully.

Christ! Stocker's admission called Fred to the truth: *This bloody gunner had all the cards in the pack marked already! So . . . all this was . . . mere window dressing?*

He looked down the runway, towards the nearest Dakota, which was already surrounded by the RAF's turn-round vehicles and their crews. "We're going back to Germany . . . immediately?"

"Of course." The wind blew Driver Hewitt and Captain Audley away. "What did you expect, Major Fattorini? We've got a great deal of work to do." A hint of that deceptive smile, which Major McCorquodale would undoubtedly misinterpret, returned. "In fact, our work is only just beginning . . . now that we're free of treachery."

Infinitely far down the runway, close to the end Nissen hut, Fred caught a last glimpse of Number 16. "Sweet Sixteen," who had survived the kiss of death, and was now about to be kissed by two boffins from Cambridge, to encourage him to do for England what he had refused to do for his own country.

But Number 16 was no longer his problem. "What I expect, if I'm coming back with you, are answers to questions, sir. And straight answers." He switched to Clinton. "'Like, who gives Otto Schild his orders?"

The brigadier gave him a little nod. "I am not very pleased with Otto Schild right now." The blank eyes bored into him. "Was it you, or the Crocodile, who put him under close arrest, Fred?"

Fred decided to repay his debt to Otto Schild. "It was his own suggestion, actually."

"It was?" Still no emotion. "He didn't try to run, then?"

Where would Otto Schild run? Fred wondered. But then he thought that Otto Schild, being Otto Schild, might well have a bolt-hole prepared; even, if the worst came to the worst, he had information to sell to the Americans—or if not information, then the odd wild boar, anyway.

But the debt still wasn't fully repaid. "He didn't try to run. And I rather think he saved my life and Audley's, as well as Number Sixteen's, as it happens." He felt a twinge of anger as he spoke. "Or is that the reason why you aren't pleased with him? Were we all expendable, if you could get your traitor in exchange for us?"

"Major—" Stocker started to speak.

"It's all right, Tommy." The brigadier raised his hand. "This is interesting. . . . What do you *think*, Fred? Obviously, you've been doing some hard thinking."

That was true. "I think you had a plan, and it went badly wrong—because of Amos de Souza. Because you didn't trust him."

"I didn't trust anyone. Except you and young Audley." Clinton nodded. "All I knew was that our traitor—and the Russians—wanted Number Sixteen very badly. And alive, too. So I made it very easy for them to get him. But they wouldn't have got away with him." He stared at Fred for a moment. "But . . . you're right about de Souza." He shook his head slowly. "I judged that the enemy wouldn't want a noisy massacre. A quiet kidnapping, with you two as hostages, was more likely. But Amos . . . Amos blundered in. So now I have him on my conscience for my stupidity—is that what you want me to say, Fred?"

Clinton was always full of surprises. "On your conscience?"

"Oh, yes." The old blank stare was back. "Schild was there to see that everything went according to plan. But . . . you're probably right: once de Souza was dead . . . Levin probably would have shot you, too."

"Schild was your man." Fred frowned. "But it was Colbourne who took him on, surely."

"He thought he did, yes."

"So . . . where did Schild come from?"

Stocker stirred again. "I really don't see how that is important to you, Major."

"No." Clinton raised his hand. "In the circumstances, it's a fair question. And poor Amos de Souza put two and two together and made them five because he didn't know enough . . . which is a burden I must bear, because of my incompetence. So we'll start right now, anyway." He nodded at Fred. "My man, yes. Schild *is* my man."

"Acting on your orders?"

"Not to kill. I wanted our traitor alive. Though . . . perhaps Schild has saved us more trouble than he's caused, at that."

Now another installment of the debt could be paid. So he shrugged. "He said he went for a head shot because the RSM was wearing ammunition pouches, so he couldn't be sure his bullet wouldn't be deflected. It was almost the only thing he said—apart from wanting to be taken into custody."

Clinton shook his head. "Thin, Major Fattorini, thin. Gehrd Schild liked Amos de Souza, he once told me so. He said Amos would have made a good German officer—he had the Wehrmacht touch with his men, Gehrd said. And he liked young Audley too, oddly enough. So . . . he disobeyed orders, anyway."

Fred stared at him. *"Gehrd?"*

"Oh, yes. *Gehrd* Schild is his real name. Otto the pork butcher from Minden was his elder brother. Gehrd used to help in the shop when he was on leave, so he knew all about the family business. And so when Otto was killed at the very end—killed by one of our delayed-action bombs while digging survivors out, actually—when he was killed, Gehrd quietly took over his identity as he mingled with the refugees. Quietly and prudently . . . and, of course, he was well-placed to doctor the necessary documents, even apart from his acquired pig-butchering skills, you see."

Fred didn't see, but waited nevertheless.

"Gehrd was an Abwehr man." Clinton nodded. "Same rank as you, Major. Division Two—antisabotage and 'special tasks,' stationed in Northern France until the Hitler bomb plot. And then the Sicherheitsdienst and the Gestapo moved in on the German military intelligence, of course, when they went for his boss, Admiral Canaris. . . . Not that Canaris was really in on the Hilter plot. But the Nazis had been gunning for him for a long time. *But* . . . but our Major Schild was in the clear, having run his particular 'special tasks' efficiently."

"What special tasks?" Fred could understand very well why a German major of intelligence might want to swap identities with his civilian brother, whatever his tasks might have been. But if Brigadier Clinton was turning a blind eye to the imposture for his own purposes, and now he, Major Fattorini, was being admitted to the secret, he needed to know how deep the water was under such thin ice. "What was his job?"

Clinton lifted a hand again. "Fortunately nothing too embarrassing—nothing worse than Major McCorquodale and Macallister might have pleaded guilty to if things had gone the other way, let's say. But . . . since *Herr Major* Gehrd Schild no longer exists, for our purposes, that is a hypothetical question. And in any case, our concern is only with what *Otto* Schild did next, Fred—eh?"

Now he was being tested. But he didn't know enough yet. "What did he do?"

"He was seconded to coordinate Abwehr Division Three personnel, in support of the Gestapo and the civil police in certain investigations in Germany," Clinton answered him suavely. "So what do you think that involved, then?"

With teacher's help, suddenly the test wasn't so difficult. "He drew Professor Schmidt's name from the hat?" Even as he asked the question it became unnecessary. "How did you get on to him, sir?"

"I didn't. Gehrd Schild—I beg your pardon! *Otto* Schild now . . . *he* got on to *me*." Clinton watched him. "*Now* are you beginning to add two and two, eh?"

"Yes." That wasn't quite true, because the information was coming to him too fast now, as he tried to marry it to what David Audley had told him. And already, as he thought about it, there was a bone sticking in his throat; but he couldn't work out the dates and the timing. "He didn't go to Colonel Colbourne?"

"Precisely." Clinton almost looked pleased. "The truth is that the Abwehr knew about Professor Schmidt's little game from way back, is what he told me. But Canaris sat on the information. Or rather, he *didn't* sit on it, we have reason to suspect. He fed it to a man named Rosseler—*Rudolf Rosseler*—who worked for the

Russians. And that's how the Russians got on to Professor Schmidt. This is what Schild came to tell me: that Moscow had been after Number Sixteen for months, you see?"

Fred saw. And saw also that once Clinton had known that, after Schild had learned that the British were also hot on the trail of Professor Schmidt's Romano-German archaeologists, then Schild had a new master. And then the brigadier would have realized at last that TRR-2's misfortunes weren't just bad luck, but treason.

But all this brought him to what he still couldn't quite believe, even though it must be true. "The colonel, sir—Colonel Colbourne? Levin was *his* man?"

"Gus Colbourne?" The nuances of the brigadier's range of facial expressions were as indiscernible as ever. But this time he almost looked sad. "Gus Colbourne is another of our casualties, I'm afraid. Maybe not as final as poor de Souza . . . but, for our purposes . . . final, I'm afraid." He took the responsibility to the gunner colonel quickly. "Gus belongs to you, Tommy?"

"Yes, sir." Colonel Stocker took his dismissed predecessor on the chin, for the benefit of his newly appointed adjutant. "These are early days yet, Major. We've got a lot of checking still to do. But for my money, Colonel Colbourne is no traitor."

"Sir?" It galled Fred that a gunner was bemusing a snapper.

"Of course, we shall never be able to clear him absolutely. And for this war . . . of the brigadier's"—Stocker steadfastly didn't look at Clinton—"we can only use men who have no mark against them, who are utterly above suspicion, Major. So he has to go. But it's a pity, all the same." Stocker watched him digest this ultimate disqualification, until all its implications had been assimilated. "We don't know the full story yet, Major . . . although Colonel Colbourne has been very frank with us, so we do have the beginning of it, I think. And we have to talk to our people in Palestine before we can draw the picture with any certainty . . . from Bum-Titty Bay in '43."

Bum-Titty—? Suddenly Fred was hideously back in the Teutoburg Forest, gaping at RSM Levin, not at the gunner colonel. "P-P-*Palestine*, sir?"

"Haifa. On the beach at Haifa, Major." The fact that Stocker understood his astonishment, and sympathized with it, didn't make his slow smile more acceptable. "Colbourne and RSM Levin went up there—*Major* Colbourne and *CSM* Levin then—to a leave-camp, after El Alamein . . . which was well-deserved, after what they'd achieved in the desert, between them." He gave Fred a slow nod. "'Bum-Titty Bay'—all those pretty Jewish girls in swimsuits on the beach . . . and most of them were already in

245

the Haganah, of course. And some of them were in the *Irgun Tzvai Leumi*—in the *ETZEL*—which is already killing our men out there, in the cause of an independent Jewish state." The nod steadied. "And . . . it seems possible that one particularly beautiful girl named Rachel may have picked up Company Sergeant Major Levin, as she picked up other Jewish officers and senior NCOs. And if she did, then it's tolerably certain that she introduced him to a man whom we know as 'Ze'ev,' who is a link-man between *ETZEL* and the Soviet Union. Because the Russians are strong supporters of what is already being called the State of Israel. Not because they like Jews, but because they see us as supporting all the Arab states, against the Jews." His lips twisted as he spoke, but he watched Fred just as sharply as Clinton had ever done as he did so. "What *ETZEL* thinks 'Ze'ev' is doing is getting them arms and ammunition. But what we think is that he's also taking orders from Moscow. And in '43 Colbourne was marked down for special assignments in Europe, because of his record in the desert. And Levin had been his right hand, through thick and thin, in operations in Syria and Iraq, long before El Alamein. So they were a winning team already."

God! thought Fred. *Syria and Iraq . . . and Palestine—they were all a far cry from the Teutoburg Forest! Almost the only thing that united them was that they had all once been parts of the Roman Empire, almost—almost two thousand years ago, when both were trouble spots!*

"We know that 'Ze'ev' has made other deals, you see, Major. Russian arms in exchange for treason—and the promise of airlifted material, from Czecho-Slavia and Bulgaria, through an airfield somewhere in Syria, where the locals have been bought off—Druse, probably . . . we don't know for sure." Nod. "But once Levin was committed . . . because 'Ze'ev' would have fed him with true horror stories of what was happening in Germany and Poland—even before he arrived here in Germany . . ." Stocker looked sidelong at Clinton as he spoke.

"Yes." Clinton accepted the look. "Levin was a damn good warrant officer—almost the perfect warrant officer, I would have said: brave and intelligent. *And* he knew King's Regs to the last letter of the small print." He threw the look at Fred. "So maybe he argued himself into splitting what belonged to the King of England into what he thought was due to the Promised Land . . . But thanks to Gehrd Schild, that's one thing we'll never know now, Fred."

And perhaps there were some things it was better not to know? thought Fred. But then he remembered Amos de Souza. "So what *do* we know?"

The wind gusted between them, smelling only very slightly of hot engine oil and aircraft fuel. And he knew that it had been blowing over them fitfully all the time while they had been testing him, even though he hadn't noticed it until now . . . just as he knew, beyond certainty, that they were both relaxing as he hardened his heart, as they had both long ago hardened theirs to the loss of all those simplicities of their old war, which Professor Schmidt and Number 16 had tried in vain to avoid, and which had killed Amos de Souza and Number 21 in failing to do so. And RSM Levin, too.

Clinton caught his glance down the runway, towards the ridge under its gray sky. "We know that it's going to be a bad time, for all of us. Because nothing is going to be easy for us anymore—not when good men like Levin betray us for reasons which seem honorable to them . . . reasons which may even *be* honorable. Apart from others who are already working for the Russians."

All this was only what Kyri had said, showing his teeth under his brigand's mustache long ago, thought Fred. So . . . he couldn't say that he hadn't been warned, anyway. But what he missed now was the Greek's cheerful sense of good and evil, and his trust that the first would always outweigh the second in some final reckoning.

"More to the point—we have to get back to Germany, Major," snapped Stocker. "Because we have work to do."

"Sir?" He felt the man take command. But he also felt Clinton's envelope in his pocket. "You don't want me to find the exact site of the battle of the Teutoburger Wald, I hope?"

"No." Stocker's face hardened. "I shall be going on to Berlin with Major McCorquodale tomorrow. You will be staying behind, ostensibly to pull the rest of them together before they follow me."

"Yes, sir." It hadn't been a very good joke, at that. But the thought of Sergeant Devenish at his side raised his spirits. Also, reaching Berlin finally had always been the height of his military ambition, ever since 1939. For then the war would be truly ended, he had foolishly believed. "I'll do my best to get them to you as quickly as possible."

"No, you won't. You'll make a hash of it, Major. Including, among other things, allowing Gehrd Schild to escape." Stocker drew a deep breath, and then looked down the runway towards the Dakota. "I'll fill in the details during the flight, Major. But . . . you won't be going to Berlin, anyway."

Fred felt the blood flare in his cheeks. "What?"

"Colonel Stocker will be back from Berlin in ten days. That should give you time to put everyone's back up." Clinton nodded at him. "Then you will have a public stand-up quarrel with him in the mess. And then you will use the contents of the envelope I gave to you and become a civilian."

The wind felt cold on his cheeks. Becoming a civilian was something he'd dreamed of all these years. But now the thought of it was as desolate as the airfield around him.

"You will, of course, rejoin your family firm then—you uncle Luke will put you in the right place. But in three month's time there will be a civilian vacancy on the British Control Commission in Germany, in the economic section. And the circumstances of your departure from TRR-two, as well as your name and qualifications, plus the influence I will arrange, will get you the job. So then you will be where I want you to be. Because, although this new bomb has given us a breathing space, I foresee trouble in Germany first. And I must have someone right inside the commission to keep an eye on things, Fred."

For a moment all Fred could think of, almost irrelevantly, was *so I'm not going to get to Berlin after all.* But then it occurred to him that this was a properly symbolic failure if his war wasn't ending, but just beginning. The only question was . . . *did he still want to continue fighting?*

"You aren't leaving me much choice, it seems." He stared at Clinton.

"On the contrary. The choice is all yours. I told you that you were a free man, and you are. And in a fortnight's time you will be altogether beyond my reach, if that's where you want to be. It'll be entirely up to you then to decide your own right and wrong, and whether you want to serve undercover."

One of the Dakota's engines coughed, and then came explosively to life. Colonel Stocker was already a dozen yards away, striding towards the plane as though Major Fattorini's decision was a foregone conclusion.

"Yes, sir." Because there didn't seem much else either to say or to do, he saluted Clinton. Which meant that Stocker was right—at least for the time being, anyway.

The brigadier returned his salute. "Well, then . . . you'd better be starting, Major Fattorini," he said.